Night Moves

Book #3 - G-Man Series

A Novel by Andrea Smith

Meatball Taster Publishing

Copyright 2013

Sandra –

Great seeing you in Chicago!

Andre Smith

Author: Andrea Smith

11/27/2013

MEATBALL TASTER PUBLISHING

ISBN: 978-0-578-12747-7   (E-Book)

ISBN: 978-0-9898250-8-5   (Paperback)

All characters and events in this book are fictional; any resemblance to actual persons or events, living or dead, is purely coincidental.

This book is intended for adult readers only.

Cover Design: Kim Black, TOJ Publishing Services

Editor: Ashley Blaschak Stout

Formatting: Erik Gevers

Table of Contents

Acknowledgements

Thank you to my ever vigilant street team! You ladies are the best!

I can't leave out my British friends who helped me with the lingo—I hope I did you proud! So cheers to Bev, Becs, Donna, Emma, Lisa Jayne, Joanna and Daisy! You girls are quite brilliant and smashing! I hope Easton's a bloke that gets your knickers in a twist—in a GOOD way, of course!

I want to acknowledge reviewers (who without them, let's face it: the word would not get out). I don't believe in adversarial relationships between authors and reviewers. Even though you've reviewed my books and rated some of them less-than-perfect, you've also told me *why*. You've taught me to suck it up, to not take it personally and have allowed me to walk away with *something*...Hopefully, I've managed to turn some of those 'whys' into 'well-dones' or at the very least, 'better job' on this book! *So thank you!*

A special thanks to my readers as well! I hope this is one that you truly love!

Special Note to Those Leaving Reviews!!

The British spelling of certain words during Easton's narratives and ~~dialog~~ dialogue in this book are not to be confused with my neglecting to use Spell-Check! This was done intentionally because he is British!! I just wanted to make sure that you ~~realized~~ realised that! This book has been a ~~labor~~ labour of love for me, and I hope that you get the ultimate possible pleasure when reading it! ~~While~~ Whilst the reader will find Easton's character a bit different than the G-Men in Books 1 and 2, I think you will find him to be a ~~colorful~~ colourful individual in his own right.

Playlist

"*Love of a Lifetime*" by Firehouse

"*The Search is Over*" by Survivor

"*You are so Beautiful*" by Joe Cocker
(Lindsey & Taz's Wedding)

"*Viva La Vida*" by Coldplay

"*Rolling in the Deep*" by Adele

"*Set Fire to the Rain*" by Adele

"*Where Does My Heart Beat Now*" by Celine Dion

"*Drive*" by The Cars

"*We've Got Tonight*" by Bob Seger

"*Wrecking Ball*" (Cover) by Madilyn Bailey

"*Unbreak My Heart*" by   Toni Braxton

"*Night Moves*" by Bob Seger

"*[Do - Do - Do - Do] Heartbreaker*" by Rolling Stones

"*Fuck Me Pumps*" by Amy Winehouse

"*Unbreak My Heart*" by Toni Braxton

"*Second Chance*" by Shinedown

"*All of Me*" by John Legend
(From my home town of Springfield, Ohio!!!!!)

~ **Darcy** ~

I was on my way to Darin's apartment to surprise him. We'd met a year ago tomorrow, Christmas Eve, making that *entire* year feel like Christmas. Darin officially graduated from the FBI academy in Quantico last month. He would now be given assignments as an "agent" instead of carrying the title of "agent trainee" with the FBI. He was stoked and so was I.

I was trying to finish up my degree program on-line from the University of Virginia in Charlottesville. It made it so much easier pursuing it while living at home with my parents in Georgetown, making it possible to be closer to Darin.

On-line classes were definitely not a cakewalk. I was forced to study more than I had before when attending classes on campus, but it was well worth it to be able to spend as much time as possible with my G-Man, Darin.

I had talked to him earlier in the day. He had been out on post-graduate field practice for covert operations. That's all he could tell me—or would tell me. He said he was going to shower and crash. We would see each other tomorrow for a celebratory one-year anniversary dinner date with a major fuck-fest scheduled afterwards.

I guess I should admit that I'm rather spoiled. I'm not a big fan of delayed gratification. My man and I hadn't seen each other in nearly a week as I finished my finals for the semester, turning in the remaining essay projects for my classes.

As an only child from a somewhat wealthy family, I suppose I can blame my parents for my penchant for "instant gratification." It's true. They'd denied me nothing over the years and now I'd come to detest having to wait for anything I wanted badly. Right now, I wanted Darin Murphy between my legs, so there was no stopping me.

I was totally decked-out in "fuck-me" couture, having shopped the entire afternoon with my BFF, Lindsey Dennison. Linds had been through the wringer over the past year as well, but for entirely different reasons. Our shopping trip

8

was supposed to be for Christmas and not trashy lingerie, as Lindsey so eloquently pointed out.

Actually, it was through Lindsey and Taz—or I should say Trace Matthews, that I'd had the opportunity of meeting Darin a year ago. So much had happened to both of us over this past year. Mine had been great; Lindsey's had been pretty fucked-up, at least for the first half of the year.

I was so happy for Lindsey now. She'd just had a beautiful baby girl with Taz, another G-Man in D.C. and an agent that Darin really looked up to. He said Taz was one of the best special agents in the bureau. He loved being on assignment with him. Lindsey was entirely wrapped up in her new baby girl, Harper. She deserved that happiness and, in some ways, I was a bit envious, I admit, but I certainly didn't begrudge her that. She'd been tortured nearly to death by a crazed student on campus that was in to all kinds of evil. Taz had literally saved her life.

I pulled my car over to the curb in front of his apartment complex. The winter darkness was descending as I walked up the concrete walk to the door of his townhouse. My heels clicked against the hard surface of the cold cement and echoed in the quiet tranquility of the complex. My heart did a major flutter as I saw lights on in his apartment. Darin was likely still awake, probably watching something on his flat screen in the bedroom before he fell asleep. That was his habit. He wouldn't be grumpy for long when I took off the belted trench coat I was wearing and displayed the sexy outfit underneath. I giggled silently at the thought of what he would do to me when he did.

I could hear soft music from the stoop as I pulled the key he had given me to his apartment a few months prior out of my coat pocket. I wanted to boost the effect of the surprise. He was probably stretched out on his massive, leather couch, dozing off to one of his music satellite channels.

I slipped the key into the lock noiselessly and slowly opened the front door, stepping inside quietly...ready to rock my man's world. Nothing prepared me for what I saw taking place on his leather sofa once I was inside.

Darin's ass was up in the air. I watched as he plunged his dick inside someone beneath him over and over again. Whoever it was underneath, was moaning and digging her painted fingernails into the skin on his back. I didn't realize until his movements suddenly stopped that I was screaming. Yep. I was screaming loud, vulgar things. At both of them.

"You rotten, mother-fucker! You whore-hopping son-of-a-bitch!"

Probably not my finest moment…but hey, I really didn't care about that at the time.

Darin was up and off of her in a flash, his still-hard cock cloaked in a festive condom. It was then I saw the chick he'd been fucking so furiously, perched on her elbows, glaring at me as if she had the right to be indignant at my untimely interruption. It was Dee-Dee or "Dirty Diana" as she was better known throughout the bureau. Yes, a female FBI agent, whose slutty reputation for doing all the dudes in the bureau was evidently notorious. Darin had joked about it with me many times, appalled at her total disregard of her professional reputation. Now he was doing her. Fuck me.

Time seemed to go in slow-motion as my brain sorted it all out. Darin was frantically groping around for his jeans that lay on a heap of clothing on the floor next to the sofa.

I flung the key to his apartment at her, watching it bounce off of her forehead and land on her bare crotch.

"Here slut, have at it!" I screeched. I turned to Darin and in the *calmest tone possible* hissed, "I hope your cock rots off."

I stumbled out of his apartment, wet tears now streaming down my cheeks, as I tried to run in the stupid, four-inch heels I'd purchased earlier for this special occasion. I wasn't having much luck. I stopped momentarily to remove the heels, giving Darin just enough time to catch up to me on the sidewalk. He had managed to pull his jeans on for the chase, but nothing else.

"Whoa, Darce, hold up there, baby. It's not what you think."

Not what I think? What the fuck?

His hand reached for my shoulder, turning me to face him. I immediately clawed at him with the heel of my shoe, gouging his still-bare shoulder over and over again with it. He didn't even flinch.

"Baby, please? It didn't mean anything, I swear to God! It just happened. It has nothing to do with you or how I feel about you."

10

"How can you say that?!" I screeched.

"I'll make her leave, we'll talk it out," he pleaded. "I love you, Darce."

"Fuck you, Darin," I hissed. "It's over. We are done. Don't ever call or come around me again. Do I make myself clear?"

I looked up into his dark eyes and saw the tears welled up in them. Too fucking little, too fucking late. He started to reach for me again, but something in my eyes must have registered with him because he stopped and drew back. My tears had dried up. All I felt was coldness in them now as I directed an arctic glare at him. He felt it too, taking a half-step back from me.

"Do I?" I repeated, my voice having a steely edge to it that even I didn't recognize.

He nodded slowly, swallowing the lump in his throat. The realization had hit him with full force. I watched as the comprehension sunk in. Darin Murphy had fucked up in a big, big way. No one, I repeat, *no one* breaks Darcy Nicole Sheridan's heart. It's just not done.

Chapter 1

The flight attendant in first-class roused me from my sleep gently.

"We're preparing our initial descent into Belize City. I need for you to bring your seat into the upright position and fasten your seatbelt now."

I kind of wanted to kill her. Just a little. I settled for smiling at her and obliged, groggy as I was, to comply.

It was Christmas day in Belize. I was relieved to be spending it in another country, not back in the U.S., where everything had imploded as far as my love life was concerned. My parents were spending the holidays in Cancun. I had quickly decided to get away, only not with them. I was not up for the pummeling questions I knew would be forthcoming if my mother and father knew what had happened with Darin. I barely had the strength to make the last minute call to Lindsey, seriously not in the mood to go into the details with her at the moment. I was just too raw.

She'd freaked like I knew she would when I simply told her that it was over with Darin and me and that I wasn't going to provide any details to her at the moment. I told her I'd booked a flight to Belize, leaving Christmas Eve morning; I'd discuss everything with her upon my return. She wasn't happy. She'd attempted to pry, but I told her I needed to get packed and quickly ended the call.

As soon as I walked into the terminal, I collected my luggage and arranged for a ferry to San Pedro. I was booked at a beach-front villa at the Grand Colony. My parents had taken me there after my high-school graduation. I remembered how totally beautiful it had been; the beautiful blue water and white, sandy beaches. And that was something I desperately needed right now.

I could forget about everything, being thousands of miles away from D.C. I could forget the pain and betrayal of what Darin had done to me. If I had to, I'd drink myself into oblivion to forget. Of course, I'd be drinking fancy, tropical drinks delivered to my villa by a very hot, sexy Belizean dude.

Is "Belizean" a word?

Anyway, all I really wanted was the ability to numb myself from the hurt and betrayal I was trying to deal with. It was a first for me. I'd never been broken. I was always the breaker never the breakee. This was new ground for me.

After I was settled into my beach-front villa, I opened all of the shutters to enjoy the warm sunshine trickling in and the soothing, salty, ocean breeze. I stood at the open window and reveled in the tranquility of this extraordinary place on earth. I hoped it would help to heal my broken heart, at least for now.

My phone rang from somewhere in my handbag. It was probably my parents calling from Cancun to wish me a Merry Christmas. I fumbled around until I found it. Sure enough, it was Mom. I knew she'd worry if I didn't answer and commence blowing my phone up until I did.

"Hey, Mom," I greeted, making sure to put my game face on and throw in some fake, red-and-green cheer. "Merry Christmas!"

"Darcy, what's wrong?"

Shit.

"Nothing's wrong, Mom. What could be wrong? It's Christmas," I reassured her with a grin plastered to my face, hoping like all hell that the explanation for my "Worst Breakup of the Year" award wouldn't break through my lips.

I totally cracked 2.5 seconds later.

For the next ten minutes, I shared the whole story with her, including the fact I was in Belize alone on Christmas. I told her I needed to be alone right now.

"Nonsense, darling," she argued. "Your father and I'll change our plans and join you in Belize tomorrow. Where are you staying?"

"I'm at the Grand Colony in San Pedro."

"Wonderful, darling. I'll call you back once our plans are firmed up. Stay put, okay?"

Where the hell would I go?

"I'll be right here, Mom."

13

"Please know this isn't the end of the world. It's better you found out now rather than later what type of man Darin is."

I doubted if the pain could be any worse, but Mom needed to know that I'd get through it.

"I know Mom, and you're right."

"Good girl."

I changed into a summer dress complete with flip-flops, to take a walk on the beach, letting the warm tide wash over my feet in the wet sand. I let my long hair down so I could feel the wind whip through it. It was therapeutic and calming. The ocean had a way of making everything seem so very small and inconsequential, putting things in perspective.

I was enjoying the relaxing solitude when I noticed a couple coming down to the beach about twenty yards from me. The man was tall, probably around 6' 3" and extremely handsome. I could tell that from a distance. He had very dark, thick hair and a lean, but muscular build. I noticed he had a five o'clock shadow gracing his tanned face, his features were finely chiseled. I smiled to myself as I noticed his very rugged looks conflicted with the air of aristocracy he had about him. How in the hell I could presume that was beyond me. He wore sunglasses, but I imagined his eyes to be either blue or green. He wore a white linen shirt, the sleeves rolled up to his elbows and the top few buttons unfastened, showing his muscular broad chest with a pair of khaki trousers. That was one fine ass he had going on.

I noticed the young woman with him was now staring at me. She obviously noticed that I had noticed, and didn't appreciate it by the body language she was giving off. She was shorter than I was, probably about 5' 2" or 5' 3" to my 5' 7" height. She was built nicely, had medium-length blonde hair and a gorgeous tan. She was wearing a bikini that left very little to the imagination. As soon as I knew I was busted, I looked away. I could hear the man's deep, rich laughter as I did. Blushing furiously, I turned and headed further down the beach.

A couple in love no doubt. Here I was, just a loner with heartbreak in a tropical, romantic place like Belize. What had I been thinking coming here? I'd have been better off holed up in some hotel in London watching the rainy drizzle outside my window. At least the rain and I would have something in common.

My thoughts were interrupted when I heard a raised voice down the beach where the couple had been.

"I'm sick of the way you're always scoping out other chicks! It might be nice if you paid some attention to the girl you're actually with once in a while!"

What in the hell?

I glanced back and then around. There were no "other chicks" on the beach except for me.

Really?

The girl was totally gorgeous, looking like Vacay Barbie, so her insecurity really didn't make much sense to me. I watched as he pulled his sunglasses off and faced her, his index finger jabbing the space in front of her as if reprimanding her. He obviously was saying something to her in a calmer voice, making it impossible for me to hear. I saw her shrink back from him, then whirl around and run back down the beach in the opposite direction, presumably back to their own villa.

The guy put his sunglasses back on, turning to gaze down at me. He saw that, once again, he had my attention. Busted #2! I hurriedly turned away from him and started walking further down the beach, feeling his eyes still upon me. A tingling sensation enveloped my whole body as he did. It was my turn to laugh softly as I put distance between us.

Once I'd finished my walk on the beach, I showered and changed for dinner. I decided I wasn't going to hole up in my villa and order room service. I was damn well secure enough to dine alone (which would definitely be a first experience for me. But what the hell, right?).

I chose a clingy cobalt-blue cocktail dress that covered the necessities, just *barely*. It clung to my curves, and damn near lifted my breasts up over the top. I worked hard on keeping my body in shape, so why not flaunt it? It wasn't as if I'd ever see any of these people again.

I accessorized with silver earrings and a slave bracelet. I slid my freshly-pedicured feet into a pair of black, 4-inch, spiked, Louis Vuitton summer sandals. They were hot. Poor Daddy! They'd set him back somewhere in the neighborhood of eight hundred dead presidents. I tried not to over-do it with his and Mom's generosity, but like I said, I was their only child and if it made them feel good to indulge me, then why spoil it for them? My mother had been 42 years old when she had me. She referred to me as her and Daddy's miracle surprise.

At 64 years of age, they both still possessed a youthful air about them. I knew the truth, though. My parents had been "hippies" in the late sixties, early seventies. That's right, bona fide, sign-carrying, Vietnam-protesting hippies. I had a hard time with making that connection too. It was only because of Mom's slightly younger sister Bridget that I'd found out about it.

Apparently, my mother attended Antioch College in Yellow Springs, Ohio, which to this day, she claims, is a town still lost in the "sixties." My father had attended nearby Wittenberg University in Springfield, Ohio but they didn't actually meet until August of 1969. Guess where?

WOODSTOCK! (A three-day concert held in upstate New York—I had to look it up.)

It's so hard for me now to picture my parents as war-protesters or hippies. They blend in very nicely with the country club set and international travelers. I suppose youth has a way of putting different perspectives on things before it's time to bring home the bacon. I'm only grateful that I'd been a late-in-life baby. I can only imagine what my life would have been like if I'd been born as a result of their "hooking up" at Woodstock. God! I'd be like in my early forties and would probably have some Bohemian name like "Moon Shadow" or "Rain Flower."

I took a deep breath, putting all of that out of my mind as I realized it was time for me to leave for dinner. I left my villa, clutch purse in hand and walked the lonely distance to the resort's high-end restaurant. I'd made a reservation for one. Don't think that wasn't extremely difficult. Fuck it. What doesn't kill you makes you stronger and all that jazz.

Luckily, I passed a Tiki bar on the way up to the restaurant. I stopped and ordered a Mambiscus, one of the tropical favorites in Belize. It was delicious with coconut rum, coconut liquor, apple liquor and peach liquor, along with watermelon juice and some other various non-alcoholic mixtures. I slurped it up in no time flat, getting the tingling buzz of relaxation from the alcohol content. I adjusted my dress downward to shield my said necessities from a mix of perusing male eyes sitting at the outside bar.

As soon as I arrived at the restaurant, I knew this had been a mistake.

It was packed as hell, so naturally I had a wait time for my "table for one"—which, with my current luck, would probably end up being right outside the Men's room. I was invited to sit at the bar with an electronic device that would light up and vibrate when my table was ready.

Luckily, I found an empty stool at the bar, and proceeded to plop my ass down on it without giving everyone in the house a show. There was an older guy to the right of me, and a younger guy in business dress to the left of me on his cell phone. I gave the bartender my drink order and then took a look around the bar and restaurant, swiveling the bar stool to do a full panoramic view.

Shit!

It was him! The hot guy from the beach earlier. Guess who was with him? Yep! The petite blonde that had been with him there and had stomped away after accusing him of gawking at other chicks.

Double Shit!

They were already seated; nibbling on their appetizers, while Blondie had her small notebook computer opened, occasionally entering data while he spoke to her.

What's up with that?

I was still gaping their way when "gorgeous" happened to look over at me. I could see instantly he drew the connection with me being the one on the beach earlier. I felt myself tingle as his gorgeous eyes, now without sunglasses to mask them, perused my body up and down as I sat cross-legged on the bar stool. I hurriedly spun my bar stool back around, presenting my back to them. There was a mirror over the bar and I couldn't resist searching him out in the reflection and noticing he was still very much checking me out.

God, he looked so hot in his dinner suit. He was impeccable from every angle and trust me; I was checking each and every angle out in that mirror! He was watching me watching him. I wanted to turn my head, but I seriously couldn't! I was freaking mesmerized with his looks and his charisma that seemed to seep from every pore in that oh-so-lovely body of his. I was lost in the moment, gazing at him gazing at me through the mirror behind the bar.

All of a sudden, Blondie turned her head, obviously aware that he'd stopped paying any attention to what they were doing. Her eyes met mine in the mirror and shot a whole new set of icy daggers at me, which didn't diminish a bit in the reflection. I wasn't going to give her the benefit of breaking my gaze first. Finally, she turned back to look at him. My eyes dropped as the bartender placed my drink in front of me. I focused my attention on that, sipping the delicious nectar of this tropical drink.

Already, I was feeling light and giddy, probably because I hadn't eaten a thing since I arrived in Belize. The older guy next to me turned his attention to me, his eyes flickering over me from top to bottom.

"On vacation?" he asked, trying to give me an appropriate opening line.

"Yep," I answered, sipping my cocktail.

"Me too," he replied, scooting his bar stool just a tad closer. "I'm here all alone taking a much needed vacation from my wife and grandchildren," he explained, as if I were minimally interested.

"That's nice," I replied, trying not all that hard to sound condescending.

He bantered on a few minutes longer. Most of the conversation didn't even sink in to my brain until his hand reached over and rested on my bare thigh.

"Yep," he continued, "I have a stressful job as a CEO in the States. My wife's taken to raising my low-life son's children, so it's like starting that crap all over again. Thought I was done with all of that once I hit fifty. But no, wifey says it's for the children; can't be selfish when it comes to the children. I wish she cared about my well-being as much as she cares about 'the children's' well-being, you know?"

"Well, actually, I don't," I replied, politely moving his hand from my thigh and placing it back on his own. "I'm 22, and I honestly can't fathom what your life is like. I'm sorry."

"Aren't you a call girl?" he asked, looking totally perplexed. "Aren't you paid to listen to my sad tales? Oh, I get it, cash first, right?"

I think my mouth would have dropped open if that initial reaction wasn't swiftly followed by rage-studded humiliation. "Fuck you, old man," I said. "I think you've stepped into a generation you don't know *a damn thing* about."

I was about to say more, tell him to fucking turn away and leave me the hell alone, when the bartender approached with a fresh drink in his hands for me.

"It's from the gentleman over there," he said with a nod towards the table where "gorgeous" and his pouty wife and/or girlfriend were sitting.

"He said for me to tell you to enjoy, and that he finds you most beautiful, Miss."

I couldn't help myself, I had to turn and see if he really had enough gall to send a drink to me in front of his wife, girlfriend—whatever the hell she was to him. And I saw it, his eyes on me, gazing with an intensity that made me shiver in the balmy air. I also saw her arctic gaze, sizing me up in her mind, trying to figure out just why he'd made sending me a drink an issue that she wasn't comfortable with.

I gave him a saucy wink (which I never would have done if I wasn't already feeling really, really buzzed) and swiveled back around to face the bar. Of course, my very astute vision allowed me to watch what was happening from behind in the bar mirror without them noticing.

Blondie stood up, pushing her chair back abruptly from their table, banging it into the man sitting at the table next to them. She threw her linen napkin on her plate, grabbed her notebook and handbag, and then stomped off quickly.

I watched closely in the mirror, trying to ascertain his reaction. There was none. None whatsoever. He sat there cool, calm and collected, and finished his drink as if her storming out of there meant nothing to him.

Probably a player…

Just then, the beeper I'd been given beeped and lit up like a Christmas tree. I collected my drink from the bar and walked over to the Maitre' D, handing him the beeper.

"Right this way," he said, nodding for me to follow him. You can imagine my utter surprise when he pulled the chair out that Blondie had recently vacated, indicating for me to take my place across from "Gorgeous." A fresh place setting had been delivered. All signs of the blonde had vanished.

"Wait," I sputtered. "This is a mistake. I need a table for one."

I looked across the table as this smokin' hot man stood up, flashing his exquisite gray eyes at me, smiling slightly, reflecting a dimple.

Oh. Wow.

"If you'll excuse my boldness, Miss. I made the request on your behalf, hoping that you might agree to have dinner with me this evening."

"I thought you had a dinner companion for the evening," I replied, hearing an audible sigh from the now-growing-impatient Maître' D behind me.

"Plans change," he replied with a smirk, tilting his lips. "Join me?"

He was gorgeous, sexy and had to be in his early thirties, likely very worldly, too. What the hell. I lowered myself into the chair, nudging it closer to the table in an effort to shield my bare thighs from his bold gaze. He wasn't even trying to hide the fact that he was looking. The Maitre' D left, telling us our server would be with us shortly.

"Gorgeous" took his seat across from me once I was situated. "My name's E.J.," he said in a rich, sensual voice. I released a sigh, thinking how his voice could make even initials sound sensual and slightly dangerous.

Jesus, he even had a British accent.

"You were given initials as a name?" I blurted, unthinkingly.

"Not exactly," he replied, giving me a dazzling smile. "It's just what I go by for now, and you are—?"

Oh shit. He wants my name and all he's giving me are initials. Let's see...

"Nicole," I replied, returning his smile and holding my hand across the table.

If he can use initials, I'll use my middle name.

He took my hand in his and raised it slowly to his sensual mouth, brushing his full lips across my knuckles gently. I shivered at the feel of his touch. Wow!

"Nicole—a beautiful name for an extremely beautiful woman," he said softly, his eyes boring through me. He had thick, dark hair that he wore slightly longer than the current norm, yet I could tell his haircuts cost plenty. His piercing silver-toned eyes unnerved me. I pulled my hand back, clasping both of them in my lap.

His elbows rested on the table, his hands clasped together, supporting his chin as he gazed across the table at me. His shirt was Armani. I imagined his whole wardrobe was couture. His nails were neatly manicured. No sign of a wedding ring or a tan line where one had been. Good sign.

"So, why did Blondie run off?" I asked, wanting to break the silence.

He laughed a deep, rich laugh and I liked the ways his eyes danced when he did.

"Her name's Lacee," he explained. "I'm afraid you pissed her off."

"Me?" I asked incredulously. "What did I do?"

"You were on the beach and then you came in here."

"So?"

"She didn't like the fact that I noticed you."

Our server interrupted us at that moment, handing out menus and asking for drink orders.

"Just a sec," I said, signaling the waiter to hold on for a quick minute. "Before I dine with you, I want to know if Blondie—Lacee—whoever the hell she is, happens to be your wife, fiancée, girlfriend, fuck-buddy, whatever. I don't like playing the part of a protagonist in some type of drama you've got going."

E.J.'s face grew serious as he instructed the waiter to come back in a moment. He leaned in close; his eyes had darkened at my accusation. I could tell he was ready to clue me in.

"Lacee's my executive assistant. If she were my wife, fiancée, or girlfriend, I can promise you, Nicole, that I wouldn't have sent the drink over, or invited you to have dinner with me. I don't make it a habit of engaging in melodramatic games, I assure you. I'm unencumbered as far as relationships go at the moment. Are you clear on that?"

He left out fuck-buddies...

"So, if Lacee's your executive assistant, why does she care who you notice at the beach or in a restaurant?"

He shrugged, taking a sip of his drink before answering.

"Let's just say Lacee would like to be more than an executive assistant to me. I simply don't reciprocate those feelings. It's not going to happen."

"I see," I replied, processing that bit of info.

He is so doing her...

E.J. motioned the waiter back to our table. "Are you ready to order?"

"I think so," I replied, my face hidden in back of the menu, so that he couldn't see my smile.

Surprisingly, having dinner with him turned out to be quite entertaining and comfortable once we got past the Lacee issue. E.J. mentioned something about owning a company that did various consulting and programming for global government entities. He didn't elaborate, so I didn't dig any deeper.

"It's my turn to grill you now. You know everything you need to know about me at the moment and I know nothing about you," he said, his eyes studying me with obvious interest as we were having an after dinner liqueur.

Oh God! What can I tell him that doesn't make me sound so...collegiate?

22

"Well, I'm from D.C. I'm finishing up my degree in International Marketing next semester and I'm here in Belize because I caught my boyfriend fucking a skank on his couch. That pretty much sums it up in a nutshell." I giggled and threw back the rest of my second liqueur, loving the nice, warm buzz that was re-emerging since dinner.

I saw E.J. frown slightly while he digested my one-paragraph's worth of information. Maybe he thought my language was too brash. Or he thought I was getting drunk—which, of course, I was.

I saw him signal for the waiter to bring the check.

He thinks I'm fucking pathetic.

"Are we leaving?" I asked with a slight slur.

Face palm.

"I think it's time to get you safely back to your villa. I'll walk you."

"No, really, I'm fine. It's not necessary," I argued.

"I insist," he said in a very no-nonsense tone, placing his hand on my elbow as he guided me through the restaurant towards the exit.

Once outside, I realized there was no way in my current state I could navigate my way back to the villa in these heels. I stopped, leaning into E.J., and took my shoes off.

"There—much better," I said, slinging them over my other shoulder as I leaned into his strong body, breathing in the salt air and his musky, masculine scent. He had an arm wrapped around my shoulder as we walked toward the beach to my villa. The breeze off of the ocean whipped my hair back from my face. I felt the sand now under my bare feet and it was warm and moist. Suddenly, E.J. stopped and pulled me closely against him. I immediately dropped my shoes onto the sand and looked up into his face, trying to understand why we had stopped.

"Such beautiful hair," he commented, taking several locks and rubbing them between his fingers. He dropped the locks, and moved his thumb to my face, gently grazing it back and forth against my cheekbone.

23

He gazed into my eyes and I felt butterflies in my belly. I hadn't felt butterflies in a really long time. The way he studied me at that moment made me feel as if he were debating something.

I melted against him, raising my face upward to his, closing my eyes, wanting only to feel his full, sensual lips on my own. His lips captured mine, very gently at first, but as we continued, his tongue found mine and our kiss grew in passion. His tongue teased mine, his teeth nipped at my lower lip as I wrapped my arms tighter around his neck and molded my body to his. I felt his hands lower to my butt, gripping and aligning every inch of me to every inch of him. *Every* inch.

I was on fire for this man and wasn't sure why, aside from the obvious. I mean, he was sexy, single, gorgeous and in the perfect place at the perfect time— did I mention just how fucking sexy he was? I wanted him to fuck me—yes I did. Right here. Right now. On this beach. I wanted another man's cock inside of me. I couldn't explain my rationale at the moment, only that having another man fuck me would give me a sense of relief, knowing it wasn't Darin who was the last one there, if that made sense. Hell, it made sense to me in my current state of mind and I was determined.

I pulled back a bit and lowered my hand, cupping him while gently massaging his erection which seemed enormous. He stopped kissing me suddenly and pulled back.

"What are you doing, Nicole?"

Isn't it obvious?

"I—I just thought we might want to take this to my villa," I stammered, confused by his reaction.

"I see. Well, let's find your villa, okay?"

"Sure," I said, stooping down to pick up my shoes from the beach, shaking the sand out of them. I smoothed my dress down, feeling my cheeks flush as he continued his relentless observation. "Follow me," I said, heading down the beach towards the cluster of villas.

When we reached mine, I fumbled for the key in my clutch. I was inexplicably nervous now, as if I had totally lost my buzz. I finally found the key

24

and inserted it in the lock when I felt his hand gently on my arm. I turned to face him and saw an edge of humor in his expression.

"Thanks for having dinner with me. I enjoyed this evening more than you know. Perhaps we'll meet again."

Seriously?

"What? I thought…," I couldn't finish that thought. I was dumbfounded and a bit humiliated if I had read his apparent brush-off correctly.

He pulled me close to him, capturing my hands in his, raising them up to his lips where he kissed them both.

He leaned, his lips brushing my ear. "Baby," he said in a rough whisper, "I want to fuck you in the worst way possible. What I don't want is to be some *revenge* fuck of yours in order to get back at your cheating boyfriend, who you'll most likely get back together with before you touch down in D.C. I'm not that guy, love. When I fuck you, there will be no doubt in your mind as to whom you're with and why you're with me, understand?"

I swallowed nervously, nodding my head. He lowered my hands and cupped my chin, kissing my lips again softly and sweetly.

"Get some rest."

And then he was gone.

Chapter 2

I woke up the following morning to a grueling headache, cotton mouth, and nausea that had the room spinning. My parents were due in early this afternoon, and I needed to get my shit together before that. My mother would be grilling me on more details of the whole Darin thing, which caused me to dry heave again.

I finally managed to pull it together and jump in the shower. I couldn't shake the whole incident with E.J. the previous evening. Did I completely misread the guy? I know I was shit-faced, but still, I knew how it felt when our bodies were pressed together. I felt his hardness while we were kissing, there was no mistaking that. I couldn't help the feeling of total rejection that seeped in now in the light of soberness. I couldn't possibly deal with double rejection; first Darin, now E.J. Yeah, I knew it was not the same thing, but rejection in any form is still *fucking rejection!*

After my shower, I dressed in shorts and a tank top. I ordered room service for breakfast and popped some Advil for my headache. I went to the exercise room on-site and worked out until sweat was pouring down my face and back.

My mom called right before I was heading out with my poolside supplies to get some sun without sand. She let me know that she and Daddy had not been able to book a single villa at the resort. They were staying in one of the two-unit condos just down the beach from me. Truthfully, I was relieved. I loved my parents, but having them hovering over me while I was here was not going to help. In particular, it would definitely cramp my style if I wanted to hook up.

I headed down to the Olympic-size pool that was just up from the beach. Luckily, this resort was not kid-friendly, so no worries about having screaming, whiney kids splashing and pissing in the pool. There were a scattering of people on chaise lounges and in the water. I located a chaise with a table next to it for the pool-side cocktails I'd be ordering later. (Hair of the dog and all that.)

I got settled in the chaise, pulling off my beach cover-up so anyone who cared to feast their eyes on my new Agua Bendito Brazilian-cut monokini (which was almost entirely comprised of criss-cross strings and not much else) could do so. I had sprayed on sunscreen before putting it on at the villa. I dug my iPad out to read a steamy novel I'd downloaded, adjusting my sunglasses on my nose to look around and see if anyone interesting was pool-side.

Un-friggin'-believable.

Lacee was stretched out on a chaise right across the pool from me, in a hot pink string bikini that should have been illegal in at least forty-one states. She was on her back, her already-tanned skin glistening with oil, one leg propped up on the chaise; her light blond hair was pulled up in a perky ponytail. She had sunglasses on, which made it impossible to know if she had noticed me. Oh hell—who cares! I continued to glance her way, silently smirking at the way her boobs were spilling over the teeny-tiny triangle of material that barely covered anything!

Uh oh!

There was no doubt in my mind she was now glaring at me behind her shades. I quickly pulled my iPad up, blocking her view of my face at least. I tried my best to put her out of my mind as I started my book.

Hmm—wonder where E.J. is right now? Maybe I should consider going blonde…

After a very colorful argument with just my thoughts in general, I forced myself to re-read the words on the current page for the third time. I hadn't read more than a few pages when I heard a chaise being scraped against the concrete surface surrounding the pool as it was moved right next to mine. I peered up from my iPad observing a young, well-built, blond guy getting settled into it.

"Hi there. Hope you don't mind me sitting next to you. It looks like you're alone here, too. Thought you might enjoy some company. I'm Eli." He pulled his T-shirt up and over his head, tossing it to the ground next to his chaise.

I raised my sunglasses to get a better view of this friendly and totally ripped dude.

"Not at all, Eli," I said, providing him with a dazzling smile. "My name's Nicole."

Might as well continue with the charade.

"Nice to meet you, Nicole. I can tell you're from the States. For a quick sec, I thought maybe you were from France or Spain. You've got that European look going on, you know?"

"Really? You know, I was contemplating going blonde."

"Oh no," he said quickly, "I think you're gorgeous with your dark brown hair and sapphire-blue eyes. It's my favorite combination."

"You're too nice, Eli," I cooed, flashing him another smile. I was checking out Lacee in my peripheral vision; she was still over there all by herself. I made sure I put a giggle out there for good measure. I saw her squirm in her chair, and then she rolled over onto her belly.

Eli and I chatted for a few more minutes. He was from Denver, Colorado and was actually going to be interviewing for a position with the resort the following day. He said winters in Denver were not his thing; he much preferred sand to snow. I filled him in on just enough, not mentioning the thing with Darin, only that I was meeting my parents here for winter break. He was a few years older than me. He'd stayed on in Colorado after he graduated from the University of Colorado several years back.

"So, Nicole, are you going in the pool anytime soon?" Eli was watching me with his boyish grin going on strong.

I glanced over at the gorgeous pool. "Well, I'm not sure. I think this suit might be 'dry-clean only.'"

"What?" he asked; his voice incredulous. "I think you're full of shit. I think it's time we find out if that suit can take being wet."

Before I knew what was happening, Eli took my iPad from me, and placed it on the table. He scooped me up into his strong, muscular arms and headed towards the pool. I was laughing and kicking in faux protest, making enough noise to draw Lacee's attention, I'm sure.

"Eli," I squealed, "put me down. I don't want to go in just yet! Pretty please?"

"Too late, beautiful," he replied, laughing. "You're going in, baby!" He jumped into the pool with me still in his arms, shrieking and giggling as we both went under the water and sprang back up. Eli let go of me, laughing, and dared me to race him to the end of the pool.

My sunglasses were still on and as I looked over at Lacee, I saw that E.J. was standing right there, next to her chaise. He had observed the whole thing with Eli and me; his expression was unreadable. Lacee's not so much, as a slow smile graced her full, pouty lips.

E.J. wasn't dressed in pool garb. He was dressed casually in a pale blue polo, and cargo pants. He looked magnificent. I watched as he apparently instructed Lacee that she was done at the pool. She quickly gathered her towel, sandals and suntan oil, getting up from the chaise, where I heard E.J. instruct her in a brusque tone to put on her cover-up. He, apparently, was not happy with her. Again.

I turned my attention back to Eli who was swimming towards me now, dipping beneath the surface of the water where he grabbed an ankle and pitched me up in the air, causing me to fly a few feet and go under. When I sputtered to the surface, all signs of Lacee and E.J. were gone. I felt a bit deflated.

I finally managed to escape Eli's attention in the pool and climbed out, going back over to my towel on the chaise. He followed a few minutes later, shaking his wet blond locks on me as he passed my chair with a laugh.

"You're a brat," I said, drying myself off again.

"Are you mad?" he asked, seriously thinking that I just might be.

"Well, you can make it up to me if you bring me a frozen strawberry daiquiri, how's that?"

His replying grin was fully-watted. "You've got it, babe," he said, grabbing his wallet from beneath his towel and heading over to the Tiki bar. I settled back down in my chair, relaxing and letting the sun soothe my raw nerves. Why did this whole thing with E.J. bug me more than the deal with Darin? It was like I wasn't even thinking about Darin any longer; not so with E.J. though.

Eli and I enjoyed a couple of daiquiris over the next hour. I was feeling fairly relaxed when my cell phone rang. It was Mom.

"Hi Darcy. Daddy and I will be at the resort in about an hour and a half. We're staying in Unit 12B in the Coconut Grove Condo complex. It's just east of the villas. Do you want us to come to your place, or do you want to come to ours?"

"I'll come to your condo, Mom," I replied quickly. "I'm at the pool right now, but I'm heading back to shower and get changed."

"Okay, darling. Why don't you stop by the condo around dinnertime and we'll go together?"

"Sounds great, Mom. See you then."

I turned to Eli who was reading a magazine. "Got to go. Meeting the parents and I gotta' get ready. It was good meeting you. It's been…interesting." I shot him my famous smile.

"Do you have plans for dinner?" he asked.

"I'm having dinner with my parents," I deadpanned.

"Oh sure, right." He quickly put on his shirt, and grabbed his shades that were lying idle on the small table between us.

Ah, fuck.

"I mean, if you'd like to join us, I'm sure they'd have no problem with that—"

Except he thinks my name is Nicole…

"I'd love to, if you're sure it's okay with you."

"Sure," I shrugged like it was no biggie that I was kind of inviting a guy I'd just met. But the hell with it. This was my vacay and he seemed like a pretty chill guy. Maybe a little lonely…and I knew what that was like.

We exchanged cell numbers and I promised to call him once I was ready so that he could pick me up at my villa and we would head to their condo together.

Once I got back to my villa, I showered, shaved, and gave myself a facial. I went through my closet, selecting a newly purchased Stella McCartney designed cocktail dress. It was a clingy, silhouette-enhancing two-tone dress. The major portion of the dress was Fern-green; the side inserts at the waist to the top of the hips were black mesh.

It was sexy, yet conservative enough not to upset my parents. Yeah, the ones that used to wear tie-dyed shirts with peace signs, love beads and bell-bottom jeans that were frayed because they dragged on the ground—those parents. I put on a pair of new Prada open-toed strapped heels, and a clutch shoulder bag to match. I left my hair down, taking pains to straighten it flat; humidity was not my friend. I was ready to call Eli, but I wanted to check in with Mom first. I needed to clue her in on what was happening. She answered her cell phone sounding kind of flustered.

"Mom? It's me. Did you guys get in okay?"

"Yes, we've been here for over an hour now."

"Is something wrong? You sound kind of frazzled. Does the condo suck?"

"Oh no, it's not that. As a matter of fact, it's breathtakingly beautiful with a great view and a lovely outside terrace that's to die for. It's just that it's a double and the people in the "A" unit are kind of noisy. The walls must be kind of thin, I guess."

"Noisy? Do they have kids or something?"

"No, no—they're noisy and seem to be on some sort of a sex marathon, as far as I can tell."

I had to giggle at the way she described it. "Well, Mom, maybe they're honeymooners or something."

"God—I'd hate to think so with the language and tone they're using! They sound like two people that hate each other, but decided to fornicate all afternoon for the hell of it."

At this I burst out laughing. Yeah, my mom didn't usually talk that way. As in: at all. And it was kind of hilarious as hell hearing her use the word 'fornicate.' "Mom, why don't you call the office and see if the property manager can request they hold it down?"

"I tried that," she replied with a sigh. "It seems that this particular condo is owned by the guy currently inhabiting Unit A. In fact, he owns all four of them on this beach. The property manager was not inclined to make that call. In fact, he said the owner specifically wanted the unit free of guests while he was using it this week, but apparently a clerk made a mistake in letting us rent it, so I was told I should be grateful and I was advised to keep a low profile."

"Well," I said, trying my best to console her so that we could change the subject, "we'll be out for dinner soon, so maybe they'll get it out of their systems."

"We can only hope," she replied. "Are you ready to come down? Your daddy found a seafood restaurant down the main road that he'd like to try. We made reservations and since we have a rental car, no sense in not putting it to use."

"Sounds good to me. There's one thing, though. I met a really, really nice guy at the pool this afternoon. His name's Eli and I invited him to come along with us for dinner. Is that okay?"

I could feel her smile over the phone. "Well, of course, darling. He's more than welcome to join us this evening. I'm glad you're getting back out there and not sitting around crying over Darin."

"Great! There's just one more thing, Mom; can you and Daddy refer to me as 'Nicole' instead of Darcy?"

Silence from her end.

"Darcy Nicole, what are you up to?"

"Nothing Mom—it's just that, since I've been here, I've been introducing myself as Nicole instead of Darcy."

"Why would you do that?" I could almost feel her churning over thoughts in her head about how her daughter was probably having personal identity issues.

"I don't know. Maybe I just wish I *was* a 'Nicole' instead of a 'Darcy.' The name Nicole sounds so much more together, you know?" She was *so* going to speed-dial her shrink after she got off the phone, probably wanting to make an appointment for me as soon as this trip was over.

"I'm not going to be a part of any game you're playing so, to answer your question, no. And I think I can speak for your father as well on this. Your first name is Darcy and that's what we call you and will continue to call you, understood?"

I rolled my eyes. It really wasn't *that* big of a deal, I thought.

"Sure, Mom. I'll explain it to Eli before we get there."

"That's my girl," she said. "Deception almost never works out, remember that, okay? It's always better to speak the truth than have your deception come back to haunt you."

"I know, Mom. You're right of course. Eli and I'll see you and Daddy soon."

"Not soon enough for me," she replied, her tone now totally exasperated. "They're at it again next door. Hurry up and get here so we can get the hell out. You're daddy doesn't seem to mind all the racket, but I sure do. He probably has plans for me tonight after hearing all that dirty talk next door for the past couple of hours. My God, the language…" I could practically feel her cringing.

"Okay, Mom," I replied, smiling.

Chapter 3

I called Eli and he was at my villa shortly after, looking fantastic, I might add, in a summer sport jacket and cotton trousers. His blond locks were gelled, and slightly spiked, which was a good look for him.

"You look great," I said, motioning for him to come in and take a seat. "I need to explain something to you before we meet my parents."

"You look fabulous, Nicole," he said, studying me from head to toe. "Stella McCartney?"

"It is—but listen, you need to call me 'Darcy' not 'Nicole.' Just for tonight, okay?" I saw him quirk a brow. I needed to explain this to him.

"You see, my name's Darcy Nicole Sheridan. I've been—well…going by my middle name since I've been here at the resort for…personal reasons. My parents will be calling me Darcy and I just thought you should know."

"It's fine. I get it," he responded, shaking his head slightly.

"You do?" I asked, frowning in confusion.

"Sure. Hey, whatever makes you comfortable is fine with me. I don't question the way people handle things in their personal lives and I certainly don't judge."

Judge what? Wait a sec…

"Eli, how did you know this was a Stella McCartney design?"

He shrugged. "I was in Milan for her fall show," he replied nonchalantly, as if he'd just told me he was at a Bronco's game or the U.S. Masters Tournament. He watched my puzzled expression with amusement.

"Oh, somebody's 'gay-dar' seems to be on the fritz, I see."

"Eli," I said, the shock apparent in my tone, "you don't *look* gay. I mean, it never crossed my mind…"

"Ah hah, I see some stereotypes at play here, beautiful," he teased. "And may I add that you don't look *butch* either?"

Rewind. What?

"What?"

"You know, '*butch;*' the stereotypical description for a *lesbian*?"

"Holy hell—you think I'm a lesbian?"

Now he was now the one flustered…getting up from the couch, and running a hand through his thick mass of blond hair. "I guess my gay-dar's on the fritz as well."

I burst into laughter as I saw how totally clueless we both had been. Eli joined me and we continued to laugh until tears were rolling.

"Okay, okay," I said, still giggling. "I want to know why the hell you thought I was a lesbo."

Eli rubbed his eyes and tried to compose himself enough to explain. "I was watching you from outside the pool area before I even came in," he said, starting to chuckle again. "I mean damn, girl, the way you were checking out that blonde across the pool from you left no doubt in my mind. Since I didn't see any interesting males around, I thought it might be nice to hang out with one of my own." He dissolved into laughter once again.

I gave him a hand gesture that was definitely not mom-approved. "One of your own, huh?" I playfully tossed a few couch pillows at him.

"Sorry, sorry," he laughed, shielding himself from the barrage of pillows. "But hey—we can still hang out, yeah?"

I loved the idea of having a gay male BFF.

Let's be honest here, folks. It's every girl's *dream* to have a gay guy bestie, right? I mean, I'm a huge fan of "Sex in the City." Carrie Bradshaw had Stanford

Blatch; Charlotte York had Anthony Marantino and I definitely wanted a Stanford Blatch or an Anthony Marantino of my own!

"I don't know," I said in a teasing voice. "Are you sure you won't mind hanging out with a straight female?"

"Mind? Of course I don't mind. Every gay guy wants a gorgeous, straight, female to drink daiquiris with him poolside. It's the American dream. You're like the ultimate hot-guy bait. Don't you know anything, girl?"

"Well, now that we've settled *that*, let's go meet my folks."

"Showtime!" Eli said, taking my hand as we left to walk down the beach to their condo.

Dinner with Mom and Daddy went well. They both seemed to like Eli a lot. Daddy and Eli talked sports (yes, gay guys enjoy football like anyone else). It was nice having Eli with us because Mom didn't bring up Darin's name at all. I was grateful for that. I knew she presumed Eli was a romantic interest for me, which was fine. I didn't feel any explanation was necessary.

After dinner, they invited us back to their condo to play euchre. Mom poured a glass of wine for all of us, and it was adding to the buzz I'd gotten at dinner. I wasn't used to wine. I was never sure how it would hit me. I realized it was affecting my ability to play euchre when Daddy sighed for the third or fourth time at my throws. He was so damn competitive at everything.

"Let's change partners, Denise," he suggested. "You take Darcy; Eli's mine." For some reason, that struck my funny bone and I started giggling uncontrollably. I felt Eli kick my brand new pair of Prada's from underneath the table.

"Darcy, are you alright?" Mom asked, her brow furrowed in concern.

"Squueeekhehe," I giggled, nodding my head up and down affirmatively.

"No more wine for her, Denise," Daddy replied, taking a serious tone. I changed places with Eli and we started the next game. We were just a few rounds into it when a loud, banging noise against the wall started. It was rhythmic, getting louder and faster and then the moaning started.

"Oh dear God, Martin, they're at it again," my mother hissed, throwing her playing cards down on the table. I looked over at Eli and saw a slow grin appear. The female was moaning loudly and as she continued on, her tone got shriller.

"I swear that broad's going to break glass one of these times," my father said with a laugh, shaking his head.

"Martin!" my mother scolded. "We have guests."

"Then they'll hear for themselves in about twenty seconds." We all strained now to listen and sweet *Jesus,* my father was right! That bitch's moans reached a high soprano pitch that rivaled anything Renee Fleming could've belted out.

"Are you sure there's even a man in there with her?" I asked, giggling. "All you can hear is her screeching and moaning."

"Oh yes," Daddy answered; "Trust me, he has his moments too."

"I mean, the vulgarity they scream," my mother commented again. "Disgusting."

Everything had pretty much quieted down next door for the time being. I wasn't in the mood to continue playing cards.

"I'm really sorry you had to hear all of that, Eli," my mother said, patting his shoulder.

Ahh...Geez. She probably thinks it gave him ideas.

"I'm tired of cards, Eli. Let's go out on the terrace. I could use some salt air to sober up a bit," I said with a sigh.

"Great idea, darling," my mom replied, starting to clear the table. "You two enjoy the ocean view. It's spectacular."

I found my shoes under the table where I'd kicked them off and slid back into them. Eli held my chair out for me like a perfect gentleman. He was scoring so many points with my parents. I could tell by the looks of approval that passed between them all evening. I had to bite my lip to keep from laughing out loud at the thought.

Eli opened the French doors leading out onto the large terrace, and I walked out onto the wooden floor. We could hear the waves splashing against the break wall on the beach. The stars were out, casting their reflection against the ocean. It was magnificent.

"Mmm," I sighed, leaning against the rail as we both looked out over the water. "I love the beach, the ocean, the sand—all of it. I so envy you. You get to work here all year round."

"I haven't got the job yet, and I have no applicable experience. It's kind of a long shot."

"Yeah, but I mean they wouldn't have flown you here unless you had a good chance of being hired, right?"

"Wrong. I paid my own way. Nothing's guaranteed."

"What will you do if you aren't selected then?"

"I'm not sure. I don't have a Plan B yet."

"You could always move to D.C., you know? I'm sure my father could use you in his business. That's where I'm going to work after graduation."

"What kind of business is it?"

"He owns a consulting firm for international marketing and communication. He founded it more than twenty-five years ago. It's called "Sheridan and Associates." I'm going to be one of the associates soon. My father promised me a position before he retires. He eventually wants me to run the whole show there."

Eli let out an impressed whistle. "That must be nice…to have a career waiting for you. I don't know, we'll see," he shrugged. "I have my heart set on staying here, you know? I studied International Culture and can speak Spanish fluently. I'm not sure those skill sets would fit your father's business."

"What do you mean? You're bi-lingual and he does international marketing, for Christ's sake! Of course you'd be a great fit. I mean, it's something to consider as a Plan B, right?"

"Sure, sweetie. Hey, do you wanna do something for New Year's Eve?"

"*Hell* yeah. I have the perfect outfit."

"Somehow, I knew that," he chuckled, giving me a hug. It was in that brief moment of silence we both heard a male voice clear his throat from the next-door terrace. I leaned over the rail just a bit to have a look.

Oh. My. God.

I felt my heart race, as E.J.'s eyes looked over into mine and a slow, sardonic grin graced his handsome face. I realized that he'd been out there the whole time, eavesdropping on our conversation. Holy shit! I backed up quickly so the wall between the two terraces obscured his view of me.

"What?" Eli mouthed to me, looking confused. I didn't answer him, just shook my head, putting my index finger up to stay quiet. A moment later, I heard the terrace door from next-door open and a female voice.

"Are you coming in to bed?"

"Be right there, Lacee," his soft, sexy voice replied.

Skank!

I turned and went back inside the condo, Eli following behind me, still trying to figure out what the hell was going on. "I'll tell you about it when we walk back to my villa. I'm ready to go."

We said goodnight to my parents, who ended up inviting Eli to breakfast the following morning. Seriously, I was pretty sure I was going to have a sore jaw the following morning from trying to hold back all the laughter at the thought that my parents were currently thinking Eli and I were some kind of an "item."

Eli and I walked down the beach towards my place. I told him about my meeting up with E.J. and introducing myself as 'Nicole,' and the rest of it.

"Is there someone special in your life?" I asked, after we'd walked several paces in silence.

"There was," he replied. "It was over before I left Denver, though. I guess I came here for the same reason as you, to heal. Only difference is, I want to remain here permanently. There's no way I'm going back to Denver."

39

I looked over at him, tucking a stray piece of hair behind my ear. "Then don't," I replied. "Seriously, if this thing doesn't work out for you, you should come and work for my dad with me in D.C. The guy friggin' loves you, and Denver doesn't want you anymore."

He nudged me in the ribs, and I gave him a wink.

"So," I said with finality in my tone, "if the job interview doesn't go well, I'm considering you as a gift shop item and am taking you back to D.C. with me."

I really liked Eli. He was easygoing, gorgeous, and I just felt, I don't know…*effortless* around him. Like I didn't have to try and impress him. Plus, I kind of wanted to see the girls at the office completely fall all over themselves as they'd try to get him to go out with them.

I may just have to bring my camcorder.

"Yes, ma'am," he said with a salute and a grin. We'd reached my villa by this time.

"Be by early in the morning to pick you up for breakfast. Sleep well."

"Night, Eli," I said, closing the door to my villa behind me. "You do the same."

Chapter 4

Of course I wasn't completely ready the following morning when Eli came by the villa to pick me up for breakfast. I invited him in while I rushed to finish up with my make-up.

"Okay, I'm ready," I said, slipping my sandals on as Eli opened the door for me, following me outside the villa.

Now timing's a funny thing. If this was a movie, who do you think would be jogging past my villa on the path, looking totally sexy and hot, just as Eli was closing the door behind us at this early morning hour? You guessed it: E.J. And he was without his skank, Lacee. He looked over at me and Eli and in that brief second I could've sworn a dark scowl crossed over his face. And then he was gone.

Breakfast with Mom and Dad went well. They were taking to Eli as if he was going to be their son-in-law some day. I supposed eventually I'd have to explain the relationship. Now wasn't the right time.

My Dad coached him on his interview scheduled for this afternoon with the resort. They were chatting together as if they'd known each other forever. My mother was talking to me about going shopping this afternoon—my favorite thing. She mentioned having dinner tonight, alone, which was kind of strange. I was sure they loved Eli, so I was sure it had nothing to do with them giving me some sort of parental lecture on "taking things slowly." It sounded as if they wanted to have some sort of a serious discussion with me.

Mom and I shopped all afternoon. I'd told Eli to call me later in the day to let me know how his interview had gone. He promised he would. Back at the villa, I had some time to kill before meeting my folks for dinner, so I called Lindsey. I missed my BFF, since I hadn't talked to her in over a week.

When she answered the phone, I heard all kinds of chaos in the background.

"Hey Darce, where the hell you been?" she asked, with an irritated tone

"Your phone works as well as mine," I responded with a laugh.

"I know that. I guess I just wasn't' sure what to say to you. I mean, I hate what Darin did to you and trust me, I told Taz everything and he's royally pissed. I had to beg him to just stay out of it and not say a word to Darin. You don't need that S.O.B. thinking that he broke your heart or anything."

"Thanks, Linds. Actually, I'm thinking maybe he didn't break my heart after all."

"Oh?"

"No, it's not like what you're thinking. I haven't met anyone else. Well, actually I *have* met a really great guy, but he's gay."

"Shut up!" she shrieked. "What are you thinking?"

"I'm thinking that it's really great having a male BFF, that's what I'm thinking."

"He's not going to replace me, right?"

"No one could replace you." I was hearing all kinds of commotion in the background, including a dog barking furiously. "Where the hell are you?"

"Oh," she laughed, "we're over at Mom and Slate's. Mom bought a puppy for Bryce. She thought it would help him kind of get over his jealousy thing with the new baby. The dog's hyper as hell and Slate's having a fit. Want me to call you later?"

"That's okay, Linds. I'm going to dinner with my folks. They came in from Cancun yesterday and we're hanging out. I'll talk to you as soon as I get back to D.C. I've got a lot to tell you."

"I can hardly wait. I'm so happy you're dealing with all of this. I miss you!"

"Miss you too. Give Harper a kiss for me and tell Taz hey."

"I'll do it. Love you."

I smiled after our call ended. I was ready to go back. I no longer feared seeing Lindsey, Taz or anyone else that reminded me of Darin. How could this be? Why did I no longer feel destroyed and heartbroken? Maybe it was meeting Eli, or the feelings that I'd felt when I met E.J. that provided proof that I hadn't really loved Darin the way I thought.

As I reflected, I realized that I'd never once felt the butterflies in my gut that I felt when I was with E.J. that evening. I thought that it was just about a good ol' rebound fuck, now I knew that it was something different. It was something very foreign to me and I liked the fact that it was scary on top of that. I wanted to pursue those types of feelings, and the way I looked at it, if it happened with some stranger hundreds of miles away, it could happen again with an appropriate man. I wasn't into pining for man-whores and that's exactly what E.J. seemed to be.

I dressed for dinner. Mom and Daddy picked me up on the road on the other side of the villas. We were going to an Italian restaurant tonight. My parents were unusually quiet on the ride to the restaurant.

What's up with this?

We were seated, waiting for our appetizers, when my father cleared his throat nervously and said, "Darcy, it's time we talked about your future. Some things have changed and I want to discuss them with you tonight."

Okay. Not a good sign.

"Am I in trouble, Daddy?"

"No sweetheart, nothing like that. It's just that, over the past couple of years, your mother and I have noticed that it may not be prudent for you to assume a top level role at Sheridan & Associates so soon after graduating."

"I don't understand," I replied, looking back and forth between them. My mom wasn't making eye-contact.

"Daddy," I interrupted his next sentence before he began, "cut to the chase, please. Have I done something wrong?"

"No, it's more about what we've done wrong. Your mother and I have come to realize that over the years, well, we've spoiled you rotten, to be perfectly honest. You spend money as if you have an endless supply of it, and you don't appreciate the value of earning your own living. Even in high school, while many of your friends held summer jobs, you spent your time at the country club, traveling, or shopping. It's really our fault, not yours."

Okay. Freeze frame.

You know that scene that most parents have with their teenage son or daughter, where they're all sitting around the dinner table, and the parents are laying it into the poor offspring about how they need to grow up?

Well. That's what was happening to me, right now, except that I was their *twenty-two-year-old* offspring. And that talk was way past due—according to them.

…Shit.

"But Daddy, I never knew that's what you expected of me. I mean, on the plus side, I've never been arrested or anything. I've kept my grades up at school." I gave him the ol' daddy-I-love-you smile.

"I realize that, Darcy," he cut in, "but I'm afraid you're not mature enough to come into my firm at a high-level position. I expect you to earn your way to the top, if that's truly what you want, just like anyone else. It's with blood, sweat and tears that your mother and I built this company. I'm not inclined to simply hand it over to someone who's had everything handed to them over the years, and again, I take full responsibility for that."

Geez, lay it on thick, Dad.

"So, basically you're punishing me for the fact that you and Mom spoiled me?" Lame attempt, I know. But right now, I was grabbing at pretty much anything to protect something that was pretty damn important to me. You know—a six-figure salary with job security and all.

I was incredulous at this turn of events. I mean, yeah, sure, I got everything I wanted, but I still treated them with love and respect! I'd never rebelled against them. Of course, I guess I never had reason to, given the fact I had everything I wanted.

"This isn't a punishment, Darcy Nicole," my mom spoke up, finally making eye contact. "This is a life lesson that both your father and I learned along the way on our own. Neither of us came from wealth. Nothing was handed to us. We worked hard, we studied, and then we built this business together. After you were born, I left the company to raise you and make you a priority. Perhaps I did too much."

"Mom," I gasped, "how can you say that? I feel as if you're both viewing me as some monumental failure!"

"That's not true," my father interjected. "This is an opportunity for you to carve your own career, to have your own dreams and to work to make them happen; if not at Sheridan & Associates, then perhaps somewhere else. The point is, that it's in your hands, and you'll be the one to decide what you want and how to get it without our intervention."

"I see," I whispered, feeling totally deflated. I needed time to digest all of this. I couldn't dispute a lot of what they said. It was painful, though, to think about how they saw me. I was a disappointment to them.

"Darcy," my father said, interrupting my thoughts, "it's *because* we love you so much that we want to take this route. I hope you understand that."

"Yes, Daddy," I replied, clearly defeated. "I think I do."

Chapter 5

I immediately phoned Lindsey as soon as I got back to my villa. I needed my best friend's comfort right now. I was shocked at what my parents had done to me this evening. They knew I was already in a delicate state with all that had happened with Darin. I was trippin' over the fact they'd dropped a bomb on me like that when I was already down. Shit! My call went to her voicemail. I wasn't going to leave a whiney message for her. This required one-on-one communication.

I pulled up Eli's number and called him.

"What's up, Darce?" he answered.

"Are you busy, Eli? I really need someone to talk to right now. It's kind of important."

"Sure, be over in just a few. Are you alright?"

"Not really."

Eli was knocking on my door in less than ten minutes. I rushed to open it, trying to keep a brave face. He was standing there with a bottle of wine in one hand and a very concerned look on his face.

"What happened?" he asked softly.

That's when I lost it. The tears started flowing. I sat next to Eli on the couch and let it all out. I told him about the talk my parents had with me at dinner, and I finally told him everything that I'd been holding inside about Darin and what he'd done to break my heart. He sat there and listened, not interrupting, letting me vent just the way I needed to.

Later on, I was curled up next to Eli and still mulling over the whole ordeal with my parents as we watched some mindless T.V. I felt better after having spilled everything and, as it turned out, Eli was a great sounding board. He just listened, quietly…letting me vent without interrupting.

"You should've heard them, Eli. They painted me as this…completely spoiled brat; a major disappointment to them. Then they took all of the blame for it," I admitted quietly. "I mean I can't believe I'm as bad as all that." I looked up at his face and saw he was fighting back a smile.

"Eli?"

"Hey, Darce, I mean, I've known you for what? All of ten minutes? But I've gotta say, you might stop and give some thought to what they said tonight."

"Eli!"

"Well, come *on*. Put it into perspective, okay? You *are* a tad spoiled, right?"

I gave a reluctant nod, swallowing my pride down with a big chunk of self-awareness.

"Well, your folks are assuming responsibility for that portion of it. I think now what they really want is for you to step up to the plate and take responsibility for your adulthood. They want you to make your own success, and along the way, accept the consequences for your own failures too. It's called Life 101." He nudged my shoulder. "It's time you either step up, or step off."

I looked over at him through my damp eyelashes and knew he was being sincere and, most importantly, he was being a friend; telling me how it was instead of stroking me and trashing my parents for throwing me into the water to sink or swim.

"Is this where I'm supposed to say 'I don't think we're in Kansas anymore, Toto?'"

He smiled and nodded. "Yeah, it's time you found your way all by yourself. Of course, it wouldn't hurt for you to have someone traveling that yellow brick road with you for company." He waggled his eyebrows.

"What?" I sat straight up looking at him for some indication as to what he meant.

"You didn't even ask how my interview went today, Darcy girl."

"Oh, Eli, I'm sorry! You're right. Once again, it had to be about me, didn't it? So, will you tell me how it went?"

47

"Suffice it to say, I didn't get the job. But truthfully, maybe that's for the best since Plan B is looking pretty damn good right about now. That is, if you aren't totally estranged from your folks at this point."

"Are you serious?" I threw my arms around his neck, giving him a bear hug. "You're coming to D.C? That's so fucking awesome! Let me know if you need a place to stay. Seriously, you have no idea how much I needed some good news!"

"Whoa, hold up there, sweetheart. I'd like to discuss this with your father to make sure his company could use me. I don't want to be a charity case or anything. He did mention his firm hires interns and that there were openings, but I want to make sure he wasn't dangling that carrot in front of me in order to appease his somewhat-spoiled daughter."

"Shut up," I laughed, smacking his shoulder playfully. "I'm sure my dad thinks you're good husband material for sure, but do you really think I'm so unappealing that he'd use bribery?"

"Hmmm, I don't know, Darce. I'm willing to bet the guy that finally snags you is going to have his hands full. Chicks like you make me pretty fucking thankful I'm gay."

"Oh really?" I taunted. "Like you're not high-maintenance at all?"

"Can't hold a candle to you, sweetheart. Now, let's figure out what couture we're wearing tomorrow night for the big New Year's Eve bash at the clubhouse. Because I'm *so* not the clashing type."

Eli and I spent an hour going through my wardrobe. And after my sob fest, I think we both needed the therapy that only silk shirts and red-soled shoes can provide. After that, we went over to his villa and completed the calming process. Talk about a clothes whore! I told him he better never say another word to me about *my* clothes addiction. Dude had way more clothes in his closet than I had in mine.

"Did you bring everything in your closet from home thinking you had that job, Eli? I mean a tuxedo, really?"

"Don't be ridiculous. I brought the essentials for a week at a resort for multi-occasion dress," he replied, inserting a slight lisp to be funny. "Besides, the New Years Eve gala is black tie."

I rolled my eyes at him, digging back in and finding he loved shoes every bit as much as me. I knew right then and there that this was the beginning of a *very* beautiful relationship.

Eli shared the details with me on his recent break-up. Seth was Eli's former partner, still living in Denver. They'd lived together all during college and had plans to start up their own business in New Orleans once they'd graduated. They'd saved to invest in a cruise boat that would cater to people with alternative sexual preferences—within reason. The ship would be for weekend cruising around the Gulf.

Then, three months ago, Seth started backpedaling on the idea. Eli said he knew something was wrong. He decided to follow Seth one day and discovered the love of his life was involved in a lifestyle Eli had never fathomed. Seth, dressed in drag, went to a seedy hotel in Denver. As it turned out, Seth was involved with a group of men that practiced BDSM to the hilt. Eli described some of the toys of torture Seth was enjoying when he'd busted in on him and his friends in that hotel room. All Eli could do now was try to rebuild his life and move on.

We talked about our families. Eli's family lived in Montana; that's where he was raised as the youngest of four. He had two older sisters and one older brother. Eli said his family had always been supportive of his lifestyle. He'd come out in high school and they were down with it. His family had loved Seth like one of their own. The way Eli told it, their break-up crushed his family nearly as much as it had him.

"You know, Eli," I said, "I think you'll find D.C. to be fairly liberal about alternative lifestyles. Maybe you'll find someone to love there."

"Maybe we both will," he replied softly. "So, are you hoping to see your hottie at the New Year's Eve shindig?"

I shrugged impassively. "I don't care one way or the other," I lied.

"That's bullshit and you know it, girl. Don't worry though. You'll turn his head regardless of what you're wearing. I have a feeling when the dude looks at you, he's not picturing you clothed anyway." He winked over at me.

"Ha, and what makes you say that?"

"I'm gay, not cold-blooded, sweetheart."

"Well regardless, you know he'll have Lacee clinging all over him, as always. You know the one he says is his executive assistant? Executive assistant, my ass."

"I'm glad to see you don't care one way or the other about it. It looks like this party's going to be fun. Hey, maybe I can be of help to you on the Lacee front," he said, tossing me another one of those, what I was beginning to recognize as Eli-trademark, winks.

Oh yeah. Definitely a beautiful relationship in the making.

We finished with our wardrobe selection for the following night. We had plans to work out together in the morning, and then hang by the pool until it was time to get ready for the party. My vacation was turning out to be better than I'd ever expected.

Darin who?

Chapter 6

I was putting on the finishing touches to my hair and make-up when Eli arrived, looking like someone I'd have every intention of hitting on. *If he were straight, that is.*

He, naturally, was wearing his Calvin Klein tuxedo, with a two-button notched lapel, satin besom pockets with the pleated trousers that went with it. His thick, blond hair was fashionably tousled and he had his five o'clock shadow going, which was the perfect touch for this evening. The guy could be a runway model.

"*Hello*, gorgeous supermodel," I said as I gave him a quick hug after letting him into the villa. During the quick embrace, he managed to reach the part of the zipper at the back of my dress I'd had trouble with before.

"Don't tell me, let me guess—Jovani?" Eli suggested, once again guessing the designer who was responsible for tonight's dress, as he finished zipping up the form-fitting material.

"Dude knows his designers, I'm impressed," I replied with a wink. My mother had actually purchased this for me when we shopped the other day. It was indeed a Jovani; a sexy strapless little black dress that had a sheer overlay with a wire hem ruffle hemline, and a rosette with jewel embellishments. It was short, my mother had a bit of an issue with that, until I promised her I wouldn't bend over the whole evening.

"Bend over? You better not even sneeze," she'd clucked, giving in as usual.

I had a black, Spanish-lace wrap in case the evening got chilly, and of course, black stilettos and clutch. I had piled my hair up on top of my head, letting wispy cascades escape to frame my face, and wore long, silver drop ball earrings.

"You, sweetheart, look magnificent, I might add," Eli remarked, giving me a kiss on the cheek. "I'm sure you'll be quite the distraction tonight. Mission accomplished."

"Hey," I said, turning and leaving the room to grab my wrap and clutch, "that remains to be seen, Mr. Chambers. Do you dance, by the way?"

"Do I dance?" he asked, giving me a major eye roll. "Do I dance? You really need to ask?"

"I'll take that as a 'yes' then. Good—because I *love* to dance and shake my stuff, if you know what I mean."

"I'm not sure how much you can shake in that number," he commented. "You're virtually overflowing at the top."

"I know, right?" I giggled. "Let's go."

∞ ∞ ∞ ∞ ∞ ∞

Dinner and dessert had been served. My parents had dinner with us and then begged off for the rest of the evening, saying they were going back to their condo to relax and have a couple of nightcaps. My instincts told me they thought Eli and I wanted to be alone. I should probably have told them about me and Eli at this point, but it seriously was just too fucking entertaining to see them fawn all over the poor guy.

The band was awesome, playing a mixture of soft, classic, and alternative rock. Eli and I had fast danced a couple of times. I wanted to dance to a couple of slow songs that I absolutely loved, but Eli refused, saying that my tush and va-jay-jay would be exposed. He was kidding, I'm sure. When we sat back down at our table after leaving the dance floor, he ordered more drinks.

"Why the sad face, pretty girl? Disappointed that your hottie hasn't shown yet?"

"Not really," I lied, tossing down the rest of my cocktail, trying to appear unaffected.

"Well, get ready to lose the frown," Eli said with a grin. "Check it out at three o'clock," he finished with a nod. I immediately turned to my right—nothing.

"*My* three o'clock," he laughed.

"That's not the way you're supposed to do it, Eli," I hissed, now coyly looking to my left. And *there he was*, without that fake blonde who he usually always came equipped with, I'd like to add.

E.J. was dressed in a black, Dior tux that was custom-tailored to fit perfectly to his lean, masculine build. His hair had been trimmed a bit, and it was somewhat disheveled—maybe from the ocean breeze that had whipped up this evening, or maybe from something else. He had an almost predatory thing going on tonight, much different than the persona he'd presented previously. I was even more curious now than ever. I hadn't intended to stare, but when his gaze locked onto mine, I could feel myself blush at being busted. A-fucking-gain.

A slow, sardonic smile spread across his full, luscious lips. His smoldering gray eyes seemed to undress me with their intensity as they gazed sensually into mine. He turned around to the bar when his drink was placed in front of him.

"Stare much?"

I startled a little bit, hearing my friend's voice as he brought me out of my E.J. trance.

"Oh. Sorry, Eli. My God, how obvious was that?"

He let out a low whistle. "Major obvious."

"Thanks for your words of reassurance," I replied, dryly. "I'm just trying to figure out why Blondie isn't around."

"It's as if you have mental telepathy," Eli sighed, nodding his head towards the entrance door of the club. There she was, all decked out in a ruby-red sequined party dress. It was tight, strapless and her huge breasts were spilling over the top of the scalloped bodice. Her blonde hair was gathered up into a messy tangle of curls that cascaded around the crown of her head. She wore black stiletto heels that made her about four inches taller.

"Fuck me," I commented, a bit louder than intended.

"No worries, doll. I've got this," Eli said, standing up and heading towards her in his gorgeous blond glory. *Oh yeah*, he was something else. He wasn't gone more than thirty seconds when a fresh drink arrived for me.

53

"The gentleman at the bar sent this over, Miss. He wonders if he might join you for a moment." I was totally dumbstruck, but I managed a nod 'yes' to the server, swallowing nervously. I took a sip of my drink and, within moments, E.J. had taken the seat vacated by Eli.

"You look exquisite tonight, Nicole," his sultry voice floated to my ears. "You know, I don't even know your last name," he continued.

Why do I suddenly feel as if I'm the prey...?

"Maybe it's better if you and I remain on a first name basis, E.J.," I replied curtly, taking another sip of liquid courage. This man unnerved me and, for whatever reason, I wasn't comfortable with it. Sexually, hell yes I wanted him, but something about him also sent warning bells to my brain.

"As you wish," he said, lowering his gaze to the swell of my breasts. I squirmed a bit in my seat, crossing my leg, which in the 4-inch heels I was wearing, caused my knee cap to bang against the underside of the table.

Fuck, that hurt!

"Are you alright?" he asked, quirking an eyebrow in slight amusement.

"I'm fine," I said. "So, will *Lacee* be joining us at the table?"

"I hadn't planned on inviting her, unless you'd like me to do so. Are you interested in ménage?" He smiled wickedly at me.

I nearly spewed the last sip of my drink onto him as I choked on his words. "I beg your pardon?" I hissed, trying my damndest to compose myself.

Another flicker of amusement crossed his face. "I didn't mean to offend or shock you. I guess I was simply trying to understand your reason for asking about Lacee. I thought I was perfectly clear that she's my assistant, who occasionally travels with me on business."

"Oh, I think she's a little more than that. You forget how thin those walls are between the condos. Actually," I said, shifting in my seat, "it doesn't matter. I just don't appreciate being lied to."

"When did I lie to you?" he asked, quirking that beautiful brow once again.

54

"The night…the night we had dinner," I stammered. "I asked if she was your fiancé, wife, fuck-buddy, girlfriend—whatever, remember?"

"Absolutely, and as I recall, I told you she wasn't my wife, fiancé or girlfriend. Where's the lie?"

"It's a lie by omission," I shrugged, trying to hide the fact I was getting a little pissed. "You didn't admit you were fuck-buddies and you should have."

"Whatever Lacee and I are together physically is really not the issue. I'm not emotionally involved with her and there was never a vow of monogamy. I don't sleep around, Nicole, but I do have needs. I can assure you that my dick has never entered Lacee unsheathed. You've nothing to worry about. Can you say the same to me about your fuck buddy?"

"I'm sorry, say again?" I leaned forward, not having any freakin' clue what he was talking about.

His eyes grew harsh as he nodded to somewhere behind me. Eli and Lacee were on the dance floor on the other side of the room, molded together in a slow dance to the band's instrumental song.

"Eli's not my fuck buddy," I said, turning back to face him with a haughty look.

"Oh really?" he asked incredulously. "It seems I recall him loitering around your villa one morning recently. I presumed he'd stayed over."

"Whatever we were doing is none of your business," I quickly informed him. "You weren't interested, remember?"

"So, of course you found someone else to fuck posthaste." The pissier he got with me, the more aristocratic British vocabulary crept into his voice. The words, I loved. The tone? Not so much.

I took a long sip of my drink. "For your information, Eli's becoming a good friend. He's not interested in having sex with me, so there."

"I find that very difficult to believe." He gave me a wry look.

"I'm not his *type*, if you catch my drift." His look of disbelief went to confusion and then, yep, there it was: realization.

"Oh. I see," he replied softly, a quirk of a smile appearing, along with that gorgeous dimple.

"And, for the record, I'm offended that you obviously think I'm some slutty skank. Just because I was kind of drunk and...*lonely* the night I grabbed your junk, *doesn't* mean I make a habit of doing that. I think I shared with you the fact that I recently ended a one-year relationship that was monogamous—at least on my part, anyway."

"Indeed you did, which I also explained at the time was the reason things didn't go further with us. It didn't mean forever, though."

Now it was my turn to be puzzled. He saw my frown and the corner of his mouth curled into a cryptic grin. I was mesmerized by that grin. There was something refined, powerful, and there it was again: *predatory* about it. My reverie was broken when he glanced at his Rolex.

"It's nearly midnight. Take a walk with me out onto the veranda, Nicole."

I nodded, despite the fact that his request was a border-line order, allowing him to take my hand as he quietly led me out through the French doors that led to the veranda. We walked down to the end, where it turned and continued on to the side of the building. It was quiet and we were alone.

Without warning, he pulled me against him, tilting my chin upward with his long fingers, he studied my face in the moonlight. His eyes were extraordinary...dark smoky gray. He lowered his mouth to mine, his full lips working mine into complete obedience; his tongue found mine and I kissed him back with a startling hunger. It unnerved me what he was evoking from me; I didn't even know this man and, here I was, willing to take anything and everything he was giving.

His hands lowered to my hips, gently massaging them, before moving to my ass and pulling me to him where, once again, I felt his rock hardness against my abdomen. His hips gyrated slowly, causing me to bite down on my lower lip to keep from moaning at the feel of his cock—his very impressive cock, I'd like to add.

Jesus!

He backed me up, pressing me into the side wall of the building, his hands now fisting the material of my dress, slowly inching it up my hips, and exposing my black silk thong. I felt his hands on my bare ass now, gripping the bare skin. A moan finally managed to escape my kiss-abused lips, quietly pleading with him.

"Shhh…" he brushed his thumb across my bottom lip, and my tongue reached out to it. I heard his quick breath, inhaled through his teeth. I felt him lean more into me, taking his other hand and resting it on the wall next to my head. His mouth was next to my ear as he whispered, "I'm going to make you come. Right here. Right now…and you *will* come, love."

I moaned again at the forbidden thought of it. Nodding, I pressed myself harder against his erection. My hands were firmly planted on his shoulders, my fingers digging into them with the pleasure he was providing. I felt his long fingers dip beneath the elastic of my thong, then instantly they were gently teasing the soft, moist folds of my sex. I drew in a sharp breath as his thumb and forefinger rolled my clitoris, squeezing gently, which sent an electric shock wave through my entire body.

"Oh God," I moaned, my breathing now coming faster. He thrust a finger up into me, and then another, while he rocked the heel of his hand against my clit. I felt his fingers inside of me, expertly locating my swollen G-spot, and applying pressure against it rhythmically as my hips started gyrating in a circular motion around his hand.

"Mmmm," I moaned, my voice husky with pleasure. His lips imprisoned mine, his tongue tracing my lower lip.

"Your pussy's so wet, love; wet and ready for me. I'm going to kiss it one day, Nicole." He told me, his British accent thicker now. "Would you like that?"

"Yes," I whined, continuing to roll my hips. "Don't stop," I breathed, as his fingers continued fucking me with a slow, deliberate vengeance. The sweet sensation of an orgasm was now unfolding at his fingertips. My body shook with the release. I cried out with pleasure, moving my hips harder against his hand as it unleashed around me. My fingernails were digging into his shoulders, and I bit my lower lip as I kept coming and coming around his sexually menacing fingers until I was totally spent.

"Oh God," I rasped. "Jesus Christ." I slumped against him, catching my breath. My limbs had turned to jelly; my face was flushed with afterglow.

E.J. pulled his fingers from me, and smoothed my dress back down over my hips. Never taking his eyes off mine, he brought his wet fingers to his mouth, making me watch as he sucked on them. From inside, we could hear the final countdown chant of the partiers to midnight.

"Five...Four...Three...Two...One! Happy New Year!" From somewhere, fireworks went off in beautiful displays on the beach. E.J. pulled me back against him, and lowered his lips to mine in an almost savage kiss. I finally got with the program, wondering why he had gone from gentle to wild on my lips. They were tender by the time he pulled away.

"Happy New Year, Nicole," he said softly. Just then, we found ourselves illuminated in the dark by headlights from a car pulling up alongside of the building. It was a black, stretch limo. No one got out immediately.

"That's for me," E.J. said nonchalantly, like he was already forgetting what just happened. "I'm headed to the airport now. I'll see you again, Nicole. Behave yourself and I mean it."

"What?" I asked, standing there completely confused by his exit. The chauffeur got out and opened the passenger door for him and I watched as he disappeared inside the car. I stood there in a complete stupor, watching as the limo backed up the drive, and faded quickly into the night.

What the fuck just happened?

Chapter 7

Yep, it was Friday the 13th alright. Not one of my favorite things, even though I don't particularly ascribe to being a superstitious person. Conversely, there had been some very bad things happen in my life on Friday the 13th. Without a doubt.

Just some of my anti-Friday-the-thirteenth examples:

1. On Friday the 13th in 1998, my sweet little kitty named "Scamper" got hit by a car and killed.

2. It was on a Friday the 13th that I first ever got my period.

3. I lost my virginity on a Friday the 13th to Jamie McWilliams and it was the worst experience of my life!

4. It was also on a Friday the 13th that they crowned our high school Homecoming Queen and I only made it to first runner-up. And just between you and me, I deserved that crown more than Sheila "Married to my Pom-Poms" Deming!

So you see why I'm not a big fan of Friday the 13th? Of course, Lindsey had pooh-poohed my objections to her having the rehearsal dinner held on this day.

"Our wedding's on the 14th, Valentine's Day, Darce. The whole point of the rehearsal dinner is to prepare for the wedding the following day," she pointed out, when we'd had lunch a couple of weeks prior.

"I know, but couldn't you have it two days ahead, like on the 12th instead of the 13th?" I'd whined.

"Don't be ridiculous," she replied, giving me a major eye roll. "Besides that, Taz's brother Easton won't be arriving until the morning of the 13th, so that wouldn't work anyway since he's Taz's best man."

I shook my head. "I still can't believe Slate's not going to be Taz's best man. They're best friends. That's crazy."

Lindsey sighed as if tired of explaining. "Darce, my grandfather's dead; my dad's either dead or on the run, so Mom insisted that Slate be the one to give me away and that *no* bride should have to walk down the aisle alone. So, having my step-father escort me down the aisle makes perfect sense. Besides it solved the problem Taz had with his father being so adamant about including his older brother in the ceremony. Problem solved."

I wrinkled my brow in confusion. "Yeah, what's all that about with Taz's father? I mean, what's the deal with his whole family anyway? Does he hate his brother or something?"

"No, nothing like that. I guess they're just not close. Actually, Easton is his half-brother. He's 33 years-old, and has spent the majority of his time over in England with his mother, since she and Taz's dad divorced. I guess she's a real bitch too, and from some sort of wealthy British royalty. Easton spent summers in California with his dad, though. But, with Taz being three years younger and all, they just really didn't have a lot in common."

"Huh," I said, "Sounds like there's a lot of water under *that* bridge."

Lindsey had snorted. "I think there's a whole lot more to the story than what Taz has shared with me. I get the idea that Easton's a spoiled prick. Apparently, he used to pull some shit during those summers he spent with Taz and the younger sister, Paige. He didn't elaborate much, but I'm sure I'll get it out of him sooner or later."

"Where does Easton live now?" I asked.

"All over, I guess. He's some kind of wealthy mogul. Actually, he's kept in touch with Taz somewhat over the years. I guess he was in D.C. a couple of years ago and they hung out for a week or so. Taz says he's quite the ladies man, too," she added, giving me a wink.

So, against my objections, the rehearsal dinner was to be held at the Country Club my folks belonged to on Friday the 13th. Eli was escorting me. Yes, that's right. I need to catch up here.

I'd found an apartment in D.C., so it actually kind of worked out perfectly when I found out Eli *would* be moving to the same city, because I wanted someone to live with and Eli was…well, *Eli*. My parents now knew the whole story about Eli's being gay, which of course disappointed them as far as being husband material for me. Not me though, because their faces when they found out? *Freakin' hilarious!* I mean, they were still crazy about the guy—who wouldn't be? Plus, I think they felt better having me out on my own knowing Eli was looking out for me.

I had finished my on-line classes and officially would graduate in March with a B.S. in International Marketing. Eli and I had both started entry-level positions as Management Trainees with my father's company. Eli was working for the Director of Customer Relations. I was working in the Public Relations group. We learned how to prepare press releases, presentations, advertisements, and designed booths for clients participating in trade shows and technical training sessions. Both of us hated our bosses.

My boss was Jon Rollins, a tall, lanky guy in his mid-forties with acne scars and a crew cut. Eli worked for Leanne Harshman, a self-proclaimed cunt that was banging Rollins. Eli said she was a royal bitch if she didn't get her way. Both of our bosses liked to micro-manage. We'd bitch about it at home after work, along with complaining about our lack of love lives. I no longer felt any sorrow about the break-up with Darin.

It was strange that my thoughts occasionally drifted back to New Year's Eve with E.J. I wondered if we'd ever see each other again. And that question bothered me because, after the stunt he'd pulled, I should've blacklisted the guy from my mind altogether. But *God*…those fingers. And his voice as he whispered dirty promises…

I shook those thoughts from my mind for the hundredth time, at least. It had been over a month ago. I needed to move on and focus on tonight's rehearsal dinner.

There, I was ready. Glancing in the full-length mirror, I assessed my dinner dress for tonight. It was an Anne Klein simple black dress with a squared neckline trimmed in royal blue. I'd accented with royal blue earrings and necklace. My hair was down and straightened flat.

Eli called from the hallway, reminding me that we needed to leave now or be late. "I'm coming," I hollered out, slipping my heels on and grabbing my coat. Why Lindsey picked February for the wedding was beyond me! She was all into having it on Valentine's Day, though. And the dresses were gorgeous, so I was fairly excited about the event. It was going to be a small wedding in a Methodist Church. I was maid of honor and Jill was a bridesmaid. Easton was to be the best man, and Gabe a groomsman. Lindsey had won that battle, putting her foot down and explicitly informing Taz that Darin was not only out of the wedding party, but not to show his cheating face at their wedding either.

Eli let out a whistle when I joined him in the entryway. "You look fabulous as always, Darcy," he complimented.

"Ditto," I replied, buttoning up my coat. "Now, let's do this."

A valet greeted us as we pulled my Mercedes up to the arched overhang at the entrance to the club. We proceeded inside and were directed to the "Wisteria Room" where the bar was set up for pre-dinner cocktails and appetizers. Soft music was being piped into the banquet room. Eli took my coat for me, once we were inside. I immediately saw Lindsey's grandmother and Slate talking to a man and woman I'd never seen before. Taz's parents maybe?

Eli returned with our drinks and I all but slurped mine down.

"Easy," he cautioned, with a smile in his eyes. "Nervous much?"

"You know I hate Friday the 13th," I replied, "Nothing good ever happens for me on days like this."

"I'll get you one more if you promise to sip, and not slurp."

"Fine," I said, shooting him an innocent look, as he began his trek back over to the bar. "But make it a double."

Taz and Lindsey had just come in, so I hurried over to them, giving Lindsey a hug.

"You both look gorgeous," I said, hugging Taz now. "I'm so very happy for you."

"You aren't drunk are you?" Lindsey asked, cocking an accusatory brow. I gave her a very offended look. Taz chuckled as he leaned in to give me a brotherly kiss on the cheek. "You look hot as always, Darcy," he said.

Eli returned with my drink and greeted them both. We chatted for a few minutes, and then I asked about Jill and Gabe.

"They should be here any time now," Lindsey replied, with a hint of nervousness. "They had a slight delay in Philly."

"Calm down, babe," Taz soothed her. "They'll be here. Let's go over and say hi to Mom and Dad, okay?" She nodded and they made their way over to where both sets of parents were, well except Slate was the stepparent, obviously. Standing there while Eli chatted with someone nearby, I leisurely looked around the room for a face that resembled Taz's as I wondered what his seemingly-absent half-brother looked like, and when he'd make his appearance.

By the time I finished my second cocktail, I knew I needed to make a trip to the Girl's Room before we sat down to dinner. When I told Eli where I was going, he opted to join me. We rambled down the carpeted hallway and around the corner, where I knew there were a set of lavatories that served the banquet rooms in this wing of the club.

As we rounded the corner, there was a line of women waiting outside of the Ladies Restroom, complaining about the door being locked. One lady was lightly tapping on the door, asking repeatedly if anyone was in there.

"Looks like the little boy's room is free," Eli commented, "Be back in a flash."

"What's the hold-up?" I asked, as I took my place behind the last lady in the line. "I know there are several stalls in there."

"Someone has the main door locked," she said, clearly irritated. "It's been nearly ten minutes now. Some of the others went to find facilities in the other wing. This is my first time here and I don't feel like getting lost in this mammoth building, or I'd do the same."

Just then, the woman at the front of the line started banging loudly on the door. Frustrated, she huffed off saying she was going to find a manager to get the door unlocked. A couple of guys came out of the men's room and waited with their respective dates for the evening, asking them what the hold-up was in getting inside. Eli returned to me, clearly puzzled that the line hadn't moved at all.

Just as the pissed-off lady was coming back with one of the staff following closely behind her with a key ring, we heard the sound of the lock being turned on the door. By this time, Lindsey had come up behind me.

"What's going on?" she asked, taking her place at the end of the line.

"I guess someone's locked the door so no one else can get into the ladies' lounge," I replied with a shrug. The door opened and, I swear, my heart stopped for a slow-motioning second as I saw the guilty party step into the now-crowded hallway.

"Good evening, everyone. Sorry about the inconvenience," the familiar, masculine, sultry voice floated to my ears, sending shockwaves. It was *E.J.*, impeccably dressed, smiling as he straightened his tie and smoothed his jacket into place, walking down the hallway towards us.

"Oh my God," I hissed, once I closed my gaping mouth. I heard Eli's amused snicker. E.J.'s smile faded slightly when he recognized me in the line. His lashes lowered to half-mast and then I heard him address Lindsey.

"Lindsey," he greeted, "See you at dinner."

"Let Taz know I didn't fall in will you, Easton?" She gave a small giggle then turned back to me, seeing my shocked reaction.

"What?" she asked, furrowing her brow.

"Easton?" I sputtered. "That's EASTON?"

"Yeah, Taz's half-brother, he got in this morning."

"That's *E.J.!*" I hissed. "You know—the one I told you about?"

"No!" Lindsey said, clamping her hand over her mouth.

I gave her a look. *The* look.

"The man-whore who finger-fucked you to a mind-blowing O?"

"Why not say it a little *louder*, Lindsey? I don't think the east wing heard you," I hissed.

"Oh shit, sorry," she said, pressing her fingers against her lips.

"Fuck," I heard Eli murmur behind me. I turned back around to face him and that's when I saw *her!* Fucking *Lacee* was now coming out of the restroom, fixing her hair and at least having the courtesy of looking a *little* sheepish until she saw me. In that moment, her expression morphed to haughty as her blue eyes flickered recognition. A cat-like smile graced her lips as she passed by, nodding to Lindsey as she made her way back to the banquet room.

Friday. The fucking thirteenth.

Chapter 8

Everyone was gathered in the church waiting for the wedding procession to begin. Above, in the choir loft, the organist and vocalist had begun the song that was to be Lindsey's wedding march, "Love of a Lifetime," by Firehouse. The vocalist was doing a damn great job of sounding exactly like C.J. Snare from the band.

Lindsey had picked the entrance song; Taz had picked the song for the exit procession—the one where I'd be escorted out by Easton. Who knew Taz would be such a romantic and pick "The Search is Over" by Survivor? We'd all been given our cues as to what lyrics of the songs signaled our entrance down the aisle.

I fixed an errant wisp of hair for Jill, as she stood nervously in the vestibule of the church waiting for the lyric signal. We needed to pace ourselves so that the song finished as Lindsey and Taz ascended the steps to the altar.

"You look beautiful, Jill," I whispered to her.

"I'm shaking like hell, Darce. I hate having to be first out of the gate."

"It's not a horse race, hun," I reassured her. "You'll be fine.

"We'll make a wish and send it on a prayer..."

That was Jill's cue as she started up the long, white satin runner that had been placed on the marble-tiled floor of the church aisle. I could see her bouquet shaking just a bit as she proceeded. Jill was keeping the proper pace and was halfway up to the front where Taz, Easton and Gabe were standing next to each other in front of the steps to the altar, facing the back of the church, waiting for the beautiful bride.

Lindsey's dress was an exquisite winter white satin gown that was form-fitting, but flared out slightly at mid-calf; there was a bustle in the back where the long train was attached. The front had a low-cut square bodice, with capped long tapered sleeves, appropriate for a winter wedding. Sammie and I had helped her

66

with her hair, piling it on top of her head, intricately weaving Baby's Breath throughout it. Just then, I heard my lyric cue.

"A love to last my whole life through…"

I started up the aisle, now understanding why Jill felt so nervous. Everyone in their pews turned to watch the wedding procession head up the aisle, waiting for the star of the event to make her entrance. I finally reached the front of the church, noticing Easton's piercing gaze as I did.

Humph—Man-whore in a tux! Damn sexy man-whore in a tux.

Eli gave me a smile and a wink as I passed his pew and turned left at the front and took my place in front of Jill, turning then to the back of the church, seeing Lindsey standing there, with Slate looking hot in his black suit, his arm wrapped around hers as her lyric cue started.

"Still, we both know that the road is long…"

Damn this song always gave me chills. Now it brought tears to my eyes as I watched my best friend coming down the aisle. The long train of her dress flowed elegantly behind her as Slate had her by the arm, walking her down the white satin runner to the front of the church, where Trace waited for her with nothing but pure love in his eyes.

Taz looked gorgeous in his long-tailed, black tuxedo, as did Easton and Gabe. The cummerbunds matched the color of the gowns Jill and I wore. They were floor length, midnight-blue satin, with plunging necklines and long tapered sleeves. Our flowers were white roses mixed with dark-blue carnations that matched the gowns. I watched in awe as Slate took Lindsey's hand and placed it into Taz's outstretched one. The song was just finishing up as Taz and Lindsey, hand-in-hand walked up the three steps to where the minister waited.

Forever in my heart, I finally found the love of a lifetime.

That was my cue to go and take Lindsey's bouquet from her so the prayers and vows could begin. When she turned to me, I saw tears of joy in her eyes as I gently relieved her of the gorgeous, overflowing wedding bouquet.

The minister started the service, letting everyone know the purpose for which we were gathered here today…blah, blah, blah. I wanted him to get to the good part. I knew Lindsey and Taz had composed their own wedding vows in secret from each other. What I didn't understand was why she refused to share what she'd written with me, her best friend, for Chrissake! Naturally, I suspected she thought I'd roll my eyes over that kind of stuff, but really? Would I do that to my best friend? Well, definitely not on *purpose*, anyway. Oh good, it was time. The minister announced the couple would be exchanging their vows. They turned to face one another. Taz went first. He cleared his throat, taking her hand in his.

"Lindsey Erin Dennison, I love you. You are my best friend. Today, I give myself to you in marriage. I promise to encourage and inspire you; to laugh with you and to comfort you in times of sorrow and struggle. I promise to love you in good times and in bad; when life seems easy and when it seems hard; when our love is simple and when it's an effort. I promise to cherish you, and to always hold you in highest regard. I promise my faithfulness and devotion to you. These things I give to you today, and all the days of my life."

I could tell Lindsey was crying. She could be so emotional at times, especially where Taz was concerned. Their love was the real deal, no doubt about that. She paused for a moment, brushing a tear from her cheek and then raised her head to him, gazing up into his eyes.

"Trace Michael Matthews, because of you I laugh, I smile, I dare to dream again. The sun smiles on us today, our wedding day, and how can it not? For our love is stronger than forever and our hearts beat together as one. I look forward with great joy to spending the rest of my life with you. I promise to be a true and faithful partner from this day forward, in all life's circumstances, as we face them together. I will always be there for you, to comfort you, love you, honor and cherish you. This commitment is made in love, kept in faith, and eternally made to you. I love you."

Crap. And there goes my mascara…

The minister had a bit more to say, then he motioned for Easton to bring the wedding bands up to the altar. Taz slid Lindsey's wedding band on her finger, lifting her hand and kissing it as he did. She placed the plain gold wedding band onto his finger, smiling up at him adoringly.

The minister then said all the usual stuff about the power vested in him through the District of Columbia, pronouncing them husband and wife. He then instructed them to kiss. Once finished, they turned to face the congregation and the minister introduced them as Mr. & Mrs. Trace Matthews. Everyone clapped. I looked over at Easton and he was watching me with those intense, gray eyes as he clapped for the newlyweds.

My attention turned when I heard Harper start to fuss. Constance Matthews had not let that baby out of her arms since arriving from California. Slate was holding Michael. Sammie had Bryce. The organist started the first chords of "The Search is Over" and I knew it was time to follow the newlywed couple out of the church.

Here we friggin' go…I have to touch him, as the instructions were, we had to be arm-in-arm.

While Taz and Lindsey descended the steps from the altar to start down the aisle, it suddenly dawned on me that I hadn't noticed Lacee in the congregation as I had made my entrance. I took the opportunity to gaze through the pews and didn't see her in attendance. Maybe she was only interested in showing up for the reception, no doubt in something skimpy and glittery to take attention from the bride. I scoffed internally at the notion. My mom caught my eye and gave me a smile and a wave. Daddy looked totally uncomfortable in his suit and tie, running his finger around the inside of his collar, as if it were too tight.

From behind, Jill nudged me to move as I walked to the center where Easton was with his dazzling smile, hooking his arm into mine as we followed the bride and groom down the aisle.

"Smile," he whispered to me, "This is a happy occasion."

"Maybe for them, not for me," I hissed quietly, making sure I tensed my arm so he knew I wasn't enjoying him touching me. I forced a smile at all the wedding guests who were turned sideways, taking pictures of the wedding party.

I'd been in enough wedding parties to know that the freaking picture-taking right after the ceremony dragged on for eternity. Plus, I was sure I'd be stuck in a picture or fifty with just Easton and me as best man and maid of honor. Fuck me.

Once outside the church, the photographer directed all of us to the church basement, where we could freshen up for the pictures. We were to meet back upstairs in ten minutes.

As it turned out, it wasn't as miserable as I thought it would be. Easton and I had several pictures taken together, most everything else we were in involved the whole wedding party, so I kept my distance. The final picture was the wedding party, boy-girl, boy-girl.

It was Taz and Lindsey in the center, Easton and me next to each other with Easton standing next to Lindsey, and me standing on the outside. Jill was next to Taz with Gabe on the outside. The photographer had to tell me twice to scoot closer to Easton so that he could center the photograph properly and get everyone in. I grudgingly obliged. The girls all held their wedding bouquets for this shot.

Once he had everyone lined up, smiling as instructed, the camera had a malfunction. *Shit, I wish he'd get this done.* He was working on it when I felt a warm hand caress my ass. I immediately squirmed to the outside, not daring to look at whom I knew was the culprit.

"There now," the photographer said, once again taking aim. "No, no, Darcy, you need to move back in closer to Easton. You're out of alignment again." I scooted back over, purposely elbowing Easton in the side as I did.

"Okay, one…two…three…everyone say 'cheese'," he instructed in an ironically cheesy way. Just as we all complied, I felt that hand once again on my ass, squeezing my right cheek firmly.

"Shit!" I hissed, louder than intended as the flash went off. Lindsey looked over at me with a puzzled expression.

"All finished," the photographer announced. "We'll take more at the reception."

Thank God!

Lindsey and Taz left in the wedding limo, heading to the reception taking place at one of the banquet rooms at the St. Regis in the heart of D.C. Eli and I had a room reservation so that we could party responsibly at the reception, where the live band would be performing an ensemble of mixed genre music.

Apparently, Easton had rented a limo to transport his parents, along with Slate and Sammie to the reception. Lindsey's grandmother was going to be taking all of the children home to stay with her, forgoing the reception. I could tell Constance was having a difficult time parting with baby Harper.

As Eli and I got into my Mercedes to start over to the reception, he could tell I was pissed.

"Okay, spill," he said. "What the hell happened back there?"

"I'll tell you what fucking happened. Easton grabbed my ass twice during pictures. How fucking inappropriate is that?"

I saw a smile flicker across Eli's face.

"Oh no," I said. "It isn't funny. After what he did with bringing Lacee to the rehearsal dinner last night, and the incident with the both of them doing whatever in the restroom, he's a freakin' piece of work."

Eli patted my arm gently. "Hey Darce? This is Taz and Lindsey's day, so I don't have to remind you to keep your temper in check, right? You already know that photographer's going to be snapping pictures and videos all evening long, so please, just chill? She's your best friend, too."

The thing about Eli, I was coming to realize, is that the guy knew how to drive a point home.

"You know I wouldn't do anything to ruin Lindsey's special day."

He gave me a sidelong glance, the corner of his mouth turning up in a smile. "I know sweetheart. That's why I admire your restraint. There's nothing quite like it."

"Smart ass," I snipped, turning to look out the window.

"That's my girl," he replied with a smirk. "I just know you'll come through. But listen, did you notice Lacee isn't here?"

"Yeah, I noticed at the church."

"I'll just bet you did," he chuckled. "So, what does that tell you?"

"It tells me nothing. She'll probably be at the reception all hanging out of her dress and fucking him in the restroom."

"Don't bet on it," Eli replied knowingly.

"What do you know?" I asked.

"Well, we were in the locker room before the ceremony and I happened to ask about her. *He* claims he sent her back to New York last night. Said he had pressing business for her to attend to back at the office that couldn't wait 'til Monday."

"So?"

"So, get a friggin'clue. He wants to focus on *you* this weekend."

"Fat chance," I scoffed, feeling a slight tingle in the pit of my belly.

Chapter 9

Finally the freaking picture-taking by the pain-in-the-ass photographer was over. He had pictures of the wedding party eating at the front table, the multiple toasts to the bride and groom, the bride and groom sipping champagne with their arms locked, the traditional smashing of wedding cake in each other's faces and their first dance as husband and wife.

I had tossed back quite a few Royal Fuck's—that was Crown Royal, peach Schnapps, cranberry juice with a splash of pineapple juice. It was my new favorite cocktail, I decided. I watched as Eli was on the dance floor with Jill. I fought back a smile as I watched him playfully dip her, hearing Jill laugh at the sudden move.

Sitting there in a pretty dress in the middle of a wedding crowd with a healthy dose of Crown running through my veins, I couldn't help but wonder, what with Jill getting married in the fall, whether marriage was in the cards for me. I'd never really considered it with Darin. I wasn't even sure if marriage was a dream of mine.

As another song was ending, the front man announced that the next one was a classic Joe Cocker song, "You are so Beautiful." I felt a hand touch my shoulder.

"They're playing your song, Nicole." Easton had leaned down, his words caressed softly against my ear, causing me to shiver. "Would you do me the honour?"

I turned abruptly, trying to cast a frown, but it was impossible as I gazed into his molten gray eyes that locked on mine.

"I—I think you know by now, my name's Darcy," I replied brusquely, "*E.J.* is it?"

"You sound injured," he replied. "I see no harm, no foul. My initials are, in fact, valid. At any rate, I prefer to call you by your middle name, Nicole, so that's what I intend to do." Before I could react, he had taken my hand, and led

73

me to the dance floor where the lights had dimmed for this very sexy, very romantic song.

Damn, his closeness still unnerved me. He pulled me close and I had no choice but to wrap my arms around his neck. His arms encircled me, his hands gently massaging my lower back.

God this feels so fucking good.

I wanted to fight that feeling, I swear. But just the feel of him, the nearness of our bodies and the way he smelled—just a faint scent of cologne had me almost forgetting that I kind of hated him.

"You grabbed my ass during photos," I said, looking at him with a smile forced on my lips meant for onlookers.

Easton returned the smile. "I did," he said, quietly. "And do you know what I think, *Nicole?*"

I nodded at Lindsey's mom, dancing with Slate, nearby, the smile still plastered to my face as I waited for him to continue.

I felt Easton lean in, brushing his lips to my ear. "I think you have a fantastic ass," he whispered.

I had to fight the urge to friggin' glare at him, right then and there. I promptly decided to step on his foot. *Hard.*

"Sorry, I have a tendency to try and lead when slow-dancing," I warned him. His lips twitched, and amusement glimmered darkly in his eyes.

"You have no worries there. I don't intend to allow that," he responded softly. "You'll learn to follow, I promise."

I looked up at him to see if he was serious. He quirked a sexy brow, as if challenging me to argue. I lowered my head back to his chest, feeling his hold on me tighten infinitesimally, and it made me feel secure.

What the hell is this about? Do I have some unconscious need for strictness?

After the song ended and my nerves and power of will were probably completely shot, Easton led me back to my table.

"I'd offer to fetch you another drink, but I think you've had enough alcohol for the moment. Perhaps a night cap later is permissible," he said, lightly brushing a lock of my hair from my face.

"Where in the hell did you *come* from?" I asked, my voice coming off a bit more belligerent than intended. That managed to elicit a glare from him.

"I beg your pardon?" he replied.

"I mean *where* were you raised that people talk the way you talk, act the way you act, behave the way you do? I'm really curious."

"I was born in the U.S., raised primarily in Europe from the time I was a year old. I only visited the States during summer holidays from school. I received my education at boarding schools, prep school, institutions of higher *learning*. I was educated in Europe, *Darcy*, where diction, manners, social graces and protocol are deemed as important as math and science. Perhaps they don't embrace that so much over here."

Umm? Ouch!

"Well, pardon me for asking, but I guess this illiterate *colonial* was simply curious. It certainly explains a lot," I retorted. He gave me a dazzling smile and, just as quickly, my irritation disappeared.

"Are you booked here at the hotel tonight?" he asked, swiftly changing the subject. "I don't think you're in any condition to drive."

I nodded, looking up into his gunmetal eyes.

"Good girl," he said approvingly. "I'm in the Presidential Suite. Would you like to join me for that nightcap there around midnight?"

Okay, let's freeze-frame right here for a moment. You need to know something about Darcy Nicole Sheridan, and that is, I have one of those invisible angel/devil conscience creatures that are, of course, polar opposites. This was one of those annoying times of conflict where they'd perch on each shoulder (right where Easton's hands happened to be) and argue back and forth with each other. I could actually picture them in my mind; one looked like an innocent, golden-haired cherub, the other a red devil with an evil moustache and pitchfork, forever prodding me with the damn thing to go in his favor.

I contemplated in my mind as to whether I really *should* go to this man's suite where I was fairly certain I'd have some long-awaited, fan-fucking-tastic sex, or keep a teeny bit of dignity and tell him to have Lacee service him like she had in the restroom the night before. I could practically feel the devil on my shoulder plunging his pitchfork into it indicating I should go for it, and that I'd forever regret it if I didn't. As it happened, the little devil was perched on the same shoulder Easton was now massaging gently with his long, talented fingers.

I should have given him a flat "hell no." Of course, you know what I did.

"See you then," I whispered huskily, still locked in his gaze.

"Splendid. Don't keep me waiting."

God, he's fucking arrogant.

I didn't really have a chance to mull over what I'd just agreed to before Eli pulled me back up so that we could join some train dance called the 'Locomotion' which was now starting up. Apparently, it was vintage group dance where people held on to the person's waist in front of them; bobbing up and down, kicking each leg out alternately, while some old Motown tune with the same name as the dance played. It had already started, and the line was growing, pulling people up from their comfortable sitting positions to join in as they snaked around the banquet room.

I begrudgingly obliged, still thinking about Easton and how his closeness made me feel. Let's be honest: the guy knew how to work a woman's body. That much was obvious. But there was also something else about him. It's like, whenever he and I were in the same *room* together, this livewire of sexual awareness descended upon us. And I know the guy being totally sexy, gorgeous and having the ability to do wicked things with his hands was part of it, but I still had no clue as to *why* he'd pretty much taken up residency in my head. It wasn't as if I'd only been with one man in my whole life (like Lindsey).

While I didn't proclaim to be a prude, at 22 years-old and having had my V-card swiped at 17, I could still count the guys I'd been with on 5-1/2 fingers. (The 1/2 count was a guy named Tim, who I'd let sink himself into me long enough to give me an orgasm, then told him I didn't feel right about it, asking him to stop). I know—not one of my proudest moments, for sure. But hey, I was 18—*So, hold off on the judgment, capisce?*

Regardless, I wasn't one to shy away from a good thing. At the moment, I found Easton Matthews to be totally fascinating, with a hint of danger. I wanted some of that, certain I could hold my own with what experience I possessed. What with my frayed willpower and all, Easton Matthews seemed like a *damn* good thing. Plus, I kind of totally wanted to show him what I was made of…both inside *and* outside of the bedroom.

All these thoughts went through my head as I held on to Eli's waist, listening to the music and following the line of people doing the locomotion. They had already dragged Lindsey and Taz into the mêlée; my parents were near the head of the line. Imagine that. Finally, it was over, and Eli grabbed my arm and pulled me out into the hallway outside of the banquet room.

"Okay, spill," he ordered, wiping his brow from the exertion of the dance.

"Spill what?" I asked innocently.

"Don't play with me," he replied, giving me a shit-eating grin. "I saw you slow-dancing with E.J., or Easton, or whatever the fuck we're calling him now. And then I saw you get that 'I think I need to buy more lacy/black/crotchless lingerie, preferably with sequins' look on your face when he walked away from your table." He narrowed his eyes at me. "What are his plans for you?"

"Okay, first of all? It's Easton. We're calling him *Easton* now, because, guess what? That's his actual name. Second of all, I don't own lacy, crotchless panties, but I do like the sequins idea. And last but not least, there *are* no plans, per se. He invited me to the Presidential Suite for a drink later, that's all," I shrugged for added effect.

"Oh right, that's not *all* and you know it. Be careful, sweetheart. I have a feeling you're not treading in the shallow end anymore. And I don't want to see you come out of all this with your heart a lot more damaged then when you went in."

"It's hardly going in that direction, Eli."

He offered up a smile that didn't quite make it to his eyes. "Just be careful, okay?"

"I always am. No worries."

Several minutes later, everyone was throwing rice at the newly married couple as they descended the steps of the St. Regis into the awaiting limo, heading off to the airport where they were going to honeymoon in Montego Bay. Lindsey hurled her bouquet straight at me. Luckily, Eli intercepted it before it smashed against my forehead.

It was going on midnight, so I hurried up to the room Eli and I had booked and peeled my wedding garb off. I grabbed a quick bath, dressing in a short skirt with a v-neck sweater, pulling on a pair of boots, and brushing the curls out of my hair. My buzz was still going strong as I brushed my teeth and gave myself one final appraisal in the mirror.

Just as I grabbed my handbag and key, Eli came into our room, totally blitzed.

"I think I'm in love," he said, falling on his back, spread eagle on the bed in his tuxedo.

"Really?" I asked, searching for my lip gloss in my handbag. "With who?"

"Don't you mean *whom?*"

"Spit it out, Eli. No time for a grammar lesson right now. With any luck, I'm getting laid tonight."

He looked up at me in a fog. "You're seriously going through with this." It wasn't a question.

I rolled my eyes at him as I brushed a thin layer of lip gloss over my lips. "No, *Dad*—I'm on my way to a pajama party at Gidget's house. Don't wait up," I replied sarcastically.

Eli now stood up, albeit drunkenly, and confronted me. "Darcy, I meant what I said to you earlier. I don't want to see you get hurt. You can convince everyone else that you're some totally emancipated woman who enjoys responsible, casual sex with no strings, but babe? That ain't you. And the vibes I get from Easton? It's all about variety with him."

"Men do it all the time."

"Yeah, and most of us are fucking assholes for it."

"I don't intend to have my heart broken or anything else for that matter, now tell me who you're in love with, please."

He shrugged, walking towards the bathroom. "Only the hottest guy at the reception. We're meeting in thirty for a drink at the bar. His name is Cain Maddox. Sexy, right?"

"Cain?" I replied. "I hope *that's* not indicative of anything dark. Was he a guest?"

"No-no, he was the great looking guy that was overseeing the catering for the reception. You know the one? He has that younger version of Antonio Banderas's look going on?"

I nodded, as if I knew exactly who he was referring to, when the truth was that I was completely clueless.

"Well, enjoy and don't do anything tonight I wouldn't do." I playfully tousled his hair with my hand and I breezed past him.

He shook his head, giving me one of his all-American, hot guy smiles. I smiled back and left, heading to the elevator, still feeling relatively confident as I entered and pushed the button for the top floor.

I wondered what the Presidential Suite at the St. Regis had to offer tonight besides some fantastic cock. I giggled out loud at the prospect, and then quickly looked around and above me for the security cameras. Yep, there they were. Lucky for me they couldn't read minds. I smiled, stepping out of the elevator into the massive hallway of the "top floor".

Sweet Jesus! It certainly looked different than the hallway on our floor. It was polished black marble with flecks of gold sprinkled throughout; the walls were papered with very expensive looking, sound-proofing wall coverings.

The 'Presidential Suite' was at the very end of the hallway, its set of double-doors facing the hall. It was probably the biggest of the suites.

Once again, the butterflies surged in anticipation of what lay behind those doors and what was to come once I passed through them.

 *Chapter 10*

~ Easton ~

I was still drying off in the bath suite from my hot, then cold shower. That was a routine with me; always starting with extremely hot water, then finishing with cold to get me energised again. I was fucking jet-lagged as hell, but there was no way I was passing up spending time with sexy little Nicole tonight.

My now-dry cock twitched in response to where my mind had drifted. I wrapped a towel around my waist and took another one to my damp hair, rubbing furiously at it until it was at least semi-dry before Nicole graced my threshold. I had two nights in D.C. and I sure as hell was going to make the best of them with her. As much as my instincts told me to leave the girl alone, my cock had made the decision for me.

I was a man of varied tastes. This pertained to wines, liqueurs, gourmet food, clothing and most importantly, female companionship. The diversity in my tastes for female companionship was endless. I enjoyed white, black, Latino, Asian—hell, I'd tasted them all. I was enamored with American women as well, but the bulk of my time recently had been spent in London where my activities had been pretty much limited to Lacee, my executive assistant.

Don't get me wrong, I love saucy, British women, but unfortunately, Lacee had become somewhat "territorial" over the past few months, so my supply had dwindled down to her alone. I knew that was her intent. I was well aware of the fact that Lacee had been intimidating other potential contenders for my attention. I'd said nothing because it amused me—briefly, though now it was just fucking annoying.

Lacee had grown prickly since I first laid eyes on Nicole and with good reason. She had sense enough to see that I wouldn't be satisfied ignoring the dark-haired, sultry beauty for long. Hell, she saw it first-hand on the beach that day. After the unfortunate incident at Taz's rehearsal dinner the other night, Lacee became downright insubordinate with me. It was just as well that I sent her on to New York, where I'd be going once my business in D.C. was concluded.

I'd made no secret to Lacee that my interest in her was purely physical. She'd known that going into our little "fuck" arrangement. I don't change rules mid-stream. Ever. I don't do relationships anymore, either. Not since the fiasco two years ago with Bianca Templeton had left me picking up the pieces of shattered trust. Notice I didn't say heart? That's because I don't have one that's breakable. My upbringing saw to that.

A knock sounded at the door of my suite. Still wrapped in my towel, I opened it to the sexy little prick-tease that stood there waiting.

"Good evening," I grinned unabashedly, my cock stirring beneath the towel. Her lovely blue eyes flickered down my bare chest, noticing the towel hanging low on my hips. I smirked a little when her eyes returned to my face, noting the sudden blush she was now wearing.

"I take it you're not into wasting time with having to undress, huh Easton?" she said with an impudent smile curving her full lips.

Fuck me. This one definitely has a little bite to her.

She breezed past me in the doorway, taking a few steps further down the marbled hallway to the matching foyer.

"Now, this is nice," she commented, nodding her head. She was wearing a sweater and short, tight skirt that had my cock at half-mast already.

Christ that ass of hers is fucking epic. I'll have to show her how hard an ass like that should be ridden later.

"If you'll excuse me, Nicole," I said, giving her an apologetic smile. "I seemed to have lost track of time. Make yourself comfortable in the living room please. I won't be long."

"It's *Darcy*, remember?"

I moved in front of her and gazed down through my lashes, lifting a lock of her dark, brown hair from her shoulder, fingering the silky texture between my fingers. She was looking at me with just a tinge of defiance.

"To me, it's Nicole. Allow me that single liberty, won't you?" I watched as her eyebrows arched ever-so-slightly, not sure if this was a sincere request or some form of humour I was displaying. I didn't possess a sense of humour. She'd learn that quickly as well.

"I have a feeling there'll be many more liberties you require," she replied. "But hey, whatever floats your boat, I guess," she said with a shrug, no longer concerned about it being an issue. A good indication it was all about the sex with her as well. She sauntered through the foyer and made herself comfortable on the over-stuffed, velvet sofa in the living room.

I returned to my bedroom on the opposite side of the foyer and finished dressing, pulling on a pair of comfortable jeans and a white, long-sleeved shirt. I wasn't putting socks and shoes on at this stage. Hell, what was the point? We'd be having "break-in" sex within a matter of twenty minutes, by my estimation.

But first, I wanted to learn just a bit more about her. Remember, by definition "man-whore," does not automatically constitute indiscriminate behaviour. I prided myself on conducting due diligence litmus testing prior to sexual interaction. Shortly after dressing, I went to the sideboard in the living room and poured each of us a glass of sherry. Nicole had put some music on in my absence: classical. I approved.

She accepted the glass of sherry from me and I noticed she'd shed the boots and was now barefoot as well. She had her legs folded to the side of her on the sofa, leaning in towards the centre.

"Thank you," she whispered, putting on a somewhat shy and demure persona now. I unsuccessfully stifled a chuckle.

"What?" she asked, straightening herself up, quickly rebuilding that defensive wall.

"It's nothing, relax," I replied, taking a seat next to her, propping my legs on the coffee table in front of us. "I'm simply in awe of your chameleon-like temperament."

"Thank you."

"It's a gift the way you manage to blend in at any social situation. You must know that." I could tell she wasn't convinced.

"Well, maybe it's time to suspend the *chameleon-like* behavior then," she replied, "I know why I'm here, Easton. Let's not waste time with this whole seduction-scene you've got going on. I think you've figured out by now I'm pretty much of a sure thing tonight."

"Aren't you being a tad presumptuous, love?" I asked, raising an eyebrow.

"I don't think so. You grabbed my ass during photos, then invited me to your suite at midnight after asking me for a slow dance, answered your door wearing a *towel*, and poured me a drink. And I'm still here. Now, are you going to unzip my skirt, or are we going to talk about the weather?"

I had to laugh at her genuineness with me, again extremely refreshing. "Well I appreciate your candidness for sure. But there are a few preliminary pieces of information I need from you."

She rolled her eyes, downed the rest of her sherry and sighed. "Yes, I *am* on birth control and yes, I still *expect* you to use a condom. Are we good? Because I'm about to lose my buzz here."

"Not quite," I replied, setting my glass down on the table and turning to her. "I'll need your complete sexual history: names, approximate dates, types of sexual activities involved. I hope you don't think that's invasive. I prefer to think it's circumspect."

I watched her eyes widen as she considered what I was asking. Yep, there it was. She was starting a slow burn. She was on her feet instantly, giving me an incredulous glare.

"What the fuck? Is it customary for you to grill your one-night stands on their sexual history? Or maybe you're just used to chicks like Lacee, who practically carry a certified copy around with them in their handbag or wallet— you know—*just in case* they have the *honor* of doing Easton Matthews."

I fisted my hands at my sides, trying to control the urge to lay her, along with her impudence across my knee for a lesson in comportment; but at the same time...I felt a smile twitching in the corner of my lips.

"What makes you so certain this will be a one-night stand?" I asked quietly, my eyes boring into hers. She shifted nervously now, taking a half-step back from where I sat, unsure of how to answer, clearly confused.

I rose slowly from the sofa, and approached her carefully, so as not to clue her in to the fact that she was, indeed, my prey for the night and possibly for the rest of the weekend. It wouldn't do to have her bolt on me now.

"Do you remember when I told you that I'd see you again?" I asked softly. "When I had you pressed up against the wall, and you had just come on my fingers?"

She swallowed nervously, biting her lower lip and nodded affirmatively. Her eyes were smoldering at the recollection; this was my signal to close this deal.

"I meant it," I stated, our lips nearly touching.

I encircled her stiff body with my arms, drawing her against me. I raised my hands, framing her beautiful face as I lowered my lips to hers, capturing them in a sweet, tender kiss. So far, she wasn't resisting, but I needed more. I continued to caress her lips with mine, tracing her bottom lip with my tongue, drinking in her heady scent. I felt her body relax against mine and, soon, her arms were snaked around my neck, her body molded to mine.

My tongue explored her mouth, our tongues melded together in an erotic ritual that was bringing my cock to *full* attention.

The things I wanted to do to this woman.

I lowered my arms and she allowed my hands to gently massage the swell of her perfect ass. Pulling her tightly against me, I let her feel my hard cock and she began to slowly move her hips rhythmically against it as I heightened our kiss, angling her mouth so that I could lick deeper.

When I slowly began to pull away, leaving her gasping and wide-eyed, I raised a hand to the nape of her neck.

"So then," I moved my lips to the soft place just below her ear. "Is my prerequisite a deal breaker or not, Nicole?"

She was only hesitant for a nanosecond before responding. Her voice was low and husky as she looked up at me with those incredibly blue eyes. "I'd feel better writing it down. Can I have a piece of paper?"

Chapter 11

I sat at the fancy, cherry-wood desk in the foyer and scribbled down names, dates, locations and sexual positions (the ones I could recall). Finally finished, thoroughly embarrassed, and majorly sexually frustrated, I stood up and found Easton on the sofa, his laptop perched on his lap.

"Finished?" he asked impassively, not bothering to look up from his keyboard.

He expects me to hand over details of my prior sex life? Umm…yeah, no!

"Yep, got your golden ticket right here," I said, making no move to hand it over to him as he finally looked up at me.

I firmly put on my best poker face. "But here's the thing," I told him. "I still don't understand why it is you need this, really. Once I hand this over…What? Are we in a relationship? Or fuck-buddies, maybe? And if that's the case, I really don't know how I feel about that, especially seeing as I haven't gotten a chance to sample the goods."

His lips twitched again. "'Sample the goods', love?" he asked in that sexy low voice of his.

"Yeah," I affirmed. "You know, test out the waters to see if I even *want* to have a sexual relationship with you. I mean, Lacee was your personal assistant, right? She was on your payroll, basically. Meaning: you theoretically had to *pay* her to…well…*assist* you," I could feel my cheeks start to heat up as I fumbled up that last statement. I noticed he was doing that quirking-up-his-brow thing again as I now had his full attention.

"Anyway," I quickly continued on, "what I'm saying is, before I hand over my sexual history, I want to have a test-run." God, he was raising *both* eyebrows now. "To see if you meet my standards."

Meet my standards? Oh yeah, I was so hanging myself with my own rope now.

I felt as if I needed to remind myself to breathe after I made my point to him. It sounded way more powerful then it felt. I watched his reaction as he deliberated; an unfathomable expression passed over his face, his eyes almost glinted but I wasn't sure if it was with anger, anticipation or something else altogether.

Easton set his laptop aside and rose from the sofa, coming to stand before me. A hint of a smile graced his lips.

"Come, then," he said softly, an almost dangerous edge to his tone. Taking my hand, he led me from the living room to the suite's master bedroom.

The massive, wrought iron bed in Easton's suite had already been turned down for the evening. He gently placed me on the bed, facing him as his hands expertly lifted my sweater up over my head. He unhooked my bra, pulling it from me and dropping it to the floor. His hands gently caressed my breasts, his thumbs bringing my nipples to quick attention. I watched as he slid his jeans down, noticing he was commando as his thick, long cock sprang free.

In its hardened state, it rose up, resting well past his navel. Not only that, he had a fucking piercing on the head of his dick. A Prince Albert, Prince William—whatever the fuck it was called! I'd never dealt with piercings like *that* before…and the fact that Easton had a piercing *there* surprised the hell out of me. I gasped audibly at the size of it.

He must've seen the look of surprise on my face (and okay, I'm sure there was a good dose of excitement there too) because the grin that was there before quickly made itself into a smirk.

"It's too bad you wanted to use your sexual history to barter with, Nicole," he said, stroking himself, which only brought more attention to his pierced cock. "I think you would've enjoyed feeling me unsheathed."

Well played, Easton…Well played.

The bastard was teasing me, but I damn well wasn't going to give in so quickly. I had…*bigger* things to worry about.

"Easton—I'm not sure if this is going to work," I squeaked, mentally chastising myself at being a coward all of a sudden. Had the men in my sexual repertoire all been "needle dicks?" No, it wasn't possible; five-plus guys who, for the most part, seemed average or above, but this—this was something beyond average.

"Hush," he murmured, slipping my skirt off of me, hooking his thumbs into the elastic waistband of my thong, and sliding it down past my feet. "You and I'll make it work. Trust me?"

I nodded affirmatively; what choice did I have?

Go big, or go home, right? No pun intended.

He raised me up off of the bed and placed me gently on my back, my head resting comfortably on the mass of satin covered pillows. I watched as his head dipped to my core, kissing my very sensitive skin tenderly.

"This is what I was thinking about while we were having our pictures today; about how your pussy would taste," he whispered harshly.

I never realized how much a handful of words could turn me on, but *damn*, this man knew how to use them. I relaxed against the satin sheets as Easton began a slow, pleasurable trail with his tongue, twirling and nipping at the soft folds of my sex. His tongue worked magic as it explored each and every fold with determination and expertise. My hips gyrated as he suckled gently on my swollen clit. I moaned as my body responded to him like no one before. I felt his teeth, ever so gently, nibble on the hood surrounding this engorged bundle of nerve endings, feeling pleasure seep through my entire body.

"Easton, please," I said, breathing heavily, no longer concerned about the length or girth of his cock. "I want you inside of me," I gasped.

"Be patient."

He slipped a finger into my now well-lubricated pussy, and then another, exploring me with a purpose. My legs were now wrapped around his back, as he continued the gentle probing inside, searching for that special spot. I squirmed a bit as he hovered at my apex, his lips still working my pussy, the pads of his fingers now focused on the spot deep within me. He moaned as he continued flexing his fingers, delivering intermittent pressure on the area inside of me with his fingertips.

"Oh God!" I screamed, my hips now moving furiously in response. He slowed his rhythm, pulling his fingers out and I thought I would die.

What??

"No baby," he replied, "Not yet. I want to enter you from behind."

Oh God! I don't do anal…

He must've read my look of alarm as he chuckled softly. "I didn't mean *that*," he clarified. "I promise you, this will be alright."

He lifted me up, positioning me in front of him on my hands and knees. His hands started again, massaging my ass, as I could feel myself once again craving his fulfillment. I felt his lips graze my back and my butt, his fingers resuming the pleasurable stroking of my clit. He stopped momentarily and I heard the sound of the condom packet being ripped open. It only took a few seconds for him to sheath his impressive cock. I wondered if I'd be able to feel his piercing with the condom covering it.

Easton's attention, along with his hands and lips were back on me.

"That's my girl," he said softly. "Such a beautiful ass and such a hungry pussy, too."

I felt the head of his cock as it teased the outside of my slit. His fingers were still probing my G-Spot which was, once again, engorged as I arched my back instinctively, wanting to receive his shaft deeply. He entered me slowly. I felt his hard, fullness as he continued, his hand guiding his erection more fully into me.

"How does that feel, love? Huh? Are you ready to take it all?"

"Umm, yes," I whimpered, my hips now rotating at the pleasure that was spreading through my body. I could feel myself expand for him as he thrust himself deeper inside, his moan of pleasure was enough to make me come right then, but I fought back. I wanted more of this.

He then quickly flexed his hips, forcing himself all the way in as I cried out. He continued pulling out and plunging in and it was pure ecstasy with each and every stroke.

"God, I need it harder," I groaned.

Did I really just say that?!

He obliged, backing out and slamming back into me, the ridge around the head of his cock rubbing my sweet spot over and over again until I thought I'd explode.

"Fuck, your pussy's a gripper," he said, moaning and thrusting over and over. I could feel my muscles tightening around his girth, not wanting to release him.

"You're going to milk me dry, love," he rasped, his hands now planted firmly on my hips as he rocked in and out of me. He reached a hand around front, his fingers finding my neglected clit. He massaged it between his fingers, bringing me to the crest of complete, carnal pleasure.

"I need to come," I gasped. "Make me come now, please?"

He buried himself deeply and rocked his hips back and forth causing repeated stroking of my sweet spot, while his fingers pressed a bit harder on my clit.

I…was…coming…apart.

I felt myself squeeze his shaft as the pleasurable contractions released, milking him with a vengeance as he moaned my first name over and over again. He shuddered and I felt the stillness before the storm as the throbbing of his erection released his explosive climax within me. My clitoral orgasm peaked at that moment as I cried out his name, biting my lip and tasting blood but feeling nothing but pleasure over and over again.

When we were able to catch our breath, Easton was still inside of me. He grasped me to him, pulling me up against him, his warm lips kissing the back of my neck as his fingers moved my hair aside. I shivered against him, my post-O skin very sensitive.

"Cold?"

I managed to shake my head. Lining my body with his behind me, I said in a slightly hoarse voice, "I want more."

Chapter 12

I rolled over in bed, the top sheet tangled around my legs, preventing me from seeing the clock on the nightstand. I reached down, untangling it and noticed I was in bed alone. The digital clock read 5:34 a.m. I was still naked beneath the sheets. Where in the hell was Easton?

I'd only been asleep for a couple of hours, but I hadn't heard or felt him leave the bed. Probably because, true to his promise, he'd worn my ass out. My God!…*The delicious things that man had done to me.* And there wasn't a shadow of doubt in my mind that Easton was one of those hands-on men, which I was starting to realize, may just be my favorite kind.

I'd never been in so many different positions! I'd mentally thanked my mother for forcing those three years of gymnastic lessons on me during my adolescence. I definitely wasn't complaining, though. I could literally say that I'd never been so thoroughly fucked…and fucked *well*, I'd like to add.

There hadn't been much talking between the two of us once he'd led me out of the suite's living room and into his bedroom. Well, I mean other than the dirty sex talk and moaning from the both of us. Easton just might've spoiled me for others. Still, when we finally reached exhaustion, it was evident Easton wasn't one to spoon or cuddle as we fell asleep. That was fine by me. This was a purely physical adventure and he was free to make the rules, as long as I continued getting the mind-blowing O's. I seriously felt a blush coming on as I recalled some of the things he'd done to me…the instructions he'd given me, and the discipline when I hadn't complied in the manner to which he expected. Enough of the blushing, I needed my morning java.

Shit! Is this where I should just get dressed and go?

I scrambled up and out of his bed, instantly feeling shockwaves of pain from the vicinity of my ass. It was my own damn fault. I was snatching the various items of my clothing up from the floor and pulling them on. I contemplated leaving him a note, but what the hell would I write?

Thanks for the great fuckfest? You'd better not have left bruises—LOL? Where'd you get those rocking handcuffs?

Nope. A note wasn't going to be left by me. It wouldn't be appropriate under the circumstances. He hadn't bothered to leave a note for me. Hell, for all I knew, he might've checked out already. Doubtful. All his shit was still tossed about the room. Besides, Darcy Nicole Sheridan had rocked his world every bit as much in that bed last night as he'd rocked mine. To hell with social graces, I thought, searching for my boots. Once I'd pulled them on, I grabbed my handbag, noticing the folded up piece of paper I'd stuck in there with my sexual history written down on it.

I pulled it out and placed it on the nightstand next to his bed. There. I wasn't completely remiss about social graces.

I hurried out of his suite to the elevator. All I could think about was getting home and spending the rest of the day curled up in my nice, soft bed.

As soon as I slid the card key into my hotel room door, I was startled to see a very pissed-off-and-not-trying-to-hide-it Eli, his arms folded, glaring at me.

"I'm sorry," I said right away. "I meant to call you."

He blew out a hard breath. "Do you realize you worried the shit out of me? I thought you might be lying in some dumpster somewhere. I haven't slept all fucking night!"

"Oh for crying out loud, you knew where I was and what I was up to."

"Not to mention the fact that I've been blowing your phone up, too. I was getting ready to go up and bang on the door of his fancy suite."

"I'm sorry, Eli. I had my phone shut off. I mean, you had to figure I'd be spending the night with him. What a fucking night at that," I gushed, smiling.

He raised an eyebrow at the accidental pun.

"Do you know what you're getting yourself into here?" I could tell Eli was genuinely concerned about me, but I wasn't too sure if that meant it was my *judgment* or Easton's *motives* that were up for the jury.

"Hey, I'm fine, okay? You need to chill out because you're starting to sound a *lot* like someone who just needs some Midol and a Nicholas Sparks movie-marathon."

He shot me a wry look. "Ha—you're funny when you've got fresh sex in your system. I'll have to jot that down and hang it on the fridge when we get home so that I'll remember."

"Look," he said with a sigh, running his hands through his hair, "I just worry about you, Darce. Not even fourteen hours ago, I thought we'd be having a completely different conversation right about now about this guy. You were supposed to show up at the door just like you did, except you'd be holding a shovel, your hands and clothes covered with dirt, and you'd be giving me that 'I didn't know what to do with the body' look."

"So, how'd your night go?" I asked, abruptly changing the subject. I could already tell that this wasn't a conversation I was going to win with my overprotective friend and roommate. "Did you and Cain hook up?"

He narrowed his eyes at the not-so-graceful segue, but relented. "We did," he admitted, with a hint of a smile. "Although, God knows I couldn't fully enjoy the experience, being worried about you like I was."

"Okay, lay some guilt on me why don't you, *Mom*!" I teased. "So, it was all good for both of us then, right? We both had a weekend hook-up, not too shabby at all."

"Well, I'd like to think it's a bit different with Maddox and me," he said, as he started stuffing clothing into his duffel bag.

"How so?" I asked, gathering my toiletries from the bathroom.

"I actually think he's relationship material."

"Okay, Eli," I sighed. "Point well taken. I'm not looking for a relationship. I was merely looking to get laid, and I did. And quite well, I'd like to add."

"Ah, so that explains why you're walking funny."

"Walking funny?" I asked, stalling for time.

"Yeah, like you got a cob up your ass."

"Very funny," I smirked, "Just been awhile, you know?"

God that was lame...

"Whatever," he replied. "Are we ready to check out or do you want to order room service and get some breakfast?"

"Seriously, all I want to do is go home and crawl into my bed and sleep the day away. It's back to work tomorrow, so we can't be dragging ass."

"Ummhmm, especially yours," he commented, grabbing my luggage for me.

Chapter 13

I returned to my suite a little before 6 a.m. from my morning workout. I always work out for an hour or more starting at 4:30 a.m. I'd expected to see Darcy still sleeping in my bed, but it was empty, much to my dismay. After checking the rest of my suite, it was obvious the little minx had deserted my company. It perturbed me for some reason. I generally decided when it was time for the woman to leave my bed or leave my presence entirely. This one had slipped through the cracks and I wasn't at all sure that I'd wanted her gone just yet.

I still had today and most of tomorrow left before I flew back to New York. I'd set up a last-minute business meeting with the CEO of a local corporation that was a good prospect for an acquisition or merger. It might've been nice to have enjoyed more romping with Darcy today. She definitely *was not* a 'Nicole.' Last night had proven that to me. There was nothing fragile or shy about this one. I saw a folded up piece of paper on the nightstand. Maybe she'd been thoughtful enough to leave a note or a "Thank You" for the pleasure I'd given her over and over again last night. I picked it up, unfolding it and saw that it was the scribbled sexual history I'd requested.

I smiled as I read through it. She'd answered it honestly, which pleased me immensely. Of course, I'd already had all of this information prior to her crossing over the threshold into my suite last night. Colin had provided me with a full dossier on Darcy Nicole Sheridan after I'd returned to my room last evening.

As I glanced at the rumpled sheets on the bed, my mind drifted to the exquisite night spent with Darcy. I was doubtful she'd be at 100% today, or tomorrow for that matter. I smiled, as I leaned over and picked up the purple leather rose crop from the edge of the bed, tapping it against the palm of my hand, recalling how delectable her ass had looked on the receiving end of it. She'd become so fucking wet after that and she'd come so hard. It delighted me to see

94

just how much she enjoyed the rough play of the previous night. Once again, I found myself amazed at her sense of adventure. Darcy had left the leather bustier behind in her rush to take leave this morning. It was either that or perhaps she was simply ashamed of the way she'd taken to my sexual idiosyncrasies. I doubted she'd be sharing any of the details with her gay friend or Lindsey anytime soon.

I chuckled audibly, smacking the crop against my hand. Darcy had learned quickly that punishment didn't have to mean pain. Perhaps this one wouldn't bore me straight away like the others had. My cock twitched in anticipation of our next encounter. I was hoping it would be sooner rather than later.

I guess I'd simply shower and work from my suite today. I needed the rest.

∞ ∞ ∞ ∞ ∞ ∞

On Monday at 1 p.m., I found myself sitting across the table from Mr. Martin Sheridan, quickly making an assessment of his business savvy. Colin had provided me all the biographical and financial data on him, as well as his company. The man had grown his business substantially over the past twenty-five years. It would make a nice addition to the Baronton Holdings portfolio. My job here was to convince him it was time to sell.

"I appreciate your agreeing to this meeting on such short notice, Mr. Sheridan," I said, taking a sip of mineral water. "I know when we spoke in Belize a couple of months back, you indicated you weren't thinking of selling your company for another three years or so. I'm here today hoping to change your mind."

Martin Sheridan was a somewhat laid-back man in his early sixties with salt and pepper hair, moustache, and very well-groomed. He gave me a nod. "Please call me Martin," he said, digging into his pasta salad.

"Martin, it is then," I replied. "Please call me Easton."

"Well, Easton, as I mentioned in Belize when you inquired about my firm, the reason I don't want to sell immediately is actually because of my daughter, Darcy. You see, she's fresh out of college, now working as a management trainee. I'd intended on grooming her to eventually take over the business. As it stands, I'm not sure three years is enough time, or if there ever will be *enough* time to make that happen," he said, shaking his head in irritation. I sat back, reading his body language. He was obviously showing signs of frustration with his beautiful, sexy, likes-to-be-spanked daughter.

"Yes sir, I completely understand and respect your rationale on that matter. Is your daughter interested in a career path at Sheridan and Associates?" I was subtly digging for more information. Perhaps Darcy was feeling pressured to follow in her father's footsteps.

"Who the hell knows?" he snorted, half-smiling. "She says she is. I mean, she's 22 years-old, and I know these days that's still considered practically a teenager. However, I can tell you this, when I was that age I had a helluva lot more responsibility and work ethic than what she's exhibiting. Take this morning for example," he continued. "She breezes into the office more than thirty minutes late, gimping around like she'd injured herself. God only knows what the girl was doing all weekend. I guess it's better she no longer lives at home. At least now, Denise and I are spared the worry we had when she lived under our own roof. Darcy has a bit of a wild streak. Her mother and I desperately hope it's something she'll outgrow eventually."

Certainly not anytime soon, I hope.

"I can imagine," I replied in a serious tone. It was obvious Darcy stuck to her own agenda and it was pissing her old man off royally.

"Don't get me wrong. I mean, she's our baby girl, and Denise and I have spoiled her rotten. I suppose that's why I want to stick around long enough to undo some of the damage we've done, if you know what I mean. The girl's smart as hell, she just needs some self-discipline and guidance, someone to take a firmer approach with her development. Her mother and I seem to have neglected that aspect of it during her formative years."

He put his fork down, wiped his mouth and laughed. "I'm ashamed to admit this, but for the life of me, I can't recall ever having spanked the girl, not even as a toddler."

"Do tell?"

"Darcy was a bit unexpected for us, having tried for years to conceive, we simply felt it would never happen, so you can imagine how thrilled we were at her late arrival. I suppose Denise and I overcompensated for her being the only child and discipline was a stranger to our home where she was concerned. Still, I don't think it's ever too late for anyone to learn discipline."

My thoughts exactly, Martin.

"You know, Martin, perhaps this is perfect timing for both of us," I offered.

"How so?" he asked, buttering a dinner roll.

"Well, I'm sure you've done some basic research on Baronton Group."

He nodded and I continued. "So then you know my vast holdings are very diverse, not to mention global. I employ over 2,800 full-time employees in seven different countries. My transition team is one of the most talented, widely-recognised, results-oriented staff anywhere. They've received national recognition from Global Business Review three years in a row for their proven expertise in talent retention involving the companies we've acquired. Perhaps what Darcy needs most is mentoring and grooming from expert management development staff such as Baronton can offer. No offense meant, sir, but it's a difficult position for a father to be in when it comes to making unpopular decisions involving your offspring, I would think."

"No offense taken, you've nailed that one right on the head," he chuckled. "So, what are you offering? Are you willing to be contractually obligated to see that my daughter learns the ropes at Sheridan & Associates regardless of her current lack of dedication?"

"I'll do you one better, sir. Instead of an out-and-out acquisition, perhaps you'll consider a merger of sorts; a joint venture so to speak. I'm prepared to make an offer to buy 51% of your company and personally oversee the transition team. I'd like to move one of my counter-terrorism surveillance software development firms to D.C. from London. Since your company's already approved as a Tier 1 government contractor, there'll be no issues with the merger. The benefit to you is that you'll still retain minority ownership, but won't have to be involved in the day-to-day operations. You'll be a consultant for as long as you choose on the Sheridan segment of the business. My team and I will work hard to develop all of the management trainees at Sheridan per the merger agreement. You'll be free to have more leisure time, along with the peace of mind in knowing your daughter's getting trained by the very best."

I saw the look in his eyes and I knew he was going to agree. I could already tell he was on-board.

"So, in other words, I don't have to be the one cracking the whip anymore, huh?"

"Well put, sir."

"You know, I've wanted to get back on my golf game for quite some time. Denise and I have been planning a trip to Hawaii as well. I'll get a prospectus to you next week. How soon after will you be able to provide Baronton's proposal?"

"I shouldn't think it would take more than a couple of weeks, tops."

"I think this just might work out well for all concerned," he replied, reaching to shake my hand. "I'll look forward to pursuing this merger. You've somehow managed to put my mind at ease with your plan, Easton."

"Splendid," I replied, giving his hand a shake. "I think this will be a win-win for all concerned, but for now, let's keep this confidential. It's been my experience that rumours of a merger or acquisition make employees skittish on both sides, interrupting productivity."

"You have no worries there," he assured me. "I'm not a novice by any means."

"Very good, sir. I'll be in touch."

We exchanged business cards, which listed our private mobile numbers. I paid for lunch and departed feeling the satisfaction I always felt when a negotiation went as planned.

Having attended to the business that delayed my departure from D.C., I instructed Carlos to take me to the private airfield where my pilot was preparing for our flight to New York. Back to New York for a few weeks, back to Lacee's pouting face and the surliness she'd direct towards me for banishing her from the long weekend she'd planned for us in D.C I could handle Lacee, I always had, only this time would be different. I'd handle her upon my return, not with cuffs, clamps or crops and not with a sheathed cock either. It was time Lacee focused solely on her career with Baronton and not on its President and CEO.

It was a short flight from D.C. to New York. The best kind. I managed to fall asleep on the leather couch in the cabin, dismissing the first officer's offer of refreshment. The flight time would allow for a quick power nap before I faced my staff in New York.

I was almost nine years old when Mother hired a live-in governess for me; one of the many times Mother had forbade my grandparents from seeing me or coming to our house. Mother was an only child and her tantrums were notorious. I never knew the details of her snits with my grandparents, only that during one of them, I might not see Grammy and Papa for weeks; not until one of them came begging for her forgiveness in order to spend time with me. I loved spending time with them. Life was normal—with them.

The governess' name was Gennifer DuValle; her bedroom adjoined mine through a connecting door. A door which had no lock, or I would've used it.

It happened the first time just after my ninth birthday. I'd been so enraptured with the presents Mother had lavished on me that I hadn't done my lesson plan from the previous day. Gennifer had spent most of the day sequestered in her room, drinking rum and Diet Coke, the way she always did. Mother was traveling; it was just Freda the live-in housekeeper and Levon, the groundskeeper, Gennifer and me at the estate. I noticed Gennifer took more drinking liberties when my mother traveled, not that Mother would've noticed anyway.

I'd spent the better part of the day playing the multiple video games I'd received for my birthday. My father had sent money, so I begged Gennifer to take me shopping and bought even more games. I was addicted to Nintendo. Just after tea, whilst Freda took her daily nap, Gennifer came into my room.

"Time to review your lessons," she half-way slurred, coming over to where I was and shutting off the game system.

"Please Miss Gennifer," I whined, "just let me play for a few more minutes?"

"After you've shown me your completed lessons," she said, pointing her finger at me.

"Sorry, Miss," I conceded, lowering my head. "I haven't completed them as of yet."

"What?" she hissed loudly. "Easton, your first priority is your studies. That's what I'm paid to do; to make sure you stay current with your study plan. How do you think your mother will react should I tell her I've failed in this?"

"I'm not sure, Miss," I said softly, feeling ashamed I'd put her in such a precarious position with my mother.

"Well, I'm sure," she snapped. "She'd take disciplinary measures you can be sure. Maybe even the ultimate disciplinary action by dismissing me from her employment. Then I'd starve or be forced to peddle myself on the streets of London like a common strumpet in order to eat!"

"I'm sorry, Miss," I mumbled sincerely. "I'll get to it straight-away."

"The fact remains, Easton, you still need to be punished so you won't forget your priorities again. Your mum may allow you to do as you will, but I happen to think you've lacked discipline in the past, which needs to be rectified. That pretty face of yours will only get you so far in this life. Perhaps now is the perfect time for you to get a lesson in paying the consequences of irresponsible behaviour. Don't you move," she hissed, waggling her index finger in my face.

I stood like a statue hearing her going through her dresser drawers in the next room. I was frightened by her tone, the smell of rum on her breath, and the anger in her eyes. She returned to my room carrying an armful of items I didn't recognise. She approached me, tossing the items on my bed except for a long scarf. She instructed me to open my mouth. I did as instructed, fearful to resist, while she tied the rolled-up scarf around my face to serve as a gag. I felt the panic set in that I'd suffocate.

"Breath through your nose," she instructed harshly. She grabbed both of my wrists and pulled them roughly behind my back, placing a pair of handcuffs around them so I was immobile except for my feet. I immediately pushed my body against her, trying to run for the door, though of course I had no way of opening it and no means of screaming for help.

"If you resist, I'll be that much harder on you," she warned, coming up behind me and leading me back to the bed. She unzipped my pants, lowering them to my ankles; she grasped my boxers and did the same.

"Well, what a nice little willy you have already even at your age," she said, laughing harshly. I watched as she took a stick that had long strips of leather attached to it, noticing there was a metal edge at the end of each of those leather strips. I had no clue what it was.

"You've earned a flogging, Easton," she purred. "Miss Gennifer's going to show you what happens to bad boys who don't complete their lessons."

100

She turned me around so my back was to her, then shoved me face-down onto the bed. I turned my head to the side so I could at least see what she intended to do in my peripheral vision. As she got nearer, I felt my eyes widen in horror as she straddled my legs, raising her arm high, ready to deliver the first blow of the flogger against my bare ass.

"Excuse me, sir. We're getting ready to land and I wanted to make sure you were buckled in safely."

"I'm fine," I snapped, sitting up abruptly, taking a deep breath. I should've been grateful to the first officer for interrupting the horrible dream I was having, rather than reacting so harshly.

"Sorry, sir," he apologized. "I didn't mean to startle you."

"It's quite alright, David," I said, composing myself. "Just a bit overtired from the weekend."

"Very good sir. We should be on the ground in five minutes or so."

I fastened the seat belt on the leather couch and prepared to deal with being in New York and not in D.C. I wondered how Darcy was doing, immediately chastising myself for even thinking about her. I wouldn't go there. She was a diversion for now. No more than that.

Chapter 14

God! Would this work day *ever* be over? I looked up at the clock on the wall. Shit! It was only twelve-fucking-thirty. I hadn't even arrived until eight-thirty, so four hours seemed like ten. It was my own damn fault. I should've listened to the angel on my shoulder instead of that rat bastard devil. I didn't mean it; I didn't regret the choice I'd made, though my ass was still throbbing from the lashing I'd received. Christ! Easton was a freak, but hey, I was so down for something different than the generic fucking I was used to.

You can imagine my surprise the other night after we'd had our "break-in" fuck when he'd placed a stack of boxes on the bed. I almost felt as if Easton had a soft spot and was lavishing expensive gifts on me, though God I don't know when he would've had the time. Hah! From inside one box, I pulled a black, leather bustier with a matching thong. Another box contained matching leather wrist and ankle restraints, the third box contained a beautiful purple, single rose that I discovered was also made of leather! Dude obviously had a thing for leather. I must've had a look of shock on my face because, very soon after extricating the contents, I heard a chuckle from Easton. He saw my puzzlement over the items.

"It's for play, love," he explained. "Are you into it?"

I wondered if he'd shopped at some "One size fits all" perv shop. I won't bore you with the details, but obviously, I was game for it or my ass cheeks wouldn't be burning now like they were on fire. Okay—don't misunderstand me, I was down for it all. It was new, different, and like anyone else, I was a FSOG whore, I admit it! We'd spent a delicious several hours fucking, fucking hard, and fucking harder. I was spanked several times when I'd been naughty in ways that didn't please Easton. The funny thing was, I had no clue what constituted 'naughty' behavior. I supposed I'd learn soon enough, according to Easton.

I shifted for the umpteenth time in my chair, continuing to add raw data into my computer, which was boring enough. It wasn't interesting enough to take my mind off the pain in my freaking ass!

I knew my dad was pissed when he saw me trying to discreetly sneak in at 8:34 this morning. I got the familiar 'Darcy what've you been up to?" look, and I heard an audible grunt from him as I wished him a "good morning." And *that* was never a good sign. But the truth was, I couldn't get comfortable in bed yesterday; I was restless and had overslept. Eli hadn't bothered to make sure I was up before he left for his morning ritual of meeting some of his buds for coffee at Starbucks before he went into work. Finally making it into work, albeit late, I quickly sat down in my cubicle and started this data-entry shit that I'd been working on for better than a week.

Yeah…this was so *not* what I had in mind when I went to college to pursue my Bachelor's degree.

The pain on my ass cheeks might not have even been noticeable had I been able to walk around, but being planted firmly on the thinly-padded chair at my desk only exacerbated the discomfort. I mean it wasn't like I had bleeding welts or anything; just some read streaks that, at the time they were administered, actually felt delicious. My God, I'd come so fucking hard over and over again! I'd even antagonized Easton verbally, knowing quite well by that time he'd only be too willing to dole out more punishment for the disrespect I'd shown him. I wondered if this made me some kind of a perv. I was contemplating the pros and cons of that when I decided to quit reflecting on everything Easton and find something that would make each and every reminder of him a little more…work appropriate.

I slipped from my cubicle and went down the long, winding hall to where the executive offices were located. Hopefully, Daddy was out for lunch and his executive assistant as well. As I rounded the corner to the glass-enclosed offices, I could see that the lights were out. All clear! Thank God!

I quickly and silently crept into his office, looking around in his closet for what I needed. There it was; thank God! It might make me more comfortable right now. Hopefully no one would pass me in the hallway on my way back and wonder what the hell I was doing! I'd stayed in over lunch to make up for my missed time this morning.

See, I do have a work ethic, despite those spoilage comments made by my oh-so-loving parents.

I made it back into my corner cubicle with the item, and sat back down to resume my data entry, feeling much more comfortable.

It was probably twenty minutes later when I recognized Eli's whistling as he came into my department and poked his head over the top of my cubicle.

"Hey sweetie! Glad you finally made it in," he teased. "Want me to bring you some—what the fuck?"

"Shhh," I hissed, squirming in my chair, trying to pull my short skirt down to cover the inflatable donut I was perched on. There was no way that was going to happen with the skirt I was wearing.

"What the hell's that?" he whispered loudly, trying to contain his laughter. He moved inside my cubicle, his eyes glued to the inflatable donut my sore ass was resting on. He finally looked back up at my face, waiting for some type of an explanation.

"I think you know what it is," I halfway snapped at him.

"Hemorrhoids, babe?"

"No," I whispered through gritted teeth. "I don't have *hemorrhoids!* These things have multiple uses."

"Uh huh," Eli replied. "How'd you over-sleep this morning?"

"I just didn't sleep well," I snapped, nearly flinching as I moved in my chair.

"Don't be snippy with me," he warned. He was looking at me a little more shrewdly now. "I'm sorry you're in pain."

"No, I'm good," I gave him a small 'sorry for being a total bitch' smile. "But please tell me you're cooking tonight?"

"You got it, sweetie. Pasta sound good?"

"Pasta sounds great."

"You got it. See ya at home."

Eli left just as Rollins the Retch walked by giving me the hairy eyeball to make sure I was busy pecking away on my keyboard, entering this fucking mundane bullshit. Whatever.

I ran into Daddy late afternoon as I went to the food commissary to get some iced coffee. He seemed different than this morning; he was no longer pissed, but acted a tad guilty about something. What was that about?

"Hi Daddy," I said, as I filled my cup. "Are you having a good day?"

"As a matter of fact, Darcy, this has been a very uplifting day for me. How are you? I noticed you arrived a little late looking under the weather. Is everything okay?"

"Everything's fine. Just the whole weekend wedding stuff, ya know? The partying did me in a little bit. I'm just not used to it. Don't worry; I'll be back at 100% tomorrow."

"I'm looking forward to seeing *that*," he replied, walking back towards his office.

What's that about?

I went back to my cubicle, thankful I only had thirty minutes until I could blow this pop stand. Eli would prepare a great pasta dinner, complete with the appropriate wine and we'd chat about our mundane jobs at Sheridan & Associates. Then, I'd crawl into my nice, soft bed and drift into blissful sleep.

When five o'clock finally rolled around, I was so ready to be outta there. My cell rang on the way down to the front lobby. I didn't recognize the number, but my instincts told me it was Easton, and I instantly felt butterflies in my tummy.

"I see you got my note," I greeted, hoping like hell it *was* Easton on the other end.

"I did," the familiar voice replied from the other end, "I didn't, however, appreciate the way it was delivered."

"Is that right?" I teased, hobbling down the front steps of the building, not oblivious to the odd look I was getting from a woman I passed on the sidewalk. "You know, I *meant* to leave a tip for you with it for services rendered, but I just didn't have anything less than a hundred dollar bill. Sorry about that." My smile was now turning into a full-fledged, shit-eating grin.

I heard his slow chuckle. "Keep the money, love. Just know that in the future, I won't tolerate your leaving my bed without my knowing. I've punished women for less."

Oh shit.

"Got it," I replied, finally reaching my car in the lot.

"I enjoyed this weekend; I hope you did as well," he stated seriously.

I nodded, swallowing nervously at his intensity. "It was a very unique experience for me," I said softly.

"I'll see you again, Darcy; I'm not sure when, but I will. In the meantime, you're to refrain from having any sexual activity with anyone else. Is that understood?"

I nodded, surprised at his request. My understanding was that we were now going to have sort of a no-strings-attached type of relationship. I mean, I got that he seemed to be overly concerned about his health and STDs and such, but my God, how much of a skank did he take me for?

"Why's that important?" I dared to ask. I swear I could almost hear his sexy frown through the phone.

"Because I'm not ready to let you go," he answered flatly.

"Where are you now?" I asked.

"New York."

"What's in New York?" I asked.

"My U.S. headquarters," he replied, as if it was of little consequence.

"So, as in, you have your own company then?"

"Correct."

"What's the name of it?"

"Baronton Global."

"Interesting," I replied, "So, can you elaborate on what it is your company does?"

"You'd only be bored."

"Actually, I'm interested in what you do. And it's bound to come up in conversation at some point, right?"

"My company's quite diversified in its activities; primarily involved in mergers and acquisitions in Eastern Europe and security software in the U.K. In the U.S., the majority of the focus is sub-contract work for various government agencies such as the CIA and the FBI; we maintain updates on software and hardware for Interpol as well."

"Interpol? That's pretty major stuff there," I commented, impressed, but trying not to show it. "So, are you a G-Man of sorts like your brother Taz?"

"We're half-brothers, and no, I'm not employed directly by any government; my company does sub-contract work for many govern·nents."

"I see. So, does that ever present a conflict of interest?" I asked.

"If you mean do I sell my products and resources to the highest bidder, the answer's an adamant no. My company wouldn't be where it is today if the integrity wasn't rock-solid."

Now I felt as if I'd insulted him. "Easton, I wasn't implying that you'd be unethical or ruthless or anything. I mean, I wasn't necessarily referring to countries like North Korea or Iran, but let's face it, there are plenty of countries not specifically black-listed by the U.K., for instance, yet the U.S. has them blacklisted. How would you handle such a situation?"

"Great question, Darcy," he replied. I could almost see his smile. "I take a very cautious approach in adding new clients. The particular segment of the business handling negotiations for sensitive intelligence contracts and contract renewal is handled by only one person within the organisation; the only person that has my total trust."

"Oh?"

"Yes; that'd be me."

"You mean you don't trust anyone else within your entire corporation?"

"Not to handle that arm of the business. I think you'll find my trust in people in general is not easily won, if ever."

"Wow. Someone's been burned once or twice." He didn't confirm or deny.

"I've got some pressing business to attend to at the moment...a merger that's in the works. I'll be in touch with you again, though I can't say when. Take care and remember what I said."

He ended the call. I figured I was dismissed for the moment and, if I hadn't been so tired and exhausted, I might've been rankled by his audacity, but I was so I wasn't.

Finally, I was home. I kicked off my heels, went up the stairs to the bathroom, stripping my clothes off all the way to the top. Eli was already home. I could smell the sweet, tempting aroma of his marinara sauce bubbling on the stove.

"I'm getting a shower," I yelled down.

"Dinner in thirty," he hollered back.

My shower was delicious; I dressed in a flannel granny gown that Mom had given me for Christmas. What the hell, it was comforting at the moment.

Eli and I had dinner together, which was scrumptious. I let him do most of the talking, preferring it that way.

"So when are you going to see Cain again?" I asked.

"Going to the movies this week," he answered, sounding very chipper. "Hey, why don't you and Easton double with us?" he asked, rolling his eyes at me.

"Oh that's funny," I replied, flipping him the bird. "I did have a call from Easton, I'll have you know. We will be seeing one another again, so you can lay off with the jokes."

He was giving me another one of those penetrating looks. "You're seriously going to get involved with him?" Eli asked incredulously.

"Why wouldn't I?" I asked, my voice getting snappish.

"Oh come on. You have to know what his type is like; I mean, what they're after, right?"

"Clue me in," I replied, taking a sip of the fine Merlot he'd poured for us.

"I mean, sweetheart, it's perfectly fine if you take a walk every now and then on the wild side with someone of his caliber, just please don't invite your heart to tag along, okay?"

"Don't worry about that," I replied, twisting the pasta around my fork, "I do have survival skills intact, you know?"

"Yeah?" he asked, pouring more wine in his goblet, "Well, you might want to clue your *ass* in on that before your next sexapade with Mr. Easton."

I stopped chewing immediately, looking quickly up at Eli in surprise. He rolled his eyes at me, sipping his wine. "I mean really, Darce? You've been limping around for two days because *it's been a while*? That's 5th grade lame," he said with a snort.

I gave him a semi-obnoxious glare as I chewed threw some pasta. "Why would I lie about something like that?"

"I don't know. You tell me." He met my teasing glare with a serious look on his face.

"There's nothing to tell, geesh," I snapped again, irritated I wasn't comfortable talking about it with Eli, whom I'm sure had at one time or another had experimented with some level of BDSM, though I was reluctant to tag what was done as even that.

"Okay, have it your way, or maybe I should say have it *his* way."

"Look Eli, don't dance around the issue here, okay? Say what you have to say."

Eli looked uncomfortable with the conversation, but I could tell he wanted it out in the open, so I was waiting for him to put it out there.

"Okay, is Easton into sexual torture? I mean, I'm not asking out of curiosity; I'm asking out of concern."

I immediately softened towards him, breathing a heavy sigh of relief. "No, Eli; it was nothing like that, I promise you. It was just, you know, a little rough play involving some leather restraints and a rose."

He looked aghast. "A real rose—thorns and all?!"

"No-no," I said quickly, "It was a leather crop that looked like a rose."

"I see," he replied, somewhat relieved. "And you were okay with that? Did you have a safe word?"

"The answers are yes and no. It wasn't like torture, I assure you; I enjoyed it big time. And no need for a safe word. Don't blow this out of proportion, please."

He considered that for a good sec, mulling it over. Finally, he just shrugged, but I could tell that he still wasn't ready to drop the issue. "Hey, I'm not one for lectures, you know that," he explained. "Just saying, if you're planning to see him again, go into it with your eyes wide open. It may seem fun and pleasurable right now, I get that, sweetie…and maybe that's the extent of it with him. Sometimes though, this type of sexual play can gradually escalate into something else altogether; I just want you to be cautious, that's all. Don't do anything you're not comfortable doing."

I stood up and walked over to where Eli was sitting, wrapping my arms around him tightly. "Thank you for caring. I promise I'll be careful, and honestly, I may never hear from him again. I'm not that naïve, okay?"

"Okay, Darce. Hey, you're beat. Go on up to bed, I'll clean up down here."

I kissed the top of his head. "You're kind of kickass, you know that? Thanks."

"Oh, by the way, this means you cook and clean up tomorrow. I'm not letting you off that easy, sweetie."

Once in my room, I climbed underneath my soft, warm sheets and reflected on Eli's comments earlier. Was he right? Was Easton some type of sadist who would weave an intricate web of sexual play around me gradually until he caught the spider allowing no means of escape? I shivered, pulling the covers up under my chin. He definitely wasn't in to the cuddling scene, but I attributed that to the fact I still hadn't handed over that slip of paper at the time, so it was kind of still a 'test-run.' And though I still didn't know what exactly Easton and I were…I *did* know that I wanted more.

Chapter 15

~ Easton ~

I was at the Milan Fall Fashion Preview, having made secret arrangements to surprise Bianca. She was under the impression that merger negotiations taking place in Zurich had made it impossible for me to be there. The truth was, a merger of any magnitude would never have kept me away from the woman that was mine—on an occasion such as this.

I'd met Bianca three years prior at a business exposition in London. It was typical for the hosting society to staff female models to direct visitors to the various booths and displays set up to promote their products and services. That's when I spotted the tall, dark-haired beauty with the exquisite sapphire-blue eyes. I was immediately drawn to her; it proved to be a mutual attraction. We became inseparable almost immediately; my little black book had become history.

Bianca traveled with me extensively, whether it was business or pleasure. I used my contacts in Paris, Madrid, New York and London to spearhead her modeling career. Within a year, Bianca Templeton was an 'A-List' runway model signed with the prestigious Ford Models Agency. Her dreams had come true and so had mine.

Now, two years after being signed, Bianca Templeton was the most sought-after fashion model for the top designers. The lights dimmed in the giant auditorium as the models were announced one at a time, taking the runway and presenting the newest designs of Calvin Klein, Gucci, Chanel, Prada, Rodarte and a host of others. My pulse quickened as Bianca was announced, sporting the latest Chanel evening attire for this coming fall. She still took my breath away as I gazed at her long, lovely, silken legs gracefully walking down the carpeted runway. Her eyes were searching the crowd for something or someone. Had my well-kept secret somehow filtered back to her? Not possible. Then I watched as her eyes settled on someone in the crowd. Knowing her as I did, I caught the flicker of recognition, and then the look that followed. It was a look of pure love in her eyes; the look I'd seen many times now directed towards someone else.

I immediately turned to see who the recipient was of the look I thought had only been for me. It was Christopher! It was her fucking photographer, Christopher Rolando. Fuck me! I immediately felt anger and betrayal flooding my veins as I was catching the woman I had uncommonly committed to in the act of letting everyone know that she was fucking someone else.

112

I made a hasty departure back to the flat I owned in Milan, where she was staying. I had to sort this out in my mind. I needed verification of some type. The only proof I had was a 'look,' yet I knew that was all the proof I needed. I should've have followed my mother's advice when Bianca and I had last visited. She'd told me only a fool would trust a woman like Bianca's faithfulness. She'd chided me for not having her under the surveillance of a private detective, reiterating that most women cannot be trusted. She'd asked me what type of a fool I was. I'd responded the type that trusts.

I'd torn up the flat, looking for something, anything that might authenticate my suspicion. It didn't take long to find just that. The pain still felt fresh, though it was two years ago. So many women since then, but until Darcy appeared on that beach in Belize, none of them had looked a thing like Bianca Templeton, the cheating, fucked-up whore that had made a fool out of me to the world.

My phone rang, interrupting the tortuous trip to my past. It was a welcome interruption, forcing me to put all of that pain and misery out of my mind once again.

"Matthews," I answered curtly.

"Sir, everything's in place with respect to the instructions you gave relative to Darcy Sheridan. She's under surveillance, as requested. How often do you require status reports?"

"Daily, until I instruct otherwise," I answered. "The GPS tracking's been activated?"

"Yes sir. All devices are live; Ryan Dobbs is the operative on this one."

"Fine; thanks, Colin."

Ever since the weekend, I couldn't shake Darcy from my mind. Initially, she'd sparked my interest due to the physical similarities between her and Bianca. Though Darcy was not as tall as Bianca who was 5'10", she still possessed the same long, shapely legs, ample breasts, olive complexion and beautiful blue eyes. Darcy's eyes had a bit more soul to them than Bianca's, but of course, I might be biased since I indisputably loathed the (former) model bitch.

That's right; I'd made sure Bianca's assignments dwindled to nothing within months after our tumultuous break-up in Milan. It was small compensation for what she'd done to me, in my opinion, not only with

113

Christopher Rolando, but the scheme they had going that took me less than an hour to unravel, once I'd discovered the documents in her lingerie drawer.

As it turned out, Bianca had discovered she was five weeks pregnant a month before the Fall Fashion Preview in Milan. She'd not even bothered to share the news with me. A week later, while traveling with me on business, she apparently arranged for an abortion in Amsterdam. As I gazed at the documents from the clinic she'd hidden away, I recalled that week we'd spent in Amsterdam. When I returned one evening from one of my daylong meetings, she'd been curled up in bed. She said she'd gotten her period and was cramping. I had no reason to question that; it wasn't as if I tracked her menstrual cycles. I could still almost feel the single tear that had rolled down my cheek upon discovering what the murderous bitch had done.

I'd quickly composed myself, putting the flat back in order and then made myself comfortable in the bedroom next to the master suite, where I'd lay in wait for her return. The memories of that night once again invaded my mind with vivid imagery that hadn't faded in the least over time.

"Would you like a glass of champagne, Christopher?" Bianca asked sweetly. "I feel like celebrating, how about you?"

"Of course, darling; we both have much to celebrate tonight. You were smashing this evening. I believe you were snapped more than any other model; I found myself counting."

"Really? I've worked so hard for this moment. My career's on the fast track; I'm making more money than I ever dreamt possible, plus I'm seeing the world through new eyes. Life is great! Cheers! The sound of crystal clinking had made me want to puke.

"I think you may have left out a couple of things, love."

"I'm sorry, baby," she said to him. "The thing I want to celebrate most is my eternal love for you; that goes without saying."

"Of course, we need to toast good-riddance to the little bastard you were nearly saddled with as well. That was a close one, Bianca."

"Indeed," she replied, tapping her flute against his. "That would've been a career killer for certain."

"As long as we're talking about the future, how long before you break the news to Easton that you don't love him and are leaving?"

"Christopher, you must have patience with me on that. He was instrumental in building my career. I need to deal with my departure very carefully or he could unhinge it altogether."

"Certainly he wouldn't be so vindictive if he truly loves you, right?"

"You don't know him like I do. He's had a horrid past that left him extremely distrustful of women. He's only shared a bit of it with me, but I'd guess his mother had something to do with it. Constantly ignoring him and sending him off to distant boarding schools. At any rate, it will just take some time for me to extricate myself from him."

"God dammit, Bianca! I fucking love you and the thought of you still screwing him is fucking driving me crazy!"

"Oh, baby," she said soothingly, "Easton doesn't make love to me; he rough fucks. I only tolerate it because I have no choice at the moment. Do you know he's never, even said "I love you" to me? It's always "I adore you" just like he adores all of his fucking possessions! Anyway, does it help to know that I always pretend it's you I'm with while Easton fucks me?"

"No, not at all," Christopher said, clearly irritated. "He's a despicable bastard."

"Come baby, let's not waste time dwelling on it now. Come to bed and let me show you just how much I love you. Come sink yourself inside of me, Christopher. You're so gentle and caring."

Within moments, from the next room, I could hear the sounds of their love-making. Bianca was moaning his name over and over again. My heart was shredded; the sounds of him telling her how sweet her pussy tasted and how much he wanted to bury his cock inside of her reverberated in my ears. It took every ounce of restraint I could muster not to barge into that room and rip them both to pieces, just like my heart. I'd learned timing was everything.

Several minutes later, I heard Bianca begging for his cock. I knew that he'd obliged when I heard the sound of the headboard hitting the wall in measured rhythm. I knew Bianca's vocals like second nature. I could tell when she was approaching orgasm. I'd crept from the room and, as her moans became more guttural, I knew the time was right. The door to the master suite was open; after all, they presumed they were alone. I walked through the entrance and stood at the side of the bed, as Christopher continued plunging his cock in and out of her, unaware he had an audience. Bianca's head was rolling back and forth on the pillow, her eyes closed getting ready to climax.

With one arm, I reached out, snatching Christopher up and out of her, flinging him over to the other side of the room. He landed with a loud thud, squealing a pathetic "Ummmph!" Bianca's eyes shot open and, within two seconds, the passion was replaced with pure terror. She grabbed the bedspread, clutching it up against her breasts as if it could shield her. Her hands were trembling.

I tossed the papers from the clinic onto her stomach, thoroughly sickened by my own poor judgment and idiocy. Christopher wasn't making a move, crouched down on the floor next to the dresser.

"Easton," she finally croaked, "I can explain everything, love."

"No explanation required, Bianca. I want you and your pimp out of this flat within ten minutes. I'm not going anywhere, in order to make sure it happens. I've already contacted Colin, and all of the locks to my various properties have been changed. All of my staff has been advised of your current status. You may contact Colin within the next couple of days and he'll arrange for your belongings to be shipped wherever you wish."

"My status? And just what is my status?" she snapped, some of her spirit now returning.

"You're a murderous whore, whom I regret ever having cared about. I'm happy you're gone from my life, and I'll be even happier when you're gone from my house. Now get to it." I whirled around, focusing on Christopher. "You're to leave immediately, dressed or not, I want your scrawny, limp dick out of here. Now."

If I hadn't been so devastated, I might've found it comical the way Christopher had scooped his pants up from the floor, doing a one-legged hop out of the room as he tried to get them pulled up before he fled into the night. I was right behind him, tossing his jacket to him, as he fumbled with the door handle, finally getting it opened to flee.

Once gone, I'd turned my attention back to Bianca, observing as she dressed quickly, grabbing everything she could manage and stuffing it into the designer luggage I'd bought for her. She was frantic to get away from me; I could only imagine how I looked to her at the moment, towering over her, not attempting to mask my fury.

"Really, Easton, how can you possibly not forgive me? I thought what we had together was stronger than that? I really wanted the baby! It was Christopher that talked me into the *abortion, I swear! I was so confused. I thought you'd be angry, thinking I was trying to trap you by getting pregnant. I swear that wasn't it, baby! Christopher said you would ruin me because of it. We just have to work this out, Easton. You're my life, I truly mean that!"*

"Bianca!" I yelled, causing her to jump and stop chattering. She looked up at me with those incredibly blue eyes that now appeared very sad and penitent.

"Yes?" she said timidly, waiting for me to say something.

"We're done. So just shut the fuck up and leave." I wasn't angry anymore, truthfully. I wasn't hurt. I wasn't disappointed. I just wanted revenge against the last woman who would ever make the mistake of fucking me over.

I didn't like when dark memories surfaced like that out of nowhere. It wasn't as if it happened daily. There were occasional triggers that caused them to come floating back to me. Darcy was a trigger, perhaps one that my instincts were telling me to avoid. I wanted to avoid her, but something else was at play here and I realised it was my fascination with her. Her resemblance to Bianca had definitely initiated it; even Lacee remarked about it in her usual accusatory tone. It was if I had some unfinished business with Bianca that somehow Darcy might fulfill. It was crazy, yet being drawn to her was potent.

If I possessed any decency, I'd let it go. I would simply put her out of my mind, along with the things that I fantasized doing to her. But I'd never claimed to be a decent man.

Chapter 16

It had been several weeks since I had last seen Easton Matthews. I had heard nothing from him since that phone call during the painful and blush-worthy afternoon, the day after he basically rocked my fucking world. And I was beginning to wonder if that was just a courtesy-call that guys tend to make after hooking up. You know the one: where they're afraid to hurt your feelings, so they just kind of tell you that you're great and *hint* at seeing you again? Seriously, why even call at all? Not to get all annoyed or anything, but I was trying and failing to understand that maybe this was all part of the game. And that maybe I was just *one* of the many women Easton Matthews was playing with. Dudes are just plain freakin' from another planet; I wasn't thinking Mars either, more like Ur-Anus!!

I'd been a little mopey, not to mention snappy, over the past week or two. Trust me, it didn't go unnoticed by Eli. He crept up behind me at work just this morning, seeing my new scrolling marquis screen-saver in Broadway font that read, "Men are Dirt!"

"Hmm, someone has a case of the hard ass," he commented with a grin, looking over my shoulder.

"Is there something you need?" I asked curtly.

"Just wanted to remind you about the All Employee Meeting in ten minutes. I thought maybe we could walk to the conferencing center together."

"Oh shit," I replied, "I forgot about that; what's this meeting about anyway?"

"How should I know, babe? You're the owner's daughter. I figured you'd be in the know."

"I haven't really thought about it, to tell you the truth. Besides that, my dad's been hard to pin down lately. I think he's still ticked off at me, for whatever reason."

"Well, I guess we'll find out soon enough," he replied. "Helen in Purchasing said she heard from Marsha in Accounting that it's a hostile takeover of some sort."

"Eli, I didn't realize you were such a gossip queen. Is that a gay thing?"

"Darcy, I love you, but bite me."

Eli and I, along with a horde of other employees, traipsed upstairs to the large conferencing center. It reminded me of the large theater-style lecture rooms we had at college. We found seats and waited patiently for my father to take the podium.

Several minutes later he came out, dressed in a dark suit and tie, a bit different than his usual business casual at the office. My dad was not pretentious, so I had a sinking suspicion perhaps Eli's tidbit of gossip was on target.

"Fellow employees, you know me well enough by now to realize I'm not one for long and drawn-out speeches. I'm a cut-to-the-chase individual, but I want to make my message to all of you today very clear from the beginning. Today, there's good news for Sheridan & Associates that includes opportunities for each and every employee here. This is a major announcement that I'm very pleased to share with all of you. Several months ago, I was approached by a well-respected global company, interested in buying Sheridan & Associates. At the time, I wasn't interested in entertaining any proposals for the sale of my company. I felt there was more to be done prior to my retirement."

Oh geez! Daddy, what have you done?

"Several weeks ago, I was again approached by the same CEO of this corporation, and a new proposal was submitted. I'm pleased to announce that a merger between Sheridan & Associates, a privately-owned business, and Baronton Holdings, L.L.C. has been concluded. This will bring many more jobs to the D.C. area as Baronton moves a segment of their business from the U.K. to right here in D.C. A transition team will be on site next Monday, and remain here to ensure a smooth merger with the most important resources we have, our employees. I'll be retained in a consulting position for the Sheridan segment of the business indefinitely."

I didn't hear the rest of what my father was saying. My head was spinning; I felt like a statue sitting next to Eli as he continued jabbing me with his elbow.

119

I finally turned to look at Eli, the shock apparent on my face.

"I know, right?" he whispered to me, taking my hand.

My father was now introducing the new majority owner of Sheridan & Associates, Mr. Easton Matthews. I instinctively squeezed my legs tighter together; Eli noticed and let out an audible smirk. The employees clapped like the suck-ups they were as Easton came up to the podium from the door behind the stage. Naturally, he was impeccably dressed, looking sexy, hot, and gorgeous in his double-breasted Armani suit. I heard Lynda from Payroll gasp behind me.

"Dear God, he's beautiful," she whispered loudly, to Pam McCain sitting next to her. I turned around, shooting her daggers and shushing her abruptly.

"Good afternoon, ladies and gentlemen," Easton said his rich voice music to my ears once again. "I'm Easton and the first thing I'd like to do is to put everyone's mind at ease relative to this merger."

"He's got a bit of a British accent; that's sooo hot," I heard Lynda whisper again.

"First of all, I realise a move such as this tends to make employees uneasy and fearful for their jobs. Let me assure you straightaway, there's no need for worry. The transition team Baronton has in place will make this transition smooth and seamless. You're all very valuable assets to this company, and will continue to be valuable assets to Baronton-Sheridan, the new name of this organisation."

I watched in awe as the employees in front of me suddenly relaxed, smiled, and whispered amongst each other. Easton had won them over with his charm and charisma. I looked back up to where he stood talking to my father and, as they finished, he turned and his piercing gray eyes were on me in an instant.

"Oh God," Eli whispered. "He's staring right at you, Darce."

"I can see that, Eli," I murmured under my breath without moving my lips. Our eyes locked and I was tempted to get into a stare-down with him just for the hell of it, but the whispers behind me were extremely distracting.

"I wonder if he's married," Lynda said. "Fifty bucks says Shelly jumps ship from old man Sheridan and puts in to be 'Hottie's' executive assistant."

I was boiling now. I turned around and none too quietly hissed, "Umm? Excuse me. Ladies? See, that's my father there. You know—the carrier of my DNA and all? So, if you guys would just…Shut. Up. That'd be great. 'Kay? Thanks." I caught glares from both of them.

As if on cue, Easton stepped back to the podium to speak once again. "At this time, I'd like to introduce the leader of our transition team to all of you. She'll be available for any questions or concerns you may have starting tomorrow."

The whole breathing thing got a little hard as Lacee stepped out onto the stage and joined Easton at the podium. "Everyone, this is my executive assistant and newly appointed team leader of the Baronton-Sheridan Group, Lacee Fitzgerald. Again, the minions gave a round of applause to the blonde bitch who was flashing a smile right along with her cleavage.

"Wanna bet she's banged the boss more than once?" I heard Lynda comment behind me. I was ready to go off on her when I felt Eli's hand on my arm, shaking his head as if saying "Leave it alone." Now, Lacee came up to the microphone, having to adjust it downward to accommodate her short stature.

"Welcome everyone," she greeted, "to your new family, Baronton-Sheridan Group. I'm looking forward to meeting with each of you in some one-on-one sessions that I'll be scheduling to get basic information as to your job description, scope of responsibilities and future growth plans. This transition team is dedicated to grooming all of the employees so that everyone's successful in meeting their growth potential. We're going to have a lot of fun, so relax, and let us help you become the very best at what you do. Thank you."

I think I just vomited a little in my mouth.

The meeting ended up with a few more words of assurance from my father, which I totally tuned out. I was floored he would do this to me! I was, in fact, ready to cut loose with some tears of anguish, but there was no way in hell I'd give Easton *that* satisfaction! Why the hell would he be interested in a small company like Sheridan & Associates, anyway? It made no sense to me. The more I saw how he operated, the more convinced I was he was shady.

As Eli and I walked back out through the hallway to our respective departments, I remained speechless. Finally, Eli broke the silence.

"So, what are you thinking?"

"I'm thinking that I need to look for another job and revise my career path. I can't believe my father did that."

"Maybe he had reasons of his own. Maybe he wants to semi-retire. I mean, you can't necessarily blame the guy for wanting to improve his golf game."

"But he always talked as if I'd take over, what about that?"

"I think you need to discuss that with him off-premises. That's the mature thing to do. But right now, I'm more interested in how much interaction Easton Matthews plans on having here."

"Well, I can tell you this: he'll be having no interaction with me outside of work. Bringing his blonde blow-up doll here with him like that, having her head up the transition team, what a joke."

"For now, babe, you just have to dig in and be professional about it. It's all you have."

"Yeah, well I meant what I said. I'm going to look for another job in the meantime."

I watched as Eli frowned, genuinely disturbed by my current attitude.

"Is there something you want to say to me, Eli?"

"Maybe there is," he replied. "You know, sometimes you need to take a moment and consider the fact that it's not always about you. I get that you've got that "only child" thing going on, but it's time for you to realize that just because something pisses you off, you can't simply pick your marbles up and go home. Sometimes, it's about thinking things through and making the best of them. I mean who knows? This might be a good thing when it's all said and done. Let your folks off the hook, Darcy; that's really what you need to do. This is about you making it on your own."

With that, Eli turned right and headed down the hallway leading to his department, leaving me feeling chastised for the first time ever. Maybe he knew what I needed more than I did. Friends are funny that way.

Chapter 17

I sulked that evening alone in my room, taking comfort in my flannel nightgown, eating microwave mac and cheese while sitting cross-legged on my bed watching trash television. I could hear Eli puttering around on the ground floor of our townhouse. He wasn't going to budge on anything he said earlier today. And why should he? He was right and I knew it.

Who was I kidding, acting as if I could find a career anywhere I chose? I had no experience whatsoever. I was basically what companies refer to as "unskilled labor" at the moment. My only choice was to do exactly what Eli said: suck it up, be professional, and along the way my reward would be experience and knowledge.

I'd licked the last of the runny cheese sauce from my lips when there was a tap on my bedroom door.

"Can I come in?" Eli asked from the hallway.

"It's open," I called back. The door opened slowly and Eli's face was hidden by a large bouquet of *purple* roses in a crystal vase as he sauntered into the room.

"Gee, Eli, no better way to say you're sorry, I guess, than with purple roses."

"Ha, ha, smart-ass. They're not from me. Some chauffeur just dropped them off with this. He handed an envelope to me, but I didn't have to open it to know who they were from.

> *I've been very pleased with your behaviour these past few weeks. I'd like to spend some time with you this evening. My driver will pick up you up at 8:00 p.m. sharp. We'll have dinner together and then play it by ear. Please pack nightwear. - EASTON*

"He's got to be *fucking* kidding," I managed to say, to no one in particular. Eli hurriedly put the roses on my nightstand, holding his hand out so he could read the note.

"Wow, better get waxed girlie. You only have about an hour and ten minutes before our bell rings again."

"Yeah, *as if*," I huffed, curling back up on my bed. "I have no intention of going out with him or fucking him or anything tonight—or ever! What a pompous ass!"

"Whoa, now wait a minute here. Why the sudden change of attitude?"

"Eli," I deadpanned. "*Seriously?*"

"Apparently so," he replied, sitting down on the edge of the bed, crossing his legs. "Clue me in because the last I looked, dude rang your bell good."

"Yeah, alright," I conceded. "But that was then and this is now."

"How poetic."

"Bite me, bitch," I said, smacking at him playfully. "No, really a lot's changed since then. First of all, he hasn't called me, which I find offensive, but then I rationalized…why should he call? I mean, we both knew what that night was about: a sexathon with no strings. So, I get over it, right? Then he friggin' buys the company, or the majority of the company, where I work, so now he's the boss of me."

"Actually, I think it's politically correct to say that he's now your *boss's* boss's boss."

"Okay," I reply, waving him off. "Whatever. And then he sends roses that are purple—just like that…you know…"

"Crop?"

"Yes, and then he *summons* me to be ready? Pack my fucking jammies? I don't think so. Aside from the callous treatment, I'm not going to be the one everyone accuses of banging the boss. Period. You said yourself that I need to make my own way at Sheridan or whatever the hell he's renamed it. And that's *exactly* what I'm going to do! *Without* screwing the boss."

125

"You mean the boss's, boss's, boss?"

I flipped Eli off with both hands.

He chuckled, leaning over and giving me a brotherly kiss on the forehead. "That's my girl," he said. "I'm glad you got your spirit back, and honestly? I'm proud of you."

"Why?" I asked.

"I really thought your first 'Darcy move' would be to fly over to your parent's house in that sweet little Mercedes they bought for you, whining and crying about the injustice of it all and blaming them for putting a hurdle in the way of your climb to the top, yadda, yadda, yadda. Instead, you reflected, and came to the more adult conclusion, which is sometimes you simply play the hand you're dealt. I like that."

"Aww, Eli, you know I was never really pissed at you, don't you?" I sarcastically crooned at him.

"Yeah, right," he laughed, mussing my hair. "So, what do I tell 'James' when he shows up here in that limo for you?"

I put on a horrible British accent. "Please convey my sincerest regrets to Mr. Matthews, but Ms. Sheridan won't be joining him this evening to sup. She's otherwise occupied with shaving her legs and washing her hair."

Eli and I both broke into laughter. "Hopefully, I'll think of something better than *that*. Don't worry, Darce."

I took a leisurely bubble-bath, shaving, waxing, shampooing and just relaxing in general. I heard the bell downstairs ring and nothing more. Apparently, Eli had taken care of it as promised. I couldn't get over the audacity of Easton's presumption I was to be at his disposal just like that. He didn't know Darcy Sheridan at all.

After getting dried off, I dressed in a clean nightgown and robe and wrapped a towel around my wet hair, turban style. I slipped into my fluffy, bunny slippers and padded downstairs to the living room, shocked as hell when I saw Easton sitting back, arms crossed on our sofa, with a very perturbed look on his

126

gorgeous face. Eli was sitting across from him, looking more than a little uncomfortable. I wondered if they'd been conversing all of this time.

"Well, I see Darcy's out of the shower. I've got laundry to finish, so it's been very nice talking to you, sir," Eli "the suck-up" said, reaching out to shake Easton's hand.

"It was very nice talking to you as well, Eli. Thank you for keeping me company while Darcy was getting ready."

I tried to keep all unlady-like hand gestures to myself.

Eli left the room, a small smile gracing his lips, as if he knew I could handle it. I wasn't so sure.

"Good evening, Darcy," he said, his eyes burning through me with something. "I must say, your attire may not fit in well with the restaurant I chose for us this evening. Perhaps you'd like to rethink it?"

I sat down next to him on the couch turned sideways, drying my wet hair off with the towel. "Easton, I think there's been some miscommunication. See…I haven't heard from you, and then on the day that I find out *you're my boss*, I get flowers and a signed note that says, 'Let's have dinner and pack some nightwear.'?"

His eyes danced with amusement, as if he couldn't possibly fathom anyone not doing his bidding. "What's not clear to you? I believe I mentioned I wanted to see you again. To my knowledge, I didn't confirm the date."

"Nooo, you're right, you didn't. But I mean, what are we talking about here? Is this *my* night to entertain you? And I also have to tell you, I'm not pulling one of those on a work night, anymore. Because the bigger issue is: I'm not going to be banging my boss's, boss's boss. Despite what you think, I *do* have some limitations."

Dear God—I'm rambling.

He smiled genuinely, once again flashing the dimple I hadn't seen in a while.

"I know about your limitations." The gunmetal in his eyes triggered. "I can assure you that you're not the only one I have available for entertainment purposes. However, tonight's intentions weren't entirely about that, though I'd be lying if I said I wasn't open to it."

The genuine smile from before was gone, replaced by something far more professional. "Of course, I respect your position, now that the situation has changed with the company. I suppose that's problematic."

"You betcha," I said. "I heard the whispers and murmurs behind me at the meeting today."

"About you?" he asked, now frowning.

"No, about Lacee. To put it more delicately, the consensus is that she got her position, or now what sounds like a promotion, by way of doing her boss."

"I see," he replied. "Well those employees know nothing about Lacee, so I'd say that's not a fair assessment. Lacee's very good at what she does *in the office*," he clarified. "Her promotion was earned and had nothing to do with anything else. I'm not a fool," he stated very matter-of-factly.

"I'm glad to hear that because neither am I. I plan to work hard at Baronton-Sheridan, despite the fact my father totally blew me out of the water with that announcement today. But I've thought about it. And as my good friend Eli pointed out, sometimes you just do the best you can with the hand you're dealt. I intend to make it on my own; I want no one's help. At the same time, I have to respect your authority at work and maintain my professionalism. I don't intend to be on the receiving end of gossip, snickers or horrible sexual innuendos. I hope you understand. If I succeed at Baronton-Sheridan, it'll be because of my own efforts, achievements and performance *at the office*."

"I see," he replied, calmly, considering me. His face was a blank slate. "Well, though I'm disappointed we won't be playing any longer, I respect your position and determination to succeed. I must tell you, my invitation for dinner this evening had a dual purpose. There was some business I wished to discuss with you as well."

Huh?

"I'm listening," I replied, starting to become distracted by his five o'clock shadow, his full, sensual lips, and scent of his cologne that drifted subtly over to me. I squirmed while waiting for him to elaborate. And trying to quickly reassemble my personal wall of defense against my now very off-limits boss.

"I made a commitment to your father pre-merger that I'd groom and mentor the management trainees. It's of particular importance to your father that you learn skill sets you don't currently possess."

"Like what?" I interrupted, getting my attitude.

"I'll explain, Ms. Sheridan, if allowed to do so without interruption." He quirked one of those beautiful eyebrows at me. What could I do? I nodded.

"As it happens," he continued, "Lacee assumed the Team Leader position, so I'm left with a vacancy for an executive assistant at Baronton-Sheridan. I think you might fit the bill."

"Oh, I just bet you do," I chuckled. "I'm well aware of the duties Lacee performed in her role as your executive assistant. As I just explained, I have—"

"I heard you initially, Ms. Sheridan," he interrupted briskly. "Trust me, I won't be lonely without you or Lacee in my bed. This is strictly business. It'll give you an opportunity to learn about operations, negotiating, contractual agreements, bid proposals and presentations, a very diverse background."

I flushed with embarrassment, as he was quick to put me in my place. He certainly was acting as if it was no big deal about the other. He was still going on, but my mind was wondering whether I'd cut off my nose to spite my face.

"And of course, should you accept this opportunity, there's a significant wage increase involved, with periodic performance appraisals every six months to make sure you're keeping with your growth plan."

He caught my attention with that one. My annual salary of $40,000 was not cutting it with my spending habits.

"How significant?" I asked.

"First lesson, Ms. Sheridan: it's prudent to not focus on the salary when interviewing or with being offered promotional opportunities. Your main focus should be asking about your responsibilities, level of authority, accounts, and upward movement—things of that nature to show your boss or potential employer that it's more about the job challenge and career path than the money."

"Hmm, well I guess when I reach your level of income, I'll do just that Easton, but for now, the brass tacks please?"

"The what?"

"The numbers *love*," I said, imitating his accent. His smile was back, going clear to his eyes this time.

"Your annual pay will be increased to $60K per year. You'll have a company credit card, and do some traveling."

"Traveling?"

"Yes, traveling with me to visit key customers. Is that a problem?"

"Uhh, well, no."

"Splendid," he said, his palms slapping his thighs as he stood up to depart. I didn't want him to go. I wanted to hear about my new job—and to continue to look at him.

"What about dinner?" I asked timidly. Funny, wasn't it? Earlier, I was saying how ridiculous it was for him to invite me to dinner. And now, here I was, stumbling over myself in an attempt to have him stay.

Funny? Friggin' hilarious.

He glanced at his Rolex, "I'm afraid we've missed our reservation."

"Well we could order a pizza and just kind of veg out here—talk about my job and watch some television."

He considered it momentarily and then smiled. "I guess that's something I'm not real familiar with, but it sounds like a plan to me."

"Great," I said smiling. "My treat, too."

I called and ordered the pizza. Eli made himself scarce, going out to meet some friends, as if anything was going to happen between Easton and me. It was actually enjoyable sitting on the couch, eating pizza, drinking wine and listening to Easton fill me in on some of the particulars of the accounts I'd work with under his tutelage. It gave me chills a couple of times.

"Hey are you up for not talking any more business this evening and catching a classic horror flick? Eli and I have the Chiller channel," I said, smiling. The wine was giving me a warm, fuzzy feeling. Perfect for an evening with Lon Chaney, Boris Karloff or Bela Lugosi.

"I'm not familiar with the Chiller channel," Easton replied, his smile including his dimple as he scarfed up the last slice of pizza.

"Seriously?" I asked, grabbing the remote from the coffee table. "Then you're in for a real treat. These are classic black and white movies from the thirties, forties and fifties, mainly. I'm a big fan of Frankenstein and Dracula flicks—anything with Bela Lugosi in it is pure awesomeness. You've never seen any of these?"

He shook his head. "Never watched much television," he replied with a shrug. "I grew up mostly going to live theatre, operas, concerts—that sort of thing."

"Well *dahling,*" I said in my faux British voice, "Tonight Chiller Theatre is presenting Boris Karloff in *Bride of Frankenstein* for your viewing pleasure," I teased, turning the volume up as the movie started.

"And you've seen this movie before?" Easton asked.

"Oh yeah. Lots of times. That's why they're classics. I love that you're a trash T.V. virgin," I giggled.

Easton cocked an eyebrow at me, and then settled back on the couch, propping his legs up on the coffee table the same way Eli did when we watched horror flicks together.

Easton seemed to enjoy the movie, commenting when Elsa Lanchester wakes up and meets her fiancé, Frankenstein's monster and hisses like a cat at him, following it up with a blood-curdling scream.

"I mean, really," he said, chuckling. "Has *she* looked in the mirror lately?"

This brought a fit of giggles from me because I'd always thought that exact same thing when I watched that scene.

"Ignorance is bliss, I guess," I replied, polishing off my third glass of wine.

131

"Do they end up together?" he asked.

"I'm not telling," I replied, laughing. "You'll have to see for yourself."

This is nice. This is normal...

Somehow I must have fallen asleep during the movie. When I woke up much later I was upstairs in my bed. Alone. I glanced over at the clock on the night stand. It was after two a.m. My alarm had been set. Eli must've carried me up.

Chapter 18

~ Easton ~

I drove my company SUV back to the St. Regis where I was once again staying, trying to convince my cock to get over it. Damn! The minute Darcy's soft body had encroached upon mine, my dick stood at attention immediately. I ended up watching her instead of the movie when she fell asleep next to me, unknowingly, and finally resting her head on my lap (which was a mistake). Very carefully, I found myself running my fingers softly through her long, dark hair that was so much like Bianca's. I was surprised my hard-on hadn't awakened her.

When the movie ended, I had two options: I could easily slip out from beneath her and let myself out of the apartment, or I could do something that I knew she probably wouldn't agree to. I went with the latter, taking that soft body of hers and carrying it to her bedroom. It wasn't the simple action of carrying her that bothered me. It was the fact that I *wanted* to. I was bothered by the fact that she *might* wake up with a stiff neck, and be uncomfortable. I knew that she'd sleep better in her room and in her bed. It also *supremely* bothered me that I just liked the way she felt snuggled up against me.

I admit, I was a bit taken by surprise when I showed up and her roommate indicated she was declining my invitation. That was a first. I debated whether to simply blow it off and find other company for the evening, but something inside was unsettled. I insisted on waiting for her as we had business to discuss, clearly making Eli uncomfortable. It didn't matter. I would see her one way or another. I wasn't one to be so easily dissuaded on these matters.

It was three weeks after my ninth birthday. My mother had not yet returned from her trip, but was expected in the following day. I was anxious to let her know the evil things Miss Gennifer had done. I was relieved I had only one night left without my mother's protection. That was the night Miss Gennifer, in one of her drunken stupors, climbed into my bed.

"Let's see what we have here," she whispered, the smell of rum heavy on her breath. I was groggy and confused until I felt her hand slip beneath the waistband of my boxers and grasp hold of my cock, playing and pulling it until it stood erect.

133

"Stop," I said to her, pushing her away.

"Now you don't really want me to stop, do you lad?" she crooned, "You know this feels good, doesn't it?"

I squirmed from her, but she was relentless. "I've got you nice and hard, Easton; let Miss Gennifer finish you off. I want to see if you can squirt yet. Otherwise, I suppose another flogging is in order."

My child's mind went blank; I played possum, hoping she'd just stop what she was doing and leave me alone. A therapist years later said I'd gone into survival mode, a human defense mechanism and a perfectly natural thing for a 9-year old to do. It was the smart thing to do, he'd told me. It wasn't a sign of weakness, but a sign of strength borne of the will to survive. I blocked everything out until I heard Gennifer's voice again.

"Guess your spunk's not in yet, laddie…maybe when you're ten." She laughed harshly, staggering out of my room and back to hers.

The next morning, my mother had arrived, her arms full of packages for me.

"Come kiss Mummy, Easton. I've missed you so much."

I ran to her, clutching her arms, begging her to come to the study so I could tell her what had happened. Once I'd told her everything in 9 year-old terms, I saw the anger spread throughout her entire body. Relief flooded over me. She'd banish the governess; I was sure. I was totally unprepared for the anger she directed towards me.

"You must never tell anyone what you've just told me, Easton! Do you understand me?"

I nodded, confused and upset.

"I will not have the people in my social circle thinking I'm not a good judge of character or that I'm negligent in parenting. I especially forbid you to ever breathe a word of this to your father!"

"I won't, Mum, I promise."

"You damn well better not, because if you do, I'll find out and you'll never see me, Grammy or Papa, again! It'll be as if you've killed us all by spreading such a scandalous story around about me!"

I started crying, promising her I wouldn't tell anyone.

"You see there, Easton? That's exactly the reason Miss Gennifer took advantage of you! You're weak just as your father is weak! You'd better learn how to control women, Easton. If you don't take charge, they will, and then you'll have no one to blame but yourself. Now, stop your mewling; that only proves how weak you are," she'd hissed. "I'll tend to Miss Gennifer, explaining that you'll be attending boarding school as soon as possible. I will, of course, give her a sterling recommendation along with severance pay to ensure she doesn't spread any nasty gossip around London. I swear, Easton, I can't believe I came home from a wonderful holiday only to be greeted with this!"

It was only a matter of days before I was sent off to a private boarding school in Switzerland, not seeing my mother until the following spring. My father had sent letters every week, telling me all about his work, about Trace and the activities they were doing, and how much they all were looking forward to my spending the summer with them. Those letters were my lifeline at the time.

I ran my hand through my hair, wondering what the hell had made me think about that particular memory. Maybe it was because Darcy had been surprised this evening when she learned I was a "trash T.V." virgin. I'm sure our childhoods were worlds apart. I'd bet my younger brother Trace knew all about growing up *normal*.

I was restless when I arrived back at the St. Regis. It was nearly midnight, but I didn't need a lot of sleep to be on my game. I didn't feel like being alone and my cock was still twitching because the other half of my plan for this evening hadn't come to fruition. There was a trendy night club located just around the corner from the hotel. I decided to stop in for a nightcap or two.

It was fairly crowded and a bit noisy, as I expected. I took a seat at the bar, ordering a bourbon and branch. There were a few single women at the bar. A dark redhead caught my attention immediately as she gazed over at me over the rim of her wine glass. Her skin was ivory, her eyes—even from this distance— were extraordinarily large and luminous. I decided they were probably green or blue. Her lips were full and pouty—the kind I liked gliding my cock past. She was dressed expensively, certainly not in the usual chic-but-cheap garb of a hooker. I instructed the bartender to send her a drink. Several minutes later, she carried her drink down to my end of the bar.

135

"Thanks for the drink," she said, with a glowing smile. "I'm in town on business and I just hate going to a bar alone, but the thought of staying in my hotel suite tonight didn't appeal to me either. I'm sorry I'm rambling, my name's Tiffany."

"It's lovely to meet you Tiffany. My name's Easton. Would you care to join me?"

"I'd be delighted to, Easton. Next round's on me," she replied, tossing me a sexy smile.

"Where are you staying?" I inquired.

"St. Regis," she replied with a shrug. "It's where I usually stay when I travel to D.C. Sort of feels like a second home."

"I know what you mean," I said, "It's the same for me. What type of business are you in, Tiffany, if I may ask?"

She seemed to like the sound of her name on my lips. "Of course, you may," she cooed, pulling one of her business cards from her handbag to give me.

"Let's see," I said, smiling, "Tiffany Brandt, Executive V.P., Winfield Executive Resources, Boston, Massachusetts. I'm impressed."

"Thank you," she replied, softly. "I love what I do, how about you?"

"Oh I don't think I can top that," I lied, gracing her with a wink. "I'd love to hear more about your recruitment firm. Perhaps we can have our nightcap back at the hotel?"

"I'm game for that," she said. "The noise level in here seems to be escalating. Your suite or mine?"

"It doesn't matter," I replied, signaling for the bar tender to bring my tab. "Wherever you feel more comfortable, Tiffany."

"How about you come to my suite—it's 602 in about twenty minutes?"

"Sounds like a plan," I replied, taking a final swig of my cocktail.

She pulled a pen out of her handbag and wrote "6-0-2" on the back of the business card she'd given me, fearful I might have problems remembering a three-digit number.

"I'll have a cocktail waiting for you, bourbon, correct?"

"You're amazing," I laughed. "Yes, bourbon it is."

"Alright then. I'll see you at my place in about twenty."

"I'm looking forward to it," I replied, pocketing her business card and handing my credit card to the bartender, who happened to be grinning from ear to ear. Tiffany departed for the hotel, no doubt to order our drinks and to administer a quick douche before my arrival. As if any part of me was planning to head south of her bellybutton, apart from my sheathed cock.

The bartender returned with the register receipt for my signature. "Hey man, I'm sorry, but I just need to ask you something. How'd you manage that?"

"I beg your pardon?" I asked, stuffing my credit card back into my wallet.

"That chick's been hit on at least four times this evening. I don't think she had to buy one of her drinks tonight. You show up and in and less than ten minutes, you hook up. I mean, I'm impressed. Feel like sharing your secret?"

I gave him a conciliatory smile, looking at his name tag. "Perhaps it's just timing, Jeff," I replied, standing up to leave. "Right now, I have some pussy waiting."

"Hey," he called out as I reached the door, "Let me know if she's a true redhead." I heard the sound of laughter behind me as the door closed. Men could be pigs sometimes. There was no doubt about that.

Disgusting.

I headed back to my suite at the hotel, the same one I had when Darcy had visited that night. I still had the mental picture of her wearing that sweater and tight "fuck me" skirt, looking as if she was afraid I'd pounce on her the second she made her decision to cross the threshold. She'd looked sweet, vulnerable, and sexy all at once. And completely malleable. My cock twitched at the memory. Darcy was going to be a hard act to follow for any woman and the stunning redhead waiting in "6-0-2" was no exception.

137

I loosened my tie, pulling it off, tossing it onto the sofa. I reached into the breast pocket of my business shirt and pulled out Tiffany's business card, staring at it for a moment. Part of me (the part below the belt) wanted to go to her suite in fifteen minutes, knowing it'd probably only take another ten to sink my cock into her and get the relief I desperately craved. Another part of me wasn't entirely on board with the idea.

I ripped the card into pieces, letting them scatter to the floor. I continued stripping my clothes off, dropping them along the way to the huge bathroom where, in the privacy of the large marble shower, I took things into my own hands.

How fucking pathetic was that?

Chapter 19

The following Monday, freshly rested, the new and improved Darcy Sheridan dressed for success at the office. The short, tight, skimpy skirts, the practically see-through gauzy blouses, plunging neckline sweaters and spiked heels were history, as far as my job was concerned. I'd been given an opportunity and I dared anyone there to insinuate it was because I showed ass or cleavage!

I dressed in a heather gray, wool, pencil skirt that fell mid-calf, with a pleat slit in the back that didn't go up any further than the back of my knee. I wore a black, silk long-sleeved blouse with a collar, leaving only the top button undone. I accessorized with a delicate silver necklace, small silver hoop earrings, and black two-inch pumps, wearing the recommended "nude" color pantyhose. Very professional...trendy yet conservative.

Over the weekend, I'd gone online and found a great web-site for professional women called "professionalimagedress.com" for the latest tips. With my vast wardrobe, it'd actually been difficult to find the proper length skirt. So a shopping trip was in order to purchase a few appropriate items of business attire. I pulled my hair back into a low ponytail as the site indicated, stating it provided an air of professionalism for those with long locks, and was less distracting. I was good to go!

Eli did a double-take when I came downstairs before he had left to meet his friends at Starbucks.

"You didn't tell me you got another job already. A library or museum, I'm guessing by the looks of your ensemble. Ann Klein?"

"Oh bite me, Eli. This is a new chapter in my book. I intend to be professional just like you suggested and that includes wardrobe."

"Sweetie, last I heard, you didn't work in a convent," he chuckled. "Why are you up so early, anyway?"

"I think it shows commitment on my part to go beyond the call of duty, you know? I mean, I don't want to be labeled as an '8 to 5-er' by my colleagues."

"They wouldn't dare," he said, feigning anger. "Everyone knows you're more like an '8:15-8:30ish to 4:45' chick."

"Oh, you're on top of your game this morning, Eli. Go ahead, though. You'll see I'm serious about this, especially with my new position."

Shit!

"What new position?"

"Oh, well that's the reason Easton wanted to take me to dinner last night. He has an opportunity for me at work. Since Lacee's now Team Leader, he wants me to assume her former position as his executive assistant."

"Really?" he said, eyeing me warily. "What will your new job duties entail, exactly?"

"I know what you're thinking. I thought the same thing and made sure we got that out in the open. I made myself perfectly clear on that matter, and he understood, though of course, he was disappointed."

"Uh-huh," he said, shaking his head.

"What? I did!"

"Oh, I'm sure you did, but come on, don't be naïve, Darce. Easton Matthews is a master at getting what he wants, otherwise he wouldn't be where he is today. Do you really think he's content with having just a business relationship with you after you and he did the dirty deed over a six-hour period?"

"First of all, it was a *five-and-a-half-hour* period. Second of all, Easton Matthews doesn't have a problem in the free *world* getting any woman he wants into bed. He as much as told me he won't be lonely in the sack when I made it clear there'd be no more—well, you know."

"Uh-huh," he repeated, this time with an eye roll. "Let me ask you this: is there a pay increase involved?"

"A slight one," I lied, quickly adding, "The important thing isn't salary, but the opportunities to learn from the best, to carve my career path with a clear vision of my growth potential."

"Okay, really? I just vomited in my mouth," Eli said, giving me a look of absolute and incredulous disgust. Once he got his natural facial features back to normal, he gave me the ol' best-friend look and sighed. "Just be careful, okay? That's all I'm gonna say. The dude has ulterior motives—and before you get all pissy, the answer's yes."

"Yes to what?"

"Yes, I think you're smart and capable of being groomed for that position, and for that matter, have the potential for going as high as you want within any company. Just please make sure you don't pay a price at BS."

"BS?"

"Baronton-Sheridan, that's what we all decided to call it since the new name's too much of a mouthful and sounds pretentious. Hey, how about that? I just drew a nice parallel, didn't I?"

"What do you mean?" I asked, furrowing my eyebrow in confusion.

"Easton and his company name: both pretentious, both a mouthful." He was snickering as he put his jacket on.

"Oh my God! That's the last time I fill you in on my men, I mean it."

"See you at work, sweetie. Good luck!"

I arrived at work promptly at 7:20 a.m., before any of the others in my department had arrived. I figured if my transitioning into Lacee's old job started today, I wanted to get caught up on the data entry backlog I had. By 8:30, I was completely finished with the stack of documents, and had completed my filing. Of course, the batches of documents to enter arrived almost hourly in my in-basket, but that would be my replacement's worry.

My desk phone rang and the caller-ID told me it was "E. Matthews," jump-starting the butterflies that'd been lying dormant in my stomach. But I was fairly sure it was because, despite our friendly hang-out last night, I was anxious to show him I was a professional, clearly capable of being his new executive assistant.

"Good morning, this is Darcy Sheridan. How may I help you?" I answered in a very professional tone.

His rich, silky voice still had the ability of give me goose-bumps, something I was sure would diminish over time.

"Good morning, Darcy. Are you ready to begin your mentoring?"

"Yes, sir."

"Can you come by my office now so that I can de-brief you on your training schedule for this week and next? Lacee will start working with you this afternoon, but there are a few things I think you might start on now. I've already cleared this new assignment with HR."

"Certainly, I'll be right there," I said. I grabbed my handbag and a notepad, and went up to the executive suites. Easton was occupying an empty one on the other side of the hall from my father's. It had been a conference room with an adjacent office leading from it.

As I crossed the threshold to his office, I admired how quickly he'd furnished it to his taste. Leather high-back chair, dark mahogany desk and credenza, matching leather chairs for visitors, and a conference table with more chairs in the corner. The paintings on his wall were expensive and tasteful. His office was orderly and immaculate, just like he was. He looked up as I walked in, surveying with those intense gray eyes of his.

"Please have a seat," he said, standing up.

Ever the gentleman...Well. Sometimes...

"Thank you," I said, smiling, taking a seat across from his desk.

"Uh, has there been a dress code implemented I wasn't made aware of?" he asked, smiling, still looking at my ensemble.

"Not exactly," I shrugged, mentally trying to run over and hit reverse on those damn butterflies that weren't going away. "I felt that, in my new position, some decorum might be appropriate, sir."

"Okay, well about decorum—no more 'sirs' and that's a rule I have with all of my employees. I want the feeling of family here, not some rigid hierarchy. So, you may resume calling me 'Easton.'"

"Of course, si—Easton," I replied, quickly catching myself.

"As for dress codes, I'm a proponent of business casual for the employees, and that includes you."

"But you're wearing a suit," I argued gently.

"I am," he replied, "I've got a business appointment later today. On days where I have meetings with clients, customers, important people or potential partners, it's customary for me to dress in business suits. If my schedule's clear, I wear business casual."

"I see," I replied, making notes on my steno pad. "Do you even own business casual?" I blurted, unthinkingly. He cocked an eyebrow at me and then smiled.

"Of course. I'm a man of many tastes."

Easton had me pull my chair around next to his so that we could go over his Day Planner for the rest of the week—or as he referred to it, "his diary." (Another Britishism I figured.) He provided me with a new planner of my own so that I could copy down what he had scheduled so far for the next two weeks. He showed me the special coding he had for meetings, appointments, and luncheons, which meant I needed to re-confirm on the day prior to the event.

He also gave me a list of other office equipment and supplies he wanted me to get on order, and asked that I schedule some time with Helen in Purchasing to learn the purchase requisition system here, so that I could electronically forward them on indirect spend. I was hurriedly scribbling notes on everything he wanted me to handle today and tomorrow, including getting my office next to his furnished in whatever I wanted. I had to refrain from doing a full on fist-pump when he got to the part about me having my own personal office.

He also requested I schedule some time with the Accounts Payable Department to learn how the invoices for expense spends were matched for payment, and to provide him a listing of all employees authorized to approve requisitions and the spending limits for each. He wanted a full listing of general ledger account numbers and descriptions, as well as year-to-date spending for each.

"I assume you're computer literate with spreadsheets, power point, and word processing?" he asked.

143

"I'm a whiz," I said, smiling. Just then there was a tap on the door. It was Lacee.

"I'm finished with the first group of employees from R & D, Easton," she said. For some reason, the way she used his name made the hair on the back of my neck stand on end.

"Brilliant," he said, glancing at his watch. "It's lunch time now. Lacee, would you mind sending out for sandwiches? Darcy and I are having a working lunch today. Once I turn her over to you, in say an hour and a half, you can acquaint her with the access codes to my working files and show her how to track the various metrics we're going to put in place here shortly."

"That'll be fine," she answered, not hiding her displeasure at having to be around me for the afternoon. She seemed particularly out of sorts with the close proximity of Easton and me.

"Splendid," he said, turning his attention back to me. "Ready for some fun?"

Chapter 20

I was fuming as Easton and I walked out into the parking lot towards the SUV he nodded to a little after six that evening. He flipped the button for the electronic locks and opened the door for me. As I slid into the passenger seat, all I thought about was ripping him to shreds as soon as he got in. I knew I couldn't do that. He was, after all, the head honcho. I needed to chill out for a few and collect my thoughts.

He slid into the driver's seat, throwing me a smile and pulled out of the lot. Finally, I could contain my anger no longer.

"What the hell?" I snapped. "You said earlier you had a business meeting later this afternoon and would be gone the rest of the day. Then you show back up and insist—in front of Lacee, I might add—that I have dinner with you. What's this about?"

"I can't keep a thing from you, can I?" he teased. "You and I are having dinner together at Christine's."

"You're so clueless," I snarled. "People call *me* spoiled? My God, you give the word a whole new meaning! I thought we hashed this out last night?"

"You're over-reacting. It's simply dinner, not an orgy for Chrissake. I do have things to discuss with you that are business-related, and it's not healthy for you to get all of your training in the office."

It was my turn to cock an eyebrow at him.

What's he up to?

"Did it ever occur to you I might have had other plans for dinner?"

"That's irrelevant to me."

This was going nowhere, so I simply clammed up until we reached Christine's, located down the street from his hotel. I breathed a sigh of relief

145

when he passed the hotel. I'd suspected he might've had a hidden agenda when I noticed we were going downtown.

The server handed us our menus, took our drink orders and then disappeared. The silence now was obvious. My hands were clasped together resting on the table. I was totally shocked when Easton placed his hands over mine in a gesture of affection, which up to this point, had been non-existent. I looked up at him, and was way surprised to see what I found there. He was looking at me with an expression that was somewhere between confusion and uncertainty. And with a man like Easton, I wasn't sure whether that was a good sign…or a very, very bad one.

"Easton," I said, trying to feel him out. "I'm getting some very mixed signals here." I tried to pull my hands back, but his grip was strong. He didn't release his hold.

"It's simple, I've missed being with you."

"What do you mean? We were just together last night. We spent almost all morning together at the office, we had a working lunch together, and now you've hauled me out for dinner. I'd say over the last 24 hours, we've spent more time together than most married couples."

"Don't play with me," he quipped. "You know what I'm talking about. This doesn't bode well for me."

I sighed audibly. The truth was, my body ached for him as well as for his discipline, but these newly adopted scruples of mine were wreaking havoc with my better judgment. What else could I do but be honest?

"Easton I'd be lying if I said I didn't miss the experience of being with you. It was something else, no doubt about it. But things have changed. There's no getting around that. I told you how I felt last night. I need to get my priorities in order. Nothing's a given for me anymore. I have to *earn* my success. I really want to put my best foot forward with my career. You seemed to understand that last night. It's just not a good idea."

"Yes," he replied quietly, giving what I'd said some thought while rubbing my fingers with his. "Of course, you're right. It's not a good idea, assuredly. It would cross the line you set, which by the way, I *totally* respect and admire the fact that you're putting your career first, much like me, I suppose." His gray eyes

146

studied me and my heart did a fast pitter-pat at the feel of his fingers intertwining with mine.

"I appreciate your understanding and thank you for noticing that I've taken this new role seriously. I don't want anything to jeopardize my ability to succeed," I said.

He was still holding fast to my fingers. My heart continued the pitter-pat rhythm. "Absolutely," he replied, earnestly. "You're to be commended. Still," he said, his voice dropping an octave and his lips curling into that beautiful smile that couldn't be good for my pulse, "I just can't get *that* picture out of my head."

Silence…

"What picture?" I asked finally, squirming just a tad in my seat.

"The picture of your beautiful face after I've used the crop and when my lips softly place those little butterfly kisses on that very *special* spot of yours."

Oh holy Jesus!

"Which one?" I asked raising an eyebrow, immediately regretting it.

"The one right…*here*," he said softly, brushing his thumb against that sensitive area I had on my neck, an inch or two south of my earlobe. I knew the one. He continued to lightly caress it, his eyes growing darker.

"Ahh, yes," I said, remembering the way he'd made me tingle and my toes curl just with his soft kisses on that spot. "*That* spot." I shifted uneasily.

Focus, Darcy. Disengage. I repeat: disengage!

"And then, you know, there's that *other* special spot of yours…," he murmured.

"*Easton*," I warned, my tone getting stern. I shifted nervously.

"You know the one, love? That very deep, sensitive spot inside of you that loves the feel of my fingers and cock rubbing against it. Such a shame you haven't had the pleasure of feeling my unsheathed cock. I'm betting my cock jewelry would likely put you over the edge. You've wondered about that, haven't you? When you're lying in bed at night, when the world gets slightly quieter as your

147

imagination runs a little wilder…" His hand made its way to the nape of my neck, his fingers lightly drawing shapes across the sensitive skin. "I bet you have that night on replay, along with those thoughts of yours when you saw my piercing. And then you wonder what it would feel like to have it gently scrape your clit, slowly at first, but then I'd go a little faster. A little harder. Until I took it deeper and started all over again. And again."

By this time, I could feel the wet spot in my panties. My lips were dry, so I merely nodded in agreement.

"Oh," he said, smiling again, "Let's not *forget* those very enticing nipples of yours and the way they respond when I taste them, right before I take them full into my mouth to suck. Hard. Quite a rush, isn't it?"

Oh God!

The server approached, setting our drinks down, ready to take our order.

"Darcy?" Easton nodded, as the server waited, poised to write my order down.

"Uh, nothing for me, I'm still full from lunch." He turned to Easton for his order.

"Check please."

Against my better principles, I folded. Okay, I admit it! I was putty in his very capable hands, so *shoot* me! Which one of you would have done anything differently?

I thought so…

We made a mad dash from Christine's to his hotel suite, where Easton very quickly and very expertly relieved me of my librarian clothing and proceeded to introduce me to his wooden paddle. It had tiny holes drilled in the center so that it was more aerodynamic. I was pulled naked across his lap, my bare ass soundly paddled while his longer fingers were probing the folds of my sex which grew wetter with each resounding smack.

Our banter was manic. It was a veritable kaleidoscope of mixed emotions fraught with sexual tension and sensual frenzy. Don't believe me? Here, have a listen:

148

"You'll not defy me again, do you understand?" he whispered in my ear.

"Yes sir," I breathed.

"I'll take you anywhere I want when I want, is that understood?" he growled in opposition to his tender hands, as they did delicious and forbidden things.

"Yes, Easton."

"Have you had enough?" was asked softly from somewhere in the darkened room.

"No, please!" My voice was breaking, my nerves were ricocheting.

"Take it all in your mouth. That's my good girl."

"God, I love the taste of your cock!"

"Your pussy is starving, love." I felt his tongue and hands, not being able to see him through the blindfold.

"Please…keep fucking me…Like that," I begged.

"That's it love, keep squeezing my cock that way."

"Easton," I panted.

"Fuck…," I felt his lips against my spine.

We both flopped back on the bed when finished, panting from exhaustion, breathing heavily. The after effects of our fucking always left me covered with sweat, but feeling energized as well.

Easton rolled me over to examine my ass.

"I'm going to need to rub some ointment on you so you don't chafe," he said, launching himself from the bed and heading for the bathroom. He looked glorious in all his nakedness, his cock still glistening from the wetness of our sex. He'd been right. His cock jewelry totally rocked.

He returned, instructing me to lay on my belly while he gently administered aloe and peppermint extract oil to my reddened derrière. There was something about the tenderness with which he was doing this for the first time

149

ever that was strange. He rubbed more of it on my back, lowering his head to deliver soft, butterfly kisses to my backside, and neck. I shivered from the intensity of the moment.

Intensity. That's what it was. What had happened was so *intense*. That's what I kept telling myself as I reran the events that had just happened. Correction: the most *intensely pleasurable* events so far in my life.

But no matter how I chalked it up…there was a feeling that kept coming back. A ghost-like feeling that I've always had about Easton, but considering what had just taken place…the feeling was becoming a lot more real.

This was a man who could shatter me at will. I mean, look what he'd done with my resolve to be professional. Where'd *that* go? He'd splintered it the moment he started telling me those things at the restaurant. I could already feel the slow fractures begin to confetti my thoughts.

I was attracted to him, for sure. Always. And I *did* want him—badly. If I allowed myself a slow moment to be honest, I'd realize that I wanted him the way you want to watch a thunderstorm. I mean it's something great to watch from beneath a roof and through a window, but it's something altogether different when you're standing right in the thick of it, feeling the thunder through the ground you're standing on, seeing the flashes of lightning land all around you. The intensity rocked because of the risk, the danger I was exposed to without the protection of *normal*, and without the understanding of the person Easton was. Just like thunderstorms, there was a part of Easton that frightened me. My instincts were shouting from the rooftops for me to walk away from this. There was *no perfect storm* where Easton Matthews was concerned.

∞ ∞ ∞ ∞ ∞ ∞

My second session with Lacee the following morning was more uncomfortable than the first had been. I was sitting next to her in the conference room while she worked on her laptop, showing me Easton's files, passwords for the various business entities, and weekly reports I needed to upload. I was scribbling down instructions, trying to write and watch at the same time. It was nearly lunchtime and my fingers were cramping from trying to write things down as quickly as she spit them out.

"Lacee," I finally said, "can you slow it down a bit? I need to make notes and observe and you're whipping through this so quickly, I'm not getting it all down."

She stopped immediately, looking at me warily. "I was under the impression you moved fast, Darcy. It seems to me you're climbing the ladder very quickly around here. In fact, I'll give you an extra tip. Buy some disposable douches to keep handy at the office. Pretty soon he'll want nooners."

I wasn't about to give her the benefit of seeing my feathers ruffled.

"Hold on," I said, raising a finger while still scribbling the last of my instructions. "Okay, now let me write that last one down: 'get disposable douches—keep handy.' Got it. What's next?"

She was fuming as she slammed her laptop closed and stood up, distancing herself from me. She was pacing, trying to collect her thoughts. I waited patiently for the outburst I knew was coming.

"Don't think," she hissed, jabbing her index finger into the air, "that you're anything special to him. You'll serve your time and purpose, just like all of the women before you, including me. The only thing different is that this time, he's picked a nearly carbon copy of the only woman he's ever truly loved, Bianca Templeton. Maybe for that reason, he'll hang on to you a bit longer, but love is definitely not on his agenda, I promise you that."

"Excuse me," I interrupted tersely. "My personal life is none of your business, and as far as I can tell, Easton's personal business isn't your concern either. What's your interest?"

"I'll tell you what my interest is. I've given him five years of devoted service, and the last two have included servicing him sexually. I can tell you this: it wasn't always very pleasant, as you probably already know."

"Do tell?" I replied, now curious as to what she actually meant by that.

"Oh, come on!" she snapped. "You actually enjoy his brutal games in bed? Or what about the fact that he never even bothers to kiss you while he's fucking you? And then there's afterwards, when he orders you out of his bed after he's used you and then two hours later, hunts you down in another bedroom and it all starts again with him punishing you for leaving the damn bed he ordered you out of?"

"Okay, Lacee, I'm going to interrupt you right now. You're presuming things have happened based on nothing. So, the question here is, if all of that's true, why in the hell would you tolerate it for two years?"

She was now morphing from angry to sad. Tears welled up in her aquamarine eyes.

"I thought with love I could change him," she halfway sobbed. "I didn't know what I was up against with his demons. The biggest demon of all is Bianca Templeton, but let me tell you this: his own mother has no use for him. I wish you luck."

She picked up her laptop, brushing the wetness from her cheeks. "That's it for your training today," she said, heading for the door. "You've been warned."

Chapter 21

I didn't see Easton the rest of the afternoon, which was fine by me because after Lacee's meltdown, I was extremely unsettled. My mind was seriously spent after today's affairs. Literally.

And all of it could have been avoided, that's what bugged me the most. I'd already made that decision *with* Easton. I told him flat out, and in no uncertain terms, I wasn't one to sleep my way to the top. Then, on the first day I work with him, all of that went out the friggin' window just because he managed to be a little creative with his conversation at the faux business dinner.

And then there's Lacee. Holy moly, dude! What *was* that? The girl had a mental breakdown next to a fax machine. I couldn't help thinking that if I didn't get my shit together pronto, that was going to be *me* in two years.

Fuck that!

I went directly to the gym after work, putting myself through a punishing workout before I went home. Eli had left a note on the fridge.

'Having dinner with Maddox this evening, so fend for yourself. Don't wait up!'

I smiled, glad that Eli was at least getting somewhere with Cain.

Guess it's just the three of us tonight: Me, Myself, and I! God, I so want a cat.

I went upstairs and took a long, hot shower, scrubbing the day's sweat off of me. I threw one of Darin's FBI T-shirts on that I'd confiscated during one of my sleepovers at his place, not bothering with a bra, and a pair of clean sweats, not bothering with panties. After blowing my hair dry, I brushed it up into a ponytail, mentally telling my grumbling stomach to hang tight.

I skipped down the carpeted steps heading towards the kitchen when I caught movement in the corner of the living room. My heart thudded as I shrieked.

"Oh Jesus Christ, *Easton!* You scared the hell out of me! What—how'd you get in here?" I demanded. Maybe that meltdown was going to come a little bit sooner.

"You left the door unlocked," he answered casually, as if it was still perfectly acceptable to come into someone's home if they were negligent in locking the door. "I didn't see you this afternoon, and I wondered how things went with you and Lacee."

He followed me into the kitchen, where I grabbed a handful of seedless grapes from the fridge, offering him some.

Well there went any idea of calling the cops. "Oh sure, Officer Steve. Take your time, I'm offering him some food as we speak, and we're thinking about opening up a bottle of Chardonnay. He seemed a little perturbed after the whole getting-through-my-lock thing, so I wanted to make it up to him.

"No, I'm good," he said, watching me in amusement as I popped several into my mouth to assuage my growling tummy. I picked a banana off the top of the fruit bowl on the table.

"Banana, Easton?"

"Still good, love, just waiting for an answer."

I peeled the banana, returning to the living room, plopping down on the sofa. "You seem anxious," I commented. "Is there some particular concern you have about my session with Lacee today?"

His shrug was non-committal; hands in his pockets, simply waiting for my response. He finally sat down next to me, clasping his hands together. "She left work early and quite upset," he said. "She looked as if she'd been crying."

"And that bothers you?"

He gazed over at me, his eyes searching mine. "I don't like to see any of my employees distressed," he said.

I had to scrunch up my nose to hold in an un-girly sound.

"I don't think her *distress* has anything to do with working for you. She loved you. Maybe she still does," I shrugged.

154

I watched him flinch at the thought of that. What the hell was his deal?

"She also warned me about you. She said, in time, I'd be cast aside just as she's been."

I deliberately left out the part about Bianca whomever to see if the name surfaced from Easton's lips anytime soon. Maybe he'd even open up to me about his past. Crazy and unhealthy as it was, I wanted to believe I wasn't just some shiny, new toy for him to play with until he grew tired of it.

"I never loved Lacee. I never led her on or gave her reason to believe there'd ever be anything else between us."

Screw being crazy and unhealthy. Suddenly, I was just very…tired. With that last statement, everything that Easton and I had been doing, what with my initial and powerful attraction to him on the beach, and then the scene with him and Lacee at the rehearsal dinner, followed by my knocking on his door at the hotel, and the great finale of becoming my boss and my fraying willpower that had led us *back* to said hotel…

Circles. That's all we were doing, dancing in circles around each other and the mess that it was starting to cause. Jesus, how annoying had I become? I'd made a decision that night of the rehearsal dinner that I wanted no part of this gorgeous—yet clearly out of my league man. And then I folded. Then I folded *again* making yet *another* decision to not screw him once he became my employer. Good God—I was starting to sound like one of those heroines in books who make damsels of themselves when they could've saved themselves a long time ago!

"Got it," I said, after giving myself that little wake-up call. "But you do get that you just described you and me as well, right? You never made any promises to Lacee, and here you are—*not* making any promises to me. The difference is: I'm *not* Lacee."

I took a quick breath, slowly shaking my head at the thought "My first heartbreak with Darin was bad enough. But it was a quick, clean break. However, this back-and-forth thing between you and me? It won't be a fast break. It's going to be one of those slow ones full of gray areas and *unpromises*."

"What are you saying?" he interrupted, his voice husky.

Man up, Darce.

"I'm saying fast-forward six months, Easton. At the rate we're going, you'll be my boss, and I'll still be that employee of yours who's not fooling anyone with my short, easy-access skirts that you'll have me start wearing so that we can have quickies in a locked bathroom." I shot him a quick look to see if he understood the jab. "I'm saying that I've crossed the line. And I don't want to do it again. I can't fuck a guy without developing feelings for him. I'm just not capable of it. It's not who I am."

He rubbed his eyes with his fingers as if exhausted. That was rare to see Easton anything but energetic; when he walked, when he talked, at work—in bed when he fucked, it was all about power and energy. He was different now.

"I can't give you what you want, Darcy. I don't have it to give, I'm sorry. But isn't what we have the next best thing? We enjoy being with one another—isn't that enough?"

I want to spit banana in his face! Calm down...think before you speak.

"No," I replied calmly. Making sure my face was void of any of emotion or any kind of weakness Easton could seduce."We have nothing, as far as I can tell."

He stood up, totally frustrated, turning his back to me, running his hands through his thick, dark hair in exasperation. He finally whirled back around, and came closer, lowering himself in front of me, resting on his haunches. His hands were steepled together and his gorgeous eyes shuttered as if he was trying to choose his words very carefully.

"I can't seem to stay away from you," he confessed. "You have to know my regard for you is nowhere in the same vicinity as what was between Lacee and me. With her, I could take it or leave it, not so with you," he said gently, finally looking into my eyes for some kind of understanding.

I didn't understand. I don't know, maybe it was a guy thing, or an Easton thing, but I certainly didn't get the memo about all these different degrees of caring. In my world, you either cared or you didn't. People either mattered or they didn't. You either had a future together or not.

I'm not gonna lie, something inside me snapped a little.

156

"Is that supposed to make me feel better? The fact that you have the ability to...what? Compartmentalize people and emotions on some...some *EASTON* scale? So, you've established the fact that with Lacee it was purely a physical, no strings attached thing, and then there's me. What am I? A notch above that? Maybe a notch-and-a-half? Define my role, please. What does being a notch-and-a-half above Lacee give me?"

I was on a roll now. I don't think anything save him suddenly using his necktie as a gag to put over my mouth could stop me. Don't think for a minute he probably wasn't contemplating doing *just* that.

"Let's see, it must mean I'm given the *honor* of being kissed while we fuck, and then there's also the additional perk of you not ordering me out of your bed as soon as we're finished! Oh, let's not forget that I only went home with a *sore ass* versus other more serious possibilities. Tell me—in the scheme of things, where do you see my current role taking me in my *5-year plan?* Is there *growth potential* in this position, or am I going to crash against the glass ceiling?"

I was on my feet glaring at him now, standing right in front of him. His face darkened. His eyes blazed. I'd hit a raw nerve with Easton Matthews and I didn't give a shit.

"Well, I see you and Lacee had quite a little soiree this afternoon," he snapped. "Swapping stories it seems."

"Lacee did all of the talking. For once, I just listened; and I didn't like what I heard, I'm sorry to say. Every person has feelings that should be respected. I don't give a fuck how many times you've set the parameters of the sexual relationship you had going with her, apparently somewhere along the way, she missed a couple bi-weekly memos. And that's on you, because if you *did* tell her that there would never be anything deeper between the two of you, you didn't tell her very damn well."

"It's more complicated than *that*," he replied.

"Why?"

"I don't know why. It just is. I know my capabilities as well as my limitations. I didn't intentionally set out to hurt her, and I wouldn't intentionally do anything to hurt you, most of all. I just don't have it within me to love anyone the way they expect to be loved. I'm deficient in emotional connections, I suppose."

"Bullshit! You've chosen that path for yourself for whatever reason, so please don't blame it on being emotionally deficient, unless of course you're a certified sociopath. Is that what you're telling me?"

Uh oh…

He grabbed me, pulling me up against his hard body, fisting my ponytail so that my face tilted up, inches from his. His dark gray eyes were flashing with fury that I'd suggested he was sociopathic. I suppose now was not the right time to tell him that I'd read somewhere many successful CEO's, political leaders, and influential people were certified sociopaths.

His mouth lowered to within an inch or less of mine.

"Is that what you really think? Do you truly believe that you've been *fucking* a dangerous sociopath?"

His voice was harsh and menacing as he looked into my eyes. I didn't flinch or show fear, which, of course, is what he wanted.

"No," I stated firmly. "I think I've been fucking someone who doesn't know who or what he is, much less what he wants. I think he's someone that has some baggage he hasn't dealt with, which is a shame, because he's almost perfect otherwise," I finished softly.

We stood there for a few moments…him fisting my hair, and me holding his stare.

He let out a breath we'd both been holding. Releasing my ponytail, he took a step back. "I don't want to let you go," he said, almost as if to himself.

I wrapped my arms around myself in something that would probably look a lot like defeat. I waited for him to continue.

"You're always on my mind," he said. I saw a decision glint beneath his long, sooty eyelashes. "But I know what I am and what I'm capable of, and as much as I want to, I can't give you what you want and need. I'll only hurt you in the end and I *don't* want that. I'm sorry. I'm going to make arrangements to return to London. I'll assign a very capable acting replacement for me until I return."

A quick, clean break.

I managed a nod, kind of wondering where all of my strength from before had gone. I guess somewhere in our conversation, I'd lent it to him. Because now, he was doing the very thing I asked for and wanted. Right?

I was still looking down at my 'Pretty in Pink' toenails when I felt him put his arms around me, holding me tight in the way that every girl loves.

"Good-bye, love," he whispered against my hair. "I wish it could've been different. I wish I was fucking different."

I nodded again, this time being the one to take a step back. I watched as he opened the door, getting ready to leave. Midway past the threshold, he stopped.

"She didn't love me." He didn't spare me by looking back, so I wasn't able to see the look on his face. "Lacee, I mean. She wanted to *fix* me, and there's a very thick line between loving someone and having the desire to fix them."

The door closed.

A broken sigh rattled through my lips. I wouldn't let anything more out; there was no need. It wasn't as if I had that much time, effort, or affection invested in Easton Matthews. This was different than with Darin, though. This was the pain over a hesitated decision, a decision I'd probably always hesitate over and never really be quite sure of.

The rest of the evening was spent in a fog. I curled up on the couch, feeling alone, isolated, and empty. I drifted to sleep finally, awakening much later when Eli got in and flicked on the overhead light.

"What are you doing down here in the dark?" he asked, looking concerned.

I was hoping he'd simply figure I'd stayed home, got drunk, and passed out on the sofa.

No such luck!

"Oh baby girl," he said alarmed, coming over to sit down next to me. "You've been *dumped*."

159

"Can I sleep with you tonight, Eli?" I asked. "I just don't…want to be alone right now."

"Slumber party it is," he said, pulling me up off the couch. "We can't be too loud, though. My mom will get angry and then she won't pack my 'Super Man' juice box for lunch tomorrow. And little Tommy will beat me up."

I was already fighting a smile as I headed to the bathroom to brush my teeth.

For the second time this evening, I fell asleep. Only this time, Eli was next to me, assuring me that everything would be okay.

Chapter 22

I hadn't seen Lindsey since the wedding, and had only talked to her a couple of times by phone after she and Taz returned from their honeymoon. I'd called her as I was leaving the office the following day and asked if I could stop by and visit my god-daughter.

"Well, of course," she said. "You don't need an invitation. I'm dying to show you pictures of our trip."

As soon as I'd gotten into my car, I flipped the mirror down on the driver's side to reapply some concealer around my eyes, due to lack of restful sleep. Eli said I'd tossed and turned so much he had to get up and take a Dramamine before he came back to bed. That was another one of his attempts at trying to lift my spirits. It hadn't worked.

As soon as Lindsey opened the door, her eyes flickered over me from top to bottom. I had sunglasses on because it *was* actually a sunny day in March.

"Well, come on in," she squealed. "It seems like it's been forever." She and I hugged inside the door. "Come on in the living room, Harper's taking a nap, but she should be up in another half-hour or so. She grows daily."

I took off my jacket and sunglasses and followed Lindsey into the living room. She sat on the couch, watching me as I joined her.

"What's going on?" she asked, point blank.

"Nothing's going on," I lied. "Just missed you is all."

"Darcy, I love you, but you look a bit hellish. Plus, I can see that you've recently put on some cover-up." She gave me the squinty eye, "Oh…My…God."

Bingo.

"You've been *dumped.*"

Jesus, would people stop saying that...

"What?"

"Don't deny it," she said. "Who was it? You didn't take Darin back, did you? What the hell's going on?"

"Okay, okay," I said, settling back. There was no way Lindsey and I could keep things from one another, even when we wanted to. "It *was* Easton," I replied.

"What?" she screeched.

"Shhh," I hushed her. "You're going to wake the baby up."

"I think that's my line, Darce. And she's so used to the racket Taz makes, she can sleep through an earthquake. Now, tell me how in the hell you got involved with Easton."

I gave her the short story, starting from our night together after their wedding. I left out details about our other sexual encounter because that was really no one else's business. I did tell her some of the things Lacee had mentioned, though.

"Wow," she said, sitting back and shaking her head. "I had no clue you two would hit it off like that."

"We didn't actually hit it off. I mean, he basically told me he's incapable of loving anyone."

"Well, you and I both know that's bullshit. We should talk to Taz about it."

"No, we should not," I barked. "This is BFF stuff and I don't want Taz to know about it."

"Why not? Maybe he could shed some light on why Easton's the way he is. Aren't you the least bit curious?"

"Well, sure," I replied, shrugging. "But, I mean, they didn't exactly grow up together, from what I gathered."

162

"Look," she said firmly, "it might help to know and Taz may or may not be able to shed any light, but it's worth asking. There's no reason for you to feel uncomfortable about it with him. He should be home soon and you're staying for dinner, no argument."

Lindsey had her way and we spent the rest of the afternoon looking at her wedding and honeymoon pictures, playing with Harper, and catching up on everything else. When Taz arrived home, he immediately drew Lindsey in for a long, passionate kiss, and then greeted me. Harper was on my lap and immediately smiled upon seeing her daddy.

She was three months old and starting to seem less like a newborn. I couldn't tell just yet who she favored. Taz took her from me, giving her hugs and kisses. It warmed my heart to see their interaction. I wondered if I'd ever have what Lindsey had. I was happy for her, yet part of me couldn't help feeling envious. Having someone love me the way Taz loved her was something no amount of money or power could ever buy.

At dinner, Lindsey did a fine job of giving Taz just enough information, without totally humiliating me in the process, of what had transpired between his half-brother and me.

"Oh hey, Darcy," he said, reaching over to pat my shoulder, "I'm really sorry if Easton hurt your feelings like that. I mean, we're not close, you see. He spent some summers with us while I was growing up, but I have to tell you, I don't really know him all that well."

"I told Lindsey that, but she thought maybe you knew about this Bianca Templeton or maybe something about his mother," I replied, now hopeful maybe he could shed some light.

"I don't know anything about this Bianca," he said immediately, "but there are some things I do know about his mother, none of which are good."

"Really?" Lindsey and I both asked at the same time. He nodded.

"My father was really torn up that Easton wasn't able to spend much time with us. I was just a kid, so all I really remember were discussions I'd overheard between my mom and him, or Dad being on the phone with Sophia, arguing about her keeping Easton from him. Over the years, as I got older, it was very clear to me that Sophia was a wealthy, controlling, psycho-bitch. Instead of

163

envying my older brother, I felt sorry that he didn't have a normal upbringing like Paige and me. That's about it," he finished.

I was disappointed. As much as I had initially resisted Lindsey's suggestion of going to Taz for info, I'd held out hope it would enlighten me somewhat, but it had proven fruitless.

"Taz, you did that very well," Lindsey said, a sly grin on her face.

Huh?

"Not following, baby girl."

"Baby," she said her eyes twinkling, "you're a senior FBI agent. You've got access to even the most classified information, which in this case, isn't what we're asking for. Now, despite the fact your half-brother isn't part of any past or current investigation to my knowledge, you can't tell me Trace Michael Matthews that you've never, out of simple curiosity, ran a full background on him. Are you going to deny this to your wife?"

"Shit, Lindsey," he said, "you think you know me so well, don't you?"

"You tell me."

"Christ, alright. Let me see what all I can remember, it's been a while."

Lindsey and I sat waiting for only a few seconds.

"Easton Jamison Matthews, Born in San Francisco, California, November 15, 1980 to Trace Matthews and Sophia Windsor Matthews, who has since returned to her maiden name of "Windsor," due to some royal bloodline connections. Sophia's never re-married, and claims that Easton lays claim to the title of "Baron" through British peerage records, as she's the only daughter of Clive and Lillian Windsor, whose pedigree can be traced upward to the royal family."

I looked over at Lindsey and her mouth was hanging open, matching mine. Taz continued as if this whole biography was etched in his brain. I was impressed.

"Trace Matthews, my father, and Sophia divorced in 1982, due to irreconcilable differences. Sophia returned to England with 1-year old Easton,

164

briefly living with her parents until she was deeded a large estate adjacent to their property in Kensington, an upscale suburb of London. Easton was schooled in private schools until third grade. He was home-schooled by a governess for less than a year, and then sent to boarding school in Switzerland, until he was ready for college. He graduated from the University of Cambridge in 2003 with a B.S. degree in Humanities, and completed his Master's Program at Oxford in 2005 with a degree in Business Finance. Shortly thereafter, his maternal grandparents, Clive and Lillian Windsor were killed in an automobile accident while vacationing in Madrid. The beneficiaries of their estate were Sophia and Easton, splitting a $1.6 billion coffer 50/50."

Now Lindsey and I both gasped.

"I know, hon," Taz said, looking at Lindsey with sad eyes. "It appears you picked the wrong 'Matthews,' eh?"

"Oh, Taz," she giggled. "I'm sure your lack of wealth is made up for…in other places." She gave him a flirty wink.

"Don't be so sure, Linds…"

They kissed again like the 'in-love' fools they were and Taz finished up.

"Let's see, oh yes, Easton invested a portion of his heritance in a newly-formed venture capital group that hit the mark on mergers and acquisitions. Within a year, he spun off on his own with his own newly-formed venture capital firm titled "Baronton Holdings, L.L.C." and has proven to be quite the successful entrepreneur with a diverse portfolio of both manufacturing and service industry holdings that cater to government and commercial contracts of all sorts. In 2008, Easton backed an up-and-coming fashion model by the name of Bianca Templeton, a Brit whose family was average, middle-class, taking her to A-List fame with some of the top global agencies. In 2011, Easton severed all ties for personal reasons with Ms. Templeton. Shortly thereafter, her modeling career went south. Sources indicate that Easton had planned to marry the lovely, dark-haired beauty in the near term. However, upon learning that Ms. Templeton was sleeping with her photographer, the relationship was terminated. Since that time, Easton Matthews hasn't been involved in any long-term relationships, continuing to build his empire and live a life of private solitude."

Wow!

"Wow," Lindsey said, leaning in toward Taz. "When you talk like that it's so *hot*, Trace." They kissed again.

Oh geez…yeah, I can probably kiss goodbye another night's sleep after this.

"Hey, Taz," I interrupted. "Thanks for the bio, but that still doesn't tell me why he's so fucked-up. Sorry—I mean I know he's your brother and all."

"Half-brother," he corrected. "Darcy, the worst thing you can do is think it's something you did, because I guarantee you, it wasn't. Dude has some baggage going on, and it's up to him to realize it and do something about it, unless he's happy with the status quo. My money, or lack of it, I should say, is on him. I think, once he realizes he needs to fix things in order to have you, he will. I mean, besides my Lindsey here, you're the whole package, girl."

I knew Taz, in his own sweet way, was trying to make me feel better. It didn't. I still believed there was more to it than simply Bianca breaking his heart. There had to be.

"Thanks," I replied. "Lindsey, thank you, too. I'm glad you convinced me to share this with Taz. Listen guys, I've got to head home. Oh, Taz, by the way, did you know Easton just bought the majority share of my father's company?"

I watched Taz get that slow, shit-eating grin on his face. "See there? What'd I tell you? He just needs to figure it out." I hoped he was right.

∞ ∞ ∞ ∞ ∞ ∞

It had been a little over a month since I last saw Easton. True to his word, he'd departed for London. The following Monday, his acting replacement, Colin Devers, was in Easton's office chatting on the phone when I arrived. I'd furnished my office to blend with Easton's, only a bit more eclectically. He'd approved my requisition before he left. I'd found it on my temporary desk when I finally returned to work after he'd told me "good-bye."

Colin seemed more British than Easton, if that made sense. He was mid-thirties, medium brown hair, not quite as tall as Easton, but muscularly built. I figured they probably worked out together when both in London. He had a sexy goatee as well, but don't worry, I wasn't about to go there.

I got the feeling that Colin went way back with Easton, just from little things he mentioned here and there. I knew they communicated by phone and e-mail frequently because Colin stuck to the training program Easton had outlined to a "T." He'd periodically tell me Easton was pleased with my progress. He was pleasant enough and we got along well.

Lacee's treatment of me had become benign since Easton's departure. We interacted when necessary at the office, and were civil with one another. My father and mother had left two weeks ago for a 6-week cruise. Neither of them had an inkling anything had gone on between Easton and me. Thank God!

I was feeling better about it every day. It was the right thing for us. I knew it, and he knew it. Still, I found myself thinking about him during quiet hours, admitting to myself that during the small time I'd known him how much he'd managed to infiltrate my life…and during even quieter hours, my heart.

I just needed something to keep me distracted, something that would fill up *all* hours of the day. As if my wish was granted, Colin came into my office with a folder for me.

"Darcy, will you please book flights for both of us to London on the dates listed here in this file?"

"Both of us?"

"Yes, there's a meeting of several competing contractors for contract renewal for Scotland Yard on all security software and electronic monitoring. Baronton currently holds the contract, but information Easton has gathered would indicate that an automatic renewal is not a given. Therefore, you're going to get your first opportunity to create a presentation, and to personally pitch it to the sourcing contract administrators for Scotland Yard. It's in three weeks, so you'll have plenty of time to prep. I'll coach you as needed. Contact Baronton's travel agency, and get the flight and hotel dates confirmed immediately, since it's not that far away."

I nodded my head, numbly. He continued, as if he hadn't noticed.

"In this file, there's also contact information for Baronton U.K. Since we've not consolidated this entity in the U.S. yet, you'll need to reach out to the R & D Director there. His name is Nigel Cranston, and he'll need to provide you with all of the latest tech information pertaining to devices used by the client.

167

According to Easton, the competition will be pitching some cutting-edge technology to the client. Easton requested you get with Cranston and get information on 'Night Moves' the yet-to-be-released tracking software Baronton Research is developing. Keep in mind that those individuals in R & D are a bit salty about the merger. So, if they pose any reluctance in helping you or providing information, I need to know straightaway."

He paused momentarily to assess me. "Darcy, I'm acquainted with Nigel Cranston. Pardon my boldness here, but perhaps video conferencing with him might be your best approach in turning salty to sweet."

I gave him a smile and a wink. "I'm on it, Colin," I said self-assuredly.

Darcy and Easton: Take Two.

I'll be ready for him this time.

Chapter 23

I was sitting in first class with Colin next to me going over my presentation and the figures for the umpteenth time. It had to be perfect, not that I gave a shit about the sourcing contract administrators for Scotland Yard—yes, I know that should've been my first priority, but let's get REAL here: this would be my debut performance with Easton in attendance. Failing was *not* an option!

I'd timed it at least a dozen times, made back-up slides, memorized the slides, had Lindsey video-tape a walk-through test run fourteen times, spent hours searching for the right business attire, and of course, had gone to the salon for a make-over.

Okay, now I have to be honest here. Curiosity had gotten the better of me once Taz had clued me in that Easton had been in love with a freaking runway model. So, as soon as I'd arrived home after my visit with them that evening, I'd "googled" the name 'Bianca Templeton.'

Holy fucking shit!

Okay, I'm not trying to pass myself off as some gorgeous coulda-shoulda-been-a-model, because I'd never held myself to that level, but Christ! There was no fucking denying the resemblance between me and this chick. Yeah—she was a few years older, but damn she had the same long, dark hair as mine, and though she wore hers differently, it was close enough. My face was shaped just like hers, and our coloring was the same, except for the eyes: hers were lighter blue. Even our lips were similarly shaped. Of course, I'd pulled more photos of her off the internet, becoming slightly obsessive about it, once I'd seen the initial similarities. She wore her make-up differently, but that could easily be remedied.

Apparently, Lacee had been straight with me about the whole Bianca thing. Fuck me. That son-of-a-bitch didn't give a rat's ass about me! Obviously, he was still infatuated with Bianca. I felt duped. No—I felt *more* than duped. I felt *used!* Easton's whole "infatuation" with me was nothing more than a ruse to get me to be a surrogate fuck for that trick.

Dude was apparently still hung up on her. If that's the case, I was fairly certain he kept up with her current comings and goings. I'd immediately pulled up the most recent photos, showing her at last summer's Cannes Film Festival. Bianca's hairstyle had changed, and she'd added foil highlights. What the hell— why not?

I'd handed the recent picture of Bianca to Monroe, my stylist, instructing him to make me look like that the previous day.

"Honey, I don't have that many years left in my career," he teased.

"Funny, Monroe, just do your best."

He worked feverishly, trimming my ends, putting in highlights, and finally using a gel-based straightener and flat iron.

"You'll need to flat iron this hair daily to keep that style," he warned, shaking his head. "I've no clue why you wanted to do this to that gorgeous hair of yours anyway. Seems a shame to me, but you're the customer," he sighed.

"Just needed a change, Monroe. Every now and then, change is good."

"I guess," he replied, still shaking his head.

Eli had looked me over suspiciously when I returned home that evening. "Okay, Darce, what's this about?"

"What's what about?"

"Are you entering some Bianca Templeton look-a-like contest? What's the prize?"

"Easton Matthews," I replied, dryly, looking at my new hairstyle in the mirror. I loved it. Now I just needed to do my eyes like hers.

"What?"

"You heard me," I replied, not taking my eyes from the mirror. "They were engaged to be married a couple of years ago. Hey, how do *you* know Bianca Templeton? Never mind, stupid question."

"Oh, my God," he said, crossing his arms. "So *Easton's* the dude that put the kibosh on her career?"

"Apparently so, and aren't you the little fountain of information there. I will ask how you knew all of that."

"Oh, sweetie, it was pretty big news in the industry—well, for those of us who actually follow it," he said. "I mean, she went from totally chic to totally *screwed* within months. My God, I wonder how much it cost him to dismantle her career like that."

"I don't have a clue," I sighed. "Want me to ask him when I see him in London?"

"Oh, oh—now I get it. You want to win him back, right?"

"You're delusional," I said, shooting him a dirty look."Hey, since you seem to be in the inner circle with international gossip, what's ol' Bianca doing these days?"

"Hmm—well, I heard something about a year ago that she and her current lover, Christopher something-or-other are working together. He's the photographer and she's working for some French Modeling Agency as a scout/agent. Pretty far down the ladder from the bucks she used to make, I'd say."

"Poor Bianca," I replied, very insincerely.

"Darce—"

"I know, Eli. I plan on being careful. I don't want to jump back on that roller coaster again. I'm just going to totally enjoy fucking with that man's world for a couple of days. Seems to me he has it coming, you know?"

Eli crossed his arms, giving me a glare. "It's been *weeks*, Darcy. I thought you were over it. Sounds kinda like you're up to some retaliation if you plan on going to London looking like Bianca's kid sister."

I gave Eli a wink. "You know what they say, Eli? *Revenge* is a dish best served cold. Won't Easton be surprised by my new look?" I'd giggled and gone to my room to finish packing. Eli had shaken his head in frustration.

"Darcy," Colin said, "you've been over that bloody thing a million times. It's fine, now relax and try to get your rest. The meeting's tomorrow, so you need to account for time difference, general jet lag and stress. Everything will be alright."

"I know, but this is my debut presentation. What if I screw up and lose the account?"

"First off, you won't screw up, and worst case scenario, it's a small account, so I doubt whether Easton would fire you anyway," he replied, his eyes twinkling.

"Oh, bloody hell," I sighed, closing my laptop. "I guess you're right."

He gave me a grin. "Starting to sound like a true Brit, I must say."

"It's from listening to you yammer all day long," I replied smiling. "Bad habit I picked up on the job, I guess."

Colin may have been too busy looking at my hair to have heard me. "By the way," he said, and I didn't like the puzzle-solving look in his eyes. "That's a very interesting new hairstyle you're sporting. I can see that you're going all out for this presentation in every way."

I avoided eye-contact when his glance made it back to my face. But when I looked back over at him a moment later, his attention was turned back to the magazine he'd been reading.

There was a hired limo waiting for us when the plane landed at Heathrow. I'd been to London several times, so at least it felt familiar.

"Oh, by the way," Colin began uneasily, "I meant to tell you I had our reservations at the Carlisle cancelled. We're staying elsewhere this trip."

"The Langham?" I asked.

"Uh, no. Easton insisted we stay at his manor here. There's plenty of room and he wants a walk-through of the presentation in case any last minute changes need to be made."

"But you e-mailed him all the information last week," I argued.

"Apparently, since this is your solo flight, he wants to make sure for himself. He'll critique it live before the meeting."

You don't say? So, he wants to see the presentation before the meeting? I'll give him one, alright.

"He'll be back at the manor around 6:00 this evening and dinner's scheduled for sevenish. Don't worry; you'll be quite comfortable at Easton's estate."

"Don't you have your own place in London?"

"I do. However, it's a good hour's drive from the estate. Depending upon how long our meeting with Easton goes this evening, I may try to make it back to my home. I haven't seen my fiancé for weeks."

"Oh, Colin, you've never mentioned that you were engaged. Have you set a date?"

"Indeed," he said smiling. "September 14th. We're getting married in New York."

"Well, congratulations to you and—"

"Veronica," he answered. "I call her Ronnie. She's originally from New York. She worked for Easton at Baronton's U.S. headquarters there, that's how we met. Perhaps you'll have an opportunity to meet her on this trip. I think the both of you would get on nicely."

"I'd love that," I replied. It would be nice not to be totally surrounded by testosterone occasionally.

Easton's manor was breathtakingly beautiful, as I expected. It was more of an estate in my opinion with Tudor architecture, acres of rolling grass, with various well-groomed trees and shrubs, and a long winding drive once we passed through the gates that led up to the stone overhang. Once the chauffeur had removed our luggage from the trunk, the two people from the house staff, a fiftyish woman in a black dress with a crisp white apron, along with a man around the same age in black pants, a white-collared shirt, and black long-tailed jacket where standing on the steps ready to greet us.

173

"Good afternoon Mr. Devers, Ms. Sheridan, welcome. I hope your trip was uneventful."

"It was splendid, Anna," Colin replied, taking my hand to introduce me to these two members of the staff. "Darcy Sheridan, this is Anna Johnson, Easton's head of staff here at Greystone Manor. I assure you, she'll see to your every need."

"It's very nice to meet you, Anna," I greeted her warmly, shaking her hand. "I'll try to keep my needs to a minimum."

She smiled warmly, wrapping her other hand around mine. "Now, you call on me anytime, day or night, Miss. That's what I'm here for. Giles, don't dally there," she said sternly, talking to the servant beside her. "Ms. Sheridan's in the guest suite on the east wing. Are you staying the night, Mr. Devers, or will you be returning to Chelsea later?"

"Ah, I'm not sure, Anna. If I had my druthers, I'd be off to Chelsea. I have no idea how long Easton will keep us."

"What a shame," she said, shaking her head. "I hope Mr. Matthews appreciates all that you do for him."

"He's like a brother to me, Anna. His turn will come to accommodate me sooner than he anticipates," he laughed. "Ronnie has her heart set on a four-week cruise and, to be honest, I'd prefer Easton's wrath to hers."

"As well you should," she said, shaking a finger at him. She turned to me, taking my arm. "Come dear, I'll show you the way to your suite. I'm sure you'll find it quite comfortable."

"Comfortable" turned out to be an understatement. My suite was 1800 square feet if it was an inch! It was decorated in period Victorian with a large living room, and a study off of that. A wide hallway led to the mammoth master bedroom, that had a walk-in closet/dressing room that was bigger than my bedroom at the apartment, and adjoining master bath that had yet another walk-in closet off of it, a huge marble shower, a bathing area with a huge, gold claw foot tub, and a separate room with the commode, which was a bidet. The fixtures looked to be original. My guess was this house dated back to the early 1900's. It was exquisite.

I put everything away in the closet that had built-in cedar drawers. I looked at my watch. Easton wouldn't be back for a couple of hours, so I took advantage of the break and took a quick power nap. I bathed in the luxurious tub, then dressed for dinner, making sure to do the whole routine with the flat iron which, to be honest, was starting to be a pain in the ass.

But no pain, no gain, right? I couldn't wait to see the bastard's face when he saw me and my new "look." I may just have to introduce myself as Bianca when Easton tries to give me the ol' professional hand shake.

And I *would* do that…If I wasn't so sure he could run faster than me, that is.

"Don't worry, Colin. Her screams will die down eventually. Shall we proceed with having port and cigars in the study?"

Yeah, I would pass on that one, I'd decided, while putting some finishing touches on my hair. It had taken some artistic practice, but Eli said I had it down to perfection.

"You could be sisters," he'd told me when I'd given him a live demo. I was standing in my robe with my hair and makeup done just like Bianca's had been in the photo. I slowly twirled in a circle, giving him the whole 360-degree view.

He was quiet as he studied me for a moment. "Why are you fucking with him like this, Darcy?"

"Because he *lied* to me," I answered firmly. "He omitted the fact that I looked a lot like the last woman he may have actually *truly* cared for. I mean, yeah, he told me that I wasn't anything like Lacee…but what about Bianca friggin' Templeton? And then he just walks out of my life, expecting me to never have figured it out and call him out on that kind of bullshit? Yeah…fuck that *and* fuck him. It's time a woman takes him down a few pegs."

"Careful, sweetheart," Eli replied, as he leaned up against my bedroom dresser, "You're starting to sound like one of those 'Hell hath no fury like a woman scorned' chicks who sit up in their attic, planning some poor schmuck's demise."

I considered that for a good second, looking down at the carpet. "This isn't about that, Eli," I finally said. "It's about being lied to by someone who was clearly using me as a stand-in to…what? Prolong an ended relationship? To use me as some sort of fantasy in bed, so he could fuck 'the one that got away'?" I looked back over at him.

He shrugged. "I don't know. And maybe it's *better* that we don't know." He walked over to me, putting his hands on my shoulders, "I don't get it. One minute, I could swear you love the guy, the next minute you've got this "evil vixen" thing going that I can't comprehend."

I couldn't say anything to that. *I* didn't even fully understand why I was reacting the way I was.

Eli pulled away from me, crossing his arms. "A piece of advice, Darce? When it comes to fucking someone over, don't fuck with someone who knows how to fuck you harder."

∞ ∞ ∞ ∞ ∞ ∞

I dressed in an elegant royal blue dinner dress with matching heels. I put my earrings in and took a final look in the mirror. I was ready. There was a knock on my door. It was Colin.

"I'm heading down to the drawing room for cocktails," he called from the hall. Easton arrived about twenty minutes ago. If you're ready, I'd be happy to escort you down, since this house is cavernous; wouldn't want you to get lost."

"Be right there."

Show time!

I saw the quick look of surprise in Colin's eyes when I opened the door. He quickly masked it, a smile twitching on his lips.

"You look very lovely," he complimented me. "Shall we?"

Colin led me down the huge staircase.

"We're having cocktails in the drawing room before dinner," he advised, leading me down a wide, marble-floored hallway. "After you," he nodded as we reached the doorway.

176

I saw him then, his back was to me as he poured amber-colored liquor into a glass with ice, and took a quick drink, pouring another.

Freaking butterflies, I silently cursed my tummy.

"Good evening, Easton," I spoke, watching him whirl around to face me. His eyes immediately froze when he saw my changed appearance. I saw a flicker of anger cross his smoky gray eyes, and then a forced smile as he approached us. God, he was gorgeous in his black business suit and white linen dress shirt. His tie was royal blue, nearly the same shade as my dress.

"Good evening Darcy, Colin," he nodded, setting his drink on the end of the bar.

"Would you care for a drink or a glass of wine, Darcy?"

"Wine would be fine, thank you."

"Scotch, Colin?"

"On the rocks, please."

Well, that went smoothly.

There were two love seats facing one another with a large, square cherry-wood table in the middle. The thick Aubusson rug underneath the furniture was 18th century. The grouping was arranged in front of the large, black marble fireplace that was lit. It was still chilly and damp this time of year in London; the crackling warmth of the fire was welcoming. I took a seat on one of the love seats, Colin sat down beside me.

Easton took a seat across from us with his drink in one hand, his free arm resting against the back of the love seat.

"So, the feedback I've received from Colin is that you're progressing very well in your role. Are you finding your position challenging?"

I squirmed a bit, pulling my dress down over my knees as his eyes continued to peruse me.

"It's been very satisfying. Colin's been totally patient with me," I replied, smiling over at him.

"She's being modest," Colin replied, sipping his drink. "Darcy's a natural for this role with significant growth potential. She's a keeper."

I blushed at the compliment, trying to determine if there was some hidden meaning to it. Probably just me trying to read something into nothing.

"I'm anxious to critique your presentation after dinner," Easton replied.

"I'm looking forward to your input," I said, blushing at my own choice of words and watched as a smile graced his beautiful mouth.

I wonder if Bianca ever blushed.

I took a gulp of my wine, hoping it would start seeping in to calm my nerves. Just as I took another long drink to hurry along the process, Easton broke the silence.

"What the hell have you done to your hair?" he blurted out angrily.

I choked on my wine as soon as his words were out, and then segued into a coughing spell. Colin hurriedly set his drink on the table, moving towards me, his hand smacking my back roughly.

"Really, Easton," Colin said, clearly irritated, handing me a cocktail napkin. "Are you alright Darcy?" he asked. I nodded my head up and down, the hacking slowly subsided.

"Well?" Easton asked, still waiting for my response.

"I changed my hairstyle," I retorted angrily. "So what?"

"I don't think it suits you," he said in a tone that was just short of a snarl. "Not one bit."

"Well, I happen to like it," I snapped back. "I think it suits…me." I shot him an Oscar-worthy smile.

Clearly, Colin was not comfortable with our exchange."May I freshen your drink, Easton?" he asked, standing up.

"Please," Easton replied, holding up his empty glass, not taking his eyes off of me. Colin went to the bar out of direct earshot. Easton leaned forward, clasping his hands together.

"I'd prefer you tone down your make-up as well. Tomorrow afternoon you'll be representing Baronton-Sheridan at this meeting, not Victoria's Secret. Your appearance must speak professionalism in a more conservative way." His gaze was ripping right through me.

"I assure you, I understand appropriate attire. Your critique should be directed toward the presentation I've put together. I can handle my appearance; I promise you," I replied stiffly. This wasn't going well. I wanted to jump down his throat, but he was the boss and in this situation, that was simply not an option.

"See that it's handled then," he responded, taking the drink Colin handed him.

I couldn't recall whether dinner was good or not. It was just something I managed to get through, rather uncomfortably. I noticed Easton was putting away some alcohol this evening, which was something I hadn't observed previously, in between tossing glares across the table at me.

Finally, it was time for my presentation. I was ushered into a study off of the main hall that was more like a conference room with all of the media set up, ready to go. Colin clicked a button on a remote and the 19th century oil painting of Scottish moors slid away, revealing the projection screen. He clicked another button and my title page of the presentation illuminated the screen.

Easton was perched at the other end of the long table, leaning back in the black leather chair, one foot propped up on the seat of the chair next to him, his hands clasped behind his head. He had removed his suit jacket, loosened his tie and rolled the sleeves of his shirt up to just beneath his elbows. He glanced at his watch, nodding for me to begin.

I commenced my presentation, making sure to throw in some overly enthusiastic model-sashays, as I used the laser pointer very generously when bringing attention to certain elements on the slides. Easton was clearly onto me, because not even five minutes into it, he very loudly and very rudely interrupted.

"No, no, Darcy," he said, shaking his head. "It's too hurried. You haven't put nearly enough build-up into the potential of this new, cutting edge, tracking software prior to introducing it to your audience. The audience needs to be on the edge of their seats before the slide where you announce 'Night Moves.' Didn't you consider it important for them to know there's nothing out there remotely similar? What about the fact that it's been under development for nearly five years? You've shown no stats for the beta testing that was conducted. And, what's with all the flailing of your arms when showing the slides? Your audience is not interested in seeing what's behind Door #3 here. This is a *technical* sales pitch, not a fucking *game* show."

Colin spoke up in my defense. "Easton, you were provided electronic copy of the slide presentation days ago. We even discussed it on the phone before Darcy and I made the trip here. You didn't say anything about having issues with it until now."

Easton ran his hands through his dark hair, clearly agitated. I took comfort in the fact that this probably had nothing to do with my presentation at all, but rather the way I kept baiting him.

He rubbed his eyes then looked up. "Colin, you go ahead and take off. Spend tomorrow and the weekend with Veronica, you've earned it. I'll work with Darcy tonight to get this problem fixed. I'll go with her to the presentation tomorrow afternoon and, if I don't feel she's adequately prepped, then I'll present. You deserve a few days off, take them."

Colin looked back and forth between us. He seemed reluctant to leave me in the hands of a very irritated Easton.

"If you're sure," he said.

"I am. Send my regards to Veronica."

Colin nodded, wished me a good-night and left.

"Now Ms. Sheridan, let's get busy. We've work to do here."

Chapter 24

As it turned out, my presentation wasn't nearly the disaster Easton had implied. We spent about two hours rearranging the order of the slides and created a couple more up front to draw out the anticipation of the long-awaited 'Night Moves' tracking technology. It was trademarked as "tomorrow's tracking technology—TODAY!"

Pom-poms not included!

I'd never been so glad to distance myself from Easton as I was an hour ago when he finally agreed the presentation was ready. I mumbled an obligatory 'good-night' and headed up the grand staircase to my suite. I showered quickly, scrubbing off all of the eye make-up which he'd clearly detested. Crawling under the warm covers of the Victorian canopy bed felt like heaven. I was totally exhausted. Thankfully, I could sleep late, since our appointment wasn't until 2:30 p.m. tomorrow.

I'd been asleep for a while when I felt his hands on me. At first, I thought I was dreaming, until I felt his breath on the back of my neck. His hands were on my hips, gently massaging them as I slept on my side. His torso was pressed up against me. I felt his rock-hard erection. My body tingled in pleasure, until I came fully awake, realizing my mistake was allowing him to continue.

I sat up abruptly.

"What are you doing?" I hissed. The light filtering in from the lamp I'd left on in the sitting room shed enough light so that I could see him. He was disheveled, but that only served to make him more appealing, for some odd reason. He needed a shave. His hair was tousled and his eyes were shuttered.

"You're drunk," I said immediately. I'd never seen Easton like this. "Do you need help finding your suite?"

"I'm right where I want to be, love," he said, inching closer to me. "And I'm right where you want me to be as well."

"That's *your* opinion, *love*." I began to move away. "Geez…have another drink, Easton."

With a quick panther-like movement, Easton lifted me from the edge of the bed, tossing me roughly onto my back in the center, straddling me. He pinned my arms above me, quickly clamping handcuffs around my wrists, attaching them to the spindled headboard. I was going nowhere.

"I'll scream," I quietly warned. He wasn't even touching me, save for my lower body, which he was straddling. Easton's chest was right above mine, his hands resting on the mattress on each side of me; his mouth was too close to mine and not close enough.

"You won't," he quietly replied, as we shared the same breath. His eyes were an almost hurricane gray, lit up with both challenge and dimming disappointment.

I opened my mouth to scream, to ask him what was wrong, to bite him, to kiss him, to tell him to fuck off, to ask him why he ever left. But all of that was lost when I felt his lips touch mine.

Just his lips. It was almost a phantom kiss, his lips barely touching mine, quietly making up their mind. My quick inhale must not have gone unnoticed, because he quickly took my bottom lip between his teeth and began a slow, hard suck on it. My body turned traitor as it bowed up to his, and my mouth was already raising the white flag as it tried to deepen the kiss. But he wasn't having any of it. He just kept kissing me softly, like some sort of punishment, softly nipping at the corners where I keep my smiles, wrecking me.

I could feel his breath speeding up, unveiling his self-control. Still, he wasn't giving in. I let out a frustrated moan, rocking my hips against his.

"Stop that," he told me sternly between kisses.

"*Easton*," I pleaded, again rocking my hips against the heavy weight of his.

"No." He gave me a hard nip, drawing out my bottom lip once again, sucking on it to the point of pain. "You want to play games?"

Oh…shit.

"Let's play." He lifted his body completely off of mine. Stepping away from the bed, he turned back to me and began to lift his partially unbuttoned shirt up and over his head. I couldn't help but watch his muscles stretch and flex with the movement.

He was barefoot and shirtless as he leisurely walked over to the side of the bed. I tested the handcuffs as I watched him slowly reach for the bottom of my silk, black nightie. He lifted it teasingly, making sure the pads of his talented fingers gently scraped against the skin of my thighs as he did so.

Another betraying groan stumbled from my lips as I felt him cup my panty-clad pussy, his eyes at half-mast as I felt his middle finger trace my cleft.

"Still want to scream, love?" he asked, as I felt that finger lazily masturbate me.

"Yes," I let out ragged breath, shooting him a hard glare.

"But you're so wet, Darcy," he told me, his eyes on where his hand was, watching my hips subtly lift and fall to his momentum. Easton looked up at me, giving a pirate's grin, "Or am I to call you Bianca this evening?"

Fuck. Fuck. Fuckity fuck.

He slowed his finger down, lightening it to a feather-like touch. "Tell me something…" His eyes again on the bunched up silk around my hips, "Were you trying to make me angry tonight? Trying to get back at me, perhaps, for not indulging you in on a lie that you had no business knowing?"

I wasn't quite sure what to say. I'd never seen him so intense. I remained silent.

I was so fucking stupid. What did I think would happen when I showed up prancing around apparently like a ghost of his past? Did I honestly think he'd just laugh it off, slap me on the back, and offer me a beverage as we went through my presentation, like the professionals we were pretending to be?

I was too busy thinking about what Eli had said and that he was so fucking right when I felt Easton's hands suddenly on my breasts.

I watched as he tore where the bodice met the straps, lowering them below my nipples. I closed my eyes, swallowing another moan of frustrated

183

pleasure as he began to roughly knead my now-sensitive breasts, apparently making up for his too-light touches from before.

When I managed to open my eyes, I watched as his head slowly made its way to where his hands were. Almost like he couldn't help himself. I think that's what undid me the most, because I let in a sharp breath. He gave me a soft, dark laugh at the sound…Right before covering a nipple with his mouth, and sucking hard on the tip as he used the palm of his other hand to stimulate the other. I felt his teeth pulling on my nipple as he raised his head and looked up at me.

"I just wished I knew you were into role-play, Darcy." His hand continued its pleasurable assault on my other breast.

I gasped. "What's your fucking point?"

"The point," he whispered sinisterly, "is that you'll get to finish out the day with your audience asking for an encore performance."

He pushed a little voice into his whisper, giving it an almost mellifluous, lyrical sound, "I'm going to fuck you like I would Bianca. I'm going to speak to you like you are Bianca. And I'm going to *use* you like I would Bianca."

I felt his lips on the spot right below my ear. "Are you frightened, love?"

"No." I'd made my decision the moment I sat in the hairstylist's chair. Go big or go home. Besides, I knew down to my toes that this man would never really hurt me. My heart, yes. My body? No.

Easton took a step back, quickly perusing my body, stopping momentarily on where my dress was torn, and then stopping to study my face.

I raised my chin defiantly. "Do it." I challenged him.

He looked back at me, in wonder…an easy smile resting on his lips. Something flashed in his eyes as he continued studying me, and before he was aware of it, I saw a vague and saddened disappointment reflect through his eyelashes. Before I could think too much about it, he quickly replaced it with a smirk.

"My pleasure, Bianca," he said, turning his back to me and making his way to the dresser.

184

"You've displeased me today, Bianca." I watched as Easton opened one of the drawers and took out two pieces of long, white fabric. "And I *will* punish you."

Were those always in there?

He took one of my ankles, and I obliged. It was almost sickening that I could feel myself getting wetter, even though I knew it wasn't me he was seeing anymore. He looped the fabric around my ankles, making quick work of a knot, binding me. He did the same with my other ankle. Finished, he made sure the knots were tight enough to the point where I couldn't go anywhere, but not to the point where they were uncomfortable. He assessed the handcuffs that were now beginning to tire my arms.

"Comfy?" Easton asked provocatively, his British accent stronger now.

Not waiting for my answer, he deftly unfastened his pants and I watched his hard, solid cock slip out and up. He then threw the pants hard into the darkness, somewhere the light from the bedside lamp didn't quite reach. He crawled up on the bed, straddling me, reaching up and shredding what was left of my nightwear down the middle and tossing that away, too.

"Christ, you're beautiful."

I held still, waiting for him to conclude that sentence with the name '*Bianca.'* I mean, it *was* meant for her, wasn't it? I felt him take my nipple into his mouth once again.

Maybe I just hadn't heard it.

I moaned, arching my back. God, his tongue was so fucking talented. He used one hand to plump up my breast, and the other made its way up my arms and rested on the shackle one of my hands was imprisoned by.

"I love seeing you like this," he said, nipping on the underside of my breast. "I always loved tying you up, Bianca. And watching the way your body responded to my every touch."

His hands and mouth left my body as he sat up, glaring at me menacingly. He made quick work of my panties, and I waited for him to throw those to the side too.

185

But Easton didn't do that. I observed as he raised my light blue panties up to my mouth.

"Taste yourself," he ordered.

I had never…

Waiting for me to raise my mouth to meet the slightly soaked cotton, I obliged. I looked down at him as I sucked on my own heady dampness. His eyes were darkened to an almost light black now. He slowly took them away from my tongue, balling them up in his palm.

That's when I felt his cock rub at my pussy teasingly. I didn't see him put on any sort of condom he always made sure to use. But that thought quickly disappeared as I felt warmed metal causing swift friction against my clit.

Oh. My. God.

I was panting now, meeting every shallow thrust his hips were making.

"I never rode you like this, Bianca…" He breathed. "Mmmm…you'll have to tell me what it feels like." And with that, he buried himself in me with one quick thrust, all the way to his hilt.

"*Easton!*" I gasped. My head turning to the side, as I bit my lip on a savage moan of intense pleasure.

"Christ," he moaned, pulling back. "Your pussy's always so hungry."

Easton began his next thrust, only taking it halfway. He pulled back again, rubbing that delicious piercing against my clit.

"Please, Easton…"

"No, Bianca." He looked up at me through hooded eyelids. "This isn't for you."

Wait…does that mean…?

"It's for me," he said, pouring gasoline over any stupid hope I had.

Easton then showed me a series of thrusts that I was beginning to understand were some kind of pattern. He'd make several shallow thrusts, hitting my clit each time, slowly shattering me. Then he would use one hard thrust that would have me pulling against the restraints, wanting to dig my fingernails into his back in true female gratification.

Every time I did this, he'd let out a guttural groan and tell me things like:

"Take it harder, Bianca…"

He'd tilt my hips up and tell me/Bianca, "Deeper."

"Such a tight sweet pussy, how did it taste?"

Easton would never let me have any release, though. As soon as I was just slipping right towards the edge, he'd pull back again and switch to the shallow thrusts. It was fucking maddening.

Finally hitting my limit, and once again brought to brink of what would probably be the most violent and delicious orgasm of my life…I began to beg.

"Please…," I said, breathlessly. "Please, Easton. Let me…"

"Are you ready to come, Bianca?"

"*Yes.*" Another moan trembled on my lips.

That's when I felt his hands rest on either side of my body, and I was thinking that meant he was about to bring it home.

"Yes, Easton" I murmured, licking my lips. "*Please.*"

I felt him pull back in momentum. And then pull out completely.

"No," he said, bringing my attention to his face. It was expressionless. He reached for the keys, released my arms, and quickly unfastened my ankles from their binds. I felt tears begin to drown my eyelashes as he re-fastened his pants around his hips. His hands were shaking. And then I watched as he left, never once looking at me.

The last thing I remembered about that night was the sobs that raked my body after I heard the door slam shut. I curled up into a ball and cried, never once thinking about bringing myself to release.

This was my fault.

Chapter 25

All thoughts of sleeping in a bit the next morning were quashed when my alarm went off at eight a.m.

What the hell?

I was positive I'd set it for ten-thirty the previous night. Of course, anything was possible in this creaky old mansion of Easton's. I stretched my arms outside of the bedcovers, interlocking my fingers on both hands, stifling a yawn. And then it hit me. The events of the previous night.

Maybe I dreamt it. No such fucking luck…

How in the hell was I going to face Easton today after what had happened last night? He'd freakin' played me like a finely-tuned instrument, strumming my body with his expert tongue, fingers and cock, drawing the sensual chords out of me as if he'd written the music himself. He'd purposefully brought my body to the peak of what should've been an explosive crescendo. However, with expert timing, his deceptive cadence had served to punish me with the pain of unfulfilled pleasure, leaving me gasping for elusive fulfillment and left with empty dissonance after his cruel departure.

Well done, maestro!

There was a soft knock on the bedroom door. God, I hoped it wasn't him. He was likely proud of the fact he'd totally tortured me without leaving a mark last night.

"Yes?" I called out.

"Ms. Sheridan? It's Anna. May I come in?"

"Of course," I called out, now out of bed and slipping a robe around my naked body.

She gave me a pleasant smile as she carried a tray in with coffee and juice.

"Mr. Matthews wanted to make sure I brought you something before breakfast is served," she said, setting the silver tray down on my nightstand. "Also, he left this note for you," she added, handing me a folded piece of paper.

"He's not here?" I asked, feeling some relief wash over me.

"He left earlier to attend to some business in the city. He'll be meeting you later. Can I get you anything else?"

"Uh, no. Thanks," I replied, not wanting to read the note in front of her, though I suspected she already knew what it said.

"Very good," she replied. "I'll have your breakfast ready in an hour."

"Don't go to any trouble, Anna," I called after her. "I'm not really very hungry this morning. Maybe just a bagel?"

"Of course, Miss."

As soon as she shut the door behind her, I read Easton's note:

Darcy,

I've business elsewhere, so I'll be meeting you separately at the Procurement Contracts Centre downtown. I've arranged for a car to pick you up at 1:30 p.m.

You've an appointment at 10:00 a.m. this morning at the salon to have your hair changed back to its original colour and style. Geoffrey has a picture. He'll be the one colouring and styling your hair. Please be conservative with the face paint. I've removed your eye shadows, liner, and mascara. Stick with a basic foundation and add a hint of bronzer for colour, if you must. Your lashes are fine naturally. I'll trust you to select the appropriate business attire from your wardrobe for this meeting.

- Easton

I tossed the paper onto the bed.

He's off the fucking charts!

Despite my reluctance to follow his commands, my better judgment ruled. He was the boss; he had been tasked with mentoring me into a leadership position and I had promised myself that I'd comply where it was beneficial for my career. I needed to look at this as an opportunity to learn. It was my very first pitch and I needed to focus on doing it well.

At 1:30 p.m., my hair back to its original color and style, my make-up toned down, per Easton's instructions and my business attire conservative, yet professional, a limo arrived to drive me into London for the meeting. I'd checked and re-checked my briefcase to ensure I had all of the hand-outs, slides, and reference material I'd need and then some. My only fear was at the end of the presentation where the agenda allowed for a Q & A period.

What if they asked something I couldn't answer?

Once we arrived, I immediately saw Easton standing at the bottom of the concrete steps of the building, glancing at his watch before seeing the limo pull up. He helped me from the car, checking my hair, make-up and attire. It appeared as though I'd passed inspection. There was still an uncomfortable vibe between us—at least I was feeling it. I was avoiding making eye contact with him.

"You remembered to turn off your mobile, yeah?" he asked.

"Yes," I replied, walking up the steps next to him.

"Don't be nervous and make plenty of eye contact with various people in the audience," he instructed. "When it comes time for questions, I'll be up front with you to assist with that."

I nodded silently.

"Darcy," he continued as he opened the door for me, "I've the utmost confidence in you. You've done a great job preparing. My instincts tell me you'll be successful in securing this renewal."

That's probably the nicest thing he's ever said to me!

I looked up at him, finally making eye contact. "Thank you. It means a lot to me to hear you say that. I promise that I'll do my very best."

The presentation went off without a hitch. Easton and I were out of there by 4:30, met by his waiting limo. Once inside, he praised me for the great job I'd done presenting.

"I guess I had a pretty great mentor," I replied, shrugging slightly.

Oh yeah. This situation is starting to be a whole hell of a lot uncomfy!

"Shall we celebrate victory early?" he asked.

"Isn't that bad luck?" I asked, puzzled.

"In this case, I'm willing to take the risk, Ms. Sheridan. I've texted Colin and he's meeting us as well, since he's played a large part in your training."

He instructed the driver to take us to a quaint pub not far from his estate. Colin was already seated with a mug of dark ale in front of him. The table was near a stone fireplace that had a fire crackling, taking the chill off the large room. Everything inside was made of stone: the floors, the walls, the ceiling. Even the long bar was made of granite.

"This place looks like it was carved out of a giant boulder," I commented wryly.

Easton laughed genuinely, his dimple showing. "Actually this pub has been around for more than 150 years," he said. "There used to be a working quarry nearby that employed a lot of laborers that mined in this area. This was their field office. After it closed up in the 1860's, the landowner converted it into a pub for weary travelers."

"You know a little about everything, don't you?" I asked, impressed. "It must be that *European* education."

Colin chuckled good-naturedly at my assessment. I saw a slight frown cross Easton's features, not liking the semi-smart-ass comment.

Blessedly, the bartender came over and took our orders. Easton talked me into trying their dark ale, promising it did not taste like the beer I was used to in the States."

"I'm not a big fan of beer anywhere," I said.

"Just give it a try," he coaxed.

At this point, I would've downed some rubbing alcohol—anything to get me to unwind and not feel so fucking awkward around Easton. I hated that he, once again, had the upper hand.

Surprisingly, I did enjoy the dark ale and it served the purpose of settling my nerves as the feeling of relaxation seeped in. I found myself talking easily to Colin, filling in the details when he asked about the presentation. Both Easton and I had an enjoyable time at the pub, rehashing our afternoon spent at Scotland Yard.

"When will we know about the renewal?" I asked.

"Within thirty days," he replied. "If not sooner."

"What's next on our agenda?"

He quirked an eyebrow at me.

"I mean for the rest of this weekend," I replied, fumbling for words and feeling my face warm with a blush. "Colin and I fly out on Monday. I brought my laptop so I can work from your estate over the weekend and catch up, or if you've any special projects requiring my assistance, I'd be happy to help."

Okay...they're both watching me ramble on here...

Easton cleared his throat. "Darcy, it's the weekend. You can relax," he said, then turned to Colin.

"Would you and Ronnie like to have dinner at the manor this evening?" he asked.

"Sorry, mate," Colin replied with a smile. "She's made plans for us this evening. How about we get together tomorrow night for dinner and clubbing, though? I'm sure Darcy would enjoy seeing some of London's newer night spots. Ronnie's been nagging me to take her to some new club that recently opened."

"Sounds like a plan," Easton replied, glancing over at me as I drained the last of my ale. "Darcy? Are you up for that?"

"Yeah, sure," I lied.

"I know you and Ronnie will get on well," Colin assured me with a wink. "Speaking of which, I'd better head out. So, until tomorrow then?"

"Cheers," Easton said, raising his mug.

"See you, Colin," I said, wishing he would've stayed longer.

Once we arrived back at the manor, I told Easton I was going to go up and change into something more comfortable. Easton was already preoccupied with reading his mail on the table in the entry hall.

Aaaaaand…dis-fucking-missed!

I'd decided once I was in the comfort of my suite I wasn't going back downstairs. I made a conscious effort to lock the door to my room. I wasn't all that hungry, so I showered again for relaxation purposes, and threw on a pair of sweats and a T-shirt. I climbed up onto my bed and flicked the remote of the wide-screen television. I'd found it in the drawer of my nightstand, and I'd since realized it controlled the flat-screen television hidden beneath the closed cabinet doors of the huge armoire across from my massive bed.

I was settled in comfortably when there was tapping on my door.

"What?" I called out. Probably Anna wanting to know what she could bring me for dinner.

"It's me," I heard Easton's voice on the other side.

"Yeah? What can I do for you?" I called out.

"Are you coming down for dinner?" he asked from the hallway.

"Not hungry," I called out. "I'm in for the night."

"I've got pizza coming."

What the fuck?

"Why?" I called out, confused.

"The staff's gone for the night. I don't normally cook and I thought you might be hungry."

Okay, so even though I could totally get onboard for taking the blame for last night's...adventures, I couldn't help getting a little peeved at the fact that he was trying to be all nonchalant about it. At the meeting for the presentation? Sure, I mean, that's our workplace. But I didn't know how to act around the guy when the doors were closed, and when we had an entire house pretty much to ourselves.

"What toppings?" I asked cockily. I didn't want him to think I was up here sulking or trying to figure out how to tie knots better than he did or anything.

"Pepperoni and mushrooms," he replied. "That's your choice of toppings, right?"

Fuck it, I thought. Apparently tonight was about extending the olive branch. And when in Rome...Eat pizza, apparently.

"Sometimes I like *olives* on it, as well," I called out. "I'll be down in a couple."

I jumped out of the bed and went into the bathroom, brushing my teeth, brushing my hair out, and dabbing a touch more eye make-up on.

It was subtle, okay?

By the time I got downstairs into the study where Easton's flat screen was located, I saw that he had plates, napkins and wine glasses out, filled to the brim with either Merlot or Cab-Sav waiting. Just as I entered the room, I heard the "Gong" of his doorbell. It had a real 'Addams Family' ring to it. Several minutes later, he returned with the large, flat box that held our hot pizza.

"Okay, I have to ask. Do you mean to tell me you have pizza delivery clear out here?"

"Of course not," he said, helping himself to a slice of pepperoni and mushroom pizza. "I had my driver pick it up."

"Well that's kind of extravagant, isn't it?"

He shrugged, taking a bite of pizza. "I enjoyed our pizza party together that night. I guess I just wanted it to be my treat this time," he replied.

195

I'd lied, I was thoroughly hungry, wolfing down a couple of pieces before I realized Easton was watching me with a hint of amusement in his eyes.

Oh God! Here comes that feeling of embarrassment again from last night.

"What?" I asked, wiping my mouth of the pizza sauce.

"Well, I just wanted to let you know that I checked the schedule on the television tonight and there's some sort of Bela Lugosi triple feature, if you'd care to watch it," he offered.

"Which ones?" I asked, perking up.

"*Murders in the Rue Morgue, Night of Terror,* and *Mark of the Vampire.*"

"Really? Those are my favorites." I shifted uneasily, unsure as to whether he'd mentioned this so we could watch them together, or was simply letting me know so I'd have something to watch in my room later so I'd be out of his sight. I wasn't looking to step on another humiliating land mine.

"They start in about ten minutes," he remarked. "I was going to stoke the fire and watch them in here. You're welcome to join me."

Thank God! Humiliation averted!

"Yeah, okay," I replied. "I probably won't be able to stay awake for all three, though."

I got up from the sofa and started toward the main hallway.

"Where are you going?" Easton called out after me.

"Got to get a pillow and blanket," I called back. "It's not vegging out without those two things."

I heard him chuckle as I made my way towards the staircase. At least things were starting to be a bit less uncomfortable. What happened last night wouldn't happen again. It hung over us like a pall and I wanted to be rid of it.

Chapter 26

As predicted, I did fall asleep during the beginning of the third movie, sprawled on the loveseat across from Easton. I awoke with a start to the loud clap of thunder that rattled the leaded glass windows in the darkened room.

"We've a line of thunderstorms rolling in," Easton remarked, seeing I was awake. "It's fairly common this time of year. You probably need to get some sleep."

"Yeah, right," I scoffed. "That's not going to happen easily with thunderstorms coming in." I gathered up my blanket and pillow, stretching as Easton turned the movie off with the remote. I'd no sooner started towards the hallway when a brilliant flash of light illuminated the room, seconds later the loud boom of thunder followed causing me to jump and let out a squeak of discomfort.

"Are you frightened of storms?" he asked, cocking an eyebrow.

"I used to love watching them as a child," I admitted. "Until the time lightning struck a tree, and a huge limb crashed through my bedroom window. Not so much after that."

He was beside me now, watching me carefully. "You've no need to worry. I promise nothing will come crashing through your windows here."

Once we'd reached the top of the stairs, Easton stopped and turned to me. "Have a restful night, Darcy. If you need anything, my suite is just down this hallway," he said, nodding to the left.

"Thanks," I murmured, feeling flushed. The thunderous boom of the latest bolt of lightning sent me skittering to the right to find comfort beneath the covers of my bed. I finally managed to fall back asleep as the storm passed over.

Sometime later, I was once again awakened by angry claps of thunder rattling the windows in my suite unmercifully. I let out a low screech, sitting upright immediately, forgetting for the moment where I was. My heart was pounding in my chest. Torrents of rain were splashing furiously against the windows. The wind was howling through the old stone fortress and suddenly I felt as if I'd been transitioned back in time to one of those old horror movies myself.

I stared at the closed, solid oak door, bringing the bed covers up underneath my chin. My eyes were glued on the polished brass doorknob, watching and waiting for it to slowly turn with a barely audible squeak that would alert me someone was lurking behind it, preparing to pounce on me. Just as that thought finished, a blinding flash of lightning illuminated the room and a thunderous clap of thunder followed behind. I let out a scream that rivaled that of the chick from Bride of Frankenstein.

Shit Darcy! Get hold of yourself, girl.

I clapped my hand over my own mouth to keep myself quiet as the storm continued its rampage outside. Just then, I did hear the squeak of the doorknob. I saw it turn slowly as the door creaked open. I let loose with another blood-curdling scream, not giving a damn who in the hell heard me!

"Darcy," Easton said softly, swiftly crossing the distance to my bed, looking pretty damn fine in his low slung P.J. bottoms and white tee. "I heard you scream from down the hall. Are you alright?"

"I'm sorry," I gasped, shaking my head. "I guess those movies we watched and these thunderstorms rattling outside set me off. I didn't mean to wake you, Easton."

"You didn't," he said smiling. "I was still up reading. Storms like this make it tough for anyone to sleep. Just keep telling yourself it will pass over; they always do, right?"

He was trying to ease my mind. It was actually kind of sweet. Another flash of lightning streaked through the windows and what sounded like a dynamite explosion, complete with a popping sound followed. The light from the hallway flickered a couple of times and then went out, along with the lamp I'd left on in the sitting room. I muffled another scream, diving under the covers.

"It's alright, love," his soft voice was closer. I felt the bed dip with his weight beside me. "A transformer blew, that's all. Would you like me to stay in here until we get power back?"

198

"Would you?" I asked timidly, not proud of the fact I was probably feeding into the "macho" he wore around his neck like a medallion.

"Certainly," he said, stretching out beside me on the bed. He wrapped his arms around me, pulling me close against his chest.

I could hear hail pelting against the windows in torrents, more thunder rattled off in the distance.

"You know," he whispered against the back of my neck, "they say you can know how close you are to the centre of the storm by counting the seconds between the lightning and the thunder."

"Well, I'd say we're there what with it being *on top* of us and all," I replied, snuggling deeper into him. I felt his amused chuckle more than I heard it. Another bolt of lightning flashed and I tensed up against him, poising myself for the thunder that would follow.

"Count, Darcy," he commanded softly. I felt Easton's hand sift through my hair, running his fingers through the strands gently. It was calming and electrifying at the same time. It was as if he and I had this magnetic force field between us that continually drew us together, regardless whether we wanted it to or not.

The thunder rolled out, making the room echo in reverberation. Another flash lit up the room, as Easton's lips lightly suckled the skin at the nape of my neck, causing me to shiver.

"Cold, love?" he asked, my skin felt the movements of his lips. I felt a whimper coming from the bottom of my throat.

"Count," he ordered again, his lips now making their way to my jawline as one of his hands idly played with the thin hem of my cotton shirt…

I rolled over so that my face was to his. Even in the darkness, I could see his face; his eyes were searching mine for something.

"Did you fuck me because I looked like her?" I asked quietly.

"Yes," he whispered, not taking his eyes from mine.

I sighed, somehow relieved that at least he had enough respect not to lie about it.

"Are you holding me *now* because I look like her?" I felt the adrenaline catch fire in my veins, afraid of his answer, but needing to know the truth.

"No."

He lowered his face to mine, his tongue tracing a pattern against my lips. He was gentle, taking his time, his hands now lightly massaging my back and hips. God! Was this another lesson for me? It was impossible for me to remain unresponsive to his touch. I melted against him, my lips now moving with his in a slow, sensual kiss, his tongue gently exploring my mouth, his teeth nipping, tugging ever-so-lightly at my lower lip.

His hands. His glorious hands were searching beneath my clothes for skin. He pulled the covers back exposing me fully to his eyes, hands and lips. I rolled my head back and forth on the pillow, allowing him to free me of my shirt and panties; all the while, his lips traveled a slow and deliberate path down the column of my throat, licking, nipping, and kissing me into more soft whimpers.

I felt his hand grasp mine, moving it to rest on his erection. I didn't hesitate in springing his cock free; allowing my fingers to curl around the thick expanse of it, fingering the soft skin around the head. I heard a soft moan escape his lips as my hand traveled his length, sliding up and down slowly, bringing his erection fuller and harder.

It was as if the storm outside ceased to exist for us. I heard no more thunder, no more wind or rain pelting against the windows. All I was aware of at this moment was Easton: how he looked, how he felt, how he smelled and how he tasted.

His lips pulled away from my breasts momentarily, as he looked deeply into my eyes.

Oh God!

"Are you sure you really want this? Nothing's changed from my perspective."

"Yes," I whispered, huskily. "I want you to fuck me, Easton. And I want you to know that it's me that you're fucking."

He rose up, his lips capturing mine once again for a long, sweet kiss before he once again traveled to my breasts, his hands grasping and cupping them roughly, while his mouth sucked each rosy peak. I moved both hands to his cock, increasing the pressure and tempo of stroking, hearing his moans coming louder as his hips thrust forward.

"I need to taste your sweet cunt," he murmured, moving lower where his fingers gently plied the tender folds of my flesh. His tongue swirled over my clit again and again, licking, lapping and gently nipping as I swelled for him.

"Oh God," I moaned, my hips flexing against him as he thrust a finger inside of me, his mouth still sucking hungrily from my core. Another one of his long fingers entered me, and his tongue was now thrusting slowly and deliberately in and out of my pussy.

"God, you're dripping wet, love," he said, licking my essence, as if he couldn't get enough of it. "And your pussy tastes so fucking sweet." His tongue and lips continued working their electric magic on my soft folds. My hips moved in response.

"Mmmm," was all I could manage, as my breathing quickened along with my pulse rate.

Easton lifted me up, rolling underneath me. I instinctively straddled his hips as he lowered me just above his swollen cock. He dipped me down just a bit, just enough so that I could feel the rounded ball studs swirl around my clit, as he moved my hips back and forth, teasing his piercing against my slit. I drew in a sharp breath, allowing my orgasm to release from there. I whimpered loudly as the surges of pleasure enveloped me, knowing the best was still yet to come.

His fullness was inside of me now, as I leaned forward just a bit to find the perfect angle. I rode his cock from root to tip, pivoting myself up and down slowly, going full depth onto him and grinding against him each time. His hands were fondling my breasts, roughly now. His tongue flickered over his lips and his eyes darkened with passion as he watched me fucking him. I rocked forward to back, up then down and, as I continued, I could feel my sweet spot swell against his cock piercing that was hitting it just right with each downward stroke. I could feel myself squeezing him, and his breathing was coming faster, as was mine.

"Darcy," he rasped, "your cunt's squeezing me like a greedy bitch. Are you ready for it, baby?"

"Oh, yeah," I whispered hoarsely. "I want it, Easton. Fuck me hard."

His hands immediately braced my hips, lifting me up and pushing me back down on his cock over and over again as our orgasms crashed around us. Easton groaned my name over and over again, as his cock throbbed and then emptied his climax inside of me, leaving no doubt as to whom he was fucking tonight.

Chapter 27

When I awoke the following morning, Easton was still wrapped around me securely. I glanced at the clock, noticing it was after 10:00 a.m. What happened to his morning ritual of getting up at 4:30 and working out? As the low thunder still rumbled outside, I realized he'd stayed here for me. We'd fucked throughout the night, oblivious to the storms raging outside. They were nothing in comparison to the storms that had raged in this very room. Over and over again. I felt a smile form on my lips.

I rolled over to face him, my hand stroking his unkempt hair, my fingers tracing his unshaven face. His eyes opened and he smiled at me warmly.

"Morning," he said. "I see you survived the storm no worse for the wear."

"Oh, I don't know about that," I replied, yawning. "Some British cad took advantage of the situation and ravaged me throughout the night."

"Is that right?" he asked, smiling. "Maybe it was a figment of your imagination."

"Think so?" I asked coquettishly. "Some figment. I can still feel the remnants dripping out of me," I teased.

"You *are* a crude colonial," he remarked dryly. "Come, let's hit the gym together and start our day off right."

Easton and I worked out together and then showered—separately. He insisted on making breakfast for us: fried eggs, bacon and toast. I busied myself with checking my e-mails, making a few calls back to the U.S., then went to hunt him down. He was on the phone in his study, barking angrily at someone. I stayed out in the hall, polite enough not to intrude, yet nosy enough to want to listen.

"I don't understand that at all, Devon, this should've been handled weeks ago and now you're fucking telling me you and your staff dropped the ball?"

He paused; obviously Devon on the other end was likely tossing out some excuse for whatever he and his staff had failed to do.

"That's no goddamn excuse. Women have babies all the time. Some of them have them out in the rice fields while working, stopping long enough to whelp, and then get back to their bloody harvesting. You took a six-week leave, which was sufficient time for your recovery and to stay on track with this project."

Holy shit! Devon's a 'she?'

"I'll fly out on Monday morning to handle this. Be prepared to update me on the status by 1:00 p.m. your time. Make no mistake; I'm prepared to clean house over this."

(Pause)

"I think you know what I mean. It's time for you to decide whether you really want a high-level career with Baronton, or are better suited to motherhood. Despite what feminist propagandists may preach, you really can't have it all, Devon."

Jesus, dude. Harsh much?

I guess the comforting and comfortable Easton from last night was gone. But that really wasn't what bothered me the most…it was the fact that this was a *woman* he was speaking to, whose job he was threatening to take because…what? She went off and had a baby and had the audacity to *try* and work through that for her employer and fell a little short on some things?

What the hell did he expect from the girl?!

"Excuse me, doc? Do you think it'd be okay if you just e-mail me when it's time to push? I have to make some deadlines and you're tripping up my Wi-Fi every time you come within three feet. 'Kay, thanks."

We nearly collided as I resumed my entrance to his study as he was starting to exit.

"I'm sorry," I said, backing away from him. I wasn't sure whether he was still angry over the thing with Devon and one of his companies. If so, I didn't want to be on the receiving end of it.

204

"Is there something you need, Darcy?" he asked tersely.

"Uh, well I was wondering if maybe I could get to a mall or something today. I wanted to do a little shopping while I'm here. I noticed there were several boutiques near the salon I went to yesterday, I mean if it's not a problem," I said, twisting my hair around a finger.

"Of course, that's not a problem," he replied. "I can take you or if you'd prefer, I'll have my driver take you; it's up to you."

I didn't want him going along while I shopped for something sexy and skimpy to wear tonight. After the whole deal yesterday with my hair and make-up, I preferred shopping without his input.

"If your driver's available, that'd be great."

"I'll arrange it then. He'll be ready and waiting in ten minutes," he replied, turning away from me and proceeding down the hall.

"Great. Thank you, Easton," I called after him meekly.

∞ ∞ ∞ ∞ ∞ ∞

I was enjoying a bubble bath in the lovely, claw foot tub. I'd die to have a tub like this back home. My hair was piled high on top as I relaxed against the sloped back and rested my head on the rolled edge of the tub. It was so soothing after the three hours I had spent shopping. Dennis, Easton's driver, had been a great sport. I didn't find anything I liked at the boutiques that were nearby, so he'd driven me to some other upscale shops he knew about until I found just the right cocktail dress for my night out on the town.

I'd taken my time shopping, since Dennis was in no hurry. During my little British excursion, I kept thinking about the conversation I maybe not-so-accidentally overheard earlier when Easton was speaking to Devon over the phone. I knew a man with his power and status hadn't gotten to where he was without having to be ruthless now and then, but for crying out loud, I couldn't help but feel sympathy for poor Devon, getting her ass chewed like that.

I thought about the angry comments Easton had made regarding babies and motherhood. Something Lacee had said to me that day in the conference room came to mind, something about his mother having no use for him. Maybe that had soured his view of women, mothers in particular. I couldn't imagine any mother turning her back on a child, no matter what the circumstances. I wasn't about to pry into Easton's private affairs—well any more than I already had, courtesy of Taz, that is.

I finished my bath, stepping into the shower long enough to wash my hair. After I finished, I was in my robe, blow drying my hair when someone knocked on the door to my suite.

"Come in!" I hollered out from the bathroom.

Easton sauntered in, our eyes connecting through the bathroom mirror. I watched him lean up against the wall by the tub, no more than six feet away from where I was drying my hair. He seemed fascinated by the way I held the blow dryer in one hand and a round brush in the other, using them expertly from years of experience.

Finished, I shut the dryer off, placed both items down on the counter and looked at him looking at me using our reflection.

"Secret bathroom rendezvous already, eh?" I asked.

He tilted his head, studying my reflection. "Hardly," he replied softly. Stepping away from the wall, he slowly walked over to where I was standing.

"How was shopping?" he asked, standing right behind me now.

"It was fine. I found something for tonight."

"Did you?" His hands found their way to my hair.

Even after mulling over his conversation with Devon most of the afternoon, I had to admit that I secretly loved Easton's minor obsession with my hair and the way he could never quite stop himself from running his hands through it.

"I hope you had lunch. I apologize for not asking you before you left what time you'd be back."

"I had Dennis stop on the way back and got a little something to tide me over," I replied.

206

His hands stilled. "You're upset about something." Easton's eyes met mine again in the mirror.

"No," I replied, realizing I'd been a tad curt with him. "Everything's good," I reassured him. "What time are we leaving?"

Finally, looking over at him, I saw him glance at his watch. "In about an hour. I'm going to grab a shower and get ready. It's nothing fancy tonight, so don't feel like you have to over-dress," he said, giving me 'the look.'

"I've got it handled," I replied, finally finding what I was looking for. Grabbing my heavy make-up bag, I made my way back into the bathroom.

Forty-five minutes later, my hair and make-up were finished, and I was slipping into the cute little cocktail dress I'd purchased earlier. It was a London fashion brand called 'Lipsy' that specialized in party-wear. I'd selected a short, black stretch, poly-blend dress with a ruched panel in the front and lace shoulder panels. The low-cut sweetheart neckline allowed for ample cleavage to show. The back was open with a zip fastening. I'd found a cute faux (and very fuzzy) lamb's wool bolero jacket in black to wear with it after the evening chill set in. The shoes I'd bought to go with my ensemble were black, low-cut vamp 4-inch high-heels. Smoking hot was my first thought when I caught a glimpse of them in the storefront window.

I'd pulled my hair up on top of my head, allowing curly tendrils to cascade down around my face and neck for a messy, yet playful look. I'd just fastened my dangly earrings when Easton tapped on my door.

"The car's waiting. Are you ready?"

"Be right there," I called out, grabbing my clutch and jacket, heading out the door. He was waiting for me in the hall, dressed impeccably in black trousers with a matching black, loose-fitting sport jacket. He had a white tee shirt on underneath the sports jacket and wore black pointy boots.

"Hmm," I said, giving him the onceover. "You're quite the London boy tonight, I see."

He was perusing my outfit, a slight frown creasing his otherwise perfect forehead. "I'm not sure about your outfit," he said, scratching his chin.

"What? You don't like it?" I asked, disappointed, turning my back to him so that he could finish zipping me up.

"It's not that," he continued, pulling the zipper up as far as it would go. "It worries me is all."

"What are you worried about?" It was my turn to frown as I faced him once again.

"Frankly, that some of your body parts will be made public," he replied tersely.

"I swear, sometimes you act older than my father," I said, waltzing past him to the staircase. "I'm not changing," I announced to his scowling face.

"At least hold onto the handrail," he snapped following behind me. "I don't see how women are able to walk in shoes like that. Ten to one, I'll be carrying your ass before the night's over."

"Isn't that supposed to be 'arse'?" I teased.

"Either way, the odds are still in my favour," he shot back, a hint of a smile making an appearance.

Chapter 28

~ Easton ~

I took a peek beneath my lashes for the hundredth time at Darcy's legs as the limo was taking us to meet Colin and Veronica at "Rapture," one of the newer London hot spots. It was easier to gawk this way; she presumed I was taking a power nap. Hell, I told her I was going to take a quick nap for this very purpose. It was difficult to openly admire her body if she was aware of it. I didn't need her reading things that weren't there into any of my recent actions.

Her legs were probably the most gorgeous pair I'd ever laid eyes on. I sat back, recalling how they'd felt wrapped around my torso. Her ass was epic and her tits drove me to distraction. Right now, in particular, they were fairly spilling over the bodice of that slinky excuse for a dress she was sporting. Great! Fine time for my cock to spring up and take notice! Hopefully, she wouldn't notice since she thought I was napping.

"Easton, I know you're *not* sleeping," she blurted out.

Bloody hell! Did she actually notice?

"Are you trying to avoid having any conversation with me this evening?"

Oh Christ! Yet *another* reason I didn't do relationships. Women and their *infinite* need to talk when silence would do just as well. I didn't react to her statement. I didn't want to talk pleasantries or otherwise right now. I was feeling myself slide into something I clearly didn't want and it pissed me off! Having her come across the pond was simply a bad idea. I was looking forward to her going back to the States on Monday, so I would no longer be bothered with the distractions.

"Yeah, okay, have it your way," she grumbled, uncrossing her legs and shifting away from my view, then re-crossing them and looking out the window of the limo. "You've been nothing but a pain in my *arse* all afternoon, anyway. I'm so looking forward to hanging with normal peeps tonight. You give Brits a bad name," she mumbled irritably.

I felt myself smile at her remarks. "I'm only half British, Darcy," I said, opening my eyes so I could look at her. "In case you didn't know, I was born in the States. Trace's father is *my* father if you recall?"

"So, what's your point?" she asked, glancing over at me.

"My point, *darlin',*" I said, using my version of a southern American drawl, "is maybe I get my assholiness from my American side. Have you considered that?"

She then turned back around to face me. "And *why* is it that when Brits attempt to imitate the American accent it always sounds as if everyone in the U.S. is a *hillbilly*? Talk about stereotypical generalizations."

"What's wrong with hillbillies?" I teased.

"There's nothing *wrong* with hillbillies," she replied, rolling her eyes. "It's just that there are lots of accents in the U.S., why that one?"

She was definitely in an argumentative mood this evening. In fact, she'd been rather surly all day. God—she was probably menstrual, in which case, I may send her back across the pond on a flight yet tonight…

I sighed. "Is there some particular reason why you're so snappy with me this evening? We don't have to go if you're not feeling well."

"I feel fine. I told you that earlier."

"Indeed," I replied. "But I'm not convinced for some reason. If it's an uh…a…female thing or something, I can have Dennis stop at a pharmacy before we get there."

"Yet another stereotypical comment," she laughed, shaking her head. "With men, it's perfectly fine to have a mood. God help us females though. It must be *hormonal!*"

Clearly, there's an issue here.

I remained quiet for the rest of the trip. I wasn't stupid enough to step on that hornet's nest again.

It was a week or so after my break with Bianca. My mother had come to the manor for an unexpected visit. That was usually the case, since I never invited her over. She was dying to get the sordid details, having heard the gossip trickling in from Milan via tabloids to the London socialites.

"Oh darling," she gushed, coming in to my study from the hall. "I'm so shocked to hear about the horrific scandal involving Bianca and that photographer! What a wretched thing she's done to you! Do you really believe the baby she aborted was yours?"

"Thank you for your concern, Mother. I didn't realise the news had traveled this quickly, but then I forgot how fond you are of gutter press."

"It's not trash if it's true darling. Are you telling me it's false?"

"What I'm telling you, Mother, is that it's my private business, not yours. I prefer not to discuss the particulars with you or anyone else. I'd appreciate some privacy on the matter."

"Oh Easton," she laughed, sardonically, "you must realise a man in your position has little privacy, especially when one has been played the fool like you were by that harlot. After all you did for her, launching her career, using your contacts to take her to the top, financing her training and marketing. Well, it's just shameful the way she's repaid you. Though I suppose she and Christopher Rolando will still live quite comfortably now that she's the most in-demand model in Europe. It doesn't matter how much wealth she acquires though, she'll always be Euro-trash, darling. Oh, by the way, I heard she landed an exclusive shoot for Stella McCartney's new line just yesterday. Shall I call Sir James Paul on your behalf?"

"No, Mother. You should simply stay out of it and mind your own fucking business."

"Easton! How dare you speak to me with such disrespect! I'm your mother and I forbid you to treat me so shabbily after all I've done for you, after all of my sacrifices!"

"Sacrifices?" I'd shouted incredulously at her. "What fucking sacrifices have you ever made for anyone? You've shown me nothing but selfishness, ruthlessness, and dispassion my entire life. The only positive influences I've ever had were my grandparents and my father and you used me as a weapon against all of them whenever it suited your self-serving agenda."

"I can't believe you're saying these things to me!" she screamed, her face turning red with fury. "I'm the one that tried to warn you about women and how they would use you for your title

211

and wealth, ultimately controlling you until they move on to someone else! And I was right, wasn't I? I've always tried to protect you, but you simply refuse to accept it. You've gotten what you deserved, Easton!"

"Protect me? Protect me? Mother every horrible thing that's ever happened to me was a direct result of your 'protection.' What a laugh! You're incapable of loving anyone other than yourself! I pity you, but not enough to want you in my home. Please leave."

"Oh, I'm happy to leave your home, you ungrateful bastard! I'm glad Mummy and Pops are no longer alive to see what you've turned in to!"

"Whatever I am, Mother, is certainly of your making."

"Hah, considering what I had to work with I'll take that as a compliment," she sneered. "I can't take responsibility for those traits you inherited from your paternal side."

"Oh, here we go again," I snapped. "Time for you to take a pot-shot at my part-Yankee heritage again, eh?"

"Not at all darling," she said, smiling. "What makes you think Trace Matthews even sired you? Think about that!"

Those were the last words I'd heard from her mouth over two years ago. They still echoed in my ears and turned my blood cold.

We arrived at 'Rapture,' finding that Colin and Ronnie had already landed a table in the crowded restaurant portion of it. I saw Ronnie standing up, waving us over excitedly. It appeared her dress was of the same general design as Darcy's, only in red with sequins. Good God! I knew those two would hit it off straightaway. I guided Darcy over toward them, my hand resting on the small of her back. Did I mention it was also bare?

Introductions were made and, within five minutes, Ronnie and Darcy were chatting away, giggling and sharing personal information as if they were old school chums. I caught Colin's look of love as he watched his fiancé show Darcy her engagement ring. I hoped he had better luck with his engagement than I'd experienced with mine. He'd spent a hell of a lot of money on that 3-carat ring.

We ordered fish and chips, sipping dark ale, for which Darcy seemed to be acquiring a taste. I wondered if she'd been honest with me about having something to eat earlier. The ale seemed to be providing her with a nice buzz.

212

"Colin," Ronnie said loudly over the noise of the increasing crowd, "Darce and I are going to the little girl's room. How about you and Easton finding a table for us in Club North before the bands start, love?"

"Certainly, sweets," my pussy-whipped top aide replied. "Don't get lost or I'll worry." He sent her off with a loving smile and a wink.

Christ, Colin. Get it together, man.

Colin and I snaked our way through the restaurant and into the large interior hall that led to one of the four separate clubs inside. You guessed it: Club North, Club South, Club East and Club West. According to Colin, Club North was hosting British Boy Bands tonight and Ronnie thought Darcy would enjoy the venue. He started to get his wallet out to pay the cover charge.

"Let me get this, Colin," I said.

"No argument here, mate," he said, putting his wallet back in his jacket. The cover charge was steep. Colin was paid well, but I knew the fancy wedding he and Ronnie were financing was already costing more than £40,000 and that didn't include the cruise he wanted to take that he thought I didn't know about.

Colin described Ronnie and Darcy to the fellow at the window so that he would allow them in whenever they finished up doing what girls do in the powder room. Each of the clubs had its own marquee and ticket window like an old theatre. Inside, there was a huge centre stage for the band, and a dance floor that surrounded it. The tables were outside of the dance floor and were in tiers so that even on the top tier, the band was still visible and the acoustics superb.

"How's this?" Colin asked, going midway down the sloped auditorium.

"Fine by me."

We sat down and immediately a waitress in a leopard bikini that included a long tail came up to take our drink orders. I ordered bourbon, Colin his usual Scotch, ale for Ronnie and I took the liberty of ordering a Royal Fuck for Darcy, remembering that had been her cocktail of choice at Trace's wedding reception.

"So," Colin said once the waitress had left, "you didn't give me a lot of detail on how you felt the presentation went Friday."

213

"She did well," I replied, shrugging. "Actually, she did really well. I was quite impressed. You've done a good job with her, Colin."

"Then what was all the shit you were giving her Thursday night, might I ask?"

"Just me being me."

"Yeah, yeah. I don't buy it this time."

"Why's that?"

"Dude—you're still having every move she makes tracked, calling Ryan Dobbs constantly for updates; I mean, get real."

I had to laugh at him. "You've spent too much time in that States, Colin. Christ, you sound like you're a native."

"Fuck you, too." His laugh quickly joined mine.

I didn't say anything more, but I knew Colin and he wouldn't let it drop.

"So, how have things been with her being at the manor with you?"

"She's not been a problem until today. She's been a bit cheeky for reasons I can't figure."

"Maybe she doesn't care for the host," he suggested.

"Yeah? Fuck you too, mate."

Our drinks arrived and we took a moment to take a sip. Then it dawned on me.

"Oh shit."

"What?" he asked.

"I know what's got her knickers in a twist."

"Are you going to clue me in, bro?"

Jesus Christ, he needs to stay in London for a while.

214

"I was on the phone this morning with Devon Roberts in Leeds. Did you know they missed the cut-off date on that Turkish bid proposal? That's potentially £9 million in revenue lost."

He nodded. "Yeah, I heard from Clive yesterday evening."

"Well, at any rate, I was a bit harsh with Devon. I mean, the bloody woman's still using all that 'I just had a baby and got back to work' rubbish with me. Why would she go on maternity leave and not have a plan and schedule in place with her staff to make sure this didn't slip through the cracks? I'm flying there Monday, and I forewarned her that I'd be cleaning house. I might've led her to believe she needed to get her priorities in sync as well."

"You're taking a shot against motherhood, Easton. You aren't actually going to sack Devon are you?"

"Colin, I consider myself to be a fair and impartial person. If a man had let this project crash and burn, what would my reaction have been?"

"Termination," he said, taking a long swig of his Scotch.

"There's your answer then. I pride myself on being an equal opportunity Nazi," I replied, shrugging.

"So, how does that tie in with Darcy?"

"I think she was in the hall and overhead the conversation. She's been distant and rather cold towards me ever since."

"Well, come on, what do you expect?"

"I expect, as a future manager, she'll know there are consequences to pay when avoidable and costly mistakes are made. It may not be pleasant, but that's the reality of it, after all."

"I suppose she'll get over it in a few days," he replied.

"I think I know what I need to do," I said, shaking my head.

"Apologize to her for what she overheard and tell her how insensitive you were under the circumstances?"

"No. I'm taking her with me to Leeds. She's here to learn, right?"

Colin nodded, a frown now appearing as he waited for me to continue.

"She'll now get first-hand experience in how non-performing executives are terminated."

Chapter 29

Damn! Fuck! Shit! I rolled over on the bed, hoping that it was actually the bed I was supposed to be in; my head was throbbing unmercifully, my throat dry, parched and sore. I flung my arm out to get some indication of how close I was to the edge of the bed and made contact with hard, muscled, flesh.

"Bloody hell!" I heard Easton growl. "What the fuck now? Are you going to heave again?"

Oh God! It's coming back to me!

"Easton?" I heard my weak, pathetic voice whine. "I think I may be dying," I rasped.

"Not soon enough love," he snapped, moving to get out of the bed.

Holy shit! Even the slightest of movements was causing me pain somewhere.

"Did you get me drunk last night?" I asked.

"Suge, you managed that all by yourself with no help from anyone," he replied curtly. "In fact, I did my best to cut you off, but it seems you had other means of getting what you wanted."

I managed to lift my eyelids the tiniest bit. He was standing there, shirtless, wearing a pair of gray, drawstring pajama bottoms that hung low on his narrow hips. His hands were resting on his hips and a look of pure disgust was on his face. As sick as I was, and trust me, I'd never been this hung over in my life— I still recognized how smokin' hot he looked, even when he was pissed at me.

"What do you mean by that?" I croaked.

"Your dance partner, remember?"

I slowly shook my head. "Not yet," I replied.

"I'm looking forward to when it all comes back to you. You made quite an impression on the horny lad. So much so that I had to intervene to protect your honour."

"Jesus Christ, Easton! Are we fucking back in the middle ages?"

"If we were, I assure you, I wouldn't have left him breathing."

He left the room, leaving me there to contemplate my total misery and try to recollect what the hell had happened. I remember drinking my first Royal Fuck, and then another, getting a bit buzzed. Then Easton said I couldn't have anything more to drink, so Ronnie and I went to the dance floor. Colin and Easton were being stick-in-the-muds so it was just me and Ronnie dancing with everyone else on the packed dance floor. I remember now! A gorgeous raven-haired guy came up and joined us on the dance floor. He introduced himself as Damian. Within a couple of minutes, Colin was there, dragging Ronnie back to the table, so it was just me and the dude dancing. It got fuzzy again after that. It hurt to even try to remember at the moment. As hard as I tried, I simply did not remember drinking anything after that second Royal Fuck.

I lay in bed enduring the misery. Every second seeming like an hour, my stomach still lurching, even though I suspected it was empty. There was no way I could've gotten that hammered with just one ale and a couple of Royal Fucks. It was simply not possible.

Wait a minute! Wait one fucking minute! *Water!* The guy—Damian—offered me some water after we danced. I was sweaty and told him I needed to get some ice water. He said they had some at the table where his friends were sitting on the same level as the dance floor. I so didn't feel like trudging up the steps to where our table was located. Anyway, I recalled the dirty looks Easton had been shooting the whole time I'd been dancing with Damian. Everyone at the table had straws, drinking straight from the pitcher. Perhaps this was some British custom. Damian handed me a straw.

"Drink up, poppet," he'd said with a smile. I did and was shocked at the bitter taste.

"Oh God, that's putrid," I'd gasped.

"That's London water for you," was his response. I drank a few more gulps because thirst was thirst and I needed to stay hydrated. I remembered we'd

218

returned to the dance floor, and then not too much after that. I considered the possibility I'd been roofied.

Easton was back with a tray in his hands.

Oh God! Don't let it be food!

"You need to sit up and get some nourishment in your system."

"Oh please, for the love of God, I can't," I groaned, trying to bury myself into the comfortable pillows.

"You can and you will," he stated firmly. "Tea and dry toast…the best thing for you right now."

He placed the tray beside my bed and then pulled me up, stuffing pillows behind my back for support. He brought the tray over, opening the legs on it so it straddled my lap. "Darcy, take small bites and eat as much of the toast as you can tolerate. Sip the tea, trust me, it will help."

I nodded, my eyes starting to well up. What the hell had I done? How much of a fool had I made of myself in front of my boss-cubed? He sat down on the bed beside me, watching me take little mouse nibbles of the dry toast, washing them down with sips of tea.

"Good girl," he said with a slight smile. That was the most civil he'd been to me since I came to.

"Easton? Did we, you know…fuck…last night?"

He gave me a dark look. "Oh, for the love of Christ, woman; I assure you, I'm not in the habit of taking advantage of comatose females," he growled. "Aside from that, I spent most of the night cleaning vomit off the both of us."

I cringed, my face flushing with humiliation.

"That's just it. I don't remember drinking anything after you told me no more. I'm serious. Is it possible I got food poisoning or something?"

"Doubtful," he said. "We all ate the same thing. You were the only one that got ill—and I use that word cautiously. Besides that, I saw you and that wanker you were dancing with chugging alcohol at his table with the rest of the tossers."

Huh?

"That was water," I replied belligerently. "If you noticed, there was a whole pitcher of it on their table."

"It was pure grain alcohol. I believe they call it 'moonshine' or 'hooch' over in the States."

"It was bitter," I said, "The guy—"

"Damian," he interjected.

"Okay, *Damian*," I said, "told me it was just the way the water tasted in London. If you knew what it was, why didn't you stop me?"

"I was in the loo at the time. When I returned, Colin filled me in, so I went down to their table straightaway, but you were on the dance floor again, so I waited. When you returned, you introduced me to your new friend, 'Damian' who happened to have one hand on your ass, and the other on your breast. I told you we were leaving. You called me a stuffy party-pooper. Damian proceeded to tell me to piss off, that you and he were spending the night together, at which time I cleaned the floor up with the maggot."

I looked down at the knuckles on Easton's right hand, seeing they were scraped up a bit.

"Oh, my God! Did you hurt him badly?"

"He'll live," he replied. "My concern was getting you out of there and back here. I won't go into details about the very long ride home. Suffice it to say, Dennis earned a bonus for last night's assignment."

"I'm so sorry, Easton. I'm so ashamed of myself. I owe everyone an apology and, as soon as my head stops throbbing, I'll make calls to Colin and Ronnie, too. What they must think of me!"

"Relax, everyone will forgive you, I'm sure."

"How about you?" I asked, looking up at him. He had dark circles underneath his eyes.

"You're forgiven—for now. Will you be alright while I get a shower?"

I nodded. My stomach was already calming down.

"Alright then, I won't be long. Try and finish your tea. I'll bring some water and aspirin for you when I come back. I want to make sure you keep that down first."

He left and I finished my tea and took a few more bites of the dry toast. I lifted the tray and set it aside, pulling the covers back so that I could make my way into my bathroom to pee. Somehow, Easton had gotten me into a pair of sweats last night and a T-shirt that was huge on me. It must be one of his I thought, smiling. God, I was thankful I didn't remember any more than I already had!

I was horrified when I saw my reflection in the mirror. Oh God! He saw me like *this?* My hair was a wild mess; my mascara and eye-liner were streaked all down my cheeks. I used the bathroom and then scrubbed the make-up off my face. I brushed, gargled and managed to get a comb through my hair…eventually. I felt dizzy again, so I staggered back to the bedroom to a freshly showered, sitting on my bed, arms-crossed Easton.

"Why did you get out of bed?"

"I had to use the loo and then I had to wash my war paint off," I replied. "Did you dress me in this stuff?" I asked, pulling the large T-shirt out and looking down at it.

"Actually, I asked Dennis to do that," he replied, helping me up into bed again. He laughed when he saw my eyes widen in horror. "I'm teasing you," he replied, pulling the covers back up.

"I wouldn't have put it past you," I replied, laying my head back onto the soft pillows. "Did you bring something for my headache?" I asked.

"Yes, princess," he quipped, tucking me in. "Give me a second here."

He's unusually playful for being sleep and sex deprived…

He went over to my tray and picked up a cold bottle of water and a couple of capsules.

"Here you go," he said, handing both to me. I took them, and nearly drained the bottle of water. "Go easy," he said, "I don't want it all coming back up."

When he finished with me, he took the tray and headed towards the door. "Get some sleep. I'll check on you in a bit."

"Where are you going?" I asked, wanting him to stay here.

"I'm going to clean up the kitchen since the staff doesn't come in until tomorrow. Then I have to get our flight scheduled for tomorrow."

"I'm returning to D.C. tomorrow," I said, confused.

"Your trip back has been delayed for a day. I've some business to take care of in Leeds and I want you with me. It's a short flight. We'll be up and back in a few hours."

"What kind of business is it?"

"Something that requires my direct attention. It'll be a learning experience for you, trust me."

That sounds ominous…

If Easton wanted me to learn something, I knew I was going to need a good set of reviving hours to sleep off my "London Hangover of 2013." And, judging from the dark circles that were under his eyes, I knew *he* probably needed some shut-eye, too.

I pulled down the covers on the other side of the bed, fluffing up the pillows. "Come on," I gave him an inviting smile. "I need more sleep and you *definitely* could use a nap."

He sighed, giving me the once-over. "You get your rest. I'll come back up when I'm finished."

A yawn was my first reply, the jaw-movement giving my headache some unneeded encouragement. "'Kay," I told him and settled back into my nest of sheets and covers. "Don't be long."

I rolled over on my side, thinking about that conversation I'd overheard yesterday morning between him and his employee, Devon. It was none of my business. He was the boss after all. If anything, I now knew the "hot" buttons to avoid with him. Never embrace *motherhood!*

I slipped into a restful sleep, not even waking up when Easton returned and curled up beside me.

∞ ∞ ∞ ∞ ∞ ∞

I gazed down at Darcy, now resting peacefully. Thank. God! She'd kept me up nearly all night. If she wasn't puking, she was dry-heaving and then came the redundant questions:

'Where are we?'

'Am I drunk?'

'Why'd you beat the shit out of my friend Damian?'

'Are you mad at me, Easton?'

Over and over again, I had to reiterate the same answers to the redundant questions:

'We're at the manor.'

'You're totally shit-faced.'

'Because he deserved it.'

'I'm furious with you.'

Of course, the last answer had triggered the water-works, so then I was busy trying to calm her down, assuring her she was forgiven for the moment.

The last and certainly the most difficult question she'd asked before she closed her eyes:

'Easton, do you love me?'

I didn't want to hurt her. I wasn't about to have the waterworks start again right now. That was the question that caught me the most off-guard. Even after all the others and knowing that she was completely tossed, I wasn't expecting such a deep question. I had to consider she might not be pleased with the answer.

Blessedly, she'd passed out without hearing my answer.

Chapter 30

Thankfully, I was fully recovered Monday morning, no remnants of my killer hangover left. I swore off drinking forever! Easton said that was the hangover talking, but I meant it. Well, at least for a while anyway.

I'd bathed and eaten breakfast, thankful that Anna had returned to cook. The extent of my food intake yesterday was the dry toast and tea, then chicken broth and ginger-ale for dinner. Easton was punishing me, I think.

I dressed in a teal suit that was certain to please 'Mr. Conservative's' stringent inspection. My God! He'd tossed my new Lipso dress in the trash, telling me it was ruined from *'my sick'* (I think that's Brit for *'my puke'*). I'd argued it was machine washable, to which he replied that it would go in no machine of his!

I'd called Ronnie and Colin to apologize. She assured me there was no need. She said she'd had so much fun partying with me and wanted to do it again. I told her I'd better get an invitation to her September wedding. She assured me that I would.

Easton wanted to see me in his study before Dennis picked us up to take us to the private airstrip Easton had on his property.

"Can't we just walk?" I'd asked. He rolled his eyes, shaking his head.

"It's on the other side of the woods, nearly 5 kilometers," he chuckled.

"That far, huh?"

I have no fucking clue how that equates to miles.

"That's around three miles, Darcy."

"Of course."

I peered around the corner into his study. Easton was there, his gorgeous head of nearly-black hair still damp from his shower. He was dressed in business

225

casual. Apparently, he didn't think this meeting was important enough to warrant a business suit. Still, I wanted to look professional, since I'd be meeting some of the top management in the Leeds facility, according to him.

"Come on in Darcy, please have a seat. I've printed out the financials that'll be discussed in today's meeting. There are also some productivity charts and business trends for the past four years, along with the revenue projections for this year and first half of next year. Also, if you look here, I've charted the customer satisfaction responses year-to-year for the past four years. Take a few moments and study the charts and graphs for comparison. I want you to tell me what you derive from them when finished."

Oh God! I hate this kind of shit.

"Take your time and study them," he said getting up and coming from around his desk. "I need to speak with my pilot about our flight, so you have some time."

"Okay, great," I said, inwardly hoping I could make heads or tails of these charts and graphs. This was probably some kind of a test he was giving me. I cleared my mind and separated the charts/graphs into separate stacks, based on what metric they represented. Finished there, I then put them in chronological order to see the changes or trends. I studied them glancing back and forth between each group in chronological order. I pulled my steno pad out of my briefcase and jotted some notes. It wasn't rocket science, once I understood what I was looking for.

Easton returned a few minutes later, taking his seat, leaning back in his leather chair, crossing his arms and giving me a wicked smile. "I'm ready for your high-level analysis, Ms. Sheridan," he said.

"According to these charts, it appears that Leeds has had year-over-year revenue growth in the first three years of the data provided. In Year 4, the revenue had no growth or loss, but the gross profits declined about 7% in direct proportion to the drop on the productivity chart for the same period."

"Excellent," he said, rubbing his chin. "That shows me you can read the graphs, but I want more. I want you to think like a manager. What might the possible causes be for revenue to stay the same, but profits declining along with productivity?"

"Well," I said, trying to remember what I'd learned in Cost Accounting at school. "It could be a result of payroll increases, overhead increases, or material costs, or a combination of those and the product pricing remaining the same?"

"Is that a question or an answer?"

Good God, is he about to give me detention?

"I guess they're some possibilities to consider."

"Alright, then let's dig a little deeper and tell me how the slip in productivity may be explained."

"Increases in overtime premiums, issues with absenteeism, employee turnover, paid medical leaves—I guess there could be others, but those are the ones that come to mind."

"Let me stop you right there, Darcy. You've nailed it nicely. What about the rest? The customer satisfaction surveys and revenue projections?"

"The customer satisfaction graphs were all stable. There's nothing there to indicate the performance at Leeds, as far as quality and delivery, has slipped. The forecast projections going forward puzzled me, to be honest. It looks like sales are going to drop off by £4.5 million the second half of this year—and £9 million next year."

"What does that indicate?"

"Lost business," I replied with a shrug.

"Exactly," he replied, gracing me with his smile. I beamed, feeling as if I'd won a prize for my answer. I figured he should be pissed about losing a chunk of business like that, not happy that I got it.

"Why is it important to you that I understand all of this right now? You aren't thinking about promoting me, are you?"

"Don't be ridiculous," he said.

Okay, that one stung a little...

"It's for the purpose of you understanding the reason for this meeting this afternoon and the actions necessary to stop the bleeding in Leeds."

"What actions are you taking?" I asked, not quite sure I wanted or needed to know.

"I'm going to be cleaning house. You see, the reason this facility lost what should've been a sure thing on a government renewal contract representing £9 million in annual revenue is failure to submit the bid package before the deadline."

"Wait a minute. Does this have something to do with the conversation I overheard yesterday between you and someone named Devon?" I blurted out.

"That's right," he said, resuming a business-like tone, steepling his hands under his chin. "Devon Roberts is the current General Manager at Leeds."

"The one you told that women whelp in the middle of rice paddies and then continue harvesting without skipping a beat. I see. So, she's in trouble for the loss of the government contract?" I asked, tapping my fingers impatiently on the top of his desk.

"Yes, one and the same. She bears responsibility for ensuring that bids are completed and submitted in a timely fashion. That did not happen." He swiveled in his chair, turning from me.

"Whoa, hold up there a minute. Are you telling me that Leeds is a 'One Woman Show?'?"

"I don't follow," he replied, furrowing his brow.

"It sounded like she'd been off on maternity leave when this happened."

"You must have heard the whole damn conversation, Darcy," he remarked, turning his attention back to his monitor.

"I heard enough," I replied. "So, is that correct? She was off on medical leave when the bid package was due for submission?"

"It is," he replied, stiffly.

"Well, let me ask you this then, isn't there a Marketing or Contracts Manager at Leeds who prepares the bid package? I mean, that's how it's done at Sheridan & Associates," I snapped, tilting my chin up ever-so-slightly.

"Baronton-Sheridan," he corrected, giving me a slight glare. "And yes, there's a Contracts Manager at Leeds."

"Uh huh," I replied. "Name please?"

"Clive Biser," he replied, frowning.

"So, are you going to terminate Clive during your visit today?"

"No, Clive was traveling in North America when this occurred. He'd given the preliminary data to his department supervisor to delegate to one of the administrators to audit, and then prepare for submission, once the terms and conditions were in compliance."

"Okay, so the way I see it, you're holding Devon's feet to the fire for a misstep that happened while she was out on an approved medical leave for something that wasn't under her direct control at the time."

"Being on maternity leave doesn't relieve Devon from the responsibilities of her position with the company. It wasn't as if she didn't have ample notice that she'd be gone for a period of time. Nine months' notice is sufficient for her to make sure she had an executable plan in place, assign an interim manager during her absence, and schedule teleconferences to ensure that the schedule was not slipping on anything. My God, in this day of internet magic, lack of communication isn't a viable excuse."

"Dear God! The woman worked up to her due date?"

"Yes, pretty much."

I crossed my legs and leaned forward in my chair. "So, she gives birth, and then you expect her to focus on what's going on at the company while she's recovering and taking care of a newborn to boot? I mean, it sounds as if she had a plan that simply wasn't executed. Who was the interim GM?"

"Clive Biser."

"So, Clive dropped the ball, not Devon."

"Clive got called out unexpectedly for two weeks to represent Baronton on a bidding war for a new contract with British Petroleum in Canada. He was the only one qualified to go."

"Okay, so who was to serve while he was gone for two weeks to make sure everything on his "to do" list got done?

This is like pulling fucking teeth!

"Lacee."

What. The. Fuck.

"What?"

"This is getting quite tedious, Darcy. I'm not in the habit of explaining my decisions to a trainee. We need to be off," he said, glancing at his watch, mentally brushing me off.

"Wait!" I screeched, much louder than intended. He stopped, whirling around to glare at me.

"What now?" he asked tersely (and rudely).

"I'm not going," I replied flatly, crossing my arms in front of me, taking a haughty stance.

"I beg your pardon?" His expression was stuck between puzzled and pissed.

"I'm not going until you unravel the rest of this little mystery for me. First off, what would give Lacee the qualifications to fill-in as an interim GM at one of your facilities? Secondly, if she was the appointed responsible person, why aren't you firing her ass?"

He gave a very audible, very frustrated sigh, rolling his beautiful gray eyes.

"Of course, Darcy, why shouldn't I explain myself to you? Lacee's well-equipped with that particular business segment because she worked there before working for me. She knows the products, the staff, and the contracts. The company was originally located in the U.S. When I purchased it, I had it moved to Leeds to be closer to the other sites in that particular market. Lacee was on the transition team put into place in Roanoke, Virginia, where it was originally located."

"Okay—makes sense," I mulled that over and found myself agreeing. "Continue."

"There were enough managers on site to oversee the other functional areas in Clive's absence. Lacee was simply to make sure everything on his "To Do" list, as you called it, was executed on time. If something went amiss, she was to contact me directly so that I could intervene."

"You mean chew someone's ass?"

"Exactly." He hesitated briefly, collecting his thoughts to explain the rest. "Anyway, Lacee never got there because that was around the time we acquired Sheridan and I assigned her to the transition team there, because of her past experience."

Wow!

"Then in all fairness, *you* were the cause of the miscommunication in this internet magic age, Easton. You pulled Lacee off that assignment without clearing it through anyone at Leeds."

"I fucking own the company, dammit. I don't have to clear anything with anyone, now let's go."

Oh hell no—did he just yell at me?

"No," I replied, my voice direct and calm.

His eyes narrowed as he studied my face. "What do you mean, *no?*"

"I know it's not a word that you're used to hearing. It means 'nada,' 'negatory,' 'nope,' or 'ain't happening.' Take your pick."

"I'm afraid you don't have a choice in the matter. This is part of your training curriculum, so you'll accompany me there as a trainee."

"No. I'm not going. You can fire me if you want for insubordination or refusal to adhere to a direct order—whatever. Then, you can fire yourself, because you're the one that fucked up. You're the one not willing to take

231

responsibility for that. I won't be part of a company that has so little regard for their employees. The woman gave birth! It sounds to me as if *that's* the part you find intolerable, and you're punishing her for that if you fire her. I don't know British law, but I hope she sues the fuck out of you."

I turned to leave and he reached out, grabbing my arm as I started to leave. "I own the company, Ms. Sheridan, I'm hard-pressed to fire myself," he laughed.

"Then I guess you're the only one that doesn't play by your own rules. I think they call that hypocrisy, *love*. I won't be a part of this because it's *wrong*. Plain and simple*: wrong!"*

I jerked my arm out of his grasp and fled to the staircase where I managed to get to my suite, slamming the door and locking it, just in case he wanted to go all "caveman" on me.

I went into the closet, grabbing all my clothes and shoes, shoving them into my luggage as quickly as possible. I packed my make-up and toiletries, looking in every room of my suite to make sure I hadn't missed anything. I then pulled out a pair of jeans and a sweater, changing quickly, locating my Nikes and slipping them on. I crammed my suit, blouse and shoes into the suitcase, fastening the locks. I dug out the original itinerary for the return back to D.C. It wasn't leaving until 4:00 this afternoon. It was only a little before noon. I knew the tickets were non-refundable, so they were still valid.

Just then, there was a tapping on my door.

"I meant what I said. I'm not going."

"Miss," I heard Anna's calm voice."May I come in?"

Now I felt like a real idiot.

"Of course," I called out, sitting on my bed with my luggage.

"Mr. Matthews has departed for the air strip. He asked that I see to your comfort until he returns late this afternoon. Is there anything I can get for you?"

"Yes, Anna, there is. When Dennis returns from dropping off Easton, I'll need a ride to Heathrow please."

She looked undecided. I didn't care. Easton Matthews wasn't going to keep me prisoner in his estate all day in order to dole out some form of punishment upon his return. I had stood up to him on a matter I felt passionate about. I wouldn't work for someone who had so little regard for employees. 'Family Atmosphere' my ass!

"Are you sure that's what you want to do, Miss? I think Mr. Matthews is expecting you to be here when he returns."

"I've never been more certain of anything in my life, Anna. If it's a problem, I can call another limo service."

"Oh no, no, Miss. It's not a problem whatsoever. Dennis should be back in about ten minutes. So, if you're ready, I'll take your bags down."

"No, Anna, I can get them," I said, lifting my biggest suitcase off of the bed.

"How about we both get them?" she asked, smiling at me.

Within fifteen minutes, limo packed with my luggage, Dennis was cruising the distance from Greystone Manor to Heathrow Airport. I was so ready to go home, to forget this whole trip to London (well, except for the *really* good parts). I wasn't too thrilled about the fact that, once again, Easton and I were in 'no man's land.' That whole conversation we had in his study was a bunch of bullshit. He made it look *easy* firing a woman while blaming it on the fact that, by getting knocked-up, she just wasn't living up to his professional standards.

And to me?

That wasn't okay.

Chapter 31

I was exhausted once I got back to D.C. I didn't even care to discuss with Eli the details of the drama that had unfolded over my long weekend in London. I gave him short to the point 'yes' or 'no' answers to his questions.

"Hey, uhh…Darce?" I heard Eli say, as I was flipping through channels, taking all of my passive aggression out on the T.V. remote.

"Yeah," I responded, distracted by a reality show where people were secretly using their neighbors clothes to make quilts. *Okay, really?* I sighed, and began shuffling through channels quickly again.

I then felt Eli's hands as he swiftly grabbed the remote from me. "Okay. You don't want to talk about how you came back from London, apparently with this new hobby of trying to suck the positive energy out of every room you walk into? That's fine. But for the love of *God*, don't take it out on the remote." He held it up in front of him. "It's pretty. And I like it."

"It's like this," I said with a sigh, "Easton Matthews isn't a person I care to have mentoring me, or fucking me, for that matter. I guess I had my eyes wide open just as you advised I should and I didn't like what I saw."

"So, what happens now?" he asked, a frown creasing his forehead.

"I find another job because I'm pretty sure I'm fired."

"He fired you?"

"Not officially," I shrugged, heading up the stairs to my room. "But, I defied him, so it's imminent, I'm sure. I don't want to show up tomorrow and have it made official with an audience, that's for damn sure."

"Does your dad know about any of this?" he asked.

"Hardly. He and Mom are still on their cruise. They won't be back for a couple of weeks yet. It doesn't matter anyway. My father doesn't have controlling interest in his company anymore. It's Easton's company, for all intents and purposes. I'm beat. See you when you get home from work tomorrow."

"Don't worry, Darce," he called up after me. "It'll work out."

I crawled into my bed, exhausted, wanting nothing more than to put all thoughts and memories of Easton Matthews out of my mind for the moment and maybe even forever.

∞ ∞ ∞ ∞ ∞ ∞

The rest of the week went by swiftly. I was busy registering with employment agencies and recruiters, though my brief stint at Sheridan & Associates, n.k.a. Baronton-Sheridan caused more problems being on my resume than if I'd left it off. The recruiters wanted to know why I'd left. I was reluctant to tell them I was fired for insubordination, so I simply stated there were 'creative differences.'

It didn't matter. I was still considered unskilled labor.

Eli said neither Colin nor Easton had been at the site all week. Apparently, Lacee was holding the fort down with the rest of the Baronton transition team this week.

Lovely. I wonder what the fuck she's been told.

On Friday morning, I received a phone call from Colin. He was still in London and wanted to know why I'd been a no-show at work all week. Lacee had apparently contacted him.

"Didn't Easton tell you?" I asked, puzzled.

"Tell me what?" he asked.

Yeah, right.

"I'm pretty sure I've been terminated, Colin. I refused to be a part of terminating Devon Roberts and declined to make the trip to Leeds with Easton. Haven't you talked to him?"

"Yes, briefly, several times, though he said nothing to me about your termination. I think perhaps you've jumped to a conclusion prematurely. Easton's in France at the moment, but he'll be back in D.C. this weekend. He's assigned me to the Leeds facility for the next couple of months. He's returning to Baronton-Sheridan to take over again until I'm freed up or he's assigned a new GM in D.C. Do you plan to go back to work?"

Holy shit! Easton must've gone ahead and fired Devon. Bastard.

"I'm not sure, Colin. I may not be cut out for a leadership career. At the very least, I'm pretty sure I'm not cut out to be cut-throat and ruthless."

I could hear Colin's chuckle on the other end. "Well, now that's certainly your decision to make, but the right thing for you to do is to at least go into the office on Monday and approach Easton with your concerns. If you decide to resign, then don't you agree that it should be done in a mature and professional manner?"

"I guess so," I replied, not looking forward to having to face Easton again.

"Splendid," he replied. "I'll let Easton know you'll be in on Monday and that you have some issues to discuss. Oh, and Ronnie sends her regards."

"Yeah, thanks. Give Ronnie my best."

I'm definitely not looking forward to Monday.

Chapter 32

I was sitting on the other side of Easton's massive desk, feeling his cool gray eyes boring into me with dissatisfaction. He was waiting for an explanation. There was dead silence at the moment. His hands were steepled under his chin as he continued to give me his steely stare.

"I don't know what you want me to say, Easton. I told you last week I wanted no part of whatever disciplinary action you planned on unleashing at the Leeds facility. I made that decision. I don't regret making that decision, and if I had it to do over again, I wouldn't do anything differently. So, I guess if you want to fire me, go for it."

He stood up and in three angry strides was in front of my chair, glaring down at me.

"We have a problem, Ms. Sheridan," he sneered. "I'm contractually bound to mentor and see to it that you're brought to your full potential as a manager and leader. This involves doing things that are sometimes difficult and unpleasant. You flatly refused to do something that was required of you last week. You defied my instructions and then left London before you were supposed to leave. Additionally, you chose not to show up for work here the rest of the week, not bothering to call Colin or myself to explain your rationale for that. That shows a lack of professionalism and maturity. Bundle it all together and it's pure insubordination and defiance. I don't tolerate that with anyone."

I didn't like that he was staring down at me. It served to make me feel that much more subservient, and gave him even more empowerment which, of course, is what he relished. I stood up, crossing my arms, and stared up into his eyes with my own.

"Too bad I wasn't on maternity leave. You could've used *that* excuse to fire me," I told him with a smile.

I seriously think I saw his jaw clench. But that didn't stop me from continuing because I damn sure had a point to drive home.

237

"Doing things that are difficult and unpleasant? Is that what you just said to me? I don't think you find that sort of thing unpleasant at all. I think you enjoy doling out punishment, in particular, punishing *women*. I think it gives you extreme pleasure and gratification," I said to him cockily, watching his eyes darken in anger.

"Oh really?" he asked, quirking a brow, "and what do you base this conjecture on, might I ask?"

"On my observations of you in action," I replied casually.

"Indeed," he quipped, a half-smile, half-sneer gracing his lips.

"Uh huh," I replied, saucily. "I've seen it in how you handle employees and how you handle bedmates. Trust me; I don't think my father had any clue about the type of *mentoring* you had in mind when you negotiated this merger with him."

I'm just daring him to fire my ass!

I knew immediately I'd hit a nerve when I saw his eyes darken. Maybe I shouldn't have gone as far as I had, but he needed to know I knew what he was about. I knew he wanted me at Baronton-Sheridan. I also knew he wanted me in the sack again. Apart from those two things, I had no doubt he needed to punish me for my refusal to carry out a direct order. I'd been insubordinate and there was no way in hell he'd let that go unpunished.

"You present quite a challenge here. I'm bound to fulfill my part of the agreement, yet I simply cannot make exceptions, even for you, when you so flagrantly disregard my instructions and behave insubordinately to a superior. Disciplinary action up to and including termination is standard recourse. I've not decided exactly what course of action to take with you at the moment. I've decided it requires more consideration. In the meantime, you are to resume your normal duties. I'll get back with you once I've made my decision as to what's appropriate disciplinary action."

That's it?

"That's it?"

"For now," he stated, "you may get back to work. You've got quite a backlog waiting."

He turned from me and I knew I was dismissed. I left his office, feeling both relieved and apprehensive. I was spared the humiliation of being fired from my father's own company, yet now I was forced to stress over what his final decision would be on the disciplinary action that was under consideration. I guess I'd simply have to sweat it out and hope for the best.

True to his word, I had a helluva backlog to work on and was thankful because it kept me busy. It also kept me from stewing over what he might have in store for me and it made the day pass quickly.

Eli stopped by my office around lunch time, asking if I wanted to grab a burger with him. I peered up at him over the stacks of correspondence, invoices and expense reports needing Easton's signature and shook my head.

"Can't," I said. "I'm swamped, so I'm working through lunch today."

"So, at least you've still got your job, right?"

"For now," I whispered, nodding towards Easton's open office door. "Not sure what my punishment's going to be. He hasn't decided yet."

"Uh huh," Eli replied, rolling his eyes, "Bet you'll need two inflatable donuts when he's finished doling it out."

"Shhhh," I hissed, shooing him away. "We'll talk later," I whispered. "I don't need to make him any more pissed than he already is."

"Kay-kay—see ya at the crib later."

Thirty seconds after Eli had departed, Lacee came into my office. She plopped down on one of the visitor chairs, crossing her legs. The tiny, tight skirt she'd worn barely covered the top of her thighs. She looked as if she'd taken extra pains with her hair and make-up today. Was she trying to get me to notice how enticing she presumed she was?

"May I help you?" I asked, looking up from my computer to see what the hell she wanted.

She glanced at her watch. "No, I'm a couple of minutes early. I'll just chill here for a minute."

Why don't you chill like, oh maybe somewhere in ALASKA?

I glanced at Easton's schedule and he didn't have her set up for any meetings today. Just as I was about to open my mouth to ask her the reason for her chill stop in my particular office, Easton came through the doorway.

"Ready?" he asked, presenting her with his award-winning smile."

"Yep," she answered, smiling adoringly back at him.

"Darcy—cover my calls, please. My mobile's going to be off during lunch."

I looked quickly over at Lacee and saw the smug grin on her face right before she turned and followed Easton down the hall towards the lobby.

Fucking son-of-a-bitch, man-whore, shit-stain, ass-hat!

I felt my cheeks burning with anger at the obvious implications of their "lunch date."

Lunch date? Hah! I hoped Lacee took her own advice and had a supply of disposable douches handy, so the rest of us wouldn't be exposed to the smell of sex all fucking afternoon!

Being infuriated was actually a boost to my productivity, I discovered. I bulldozed through the stack of work on my desk, finishing most everything up by two o'clock, noticing that Easton had yet to return from his lunch date. I started filing things away and got a call around two-thirty from Easton.

"Darcy, I won't be back in the office this afternoon," he said. "Did I have anything scheduled? I forgot to look before I left."

"One moment please while I check," I replied, coolly. I glanced down at his schedule and saw he had a 4:15 with Nelson Pratt, the Manager of H.R. Probably to get input on the appropriate disciplinary action to take with me. Nelson was part of Easton's beloved transition team.

I pushed the hold button, speaking into my desk phone. "You're all clear," I lied.

"Splendid," he said. "Are you making good progress on catching up?"

"I'm nearly caught up," I replied. "Just working on a week's worth of filing."

"Okay then. Good to know. I'll see you tomorrow."

"Yep," I said, ending the call.

Well, I guess he'd made it perfectly clear he was worn-out from his two-hour nooner fuck-fest with Lacee. I dug through my inbox and saw that he'd signed off on one of Lacee's travel expense reports. Maybe I should go ahead and hand-deliver it to the skank to make sure she didn't reek of sex. I'd love to throw a disposable douche in her face right about now.

I went upstairs to the offices the transition team from Baronton was using. I went down the aisles of all the cubicles until I came to hers. It was empty. Her computer was shut down, and it looked as if her desk was cleaned off.

Strange…

Just then, I saw Jason Lipscomb, one of the other transition team members coming down the aisle. His cubicle was next to Lacee's.

"Hi, Darcy," he greeted with a smile. "Looking for someone?"

"Yeah, actually," I replied as I looked back at Lacee's empty desk. "There were some questions on Lacee's latest expense report; I needed some clarification."

He got a weird expression on his face. "Oh, uh, well she's not here at the moment. She called in a little while ago and said she wouldn't be back today."

"Huh," I probably said a little too eagerly, as I tried to cover up the look of surprise on my face. "Well, I guess it can wait until tomorrow. I'll get with her then." I made sure I finished with a smile.

"Why don't you just leave it on her desk with a note of what needs clarification? That way, you won't have to make another trip up here," he suggested. "Or, if you want to tell me, I can let her know. She may be calling in later today."

"No, no—that's okay," I said. "I might be able to figure it out myself."

Again, he gave me a funny look as I made a quick departure down the hallway to the stairs.

How fucking obvious were those two? I was going to let Daddy know he'd made a monumental mistake selling off controlling interest to that man-whore with his little harem.

I stomped back downstairs and filed the rest of afternoon, furiously cramming invoices and purchase order copies into overloaded files.

Around 4:00 my cell rang. Oh shit, it was Lindsey.

"Hey," I said, trying to sound way more chipper than I felt.

"Hey yourself," she said. "How's it going? How was England?"

I couldn't hide this from her and I kinda needed to do some venting of my own. And who's a better sounding board than a girl's double-x-chromosome-carrying best friend, right?

"Oh, you know…," I drawled. "I wore the perfume I stole from you two Christmases ago for my presentation; the weather was okay. I think I may have almost OD'd on British hooch, and yeah, I slept with a guy who I promised myself I'd let go of, found out that he may just be a misogynistic asshole—who, by the way, happens to be the same guy that signs my paychecks. Oh, and I had some *amazing* sushi today for lunch. So, how's it going with you?" I studied my nails, allowing her to catch up.

4…

3…

2…

1…

"What?!" she shrieked, as only Lindsey could. "It wasn't my Dolce and Gabbana perfume, was it? Because I've been looking everywhere for it. I thought maybe I'd left it at—"

"Linds." I brought her back.

I heard her sigh through the phone. "I know, it's Easton. And I just have one question for you, Darcy Nicole. Why in the *hell* would you ask for seconds with a guy like that?"

I gave her a petulant scowl. I know she couldn't see me, but I felt that it added effect all the same. "What do you *mean* a guy like *that*?"

"Umm? A guy who we literally caught at my rehearsal dinner, screwing his assistant? And then a couple of weeks later he merges his company with your dad's, promoting you as his *new* assistant. You know—*that* guy? And I know he's my half brother-in-law and everything, but what were you thinking?"

Leave it to good ol' Lindsey to restate the obvious.

"It's complicated," I explained lamely.

"Well," was her reply, "I talked to Jill yesterday, and she'll be in town tomorrow night. Taz has baby detail, so maybe you'll be able to explain your complicated love life to the both of us at dinner tomorrow? We'll have drinks and you can unload the whole shebang to us. Deal?"

"Hell yeah," I said, clicking and dragging another file to its parental folder. "Same rules apply: Jill covers valet and overall tips, you buy drinks, and I buy dinner?"

"Yep!" Lindsey confirmed. "Oh, and this can't wait until tomorrow. Guess who's been asking Taz about you?"

"Santa Claus," I stage-whispered into my cell. "Yeah…London kind of put me on the naughty list."

"Save it for tomorrow night, lovely," Lindsey responded. "No. *Darin* asked about you."

Whaaat?

"Why?" I asked.

"I guess he's been desperately lost without you," she told me with stage effects of her own. "He's been trying to get Taz to talk to me so that I'd talk to you."

I mulled that one over.

Lindsey continued, "You know, at least he's admitting his mistake. Doesn't everyone deserve a second chance? I mean, you *did* kind of give Easton one."

Low blow.

I tried to close my gaping mouth. "Oh come on, Linds. Totally different scenarios. Easton and I…we were just physical. *Darin and I*, on the other hand, well, I was with him for how long?"

A couple of seconds went by. "You're rolling your eyes, aren't you?" I asked/accused.

"Damn, you're good," she acknowledged with a laugh. "Can I at least tell Taz that I did say something to you?"

"Whatevs," I told her, already a little mentally exhausted at the thought. "I really don't give a shit. But for the record, I don't see Darin and I going anywhere."

"You never can tell," she countered in her sing-song voice. "Meet us at Busbee's around six tomorrow night, okay?"

"I'll be there." I hit END-call.

Several minutes later, Nelson Pratt was in my office to keep his 4:15 appointment with Easton.

"He's not here," I said, as I walked over to the file cabinet.

"We had a 4:15 appointment," Nelson replied, frowning.

Duh!

"He must've forgotten, Nelson. He left with a female employee for lunch and hasn't returned."

There. That ought to stir some shit...

"I see," he said, obviously perplexed. "That's odd. Nevertheless, I guess I'll catch him tomorrow."

I finished up in the office and then headed home where I filled Eli in on everything that'd happened after he'd stopped by at lunch.

"No!" he said, obviously aghast at the situation.

"Oh yeah," I replied, shaking my head. "Do you believe he's tapping that again?"

"Honey," he said, taking my hand into his consolingly, "men can be real pigs at times. There's no doubt about it. I'm glad you're going out with the girls tomorrow night."

"I guess," I replied. "Right now I just need my girl buddies to help me with...*whatever* this is."

"Hey, what am I?"

"You're my *brotha* from *anotha*." I tossed him a huge smile and an even bigger wink.

Chapter 33

~ Easton ~

Today was royally fucked. There was no other way to describe it. I was starting to wonder why I simply didn't thoroughly clean house with all of my holdings, and make it a 'male-only' corporation. Females, with their constant struggles with hormonal imbalance, mood swings and overall bitchiness, were tiring.

I'd been hit with Darcy's hostility first thing this morning on an issue where she was clearly at fault. She was lucky we weren't in the bedroom. My palm had been twitching to find itself against the soft skin of her arse at full velocity in response to the haughty attitude she presented. I would have to think long and hard about an appropriate disciplinary action for her behaviour and insubordination.

Then, the lunch with Lacee clearly wasn't what she'd expected. I knew immediately with the way she was dressed and made up she figured I was re-inviting her into my life and into my bed. Not even close. I'd decided to invite her to lunch in order to deliver the news of the disciplinary action I was imposing, based on the information I received from Devon Roberts. I'd learned during my visit to Leeds that Lacee had assured Devon that she'd call in daily to Leeds while Devon was out. Lacee had promised her she would apprise me if there were issues in meeting deadlines or if anything was slipping. That hadn't happened. What's more, when one of the entry-level admins called Lacee to raise the red flag on the Turkish bid proposal not being finished, she'd deliberately kept it from me.

Lacee hadn't taken it well when I gave her ten days off without pay and advised her that a letter of reprimand was going into her personnel file. She'd barely contained herself in the restaurant, grabbing her handbag and storming out, mumbling profanity the whole way.

I took another sip of my bourbon and branch, relaxing against the sofa in my hotel room, trying to chill out and gather my thoughts. It was damn difficult working around Darcy again and keeping my dick from rising to the occasion every time she sashayed in and out of my office. Fuck. I couldn't keep my eyes off of her when she was leaning over to open a file drawer. I'd purposely moved all of the expense files to the bottom drawer of the filing cabinet in my office for that very reason. I enjoyed the view while she was filing.

Yeah—I know. I'm a pig, but what's the harm in appreciating her fine ass as much as possible?

She was so damn prickly with me in London, taking off like that when she knew damn well I needed to clue her in on what it takes to be a manager and eventually a leader. The first lesson she needed to learn was to take orders. I could tell she wasn't accustomed to that, but then again, her old man had given me fair warning. This morning she'd acted like she wanted me to fire her ass, almost daring me to do it. Fuck that! Darcy Nicole Sheridan wasn't going anywhere yet.

My mobile rang and I saw it was Nelson Pratt.

Bloody Christ! What now?

"Nelson," I answered, "what can I do for you?"

"Sorry to bother you after hours, Easton, but I'm not going to be in the office until after lunch tomorrow. I wanted to see if you were available in the afternoon to reschedule our meeting relative to the letter we're putting in Lacee's permanent file."

Reschedule?

"I'm sorry, Nelson, I'm at a loss. Did I miss an appointment?"

"No worries," he was quick to answer. "We were supposed to meet today at 4:15. Your assistant said you'd forgotten about it and hadn't returned from…uh…a long lunch when I went down to your office."

The little vixen. She'd said my schedule was clear for the day…

"Sorry, Nelson. Apparently, Darcy and I got our wires crossed. Yes, we can meet tomorrow. I gave Lacee the news that she's getting a couple of weeks off at lunch today. I felt it best to deliver that in a public place, off site."

"Very good point," he replied. "So, then we'll finish the letter tomorrow afternoon?"

"Certainly. Stop down anytime. I'm at your disposal."

I smiled after we ended our call. Darcy was an addictive girl who was addicted to trouble, it seemed.

I got up and refilled my glass, dropping a few more cubes of ice into it.

Well, she'd definitely found some.

Chapter 34

I took pains with my work attire the following morning. It wasn't as easy as the magazines made it sound, going from office attire to after-five attire without changing outfits. Since I was meeting Lindsey and Jill downtown, there was no time to leave work to run home and change before six o'clock.

I selected a form-fitting red knit dress and accessorized it with a red and black print bolero jacket that would hide the fact that the dress had spaghetti straps and a snug bust line, making it totally a cocktail dress without it. I pulled my hair up into a ponytail, not wanting to fuck with it since I'd overslept a bit this morning. I shoved a pair of fuck-me shoes into my over-sized shoulder bag and slipped on a pair of sensible pumps for the office. I made sure my make-up case was in my bag so I could at least freshen-up before leaving the office. It wouldn't do for Lindsey or Jill to think Darcy Sheridan was less than well-coiffed these days.

Eli had left for his morning ritual at Starbuck's. It was his damn fault that I'd overslept! He'd invited Cain for a sleepover and their fuckfest had kept me awake for hours. I'd grab some strong coffee at work. Maybe I was just grumpy because everyone I loved had someone and I had no one. Maybe it wasn't all that crazy to consider talking to Darin again. I mean, was there really any harm in hearing what he had to say?

Easton was already in his office when I arrived at work. I could hear him on a conference call with some of his GMs over in the U.K. I loved listening to the British banter usually, but this morning I was in major need of caffeine. I slipped down to the cafeteria to fill my mug and saw Eli talking to one of the transition team peeps. I smiled and shook my head as I filled my mug. Eli and his friggin' gossip.

As I turned to walk back towards the hallway, I heard him call out.

"Darce, hold up," he said, catching up to me, looking all perky and well-rested.

Pshhh—yeah, right!

"I'm surprised you can move that quickly this morning, Eli," I said, taking a sip of my hot coffee.

He blew me an air kiss. "Good morning to you my gorgeous, jealous friend." Glancing around him, he quickly added, "But never mind that, I just heard a very juicy tidbit from Rochelle over on the transition team."

"Do tell," I said, continuing down the hall.

"Well, you know when you were pissing and whining last night while Maddox and I were trying to watch The Real Housewives' of *Wherever* about Easton doing the nasty with Lacee on his lunch break?"

He definitely had my attention now. I stopped dead in my tracks, coffee sloshing over the side of my mug.

"Yes?"

"Didn't happen," he replied, a smug look on his face.

"Okaaaay, and you know this how?"

"Well, Rochelle's fucking Nelson Pratt, and—"

"Ewww!" I interjected, not really loving the visual I was getting on that.

"Shhh," he said. "Let me finish, please?"

"Sorry, yeah that was just *not* a way to start a sentence." I closed my eyes, wishing I could burn my corneas. "Continue."

"Well, apparently last night's pillow talk shed some light on the lunch date Lacee had with Easton. He took her to lunch so he could let her know she's being given two weeks off with no pay and having a formal letter of reprimand put in her permanent personnel file. She evidently fucked something up at the Leeds facility. Nelson was supposed to get with Easton yesterday to finalize the letter, but I guess Easton missed the meeting, so they're wrapping it up today."

Oh…Shit.

Eli noticed my expression and frowned. "I thought you'd think that was good news," he said, not hiding his disappointment.

"Oh sorry, Eli, yeah of course it's good news, I guess. No, wait a minute. Why the fuck should I care?"

He rolled his eyes at me, shaking his head. "Which is it Darce? Good news? Or you don't give a shit?"

"I don't know. I'm not sure anymore. We'll talk later," I said, turning off to the hallway that led to the executive offices.

"Have a nice day," he called out after me, still sounding all chipper for someone that hadn't gotten much sleep, but for the right reasons.

Bitch!

Once I was settled at my desk and signed onto my computer, I saw I had an e-mail from Easton. It was short and didn't sound very sweet.

'Would you kindly step into my office, Ms. Sheridan'

Thaaaat's not good.

I downed the rest of my coffee as liquid courage and grabbed my notebook and pen, heading into his office. He didn't bother to look away from his laptop, but he knew I was there.

"Take a seat, Darcy," he said. "I just need to finish this last sentence."

I sat down, crossed my legs, and waited. Several moments later, he stopped pecking on his laptop and turned his attention to me. His gray eyes flickered over me, as if he was seeing me again for the first time. He folded his hands on his desk in front of him and looked me in the eye. I couldn't read his mood.

"When I called in yesterday, I was given the information by you that my schedule was clear all afternoon. As it turns out, it wasn't. I missed a meeting with Nelson Pratt at 4:15. He called me last evening to re-schedule."

The butterflies were back, doing nervous somersaults in my stomach.

"Oh, really?" I asked, feigning self-disappointment with a sprinkle of surprise."You know, I bet I had the wrong day pulled up on your calendar." I

251

looked down at the floor, trying to appear repentant for making a mistake. "I'm so sorry, Easton."

He quirked an eyebrow at me, trying to decide whether he believed me or not and remained silent as I squirmed in my seat.

He's giving me the rope to hang myself. Bastard!

The silence and his perusal of me lingered until I couldn't stand it another second.

I broke. "Okay! So, I told you that your afternoon was clear yesterday when you called. I told Nelson you'd forgotten; I admit it. Happy? You can stop giving me the hairy eyeball now."

"Why would you do that?" he asked, studying me carefully.

I paused for a couple of moments, not because I didn't know the answer, but because I didn't want *him* to know.

"It's complicated," I replied, those words evidently becoming my own personal mantra these days. "I'd prefer if we could simply drop the subject. I apologize. I was wrong and it was extremely immature of me."

"I still want to know why."

If I was a woman of prayer—this is totally where I'd use it.

"Okay, fine. I thought Nelson was meeting with you to discuss what type of disciplinary action you intended to take against...me."

"And," he said, waiting for me to continue, his eyes boring into me. "There has to be more to it."

I breathed a heavy sigh. "*And* because I thought you and Lacee were having a...nooner."

"A what?"

"Hooking up during your lunch hour," I snapped.

I saw a flicker of amusement in his eyes as he stood up, placing his knuckles on the desk and leaning forward so that he was gazing down at me beneath those thick, sooty lashes.

"And would that bother you?"

I narrowed my eyes at him. "Truthfully? Yes, it bothered me yesterday. It doesn't today."

He cocked his eyebrow, which apparently was becoming his own personal non-verbal slogan with me. "I see," he replied, "So, you've had time to come to terms with the fact you've no claim on me, and I'm perfectly free to *hook-up* with whomever I choose? Glad to see we're on the same page, love."

"Well…," I stammered, "that's not exactly the case, but you know, whatever gets you through the night, Easton. I mean, we're both free to hook-up with whomever we want; that's always been the rule. It's just that you and I— well, *we* won't be hooking up…anymore." I saw him freeze momentarily. He was usually so good at hiding his emotions, but this had clearly caught him off-guard.

"I'm not certain that's your decision to make," he replied casually.

Fuck me! He DID not just say that?

I stood up now, and placed my knuckles on his desk, leaning forward in a show of defiance, giving him a glare that I'd mastered in third grade.

"It most certainly is my decision to make and I've made it, Mr. Matthews," I spat. "Unless you plan on forcing yourself on me. Cuff anyone to a bed lately?"

She shoots and…Scores!

He gazed down at me with shuttered eyes, making a show of studying his hands and using his fingers to rub his palm. "Trust me, love, you take to my cock like a fish takes to water. If ever I force myself on you, it'll be because you begged me for it that way."

I felt my cheeks flush with color at the confidence with which he made the statement.

"Are we through here?" I asked.

"For now," he replied, not taking his eyes off of mine.

I made a hasty retreat back to my office, slamming his door behind me. I didn't want to see him, hear him, or smell his masculine scent at the moment. His fucking audacity was boundless. All of a sudden, Darin Murphy was looking better and better.

I got through my morning routine without having to lay eyes on Easton again. His office had a door that led into mine and another one that led to the main hallway, so thankfully he was using that one and staying out of my way.

Right before lunch, my phone rang. It was Betty at reception telling me I had a delivery in the lobby.

"What is it?" I asked, puzzled.

"Come and see for yourself," she said mischievously.

When I got to the reception lobby, Betty nodded to the table behind her desk. There was a gorgeous bouquet of two dozen red roses in a beautiful crystal vase sitting there.

"For me?" I felt my eyes widen to the size of planets. Easton wouldn't be raising the white flag *this* soon, surely?

"Umm hmm," she said, her eyes twinkling. "Looks like someone's captured a heart," she teased.

I blushed, lifting the heavy vase of roses and headed back to my office. I placed the vase on the credenza behind my desk, taking the small envelope from the placard anxious to see what it said. I pulled the card out to read and as I did, my heart thudded; my butterflies crashed and burned:

> **Darcy,**
>
> **Unbreak my heart, baby. I love and miss you so much. Please forgive me.**
>
> **Darin**

I tucked the card underneath the vase, and was rearranging some of the baby's breath when I heard a loud whistle from behind me. I whirled around, knowing it was Eli by the whistle.

"Awww, you remembered to call him 'Sir,' didn't you?" he teased.

"Bite me, bitch," I replied with a smirk. "This is from old wood."

"Huh?"

"Darin."

"Ah," he said. "Well, hey, you can't blame a dude for knowing when he fucked up a good thing, right?"

"I guess," I replied, wistfully.

"Wanna do lunch?" he asked.

"Sure," I replied, grabbing my handbag from my desk drawer. "I need to get outta here for a bit. Let's do it. I'll drive."

"Hey, tell me something," Eli said, as we passed some cubicles on our way out.

"Okay, what?" I asked.

"This old wood of yours…," he smiled as he continued, "was it hard?"

I snorted as he laughed at his own cheezer joke.

We were chatting about even fresher office gossip he'd heard earlier relative to Rollins the Retch and his work squeeze Leanne Harshman. They'd apparently gotten into a shouting match behind the closed door of his office. He was trying to break things off with her and she was threatening a sexual harassment lawsuit. I was so engaged in the conversation I didn't notice until I was near my car in the lot that Darin was standing next to it.

Crap!

I stopped in my tracks as our eyes met. Eli continued walking, failing to notice I wasn't next to him any longer. He finally noticed Darin, and then turned back to me with a questioning look in his eyes.

"Darin," I stammered, "what are you doing here?"

"Did you get the roses?"

"Yeah, I did, but I'm not sure what to think about that."

"Hey, Darce," Eli said, "we can do lunch another time."

"Gimme just a sec, Eli." I turned to Darin. "Thank you for the roses, and we can certainly talk, but not now. I'm meeting Lindsey and Jill this evening at Busbee's. You're welcome to stop by if you want. Maybe I can break away for a bit and we can talk then."

"Yeah, that sounds awesome," Darin said, smiling.

"No promises, just a talk," I replied. He nodded.

Eli got into the car and was unusually quiet as we pulled out of the lot. I finally couldn't stand it anymore, feeling the judgment he was passing silently.

"What?" I hissed.

"I didn't say a thing."

"Yeah, but you're thinking real loud, I can tell. So, let's hear it."

"There's a Chinese proverb that comes to mind," he said. "Don't build a new ship out of old wood or you're destined to sink."

I shot him a look. "So, you think I'm a hot mess for simply listening to what Darin has to say?"

"You tell me, sweetie. It seems to me you didn't give Darin a second thought when Easton Matthews came into your life. What's changed?"

"Easton Matthews isn't capable of love, commitment, or even being a nice person. I can't deal with that."

"Hmmm—he sounds perfect for you, doll."

256

A feeling of uneasiness had seeped in after my morning spat with Darcy. Her dismissive attitude rankled me to no end. The little minx was fooling herself if she truly believed we wouldn't be fucking anymore. That wasn't her decision to make and she knew it. Already I'd gone too long without pussy and it didn't sit well at all. I'd be sinking my cock into her sweetness soon and she'd want it. I'd make sure of that.

I smiled to myself, knowing just how much she enjoyed this little game of cat and mouse, hide and seek, hot and cold. It was time to crank it up a notch as in 'Me Tarzan—You Jane' and it's time to spread your legs, love. My mobile rang, interrupting my thoughts and forcing me to put my twitching cock on hold for the moment.

"Matthews," I barked.

"Bad time?"

"No, Colin, it's fine. What've you got?"

"I had a call from Mark in R & D about some…uhm…jewelry, for lack of a better word I suppose. I'm confused, Easton."

"No need for confusion," I laughed. "I'm gifting Darcy with some titanium clit jewelry with polished onyx beads. Is there anything abnormal about that?"

"When you say it like that, I guess not," he replied chuckling. "But why have the R & D lab make this? I thought pierced clit jewelry was commercially available."

"True, however this is special. So, what'd Mark say about it?"

"Oh—yes, he has it finished and it's being couriered over to your attention. You should have it tomorrow."

"Brilliant," I replied, smiling once again. "Is that it?"

"Well, uh," he stammered, "your mother stopped in the office in Leeds, specifically to grill me on your whereabouts. She threw a fit about your estrangement and demanded to be put in touch with you."

"You told her to go to hell, I'm hoping."

"You know me, mate. I told her I'd let you know. She claims she has some important news for you. I gave her your e-mail address. I didn't know what else to do."

"Fuck."

"Sorry, mate. She can be quite insistent."

"Yeah, tell me about it. Well, I've not received anything from her yet. Was it my business or personal e-mail?"

"Personal," he replied.

"Okay. No worries. I'll handle whatever she dishes out. How are things in Leeds?"

"Everything's running great. I think it was a brilliant solution having Devon working half days in the office and half days at home. She's extremely productive and I suspect feeling guilt-free now that she's able to spend more time with her baby. The staff is rallying round her as well, so the numbers are good. I probably won't need to stay more than a couple of weeks since the transition has been nearly seamless. I'm sure you're ready for me to take the wheel once again at Baronton-Sheridan so you can return to London, eh?"

"I'll let you know when it's time, Colin," I chuckled. "Cheers."

I ended the call and decided to saunter on out to Darcy's office to see what the little chit was doing. I opened the door she'd slammed earlier, noticing immediately she was not at her desk.

Hmmm…must be out to lunch.

As I turned to return to my office, the large bouquet of red roses on her credenza caught my attention.

What have we here?

I went over to the vase, spying the card underneath it.

My blood ran cold when I read the scripted words on the card from the sender. That knob-head was going to be at the receiving end of my wrath if he thought for one minute he'd be getting into her skivvies again.

I hurried back into my office, twisting the wand for the mini blinds so I could see the parking lot. Her car was gone. Maybe she'd met him for lunch. She'd been dressed differently today, as if she had plans or was trying to impress someone. Someone other than me, it appeared.

I got Ryan Dobbs on the phone immediately.

"Dobbs," he said picking up.

"Ryan, I need you to transfer the latitude/longitude feeds from Darcy's vehicle directly into the GPS system in my computer. That way I won't need to receive updates. I'll have the data live."

"Certainly. Not a problem. For how long?"

"Until further notice," I replied, ending the call.

That pussy jewelry couldn't get here soon enough to suit me.

I picked up my mobile, and found the name I needed quickly on my contact list. An assistant picked up, telling me the bureau chief was out to lunch. She promised to have him call me as soon as he was back.

He damn well better…

I watched the digital clock on my desk, periodically checking the parking lot to make sure when Darcy returned. Finally, I was relieved to see that she'd gone to lunch with her roommate, as I saw them walking towards the entrance from her parking space, which was right next to mine. At least I knew she hadn't pulled a 'nooner' with Darin Murphy.

That's right, I know his last name. I also know where his next assignment's going to take him...

Chapter 36

I was rattled after lunch. Eli and I'd discussed it, naturally, and I knew how he felt about it. "Once a cheater, always a cheater," he'd repeated several times.

"Oh, for Chrissake! I'm just going to hear him out. He's probably the only guy that I've ever had a half-way healthy relationship with and, right now, that seems the better choice than walking this fucking tight-rope with Easton."

"Honey, it doesn't have to come down to one or the other, hello? You're gorgeous, wear couture better than any other chick I know, and you like taking risks. It's what you're about. You like walking a tight-rope because it's living on the edge and you crave that, whether you want to admit it or not."

"So, what does that mean?"

"It means find someone who likes walking that tight-rope with you and who'll adore you in spite of your flaws."

"Flaws?" I asked, my eyes flashing.

"Baby doll, you've got 'em and you know it, so deal with it."

"Like what?"

"Where do I start? Let's see: spoiled, self-centered, sarcastic, sneaky, stubborn—and those are only the ones that begin with an "S."

"Wow, how *do* you tolerate me?" I rolled my eyes, but still sported the easy grin that everyone pretty much got whenever they were in the same *vicinity* as Eli.

He threw me a mock-scowl. "Because you're also: smart, sexy, sophisticated, social, sympathetic and self-assured—*except* where matters of your heart are concerned. I can't figure out why that is, maybe you're not even sure of it, but honey, it's time you come to terms with it."

262

I knew what he was getting at and he was right. I'd avoided dwelling on it for the one "S" flaw Eli had failed to mention: scared. I was scared of the effect Easton had on me. I was afraid of the physical response I had to him as well. I'd been turned-on totally with the leather and the crop. He hadn't used those props since our first weekend together, and I wondered if perhaps I hadn't responded favorably to the play in his eyes. I was certainly a novice with that flavor of sex, but it didn't mean I wanted to remain vanilla forever...

"Darcy—"

I jumped, hearing Easton's voice; that's how deeply I was in thought.

"I'm sorry. I didn't mean to sneak up on you like that," he said, offering me a file he had in his hand.

"Oh, just day-dreaming, I guess," I replied softly, taking the file from him.

How is anyone with ovaries supposed pretend to be at war with a guy who looks like him?

"I wanted to pass this potential new customer assessment over to you for input into the system. I'll need for you to do the proper screening: Dun & Brad, credit references, annual reports, stock performance graphed out for the last eight quarters, as well as any press releases over the past five years. I need this fairly quickly if a site visit is to be scheduled next week."

"Okay," I replied, looking over the summary sheet in the file. "I see this company is located in San Francisco," I commented.

"Yes," he replied. "Baronton's looking to expand more in the private sector of security software and hardware in the U.S. This company may be ripe for acquisition. Can you stay late to get as much information as possible, since a lot of the banking references will be on the west coast?"

"Oh, well, actually I've got to be somewhere by six this evening, but I'll get as much done as possible before then," I said, starting to enter the available data into my computer.

"I see," he replied, studying me. "Nice flowers," he commented, glancing past me to the credenza. "Is today a special occasion?"

263

"Nope," I replied, enjoying the fact that Easton was obviously curious as to why they were sent and who sent them. "I'll get started on this right away. Is there anything else?"

"No," he replied a bit testily. "You can provide an update later."

I busied myself the rest of the afternoon getting all of the screening information started on the potential new client. I'd made quite a dent in it when I looked at the time and saw it was almost five. I went to the restroom to freshen up my make-up, and re-did my ponytail. I changed from my sensible shoes to the fuck-me heels I'd put in my bag, and surveyed myself one final time in the mirror. I knew I'd pass Darin's inspection. He'd always been generous with his praise anyway.

Busbee's was fairly packed with the after-five crowd when I arrived a little after six. I immediately saw Lindsey, waving me over to a booth where she and Jill were sitting.

"Jill," I screeched, as she jumped up to hug me. "How you been, sweetie?"

"If you ever phoned or e-mailed me, I guess you'd know, bitch," she said laughing. "It's all good. Just miss my girls!"

I ordered a happy hour Margarita and joined the banter with the girls. Jill was filling us in on her wedding plans. She and Gabe had nixed the plans for a big wedding, which I personally was grateful to hear. I wasn't prepared to be yet another bridesmaid or Maid of Honor. It was, shall we say, 'depressing.' Instead, they were planning to tie the knot in Aruba with a two-week cruise.

"So Darcy, anything new in your love life?" Jill asked, her eyes looking a bit mischievous. I immediately looked over at Lindsey, who was wearing a guilty look.

"I told her about the recent events with Darin," she said, holding her hand up to 'shush' me.

"You mean there's someone besides Darin?" Jill asked.

"No one important," I lied, clearly not wanting to get into all of it and ruin my mood for the evening. "By the way, I received two dozen freshly cut red roses in a crystal vase at work today from Darin."

"Oh my God!" Lindsey and Jill exclaimed together, as if they'd practiced it.

"Oh, I see. You already knew."

Lindsey giggled, already feeling the slight buzz from her drink since this was likely the first bit of alcohol she'd consumed since Harper was born. "I'm sorry, I'm sorry," she apologized, smiling. "It was just kinda cute when Darin called me last night and wondered what I thought a good ice-breaker would be to get his foot in the door with you. I happened to mention it to Jill before you got here. So, were you impressed?"

"I'm not sure that's the right word. Let's just say I felt several emotions. Then he showed up in the parking lot at lunch time wanting to talk."

"Oh," Jill said, frowning. "That's kind of lame."

"No it isn't," Lindsey snapped. "I think it's sweet."

"And why are you such a supporter of Darin's all of a sudden?"

"I just think—and Jill agrees, by the way, that the two of you are well-suited. I mean, c'mon Darce, he's G-Man for Chrissake. That's totally hot."

"Yeah, well, *cheating* isn't," I said, waving for the server to bring me another drink after I'd downed the rest of mine.

"Why are you getting so pissy about it, then? I mean, he's going to be here soon."

I raised my eyebrows at my best friend sitting across from me, knowing she truly had my best interest at heart, but what the fuck? "How did you know he was coming here?"

Both she and Jill squirmed uncomfortably in their seats.

"Well, I mean he called after he ran into you in the parking lot at lunch time and said you guys had talked and you suggested he stop by."

"You know," I said, clearly ticked off, "this is starting to sound like a little too much interference by well-meaning friends. I appreciate that you care, but in all honesty, it's not really Darin I've been thinking about lately."

265

They both exchanged looks once again. I'd be damned if Lindsey didn't have a bucket mouth. She'd evidently clued Jill in on everything.

"Lighten up," Lindsey scolded. "Darin just came in, so behave."

Behave? Umm…doubtful.

I already had an uber bad feeling about this, and an even worse feeling that it damn well wasn't going to end with me 'behaving.' I turned around, gracing Darin with a faux smile as he approached our booth.

"Hey Jill, why don't we go out on the patio and give these two a little privacy?" Lindsey said, scooting out of the booth. I shot her a dirty look that went nowhere. They both left and Darin slid into the booth across from me.

"Hey, Darce," he said softly, waving for the server. "Are you ready for another?" he asked, as I slurped up the rest of my second margarita.

"Absolutely," I replied.

Once we'd gotten our drinks, Darin began his well-practiced diatribe, taking full responsibility for his betrayal. He assured me that it had been a one-time thing, and a bad decision on his part. He said he'd likely regret it for the rest of his life. He made sure he told me that he'd not been with another woman since that night, and would do anything and everything in his power to make it up to me. He pleaded with me for another chance. He told me how much he'd missed me and realized how much he'd loved me. His eyes were sincere. His hands were clasping mine on the table as he waited. I saw the pain in his face, the pain of waiting for an answer from me that would take his pain away. I wasn't going to give him the answer he wanted. I didn't even need time to consider what my answer was going to be.

Unfortunately, I wasn't given the opportunity of answering him, because I felt a firm hand on the nape of my neck, softly fisting my hair.

"I believe," I heard Easton's voice say calmly, "this cheating prat's waiting for an answer from you, love." His hand loosened its grip, traveling down to the base of my neck in what I could only describe as a menacing caress.

Sweet baby Jesus!

That bad feeling I had earlier turned into an atomic bomb traveling through my pulse. This wasn't going to end well for poor Darin, and probably not for me, either.

I quickly looked over at Darin, who was looking very pissed as he sized Easton up. I should probably just have told the poor guy that he was *wahaay* out of his league at the moment.

"Listen buddy—" Darin interjected.

I quickly stood up, brushing Easton's hand away. I walked over to the opposite side of the table, where Darin was sitting. This had to end now before we caused a scene.

"You had your chance," I said to Darin. "You blew it. It's not like I don't give second chances. It's just that...well, you're so not worth one." I grabbed my handbag, feeling Easton's hand on my arm as he pulled me alongside of him. I heard Darin behind us cursing softly, his words unintelligible. It didn't matter. I wasn't going to build my wood out of an old boat. Or whatever the hell Eli had said.

"Wait," I said, trying to unsuccessfully pull my arm from Easton's grasp. "I'm here with Lindsey and Jill."

"You were. But now you're with me and we're leaving. We've got unfinished business to take care of at my place. You can text them in the car."

"What about my car? How'd you know where I was? And what *in the fuck* is going on?"

"You've a lot of questions, love. The only one I'm answering at the moment is about your car. Rest assured it'll be delivered to the hotel garage later. No worries."

My mind was riddled with confusion and conflicting emotions as I sat silently in Easton's car. I had definitely meant what I said to Darin. There was no going back for me with him. Easton however—he was a completely different story. I was drawn to him, for whatever reason. I couldn't explain it because I didn't understand it myself. It was as if the chemistry between us was on steroids, and yet it was more than just that. It was a bonding of sorts that was inexplicable, but strong, almost as if being on the verge of some major discovery for the both of us. It was mesmerizing...

∞ ∞ ∞ ∞ ∞ ∞

I was sitting in stony silence on the sofa in Easton's luxurious Presidential suite, watching as he paced in front of me, one hand in the pocket of his business casual trousers, the other hand raking through his thick, tousled hair in frustration. He'd barely said a word to me on the way here. I hadn't missed the occasional twitch in his cheek, as if he was struggling with some inner demon, not quite sure who to be angry with in this most recent cast of characters.

I finally saw him exhale, as if he was no longer at odds with whatever was plaguing him. He turned to face me, his hand now rubbing the back of his neck, relieving the pent-up tension.

"I have to punish you," he said plainly. "There's no other way around it."

Chapter 37

I awoke with a start; my wrists were painfully sore. Then I remembered. I felt a smile play on my lips as my fingers massaged the tender flesh on one wrist, soothing the skin that had been bruised by the handcuffs. My ankles had been bound together tightly with leather straps, which in my mind had been worse, but I'd understood the necessity of it. Easton had been about inflicting pain last night, not pleasure. Well, that's not altogether true. The pain had brought me pleasure, not that he'd intended it to, but it had, nonetheless.

I snuggled back against him, feeling his arms tighten protectively around me. He was stirring and I knew he hadn't slept well last night. He'd tossed and turned, repositioning himself a half dozen times around me, asking me if I was okay. I knew he'd been apprehensive about how I'd react to my punishment and concerned that he'd crossed the line with me or maybe with himself. But, I'd leapt across that line, hands and feet bound tightly together into his world of discipline and respect, and I understood the rules now. I comprehended this man.

I rolled over to face him, looking up into his smoldering gray eyes that were studying me intently. Was he concerned I'd flee from his bed? Not a chance. I was still naked beneath his sheets. I could still feel his cum dripping from me. My God! We'd fucked most of the night—after the punishment had been dispensed with, that is. I'd never been with a man that had a sexual appetite comparable to Easton's. It was as if he'd been on a mission to bury himself in me, and despite my reddened behind and sore wrists and ankles, I hadn't wanted him to stop.

He lowered his mouth to mine, kissing my lips softly.

"Morning, love," he murmured, his voice rough with early morning. "Are you alright?"

"I'm fine, Easton. Stop asking me that," I whispered against his lips. "I want more."

"Don't say that," he snarled, immediately disengaging from me and sitting up. He raked his hands through his fuck-tousled hair.

I frowned, perching myself up on one arm, my fingers reaching out to touch his sinewy muscled back. "What is it?" I asked, frowning.

He stood up, distancing himself from me, not bothering to hide his agitation. "For Chrissake, you can't possibly think what happened last night can ever happen again. I won't let it," he snapped. "It's not what I want with you."

"Okay, I'm definitely not following you here. I kind of thought it rocked."

He took two steps towards me, his eyes flashing. "That speaks of your needs, not of mine, at least not anymore—not with you."

I was pissed. Damn pissed! I'd been quite the trooper and was fucking proud of it. Now he was telling me what? That I *sucked* at being punished?

"You're being an ass," I snapped, hoping to get his ire up, along with anything else on him that cared to rise to the occasion.

"I *am* an ass," he spat. "You should've figured that out a long time ago. I don't want to be an ass—not with you at any rate. You didn't deserve the things I did to you last night."

"Which things?" I asked.

He was silent.

"The flogging?" I taunted. "The thin leather straps with the metal tips you flailed across my back and butt? Your aim was perfect, by the way."

I saw his quick intake of breath as my words hit home. He turned towards the bathroom to put more distance between us.

"Or the bondage?" I persisted, cockily trying to draw him back. He stopped and turned towards me, his face masked with shame. "The titanium steel handcuffs attached to my wrists, and the leather binds for my ankles making me unable to move while you fucked me raw."

"Any of it," he replied.

"Who deserved it, Easton?"

"All of them—apart from you. All of the whores I've been with, the ones I've punished in that way. Do you need names?"

"Only one," I replied, watching him with interest.

"Bianca," he snarled, his eyes flashing with fury. "It's how I wanted to fuck Bianca, the traitorous bitch. It's how I *thought* I wanted to fuck you, until I realised...," He broke off mid-sentence, agitation once again settling in as he dealt with his own confusion.

"Realized what?"

"Nothing," he muttered, going into the bathroom and slamming the door behind him, leaving me to guess how he might've finished that sentence.

I sat back on the bed, pulling my knees up under my chin, trying to figure out this complicated man. He'd been angry with me in London when I'd fixed my hair and make-up like hers. He'd succeeded in punishing me that night. Then there was the night of the thunderstorms when he'd made love to me and slept curled around me all night. He'd taken care of me the following night when I was trashed. Oh My God! I remembered him trying to get me to sleep. I asked him if he loved me...I remembered his answer now: "God help me."

Wait a fucking minute.

I launched myself off of the bed and barged into the bathroom where Easton was at the sink, splashing water on his face. He turned his face to look at me as I pointed my finger at him accusingly.

"You love me!" I yelled. "You fucking *love* me, don't you?"

He didn't say a word. He gave no verbal or non-verbal response admitting or denying. He didn't need to, because I knew the truth. He loved me.

I watched as he approached me, both of us still naked. He took me by the hand, leading me to the massive marble shower. In silence, he washed every part of my body, cleaning and polishing me as if I were his prized possession. He grimaced as though he was feeling the pain of the marks present on my wrists, ankles and butt. He was extremely gentle with me, washing my hair, and leaving soft kisses on my neck and ear lobes.

He patted me dry with a soft towel and then carried me back to his bed, placing me gently beneath the covers.

"Sleep now," he instructed me. "I'm going to shower and work from here for a bit. We'll talk later."

"It's a work day, Easton," I argued, glancing at the bedside clock. "We've got to be at work in less than an hour."

"I've got it all taken care of, love. I phoned in letting the rest of the staff know that I'd be working from here."

"What about me?"

"Call in sick," he replied with a slight smile. The first one I'd seen on his face for quite some time.

I did as instructed and then crawled back into bed and fell into a very delicious slumber, feeling the love of the man in the next room who'd become so important to me, for some very strange reason.

Later, he crawled into bed, pulling me closely against him, making me feel loved, protected, and for some reason, very secure. The tide had changed in our relationship. I knew it. He knew it. Words were not necessary because we both just knew and I was okay with that for as long as Easton chose to love me. I didn't want to analyze it, put it under a microscope, and pick it apart. He made me happy and me him, it seemed. So, for now we would just simply enjoy it.

Chapter 38

~ Easton ~

I gazed down at Darcy and my heart was heavy with the knowledge that she was right. I loved her. How in the fuck had I let that happen? That wasn't supposed to happen to me ever. I couldn't even say 'again' because this was so much more than it had ever been with Bianca. This whole thing with Darcy had cornered me into the realisation that I'd never really been in love before.

I know how trite that sounds, how utterly *female* it is to say you can love someone, but not be in love with them. The fact remains, it's true for men as well. I'd loved Bianca as one loves a prized possession, or a trophy for a performance well-executed, or a rare gem that others would kill to have, but I hadn't been *in love* with her. If I had, I never could've transformed that love into the all-consuming hatred I had for her after discovering her affair with Christopher and the abortion.

Sex with Bianca had always been about her following my orders on what I wanted and how I wanted it. She'd understood my sexual quirks, and while, not always on board with it, she tolerated it because it suited her to do so at the time. She loved the money I spent on her; the power and privilege that went along with being Easton Matthews' fiancé. The night Darcy had tried to emulate Bianca was the night I realised I felt something for her, something alien to me. I'd been infuriated at seeing Darcy trying to transform herself into the shallow and insidious Bianca. As if *that* would have endeared her to me.

In the first ten minutes after meeting her, I was fucking clueless. Aside from the obvious—that being her looks, her body, and the way her pussy clenched my cock whenever I buried myself inside of her—there was so much more to her that gave me cause to slowly come entirely unraveled by her. I enjoyed her outspoken nature, her playfulness and the fact that my wealth or power didn't impress her. I liked the way she could hold her own with me and get in my face when she needed to.

273

I liked the fact that when Mummy and Daddy pushed her from their financial nest egg, she rebounded with a determination to show everyone she had the ability to make it on her own merit, including me. She'd done a fantastic job on her debut presentation. We'd received the renewal contract three days later. Of course, being the prick I was, I hadn't shared that with her just yet.

I also loved the fact she was willing to take whatever punishment— physical or otherwise I administered without a whimper. Just as she'd done last night. She relished the bondage and the flogging; the problem was, I hadn't. I couldn't. Not with her. Not ever.

I gently lifted a lock of her dark brown hair, caressing my lips with it, while wondering where to go from here. She drove me to distraction and that wasn't a good thing. I knew what a possessive and controlling arse I was. There was no way in hell we weren't going to push against each other and have our verbal battles, and I mean often, yet I looked forward to doing just that with her. It was the very first time ever I'd regarded a woman as my equal. She was perfect for me, though I knew the road going forward would have twists and turns and be bumpy at times. We were both so imperfectly perfect for one another. Still, I was getting ahead of myself. After all, she hadn't shared with me as to whether the affection was mutual. Perhaps I was assuming too much. Maybe she didn't feel the same things I felt for her.

She stirred in her sleep, her brilliant eyes fluttering open and seeing me watching her.

"Easton," she said softly. "What is it?"

"I'm done with my work. I've a gift for you."

She eyed me suspiciously. "Where?" she asked, cocking an eyebrow.

"It was delivered a little while ago," I replied chuckling. "Come out here with me and I'll show you."

She put a bathrobe on, following me out to the living room. I handed her the small box that the courier had delivered just a half hour before. She opened it, her brow furrowing in confusion. She looked up at me, a half-smile playing on her lips.

"Is this what I think it is?" she asked coyly.

"It is," I replied, watching for a reaction.

"But I'm not pierced *there*," she responded.

"We can have that remedied if you like."

"Is that what you want?" she asked tersely.

"Not at all, love. I simply thought it would make a nice gift for you. I've heard a vertical hood piercing can significantly enhance the pleasure of orgasm, but I understand if you're disinclined to undergo the procedure. It may be a little painful, though I didn't mind it when I had my piercing done. I think it was well worth it, don't you?"

"It's not *that*," she said, clearly flustered. I had to admit it was quite entertaining to see the rare occasion when she was at a loss for words. I watched as she bit down on her lower lip trying to find the *right* words.

Christ, don't do that, love. You'll never finish what you have to say if you keep doing that.

"I mean," she continued, "how long would I have to…abstain from sex? You know, once it's pierced?" I watched her cheeks turn a flattering shade of pink.

Fuck. Don't do that either.

I stroked her hair, tilting her chin up so that her eyes locked with mine. "Just a few weeks. I'd be happy to pleasure you in other ways, if that's your only reservation. Or maybe we could simply have this beautiful black onyx re-set into a tummy button ring for you."

"No," she quickly replied, looking down at the gem. "Though…I *wouldn't* mind having a matching one for my belly-button." A corner of her lips quirked up, giving me a shy and hopeful smile.

"Brilliant," I replied, smiling. "I'll see to having another one made."

"You had this *made* for me? Why?"

"I wanted it to be special. Something no other woman has but you."

"Well, Easton, I think it's fairly safe to say, how would anyone know? I mean it's not like clit jewelry is visible to the general public." She was laughing now, shaking her head. I was simply pleased that it had gone so well.

I phoned Mark once Darcy had gone back to dress and ordered another black onyx for her tummy button ring.

"Should this one have a hot-spot?" he asked.

"Wouldn't hurt to have a back-up to be safe," I replied. "I'll need it tomorrow, so make it a priority at the lab."

"Yes, sir."

I made another call to a professional contact and let Darcy know when she reappeared that her piercing was scheduled for the following evening at my suite.

"You mean, you have someone coming here to do that?"

"You act surprised," I replied, giving her a wink. "Come on, I need to get those clothes back off of you. If we have to abstain for a couple of weeks, we'd better have a few for the road."

"I hear that," she giggled, grabbing my hand and leading me back to the bedroom.

This time I made love to her slowly and sensually. I placed my lips on every piece of her I could find, craving new places from the top of her head to the tips of her toes, enjoying every soft inch of her. I was careful to avoid those areas with marks, lifting her up and over me so that I could gently settle her down onto my rigid cock. She moved her hips in perfect rhythm, up and down, leaning forward so that my cock piercing hit just the right spot, over and over again. My hands cupped her creamy breasts, gently tugging at the nipples, raising my mouth to take one fully, suckling gently.

"Mmmm," she moaned sweetly, riding my cock slowly and deliberately. I could feel her pussy contracting around it. Our eyes locked as our climax mounted toward the crescendo that ultimately would send us both into a spiral of pulsating pleasure. "That's it," she gasped. "Keep fucking me just like that, Easton. God, baby, you make me feel so good..."

Her soft, husky voice speaking those intimate and sexy words were all I needed to descend with her into that sweet depth where we were lost in the pleasure and passion of mutual release.

Chapter 39

It had been two weeks since I'd had the hood of my clit pierced, with Easton at my side during the procedure. It had better be fucking worth it once I'm cleared for sex in another week. That was the worst part of it. I'd been spending most of my time at Easton's. I'd gone back to my apartment and picked up some of my clothes and toiletries while Eli was at work the day I'd called in sick.

Of course, he'd worried like a bitch-you-didn't-come-home-last-night older sister when Lindsey hadn't been able to reach me, and naturally had phoned Eli to see where I was. She'd spilled the whole story to him about Darin and what had happened at Busbee's. I wasn't about to be around the apartment and have Eli accidently see the bruises on my ankles or wrists. I'd worn casual pants and long-sleeved blouses to work the rest of the week.

So okay, now let's deal with the elephant in the room here, shall we? Call me a freak; call me a perv, but I'd enjoyed the punishment Easton had unleashed upon me that night.

Thoroughly. Fucking. Enjoyed. It.

What more can I say? Does that mean I have "Daddy" issues?

Please!

Does it mean I feel subservient to Easton?

Only when I choose to, and it's about the pleasure I get from it, so it's really still about me, got it?

Will Easton continue to punish me like that?

Fuck No! And I'm a tad pissed as hell about it!

"I don't understand, Easton," I had friggin' whined. Yep, that's right, *whined.* "Am I not doing something right? Not giving you the reaction you need to make it hot?"

"I've told you before, Darcy, it's not who I want to be with you. It's not happening again. End of subject."

I knew Easton loved me, though he'd never said the words to me once I'd confronted him with it that morning after my punishment. I decided I wasn't going to say it to him, either. Maybe that's what ruined a good thing. I'd been totally open with Darin; professing my love for him once he'd said it to me. (Rule #1, lovelies: Always wait until the man says it first!) What good had it done me?

Darcy's Law of the Male Psyche: Once you let a guy know you love him, he knows he's conquered you and it's just a matter of time before he's trolling around for his next 'challenge.'

Case in Point: Darin

Understand? Great—Let's move on.

Easton and I had been keeping a low profile at work. Occasionally, he'd call me into his office, shut the door, and spring his horny cock free for a mid-afternoon blow job. I enjoyed it nearly as much as he did. He'd try to get me off as best he could with his fingers, which made it easier to bypass my healing clit.

He was leaving day after tomorrow for London to conduct his annual State of the Business meeting. I referred to it as his high-powered summit. All the general managers would meet for a round table caucus to go over their current numbers and raise any concerns they had about reaching their sales goals. He'd be in London for most of the week and then traveling to Paris for another meeting of some sort. He said he'd be there for a "few" days. I absolutely wasn't going to press him for more information. I could read his body language fairly well by now.

The timing was less than perfect. Lacee was due back in after her unpaid hiatus so I was *not* looking forward to having to interact with her once again.

I was clearing my desk off right before five o'clock when my cell rang. It was Mom. I hadn't talked to them more than a couple of times while they were cruising.

"Hey Mom," I greeted. "Are you back? I'm starting to feel like an orphan."

"Yes, darling. Daddy and I got in earlier this afternoon. It was a great trip, but I'm glad to be home I think. We brought you back something, along with lots of pictures. Would you like to come over for dinner this evening?"

God, I so hated missing an evening with Easton...but—

"Sure, Mom. I'll drive over as soon as I leave the office."

"Perfect. Just know that we're having Chinese takeout. I'm too tired to cook," she laughed.

I ended the call and finished clearing my desk. Easton was still on a conference call with Colin. I stood in his doorway until he motioned for me to come in.

"Colin, we can pick this up later tonight. I've some pressing business to attend to at the moment." (Pause) "Ah, yes, I will. Cheers."

He looked up at me, smiling. "Colin sends his regards."

"Oh," I smiled. "Regards right back at him when you talk later."

"Where shall we go for dinner?" he asked, flashing me his brilliant smile.

"Well, actually, that's why I stopped in. My parents are back from their cruise and Mom wants me to have dinner with them. Since they're closer to my apartment, I'm probably going to crash at home tonight." I ran my fingers through my hair a bit nervously.

"I see," he replied. I got the feeling he wasn't pleased, but there was no way in hell I was springing him on the folks just yet. I remembered how horrified they'd been hearing Lacee and Easton carry on back in December. They'd freak if they found out the situation had changed and their daughter was now on the receiving end of his lust.

"You're probably ready for a break from me anyway," I teased. He didn't smile.

Okay. Maybe not.

"Have a nice evening," he replied, coolly. "I'll see you in the morning."

Dismissed.

He turned his back to me and started pecking away on his laptop. Okay. Whatever. Sometimes Easton Matthews could be a hot mess.

Dinner with Mom and Dad went well. First off, it was nice to have good ole Chinese take-out for a change. Easton and I were constantly eating at some high-priced, gourmet restaurant, or his butler was preparing gourmet meals for us in his suite. I'd actually packed on a few pounds I wasn't real happy about. When I mentioned that to Easton, he'd actually tried to drag my ass out of bed at 4:30 a.m. to work out with him the following morning. Hells-bells, that wasn't happening!

My parents had brought me an authentic Puka Shell necklace, a gorgeous pair of Birkenstock sandals, and a hand-embroidered silk caftan. I swore it seemed as if they were segueing back to their "hippie" days with the selections they'd purchased for me. Not that I didn't love it all.

Once we'd finished eating and I'd looked at all of the digital pictures, Daddy asked how things were going at work. For some reason I felt tongue-tied.

"I got a promotion," I said timidly.

"That's fantastic," they both said at once.

"Tell me, Darcy, how did this come about?" my father asked.

"Well, Lacee was promoted to the Transition Team Leader, so of course, that left her position open for an executive assistant to Easton. He approached me about it, basically saying that he'd personally groom me in operations management.

"Splendid," my father said, beaming.

If only he knew...

"Dad, I guess your former assistant didn't put in for the job for Easton. Why is that?"

I watched my father squirm, not knowing that I knew what I knew.

"She preferred a transfer to Finance," he said hurriedly. "Since I'm only there periodically as a consultant, there wouldn't have been much for her to do most of the time. She got a promotion as well."

"I see," I said. "Well, I guess it worked out for all concerned. I probably should be heading home. I've got laundry stacked up." I picked up my handbag, digging for my car keys.

"Darcy, wait a sec," my mom interrupted. "Is there a reason you haven't put a change of address through since you've moved from here?"

"No, I guess I never saw the need," I replied. "I mean, I don't have credit card bills or anything. I set my billing up for utilities once I moved into the apartment. What's left?"

"Well," she said, going over to the kitchen counter where a stack of mail was piled. "We had the mail stopped a few days before we left on the cruise. I noticed there were several things for you when I returned. There's a notice from your dentist that you're overdue for a cleaning, some clothing catalogs, and then this postcard from Dr. Billingsley arrived right after we left, stating you missed a scheduled appointment and has instructions to call their office immediately to set another one up."

Oh shit! My Depo shot is fucking past due...

"Honey, are you having any female problems? I mean, I know Dr. Billingsley's a gynecologist."

"Oh no, Mom. Nothing like that. I just missed my annual check-up is all."

"Well good," she replied, obviously relieved. "Make sure you call your dentist and gynecologist to get this taken care of. It's important you keep up with your preventative treatments."

No fucking shit!!

Eli was kicked back in the living room watching some freaking reality show with Cain when I got home.

"There she is, Maddox. I guess she *does* still live here, or at least makes the occasional pit stop."

282

"Shut up," I snapped, instantly regretting my mood.

I went upstairs and immediately started sorting through my clothes hamper in order to start the four loads of laundry it appeared I had. Eli tapped gently on my door.

"You okay?" he asked softly. "Did you have a fight with Easton?"

"No, no—nothing like that. My folks are back and I had dinner with them. I'm staying here tonight."

"Why the mood?"

"It's probably nothing," I shrugged. "Sorry I was bitchy. Everything's cool."

Later, as I lay alone in my bed, hoping that sleep would overtake me, I had a gnawing suspicion that everything was not okay. My instincts were on high alert.

Chapter 40

I was pulling my paper gown tightly around me as Dr. Billingsley instructed me to scoot my tush down closer to the edge of the table, my socked feet firmly planted in the cold, steel stirrups of the exam table.

Lovely.

"When was your last period, Darcy?"

"Uh, before I had my last shot of Depo."

"Umm hmm," he mumbled, putting the warmed speculum in to "have a peek" as he put it.

"When did you get the piercing?" he asked, probing around with his instrument.

"A few weeks ago," I replied, tensing up at the physical intrusion.

"It looks like it's healing nicely. You understand we can't give you another Depo shot until we get the results of the test back. It'll be just another couple of minutes. I can tell your cervix has thickened up a bit."

What the hell does that mean?

His nurse tapped on the door and then came in, handing him the test results.

"You can sit up now," he said, extending his hand to assist me. I was still clutching the paper gown to my breasts, watching his face for some hint of the news.

He took a seat on his rolling stool and made a notation on my chart.

"Well, Darcy, I hope congratulations are in order. Both of your tests have come back positive. It appears you're about five to six weeks pregnant."

"I can't be!" I hissed loudly at him. "Can't you re-run the tests? I mean, I wasn't that far past the date in getting my next shot. Certainly there's some 'carryover' time, a buffer period or something, right?"

"I'm positive you're pregnant. There's no need to re-take the tests. You'll be delivering a baby in mid-to-late January. I take it this isn't good news?" He was looking at me with compassion.

"I don't know what it is," I said, my voice sounding foreign to me. "I'm still in shock, I guess."

"Well, I'll leave you to get dressed. You should consider your options. You're still in the very early stage of your pregnancy. If you decide to terminate the pregnancy, you should do it soon. The longer you delay, the higher the risk. I'll have my nurse provide you with some informational pamphlets of clinics and counseling centers as well."

I didn't remember getting dressed or driving back to the apartment. I was in a fog…a thick, confused fog. I'd made a follow-up appointment with the doctor, and was provided a prescription for pre-natal vitamins, should I decide to proceed with the pregnancy.

Oh. My. God. Easton's going to kill me!

As soon as I got home, I ran up to my room and crawled into bed. Eli was still at work. Easton was in London. Thank God. There's no way I could've masked my emotions from him, at least for now.

I picked up my phone and called Lindsey. We'd only talked once since the night Easton had hauled me out of Busbee's. She knew we were still *whatever-we-were* to each other.

"Hey, you," she greeted. "It's about damn time you came up for air. Doesn't Easton ever give you a breather?"

"Lindsey," my voice cracked, "I'm in deep shit."

Talking to Lindsey had helped like I knew it would. She was truthfully thrilled about the idea of Harper having a cousin.

"Half-cousin," I'd corrected her.

285

"No, we're not doing halves," she argued.

"Then you think I should keep this baby?"

She shrieked loudly into the phone, causing me to pull it away from my ear.

"What the hell? Don't you even consider the alternative, Darcy! I can't believe that thought even crossed your mind!"

"I'm not sure I'd be a good single parent," I admitted, shrugging. My mind immediately started re-playing scenes from the movie, "Juno."

Can you hold on a sec, Linds? I'm on my hamburger phone.

"What makes you think Easton won't take responsibility?" Lindsey asked, bringing me back to reality.

I felt my eyes widen. "Are you serious? Easton's not a proponent of motherhood, trust me. I saw that firsthand in London."

"Even so, Darcy, you should give him a chance."

A chance to what? Fucking throttle me?

"Listen, I need you to promise me, *promise me*, you won't say a word about this to anyone, including Taz." The words fell like fallen soldiers from my lips.

"I'll promise on one condition…"

"Which is?" I was mentally flipping my best friend off.

"No more thoughts about having a—you know…"

She couldn't even bring herself to use the "A" word.

"No problem. I wasn't considering that anyway, geesh."

"You weren't?"

"Hell no! I considered the fact that I'm likely deficient in maternal instincts, but there was never any question of me not *having* the baby. For Chrissake, I sort of love the arrogant prick, you know?"

I'd no sooner gotten off the phone with Lindsey than a call came in from Easton. It had to be around 10 p.m. in London.

"Are you feeling okay?" he asked, as soon as I answered.

Huh?

"Yeah, I'm fine. Are *you* feeling okay?" I replied, wondering why he'd greeted me with that to begin with.

"You went to the doctor today. I was concerned you were ill."

"How did you know that?" I asked, putting my hand on my hip.

"The GPS in your car," he replied very matter-of-factly, as if he had every right to stalk me electronically.

"You're keeping tabs on me via my *car*?" I didn't even want to see the expression on my face when I asked that. "Sounds like someone with a little too much time on their hands."

"Answer my question, please."

"I'm fine. I had an appointment with my doctor because it's time for my Depo Provera shot—you know *birth control*?" I could feel my eyes bugging out as I carefully skirted the truth.

"Ah, yes, wouldn't do to miss that. Good girl."

Holy fuck!

I changed the subject, asking how things were going with the summit (as I called it teasingly). He said he was bored and ready to be back in D.C.

"Really?" I asked him. "I don't understand your sudden love for the States these days, Mr. Matthews," I said flirtatiously.

"I don't understand it myself," he replied. I could almost feel his smile over the phone. "Someone's got my attention in a death grip, I'm afraid."

"Yeah. I miss you too, Easy E."

"I'll see you after Paris, love. Behave yourself and I'll be in touch."

287

"By phone or GPS?" I asked, twisting a lock of my hair around my finger.

"Both," he replied. "Miss you."

I felt a warm tingle in the pit of my belly after he'd said that to me. The glow stayed with me until I heard Eli come in from work about an hour later.

What to do about Eli...

Chapter 41

The knowledge I was pregnant apparently signaled my body to start acting like it. I'd no sooner got up the following morning to get ready for work, when I made a mad dash to the bathroom to throw up.

Three times.

Eli heard me and, when I came out into the hall with a wet wash cloth dabbing at my mouth, he stood there, arms-crossed, leaning against the wall.

"Stomach flu?" he asked.

"No—I think those fish sticks that I had last night didn't agree with me. I'll be fine."

"Uh huh," he replied, giving me the once-over.

Later at work, I was in the middle of going over some figures with Lacee, when the nausea struck me again. I made a mad dash to the restroom and unceremoniously heaved again. Damn! This was going to be a bitch. By afternoon, I felt normal again. Hopefully this wouldn't be an everyday thing. Of course that was only wishful thinking…

Like clockwork, every morning I'd throw up before leaving for work and then wave two of the nausea would hit around mid-morning.

On Friday, I was at my desk, desperately fighting it back with a box of saltine crackers and a can of ginger ale I'd brought from home, when Lacee flitted into my office.

"Here are the files you requested for the presentation," she said, slapping a pile of thick folders on the corner of my desk. "Christ, you look green. You've been puking around all week here."

I looked over at her, narrowing my eyes in an attempt to scare her off.

"Sorry," she said. "It's just that the walls to the restroom down the hall are thin. We've heard you retching in the morning—Oh, my God."

Her eyes widened as the suspicion as to the cause of my illness sunk in. "Its morning sickness, isn't it? You're pregnant, aren't you?" It was an accusation, not a question.

"Don't be ridiculous," I lashed back at her. "It's a stomach flu that's been going around. Eli had it first," I lied. There's no way in hell I'd let her know the truth.

"You'd better hope that's all it is," she murmured, losing some of the haughty attitude. She looked around to make sure no one was out in the hall and then softly closed the door of my office. She came over to the side of the desk, taking a seat.

Lacee's expression was almost sympathetic. She looked sincere and compassionate in that moment. It took me a second to wrap my head around that.

"Listen," she started quietly, "I know you and I got off to a horrible start. I realize now my resentment of you wasn't fair. I mean, it wasn't your fault Easton was drawn to you and not to me. I'm so over it, Darcy. During the last couple of weeks, I had a lot of time sitting at my apartment to reflect on the past few years of my life and to think about where my future's going to take me. The "faux" relationship I had with Easton was so one-sided, and so unhealthy. I never want to be the person I was with him again. I was drawn to his looks, his power, and of course," she continued, a hint of a blush coloring her cheeks, "his sexual prowess."

I shifted uncomfortably, hoping the wave of nausea I was feeling would subside long enough for Lacee to get to the point.

"Anyway," she continued, "I don't know the specifics of your relationship with Easton and it's clearly not my business. I will share with you something that I do know, and you can take it for what it's worth. Shortly after I was assigned to work for Easton, his ex-fiancée, Bianca Templeton, made it a point to contact me. I'm not sure exactly why, other than she had seen Easton and me out one evening, and it turned out to be a very uncomfortable situation." Lacee paused for a moment and I could see a look of pain cross over her face. "In fact, it ruined the rest of my night and carried on well into the following morning."

Oh God! He had punished her...

"Bianca called me at the office the following day and warned me never to cross Easton. She said he had singlehandedly ruined her reputation and her career. She said it had been worth it just knowing she'd never have to tolerate his abuse again. She started sobbing over the phone and told me it was too late for their baby, but it wasn't too late for her."

My head snapped up at Lacee's words. "What did she mean by that?" I asked, interrupting her monologue.

Lacee looked me directly in the eye and continued. "Apparently Bianca was pregnant with their child. When Easton found out about it, he forced her to have an abortion."

"Whoa, wait a minute." I tried to find the right words. "How could he force that? I mean, I get that he's a control freak, but even I can't believe he'd carry a woman kicking and screaming into an abortion clinic and hold her down while they performed an abortion against her will."

"I'm only telling you what she told me," Lacee replied with a shrug. "She said Easton told her something to the effect that his royal bloodline needed to stop with him. He would have no heirs, period."

I was silent for a moment, tossing this around in my head.

Lacee leaned forward. "I mean, she didn't say this right out, but the impression I got from her was that she had two options: get the abortion or spend the next eight months in fear for her own life. She chose the first one."

Okay, *that* took a long second for me to swallow my WTF moment.

"Did you ever ask Easton about it?" I asked tersely.

"Are you serious?" she asked incredulously. "Easton has zero tolerance for prying. His private stuff's just that: private. I wouldn't have dared to share with him the fact I'd even talked to her, let alone have divulged what she told me. Besides that, I had no aspirations of marriage or children back then. Now it's different. Now I realize what normal is and, frankly, it's a helluva lot more appealing than his dark moods and idiosyncrasies."

She stood up to leave. "I just thought you should know," she said, walking towards the door. "I wish you luck, Darcy. I hope you kick that stomach flu real soon."

When I got home Friday after work, I immediately turned my phone off and climbed into bed. I needed to think, to reflect on what the hell I was going to do. Fuck me! Did I love Easton? My heart said I did, but did I *know* Easton? My brain said not well enough to dispel the possibility that Lacee was being honest—or that Bianca had been honest with Lacee.

I was still contemplating my next move when Eli tapped on my bedroom door. "Darce, can I come in?"

"Sure," I called out, pulling my covers up to my chin.

"Do you wanna talk about it?" he asked, taking a seat on the edge of my bed.

"What?" I asked, feigning ignorance.

"You've been puking every morning, doll. Doesn't take a genius to figure out something's going on and the possibilities are few."

I looked up at him and busied my hands, plucking at some random threads on the comforter. Sighing, I confessed solemnly. "I'm in trouble, Eli."

I was shocked when I heard the low rumble of his laughter following my admission.

What's funny?

"Sweetie," he said, crossing his legs. "This isn't 1955, and you're not sixteen years old. I think it's okay for you to say words like: pregnant or knocked up."

"It doesn't matter what words I use, the end result's the same: I'm in trouble!" I must've changed the expression on my face to one that he'd take more seriously.

"What do you want to do about it?" he asked, taking my hand into his.

I looked away. "I want to have the baby, of course. I just don't want Easton to know about it."

"What the hell do you mean?"

"I *mean* Easton doesn't like pregnant women, or babies for that matter. I know this firsthand," I replied, sitting up in bed.

I saw Eli frown. "Wanna clue me in?"

I told him everything, what had happened at Leeds, and what Lacee had shared with me just today. He listened to everything, taking it in and giving it objective consideration.

"Well first off, I would take anything Lacee said with a grain of salt. Seriously, it's occurred to you she just might have her own agenda on this, right?"

I nodded, still not convinced Lacee would take a grudge against me or Easton to that extent. I had to find out more. But how?

"Where's Easton now?" Eli asked.

"I don't know—London or Paris. He's back on Tuesday."

Eli stood up, giving me one of his stern looks. "You need to think long and hard as to how you're going to handle this with him, Darcy. In the meantime, I'm going downstairs to make you some chicken soup. I hear it's good for the soul." He finished with his signature wink.

Chapter 42

I'd survived the weekend, despite Eli's constant hovering and Lindsey blowing up my phone, both of them on the same mission: what are you going to tell Easton?

Fuck—I don't know!

[Seriously, what would *you* do at this point? Let's get this out of the way because I need to admit something. This relationship between Easton and me? It's a hot mess, I know. But hey, I'm fairly sure I'm in love with him. I will not, however, cop to *insta-love*.

Insta-lust? Yeah, no doubt about that! Somewhere along the way, it became super intense, equipped with a whole lot of angst and a lot of back-and-forth crap. And then, it just kind of...*morphed* into this kind of lopsided relationship. Add a baby to the mix? So not good.

But, I digress...]

Thankfully, the pregnancy gods were with me on Monday. It was the first day I had no hint of morning sickness or fatigue. Maybe I was home free from that part of it. I got to work early to get a head start on the files Easton had uploaded to our shared drive. He'd phoned me Friday morning and told me he was preparing to leave for Paris the following day and he'd have the summit meeting input/output reports to me over the weekend. He asked that I put it into a summarization template, which Lacee had trained me to do.

Damn! There was a shitload of them waiting for me as I logged into our shared drive. Of course, they were in various types of files, which made consolidation that much more difficult. Some of the sites had done spreadsheets, others had used power-point, and still others had submitted text documents. Geez, too bad I couldn't have some sparkly caffeinated coffee right now. This was going to take a while. There was one file that was different than the others I noticed right away. It was a text file that had been saved as the header on Easton's personal e-mail account, showing the date and how many unread e-mails he had. WTF?

I opened it and it appeared Easton had saved an e-mail string to notepad. As I skimmed down through it, it was obvious he hadn't intended on moving this particular text file to our shared drive. I scrolled down to the bottom and started reading up from there.

It was from his mom.

Her e-mail had arrived in his personal email account several weeks back. She had put "Your Father" in the subject line. Knowing that Easton hadn't intended to send this file with the others, I did what any other professional assistant would've done and deleted it before I read any further.

Yeah, right! You know that didn't happen...

I read through the e-mail threads. His mother initiated the email in an attempt to open the lines of communication. It sounded as if they hadn't talked in a very long time. She said his father was ill, very ill. *What??* She apologized to him for keeping him in the dark for all these years about his real father, but she felt it was time he knew the truth and paid his father a visit before he passed. His father had never met him, though he knew of him. She pleaded with Easton, mentioning that he was the only son and should carry his title with pride. She said it was his father's wish to meet his only son before he died.

Holy shit!

I read further up seeing Easton's response: "No." It was simple and to the point, leaving no room for argument.

Apparently, his mom hadn't taken the hint, because she'd responded back that she didn't blame him for hating her, and doubting her word, but swore she was being honest with him. She apologized for the shock and anger he must be feeling, but asked him to contact the man who had raised him as his own, Trace Matthews. He would validate her story.

Easton had responded a couple of days later, saying he'd talked with his father and they could both rot in hell as far as he was concerned.

Geez!

She'd replied back that, since he now knew the truth, he needed time to digest it, and she understood. She begged him not to take too long because his

295

father only had weeks to live and he was the only man she'd ever loved. She wanted them to meet. If Easton agreed to do so, she promised she'd never bother him again.

Easton had replied back to her that it would be worth it as long as she kept that promise. He told her he'd be in Paris on the 25th and 26th. He said he would contact her prior to his arrival. She'd confirmed back her gratitude, blah, blah, blah.

Not good.

Today was the 26th. He'd be back tomorrow. God only knew what kind of a mood he'd be in. I was fairly certain his mood wouldn't accommodate any greeting from me that included, "By the way, guess who's gonna be a daddy in seven-and-a-half months? And while we're on the subject Easton, what'd you think of your *real* father?"

I hurriedly deleted the text file and tried my best to concentrate on the task at hand. I couldn't screw up his summary report, or he'd have good reason to bring a leather crop to my ass. I smiled at the thought.

That evening, after enjoying a dinner cooked by Eli, I debated as to whether or not to call Lindsey to see if Taz had spoken to his father lately. I wondered if Trace Matthews Sr. would've shared the topic with Taz. Was it possible Taz already knew? It was hard to tell when G-Men were keeping things from you. I'd learned that with Darin. Just as I was having that thought, my cell rang. It was Lindsey. How weird was that?

"Hey Linds," I greeted, smiling and hoping it carried through in my voice. I hoped she wasn't going to ask me for the millionth time when I was going to tell Easton, or if I was going to tell Easton. I didn't want to think about it at the moment.

"Darcy, guess what?"

"What?" I responded hesitantly.

"Taz just told me Darin got transferred. You wanna guess where?"

I felt my heart start beating again knowing her 'big' news had nothing to do with Easton.

"I give—where?"

"A freaking satellite office in Fairbanks, Alaska!"

Well that's a bit anti-climactic...

"Really?"

"Oh yeah. And he's *freaking* pissed about it, too."

"Hmm," I replied, twisting my hair. "Well, maybe he put in for a transfer on account of me breaking his heart. I mean, you don't work for the FBI and get much farther away from DC than that."

We both giggled in unison. I knew the truth, though. I wasn't sure how he'd managed it, but this had all the earmarks of something accomplished by my incredibly controlling and possessive Easton.

"So, anything new with you?" she pried.

"Nope. It's all good for now. I'll call you when that changes, Lindsey."

I heard her give me a one-syllable laugh. "I get the hint. That's all I wanted to tell you anyway. Talk to you soon."

I shared the latest news with Eli as I helped him clean up the dishes. He was snickering in delight. "You know, dude deserves going there and freezing his cheating balls off," he said with a laugh. "Hey, you've gotta know your man had something to do with that."

"I think I'm going to take a leisurely bath and then get to bed," I said, yawning, and thinking at the same time how I kind of loved when someone referred to Easton as being mine.

"It's only eight o'clock, Darce."

"I know," I said, smacking Eli's behind. "But the way I figure it, the sooner to bed, the earlier tomorrow gets here and I get to see 'my man'."

Eli made the finger down his throat gagging gesture as I left to go upstairs.

An hour later and freshly showered, I crawled beneath my sheets and drifted into a restful sleep. I thought it was the next morning when I awoke until I realized it was still pitch dark out and it wasn't the irritating buzzing from my alarm clock that had awakened me, but the sound of loud voices from downstairs.

Shit!

I hoped it wasn't Eli and Cain arguing. They'd never done that before, but these were clearly male voices.

"Dude, it's fucking two in the morning and you've already woke my ass up. You're not waking her ass up too," Eli said in an extremely loud voice.

"I'll see her right now, or your fucking arse is fired, Mr. Chambers."

Easton.

I scrambled out of my bed and rushed through the hallway and down the stairs.

"What the hell's going on?" I said, my voice quivering. Why was Easton here? Why did he look drunk? What the fuck's going on?

"Evening, babe," Easton, said, a clumsy smile adorning his face.

"He's trashed," Eli said, waving his hand. "I can't believe you didn't hear him leaning on the doorbell."

"I've got it, Eli," I said. "Go on back to bed."

"You sure?"

I nodded, walking over to where Easton was now leaning against the closed front door. Eli gave me a second look, debating as to whether to leave me down there with Easton. I nodded to him again and he reluctantly went back upstairs.

"Easton, it's the middle of the night," I explained to him, wrapping my bare arms around myself against the downstairs chill.

"I'm still on Paris time, love. Its morning," he said and then laughed. "Time to get your arse up and outta bed."

"No," I replied, carefully. "I'm taking this *arse* back to bed because, you see, I'm on U.S. time and it's still the middle of the night. Now, what can I do for you?"

"Not a thing. Just wanted to come by and let you know I was back is all." Even in his stupor, he gave my body a slow perusal, looking like he wanted to devour me right then and there.

"Easton," I said, interrupting those thoughts. Upon hearing his name, his eyes traveled back to my face and that's when I noticed it. I'd seen him drunk before, but that's when he was angry. This time his guard was completely shot. The emotionless façade he usually wore was absent, and he appeared vulnerable at the moment. Something had unhinged him.

"Do you want to sleep with me tonight?" I asked softly, forgetting what I initially was going to tell him.

"Do you mind, love? I'm in need of company, it seems," he halfway slurred.

"I am, too," I said, moving closer to him. He threw his arm around my shoulders and we trudged upstairs to my room. Easton quickly shed his clothes and crawled beneath the covers, drawing me up against him.

"You know, I've not been with anyone else since you," he murmured against my neck. "God knows I've wanted to, but whatever the fuck it is about you has kept me from it. It's bloody rubbish, too."

"Really," I whispered back. "I kind of think it's nice. I love you too, Easton."

I felt his soft, warm lips kissing my neck and my special spot he savored beneath my ear. He pulled me closer against him, his arms wrapped around me possessively. Several minutes later, I heard his deep, even breathing. He was at rest…for the moment.

Chapter 43

My morning sickness was back with a vengeance Tuesday morning. I barely made it to the bathroom before hurling. I was still kneeling in front of the toilet when Easton came sauntering in the bathroom looking gorgeously disheveled—and gorgeously naked.

"Are you alright?" he asked, raking a hand through his tousled hair.

I looked up from the toilet as I pushed the handle to flush it. "I must have that stomach bug that's being going around at work," I lied. "Better keep your distance."

He grabbed a clean wash cloth from the shelf and ran cold water over it, squeezing out the excess. He knelt down, lifting my hair and pressed the coolness against the back of my neck.

"Easton," I said in a low voice. "You're standing there naked. Eli and I share this bathroom, you know?"

"I'm sure it's nothing he hasn't seen before," he replied, giving me a wicked smile.

"Still," I said, gesturing at his lower and impressive…regions, "I'd prefer he not get the full, panoramic view, if you don't mind."

Easton helped me up from the floor.

"I don't want you coming in to work today," he said briskly. "You're to stay in bed and rest until you kick whatever it is that's ailing you, is that understood?"

That could be a while…

"Yes, sir," I said, trying my best to present him with a smile. He went back to my bedroom, giving me some privacy while I finished up in the bathroom.

When I got back to my room, he was sitting on the bed, fully dressed, putting his shoes and socks on.

"So," I said, "I got the summarization finished yesterday. It's on our shared drive."

"Excellent," he said, looking around for his other sock on the floor.

"How was your trip?" I asked, cautiously.

"You saw the minutes of the meetings and the figures. It went well."

"I meant your trip to Paris," I replied, studying his reaction.

He immediately looked up at me from where he'd been putting his other sock on. "Why do you ask?"

"No reason," I faltered. "I just wasn't sure if you had anything for me to summarize on that meeting. Did you send more files?"

"No," he replied abruptly. "My trip there was personal business, meaning it's none of yours."

"Sorry," I said, climbing back into bed. "I wasn't trying to be nosy."

Easton stood up, rubbing his sexily unshaven face. "I've got to go back to my suite to shower and change. I'll phone you later to see how you're feeling."

"You know, if I feel better later, I'll go ahead and come in to work."

"No. You're to do as I instructed. No need in passing whatever bug you've picked up on to the rest of the staff. It hinders productivity."

You've no idea...

"Okay, whatever," I said, mentally flipping him off. "You're pretty grouchy this morning for being the one that interrupted my sleep—not to mention Eli's."

His expression softened momentarily. "I blame it on jet lag and too much bourbon on the trip back. Am I forgiven?"

"I'll think about it," I said, hugging my pillow to me.

301

He leaned over the bed, brushing a soft kiss on my forehead. "Don't pout, baby," he gently admonished. "I'll make it up to you when you're feeling better, I promise."

With that, he was gone. Leaving me laying there wondering where that vulnerability I'd glimpsed the night before had gone. Probably tucked away with the rest of the emotions he kept securely locked up in the back of his mind.

Ten minutes later, Eli was in my room asking for the skinny on what had happened during the night.

"I didn't hear the sounds of any squeaking bed, so I guess that means our shit-faced boss couldn't get it up, huh?" He let out an overly enthused sigh. "Happens to the best of us, really."

"Eli," I said, rolling my eyes, "all we did was sleep. Then, of course, this morning he witnessed my stomach bug."

"You're gonna have to tell him sometime, Darce. Is that the only thing you haven't told him?"

I wasn't about to tell *anyone* what I'd seen on that e-mail string. I was halfway ashamed I'd seen it. Easton clearly wasn't going to fill me in on it. Trust issues I guess.

"As far as I know," I shrugged, lying. I shimmied down deeper into my bed. "Anyway," I continued, yawning, "I think I'm going to get a little more sleep while I can."

He gave me a sympathetic smile. "Okay, sweets. I'll see you when I get home. Feel better."

If only I could…

Chapter 44

~ Easton ~

Bloody hell. I'd acted like a twat going over to Darcy's place at two a.m. and causing a ruckus with her roommate. What the hell had I been thinking? I'd needed to be close to her and, somehow, she'd understood. This feeling of needing someone for comfort was foreign to me. It was a sign of weakness. I'd been told that over and over again as a child.

As I reflected back, I realised that Trace Matthews, Sr. was a good man. His second wife, Constance, was very good to me as well, never showing favouritism amongst her children over me while I visited, always making me feel welcome and secure. God knew I'd taxed their patience on numerous occasions, simply for the sport of it.

My mother had always complained upon my return that it would take months to get things with me back to normal again. She hated that I'd been given chores to do, the same as Trace and Paige during what she termed was supposed to be my "summer holiday." I hadn't minded doing the chores. I respected how hard my father worked at his bottling plant and, for once, I felt as if I fit in somewhere. Ultimately, that feeling would wear off once I returned to England and had grandparents and a host of servants fussing over me.

The first person I'd ever intentionally hurt was my younger half-brother, Trace. It was the summer before my freshman year of college. I'd wanted to spend it in Napa with my father to avoid all the matchmaking my mother was conducting with various British socialites. Trace had just turned sixteen at the time and was driving. He was also courting his first love, Brittany something-or-other. He was head-over-heels in love, though I tried to counsel him it was simply a case of lust. He'd assured me it wasn't. She was still a virgin at nearly seventeen. She'd been putting him off, telling him she wanted to wait to make sure they were really in love and committed to one another. I'd scoffed at the ludicrous notion, telling him to wise-up, it was simply a matter of him not taking charge of the relationship and being unfamiliar with the art of seduction.

I took it upon myself to show my younger brother the errors of underestimating the female mind and libido. I'd learned this lesson myself at the age of fifteen when my mother had encouraged one of her friends at the club to properly teach me how to please a woman. I'd accompanied Margaret Middleton on a long weekend to the French Riviera. It had been a very educationally charged weekend for me. So, having that in mind, I decided to pay a visit of my own to Brittany Something-Or-Other's house. Suffice it to say, her cherry didn't remain intact after my third secret visit and she was literally begging me to fuck her daily until I left. By this time, I had grown bored with the whole game and admitted as much.

Unfortunately, Brittany succumbed to a major guilt trip, confessing everything to Trace, sobbing and crying for his forgiveness. When our father returned home late that afternoon from his company, he found Trace and I in the front yard, beating each other to a pulp, whilst Paige stood nearby, screaming hysterically for both of us to stop. The rest of my summer visit was a bit strained. Before I'd left to return to Europe, my father had sat me down and asked what had motivated me to hurt my younger brother that way. I'd shrugged and said it was better he find out now she had the heart of a whore and toughen himself up for the road ahead. I recalled how he'd looked at me, not understanding how callous I'd become at eighteen...

Only now, I knew the truth: Trace Matthews Sr. wasn't my father. He'd known that shortly after my birth. As far as I was concerned, he deserved my hatred every bit as much as my blasted mother.

When I'd phoned him at her urging to validate her story, he'd become upset, reluctant to confirm what she'd told me in her e-mail. He'd finally realised I was relentless, so he admitted the truth, telling me some shit about my not being his son by blood, but certainly being his son by love. What the fuck? Love's such a fleeting emotion, triggered by a host of temporary human cravings/desires: acceptance, security, carnal satisfaction, self-esteem, comfort, procreation, and money.

When I stopped to think about it, I realised I didn't *need* love to satisfy any of those cravings or desires for myself. My wealth pretty much guaranteed acceptance, security, comfort and carnal satisfaction. I didn't give a worry about self-esteem as long as I had the rest. Procreation was no longer a desire or dream for me. In light of the recent turn of events, I was thankful Bianca had taken the path she had several years back. I was grateful my lineage would stop with me. It was a burden I'd wish upon no one else, bastard child or otherwise.

Once I reached the office, I was relieved Darcy wouldn't be in her adjoining office to distract me. I had the summation to put together and review, and then there were plans to be made, transitioning of resources. I was going to move my office. This game with Darcy was over.

I needed to leave, and not because I didn't love her, but because I *did*. The sad truth was I was ill-prepared to know how to sustain a loving relationship. I didn't know how to trust it because the few times I'd allowed myself to feel love, i.e., my mother, the man I thought was my father and then Bianca (to a lesser degree), they'd all turned toxic. I didn't want that for her. Better for both of us to cut our losses now before we became too invested in one another.

I got Colin on the phone.

"How are things going in Leeds, Colin?" I asked, leaning back in my leather chair.

"Right on course, Easton."

"Brilliant," I replied. "Do you think you're still needed there or can Devon handle it with her reduced hours on site?"

"Devon's got it," he replied. "Why?"

"Here's an early wedding present for you and Ronnie," I said, propping my feet up on my desk. "She's been quite vocal about wanting to be closer to her family in the U.S., yeah?"

I heard Colin chuckle. "You could say that, mate."

"I'm reorganising. I'm going to be moving my office to the headquarters in New York. I want you to take the lead position here in D.C., for however long you want it. You've moved around enough. I'm sure Ronnie would like to have her husband around more often."

The silence was thick on the other end. This had to be good news for Colin. I was puzzled by his lack of immediate response.

"Colin?"

"Oh yeah, Easton, that's fabulous, though being that Ronnie's from New York I'm sure she'd much prefer my taking an office there," he chuckled.

I swiveled in my chair, laughing. "Hey, at least she's going to be on the East Coast now and not across the pond, for Chrissake."

"Oh, she'll be thrilled, mate. I'm grateful as well, though a bit surprised…"

305

I knew Colin wanted more information. He knew me better than anyone, but I wasn't comfortable in providing details because, to be honest, I wasn't good at understanding my own actions or decisions at times. When my actions or decisions had nothing to do with business, that is.

"Splendid," I replied, not feeling nearly as enthusiastic as I sounded.

"Will you be transferring your assistant to New York as well?" Colin asked, still fishing for information.

"No. Darcy will remain here. You've already proven you can mentor her as well as I can. It's for the best, I think."

"I see," he replied, I could envision the look of disapproval on his face. My own gut felt like I'd twisted a knife into it. "When do you want me there?" he asked.

"Within the next few weeks," I answered, smoothing out the silk tie I'd worn for my meeting with Martin Sheridan later. "And don't worry, Colin, this won't interrupt the cruise you've planned after the wedding."

I heard him give a relaxed chuckle. "I figured you knew about that, mate. Glad to know because the tickets are non-refundable."

"Yes, well I'm meeting with Martin Sheridan this afternoon. He's back from his cruise, so I'll make sure I clue him in on the transition, and confirm he'll be on-site full-time whilst you're honeymooning."

"Sounds as if you've thought of everything, Easton. I'll let Ronnie know the good news straight-away. Cheers."

I sat at my desk for several moments after the call, examining my motives for this decision I'd made on my own, which clearly was something new for me.

Finally, I got up and walked out into Darcy's darkened office. I noticed that one of her sweaters was hanging on the back of her chair. My fingers gently caressed the soft wool knit. I pulled it from the chair, and rubbed the sleeve up under my chin. I could smell the faint scent of Darcy's perfume.

∞ ∞ ∞ ∞ ∞ ∞

My driver had taken me to the address of the mortuary outside of Paris my mother had given me. It was nearly midnight by the time I'd arrived. Once inside, I immediately spotted her sitting in a dimly lit corner of the huge room, wringing her hands.

"Mother," I greeted her, bestowing a quick, stiff kiss to her cheek as expected. "I'm sorry I'm too late."

She took my arm, leaning against me for support. "Easton, I didn't expect your father to pass so quickly. I thought there'd be time. He wanted to meet you, to tell you things," she sobbed softly. I bristled at her casual use of the word "father" when describing the man who'd apparently donated his half of the chromosomes to my cause and nothing more.

"I'm here to keep my part of the deal," I clarified, as she continued nudging me towards the closed door of his viewing room in this gothic mortuary, which frankly reminded me of something out of an Edgar Allen Poe novel.

"But certainly you're curious as to your royal bloodline?" she asked, pulling back from me in order to gaze up into my face. "I owe you an explanation. I want you to have it."

"What possible difference does it make, Mother?"

"It's your heritage to claim, Easton. It's your birthright. Come, follow me. The mortuary has taken considerable risk in allowing us in at this time of night. We've no time to waste..."

We entered the room where his body lay in state. It looked like a fucking royal wake. I wanted to scoff out loud at the absurdity of it all. Royal bloodline, my ass. There was no French monarchy and hadn't been for more than two hundred years.

She hurried off to where the opened casket was at the front of the chapel. Floor candles and endless flower arrangements adorned the walls of the room. I watched as she leaned in and smoothed his coloured robes. I could only guess it was some sort of royal burial ritual.

I stood next to her, watching tears roll down her face and then drop into the casket and on to the body of this man who, according to her, had fathered me. I felt nothing.

"Easton," she whispered as if there were crowds of people around, "This is your father, Constantine Xavier de Conti, Marquis of the Sovereign House of Capet."

I looked at the man in the casket. He was older, much older than my mother. He still had thick hair that was graying, but I could tell it'd been dark like mine. His arms were crossed over his chest like the crossing of swords. There was a crested ring on one finger that caught my eye. It bore the royal insignia of a titled Marquis.

"Go ahead, son. Take it."

I turned abruptly, peering down at my mother. Her tears had left a wet path on both cheeks, but her eyes were brilliant as they looked up into mine, an almost pleading expression on her face.

"Take the goddam ring, Easton," she said, her voice now louder. "It's your birthright. He had no other children. Only you. He wanted you to have it. It was his last dying wish and I promised him you'd have it."

I continued watching her, wondering why it was so damn important to her that I have his ring, this symbol of royalty that no longer had significance in modern society.

She blinked several times, wringing her hands. "You're a titled Earl by blood and for thirty-five years I was nothing more than a whore to him that he claimed he loved. I'll be damned if I'll let him go six feet under still wearing it. I'm the one who earned it—for you. Now take it," she coaxed.

I reached over and slipped the ring off of his cold, stiff finger, examining it in the candlelight for a moment, before slipping it into the pocket of my trousers. I did it for her—well, maybe for me as well. The bastard owed me something, though I'd be damned if I'd ever lay claim to my royal title, or wear the ring for that matter. That was about her, not about me. She smiled up at me approvingly, leaned over, and kissed his cold lips.

"Jusqu'à ce que nous nous réunissons à nouveau mon amour, sachez que je serai toujours vous aiment Constantine," she said to ears that couldn't hear her. She brushed her fingers against his cheek and then turned to me.

"Come, Easton. I'll ride back with you. I need to tell you how it all happened."

Chapter 45

It was a perfect day.

That's the thought that kept running through my mind as I found myself completely sprawled out over what was becoming my favorite place in the 'Presidential Suite' at the St. Regis: the deliciously oversized couch in the sitting room. My "stomach bug" had not made an appearance in three weeks. I felt healthy, energetic and extremely happy with the time and attention Easton had been devoting to me lately.

Yes, I decided, being right here, right now was the perfect place to be. Kicked back on this luscious sofa, an open book perched against my knees, sneaking peeks at Easton who was sitting across the room in the overstuffed chair, pecking away on his laptop.

Shirtless.

I was pretending to be reading a book. I mean sure, I'd actually started out reading it, but every time I heard his magical fingers tapping away on the keyboard, or heard him sigh—completely unaware he'd done it, or saw him run a hand through his gorgeously disheveled hair in my peripheral vision, I had to avert my eyes to him.

My favorite was when he stretched.

Fuuuuck.

The jury was still out as to whether he was *aware* of me watching him, because I made sure to oh-so-subtly glance down at my book whenever he shifted or started to turn my way…which seemed to be happening more frequently as this Saturday afternoon dwindled by. This time, when I glanced down at the perpetual page 67 of my book, I felt his gaze linger.

Caught!

I felt my lips begin to curl up at the corners, knowing he was now staring at me. I looked up, to see those gunmetal eyes lock with my blue ones. But where I was facing away from the window, he was facing it directly, causing the 2 p.m. sunlight to reflect in his eyes, making them look like dark fireworks.

"You haven't turned the page in a while, love," he told me, as if it was a secret. "What's wrong? Having trouble with the big words?"

I gave him a soft smirk, my eyes still on his and gave the page a turn for good measure. But I saw the way he was looking at me, his eyes lowering to the thin tank top I was wearing. He was aware that I was braless, because it was he who had refused to give it back to me this morning after we'd played.

I was so on to him.

"Don't even think about it, Mr. Matthews," I scolded lightly, knowing what it did to him when I referred to him by that.

He let in a lazy inhale, his eyes now deepening to a yet un-named shade of gray. Resting his jaw on a propped-up fist, he replied, "Think about what, Ms. Sheridan? And you didn't answer my question."

I raised the book up in front of me, "Small font," I explained innocently. Placing the book face-down on my stomach, I languidly raised my now free hands to my hair and started to pile it up on top of my head into a knotted bun. The mid-June heat and humidity had found its way to the top floor of the St. Regis.

His eyes followed my movements.

"And you *know* what I meant when I said 'don't even think about it'," I told him, trying to fight back a smile as his gaze was now fastened on my exposed neck.

"I assure you, I don't," he responded softly. "Please elaborate for me."

Easton slowly stood up, leaving his laptop on the chair, open and forgotten, and began a leisurely pace towards the couch. Looking up at him, I watched as he knelt down next to where my head rested on some pillows. His hands made their way to my bun, and the elastic securing it, and gently released the heavy waves.

310

Decorating my shoulders with my now-freed hair, and tucking a piece behind my ear, he leaned in and whispered, "I like it better down."

He leaned back, supporting his weight on his calves, and gave my body a slow perusal. It was a different kind of perusal from what I was used to, though. Instead of the hunger that usually made a home on his face when he'd study me, this time it was like he was memorizing me—as if he was pocketing my curves, features, and errant freckles, planning on saving them for a rainy day.

His hands surveyed me next, distracting me from my thoughts. I watched as he took my book and casually tossed it to the floor. He then began to inch my shirt up, placing a soft kiss on my thankfully still-flat belly. And my nerves caught fire as his tongue followed his lips.

"That was a good book," I tried to fake-scowl at him, but he wasn't paying attention to my face as he quickly pushed my shirt up over my breasts, sucking in a sharp breath at my exposed nipples. Raising himself and leaning over me, he rested a hand on the back of the couch and the other on the arm. Instead of acknowledging my comment, he used his mouth to lightly lick around my hardening nipple.

"Easton," I inhaled.

"Tell me about the book," he replied, right before sucking hard on the tender tip.

I hissed through my teeth. "*God*," I whimpered.

His mouth kept nursing on my flesh, going back and forth from hard suckles to light nips. A hand now kneading the other one, lightly pinching and rolling my nipple. I felt his denim-clad knee come up and rest between my legs.

Easton's mouth released my nipple, making a slight sucking sound. "A book about God, Miss Sheridan? That wasn't the Bible, was it?" Both of his hands were now massaging my breasts. Watching his hands and the flesh beneath them, he continued. "Because if you're in need of a prayer, I'd rather first give you something to *confess*."

He moved his knee higher, to where it was now resting against my pussy. His mouth was nuzzling the side of my neck.

"Move," he whispered roughly.

My breaths were getting a little faster. "Wh-what?" I tried to concentrate on his request, but his tongue was now licking my pulse.

He moved his knee even higher against me, making me let out an audible moan at the contact.

"Move," he said again, nipping at my earlobe, the words no longer a request as they ribboned into an order. "Move your wet pussy against me, Darcy," he clarified harshly.

Holy shit.

I raised my hips, and hesitantly brought them back down, feeling the friction it caused between our clothes. I repeated the action, this time rubbing up harder against his thigh.

"Mmmm..." I mewled when he moved, pressing his knee right over my clit. My hips followed the action, and soon I began panting as we set a rhythm.

He bit down on my right nipple, soothing the abraded skin with his tongue.

My rhythm became more frantic, as I was reaching for the edge of a shallow climax.

"What's wrong, baby?" Easton asked after a sharp pull of his teeth.

"I can't...," my words stumbled. "Easton...I need...more..."

I felt his body swiftly leave mine. Opening my eyes, I saw and felt his hands on the button of my loose shorts. Quickly moving the fabric down my legs, he dropped the shorts onto the floor.

"Here," he said softly, bringing his mouth to where my panties were probably drenched by now. I felt his warm breath through the cotton before he took the wet fabric into his mouth. His eyes were on mine as he sucked on the dampness.

"Jesus," he said, letting it go, and bringing my panties down my legs. "I'll never forget how sweet you taste."

Before I could register his words, his hands were back on my hips and were picking me up and turning me over to where I was now laying on my stomach. They stayed on my hips as he slid me down to where my legs were now hanging over the arm of the couch.

Without any sort of preamble, his mouth was once-again on my pussy, sucking as his hands ran down my back before gripping my ass.

"Fuck, love" he hummed. "You're so fucking wet for me. Always for me," he lapped his tongue through my folds from bottom to top. "Just for me." He tightened his grip, flexing his fingers hard on my cheeks as he took his tongue as far as it could go into my pussy.

My hips started moving against the arm of the couch, stimulating my clit, and trying to get Easton's tongue to move deeper.

He began to slow his tongue, moving one hand around to my stomach, drifting lower to where it was now settling right above where I needed it. His tongue stopped completely.

I let out a frustrated moan as Easton asked in his low, sexy voice, "Where do you want this hand, Darcy?" I felt his fingers flex below me.

"Tell me," he whispered savagely against the small of my back.

"On my pussy," I gave him a flustered reply against the couch cushions, trying to subtly shimmy my hips to get his hand to move a *little* further south.

He obliged what felt like a friggin' millimeter down. I heard his soft laugh. His other hand was rubbing up my back. "It's already on your pussy, love."

I felt a finger lightly rub my clit before disappearing. "*That's* your clit, love. Right on top of that sweet cunt of yours." Another light flicker of his finger. "Is that where you want it?"

"*Yes.*" I was panting now; I could feel a light sheen of sweat begin to ignite my skin. "Please, Easton…Fuck. I need you to rub my clit. *Please,*" I groaned desperately.

He answered me by rolling the delicate flesh between two fingers. Another pair of fingers began thrusting relentlessly into my pussy.

The orgasm was building too fast now…too hard.

"Easton!" I was being electrified, my nerves humming with fire, my back bowing up in the intensity. For a minute, I lived in heaven. My hands curled up into fists, but not wanting to fight the stretches of lightning that reached to them.

Never in my life had I felt this amazingly satisfied, so deliciously depleted. And the entire time, Easton was showing me that he was the only one who could bring me there.

He was quietly ruining me, wrecking me, shattering me on a low pulse for any other man. He owned me, and I was happily being captured.

I felt his hands move my hair to the side as he placed the softest kiss on the back of my neck, letting my skin keep it.

"You're so beautiful," he whispered, right before lightly turning me over, and gently picking me up to cradle me as he carried me into his—our—bedroom suite.

He carefully set me down onto the soft mattress. I loved how he did that; handled me physically like I was made out of glass…but still took me to physical limits, knowing that I wouldn't break.

He unfastened his pants slowly, making a modest show of it, because he knew that I loved to watch. Through thoroughly sated eyes, I watched as Easton brought his pants down to the floor, followed by his boxers, letting me see how hard his cock was and silently letting me know that I was the cause of that.

Slightly dipping the mattress, his body hovered over the length of mine. He placed his weight on his forearms as he gazed at my face in that memorizing way he'd done earlier. Skin to skin, I let him. I didn't know why he was looking at me like that, but I loved the *feel* of it, knowing that I was being cherished to a level that I didn't yet understand.

Once again, he tucked a strand of hair behind my ear. "I love your hair," he whispered into the late afternoon. His eyes were looking straight into mine now, as his fingers brushed my lower lip. "I love your smile." I rewarded him with one, kissing his fingers in the process.

God, listening to his murmured words is amazing.

314

"I love your strength. And how you're never able to stop yourself from voicing your opinions, because I love your words." He quietly continued as his fingers swept lightly over my nipples, making their feather touches to my ribs.

"I love the way you scrunch up your nose like this," he said, making a ridiculous scrunched-up face that made me let out a series of giggles, "when you're trying to hold something back."

"And *Jesus*, love…" He brought his forehead down to mine, as his hand was now drawing idle stars on the skin between my hip bones. "I love your laugh. If I could," I felt his body draw back, and I breathed in the feeling of feminine contentment as I felt his cock tease the opening where I wanted him, "I'd make sure you'd always be laughing. And making sure that your smile was never far behind."

Is he about to tell me…?

He rotated his hips, his piercing teasing over my clit.

"Easton…" all thoughts from before were scattered across the room as I felt him tease my slick entrance.

His lips skated over my forehead. "I hope that you'll always be happy, Darcy," he whispered, right as he entered me in one full thrust.

"*Oh*…" I moaned, raising my hips. He kept the pace slow, pulling back, and re-entering me in single thrusts. He was done teasing me, but the sensations that became crumbled shards of sensation through my body kept me biting my lip, chasing the release.

"Faster, Easton," I told him, before he brought his lips back to mine.

He kept his pace. "No, love," he pulled back. "Just *feel* it." He calmed me, "Let it come to you."

"Mmmm," was my response as his lips traveled to my breasts. He didn't suck hard this time, instead went with a gentle pulling that left my flesh with just his lips.

I felt it building, my muscles beginning to shake as Easton kept his measured momentum. My nerves were beginning to fray at the ends, my brows pulling together at the delicious torture.

"Please…," staggered from my lips, almost soundless.

He changed the angle, lifting my knees, so his piercing was now brushing my clit with every heavy thrust. The release was coming faster to me now, my hands white-knuckling the sheets.

His hands made their way to my breasts. "Go over for me, sweetheart," he said both roughly and gently, right before I felt the hard pinch on my nipples.

That was all I needed.

Oh…My God!

My entire body bowed up at the orgasm, and I heard Easton's growl as I felt him fill me entirely with his own cum. I felt his teeth on the tender place where shoulder meets neck. Soothing the bite with a soft kiss, he pulled out, moving off of me. He lay on his side and brought his arm around me, bringing my back to his warm chest. I remember the feel of Easton's lips against the back of my neck, placing silent and soundless words there.

And I had never been happier in my life.

Chapter 46

I was entwined in Easton's strong arms, our bodies still damp from our lovemaking. He was fingering through the tangles of my hair that were splayed across his bare chest. I was snuggled up against him, listening to the steady beat of his heart, my finger lightly tracing patterns on his taut belly.

"I'm spent, love," he said with a sigh. "I'm definitely going to need a quick power nap after that."

"I think we both need *showers* after that," I replied with a smile.

"Later," he remarked. "I want my scent on you for a while."

I poked my head up to look at his face. His expression was serious, as if he was contemplating *something*.

"What do you want to do this evening?" he asked, giving me a slow smile. "We can go to dinner, clubbing—whatever you want."

I propped my elbow up, resting my face on my hand and studied him. "Let's just stay in tonight," I said, as I ran a finger idly on the skin of his arm. "I really don't feel like getting dressed up, and I'm thinking that curling up with that *really good book* sounds pretty tempting right now." I gave him a wry smile. "Plus, clubs and restaurants probably wouldn't approve of you being shirtless and barefoot. And I really, *really* like you shirtless and barefoot."

He quirked a brow as he gazed down at me through shuttered lashes. "What's happened to my party girl?" he quipped. "Turning into somewhat of a homebody these days," he teased.

I laid my head back down against his shoulder. "I guess I just don't need all of that any more. You've tamed me, Easton."

317

I heard his soft chuckle. "Don't go getting all domesticated on me, love," he chided. "I love your cheekiness. But if you want to stay here, that's fine. We'll order in. I've got a few things to finish up for work. Let's grab a nap."

I wasn't tired in the least, but Easton seemed to want me beside him at the moment, so I complied. He must've been exhausted, because in a matter of several minutes, I felt his warm, even breathing on my neck. As much as I hated moving away from him, I was in desperate need of the loo. I quietly and carefully extricated myself from his arms, and allowed myself a comfort break. I was still naked and decided I'd heed his instructions to shower later. My supply of clean clothing at his place was dwindling, so I went in search of the clothes he'd so expertly removed from me in the sitting room.

I shrugged them back on, pulling my wild, just-thoroughly-fucked hair up in a ponytail, slipping the elastic hair tie around it. I was thinking maybe I could actually *read* a few chapters of the book while he napped. Then we could shower together and maybe order a pizza. We hadn't had one of our "pizza and a horror flick" evenings in a while. I looked under the sofa for my book, but found my flip-flops instead, so I pulled them out and slipped them on my bare feet.

Where the hell's my book?

I looked around the bare floor and finally spotted it under the chair where Easton had been working earlier. How the hell had it gotten clear over there? He'd left his laptop on the table, the lid still opened to whatever he'd been working on.

"Way to go, Easy E," I said to no one. "You'll be bitching later when the battery's dead." I picked it up, taking it over to the desk to put it on the charger. As I prepared to close the lid, my attention was immediately drawn to what was pulled up on the screen. I felt my eyes widen and my mouth go slack as the comprehension sunk in.

It was the organizational chart for Baronton-Sheridan. I'd put the current one together, complete with company photos of the employees listed. This one had been amended by Easton just today, showing an effective date of Monday, June 17th.

Easton's photo was no longer at the top of the chart under the title of 'Acting General Manager.' It'd been replaced by Colin Devers' name and photo. I saw that my dad's name still showed as a dotted line to the acting G.M. My name and photo still showed as 'Executive Assistant to the G.M.' As I glanced through it, nothing else had changed other than Easton having been eliminated, replaced by Colin.

I slammed the lid shut on his laptop, slowly backing away from it, my mind working furiously to process the information, or lack of it at the moment.

Easton's leaving. Leaving D.C. Leaving me. Leaving our baby.

My stomach roiled at the thought. My heart was starting to crumble, taking my ability to breathe in air with it. My pulse quickened. Respiration was shallow. I felt my hands clenched at my sides, opening and closing repeatedly, my fingernails digging into my palms as I shook my head 'no.' *There has to be more to it,* I thought. I was still in a semi-trance, when I felt myself back up against a hard, warm body. I whirled around, coming face-to-face with Easton.

My eyes dropped, his nakedness registering in my mind, his cock still damp and glistening from our sex. Our lovely goodbye sex, it would appear.

"What is it?" he asked softly, drawing my gaze back up to his face. "I awoke and you weren't next to me. Not sleepy?"

He had no clue what I'd seen. I knew by the faint smile that graced his lips and his love-filled eyes.

Traitorous bastard!

"You're leaving," I said to him, making it more of an accusation than a question. "You're *fucking* going to leave me, aren't you?"

His eyes quickly skirted the room, seeing that his laptop was now closed, which meant he now knew I'd been the one to close it. And that in doing so, I'd have seen what was on it. I watched as his expression morphed from soft and loving, to shielded and masked. He was silent.

"I saw the org chart," I explained, reaffirming what he already knew. "I mean, I went to put your laptop on the desk, and it was just there in front of me," I rambled, my hands now clasped together in front of me.

"Come with me," he said, taking my hand and pulling me behind him to the bedroom. He grabbed his boxers from the floor and pulled them on. This conversation was evidently one he preferred not to have with me while naked.

319

My stomach butterflies were swarming in all directions. They were coming within millimeters of each other apparently on a crash course of destruction. He pulled me down next to him on the bed, taking my hands in his. "I was going to tell you tomorrow about Colin being assigned as acting G.M. of Baronton-Sheridan."

"I see," I replied, a feeling of dread seeping in. "Why tomorrow, Easton? Why not tell me today? Or yesterday? Why not tell me whenever the fuck it was that you *made* the decision?" My voice had regained some strength, and the anger was now finding its way inside.

"I felt I needed to reward him for his faithful service to the corporation…and to me," he continued, as if that was of any importance to me. He took his gaze from my face, now studying his clasped hands instead.

Always keep eye contact during a presentation, Darcy. Remember, our customers need to feel the honesty and the integrity that is Baronton-Sheridan…

My throat was closing up, restricting my air intake. I could do nothing but nod.

"Anyway, Ronnie's from the States and with their wedding coming up, I felt it might be best for all concerned to assign Colin here permanently. He needs to spend time with his wife. She needs to be closer to her family—"

I placed my fingers on his lips, stopping him mid-sentence."I really don't care about Colin and Ronnie right now. My interest lies in where *you're* going."

He rubbed his chin with his fingers. There was no mistaking the fact he was having a difficult time cutting to the chase.

"I'm making my office in New York starting next week…at the U.S. headquarters. The merger and acquisitions team's there and I've a host of potential companies to visit." His voice faltered just a bit. "Darcy," he said, sighing, "I'm going to be traveling extensively in the U.S. for the next several months, looking at potential prospects to acquire. These things aren't done overnight, you realise."

Huh? It sure felt like overnight when you merged with my father.

"What are you *really* saying, Easton?" I demanded, scooting further away from him. "Why have you been so secretive about this?"

"It's just that I'll be traveling so much, love. I mean it's not like you'd be seeing me much anyway, you know?"

"I guess you *are* leaving me," I responded in a voice that wasn't much more than a whisper. I quickly tried to cover up the dumbfounded tone in my voice. "Well, it's probably for the best that I found out tonight. I mean, it could've been worse. You were probably just going to e-mail it to me in the morning, letting me know that I didn't have to go through the trouble of wearing any sexy lingerie to work." I couldn't help the sarcasm that blanketed my tone.

"I was going to *tell* you, and I was going to explain," he replied with a scowl. "Calmly."

I tilted my head, and ignored the scowl. "Kind of like what I did back at my apartment, right? Before you left the first time and went back to London?"

I didn't wait for his response, exhausted at the quick turn of events of the day. As it turned out, my butterflies had been on a suicide mission as they crashed and burned, falling to the pit of my stomach in charred ashes. I turned abruptly, heading for the bathroom to grab some of my stuff. I felt myself hauled back by his strong arms.

"Listen to me," he growled, his fingers digging into my shoulders. "That's not it at all. It's just…better this way. I'm not taking you with me. I *can't* take you with me."

"Why not?" I challenged, sounding borderline pathetic. "You owe me an answer, Easton. Why the hell not?" I was glaring at him impudently now. Waiting for an answer or something—*anything*—that would help make sense out of the pain that was engulfing me.

He raked his hand through his tousled hair and turned away from me, unable to say whatever he was going to say while facing me. He moved a couple of steps away.

"Because," he faltered, "it's just that…you're not part…of my long-term plan. I'm sorry." The last part came out as a hoarse whisper.

321

Breathe, Darcy. Just fucking breathe.

"Got it," I said, feeling my hands ball up into tight fists at my sides. I quickly closed the distance between us. I didn't recognize the guttural sounds of rage I was making as I flailed my fists as hard as I could against his bare chest, over and over again.

Easton didn't attempt to shield himself, or even try to stop me. He let me continue to pummel him with all of my strength. Maybe it allowed him to feel less guilty about what he'd done.

"I *loved* you, you son-of-a-bitch! I *fucking* loved you!" My sobs cut loose with a vengeance now, blinding me with pain and rage. I tore myself away from him, not giving a shit about my things. He could trash them for all I cared. The bastard wasn't going to see me cry one more second. I'd shed the tears I needed to shed, but my audience wouldn't be Easton fucking Matthews!

"Darcy," he called out, his arms outstretched as if pleading his case, as if there was more he wanted to say. I hesitated, but just momentarily. No words followed. There were a million fucking words he could've said at that moment:

4 words:	*"I didn't mean it."*
3 words:	*"I love you."*
2 words:	*"Don't go."*
1 word:	*"Stop!"*

But he said none of them as I turned and headed towards the door. I slammed out of his suite, tears now blinding my eyes as I smacked the palm of my hand hard up against the button of the elevator, over and over again. Fuck! My handbag with my car keys, cell and everything else was still in his suite. I'd be damned if I'd go back for them. I tore the hair tie out, running my fingers through my long locks hoping to cover my tear-stained face from the general public. The humidity made my hair fan out in wispy, wavy, kinky strands.

By the time I reached the lobby, the tears had stopped. I could only imagine how I looked to the doorman, clad in tight little shorts, my hair askew and mascara running down my cheeks, making me look like some grunge rock groupie reject.

"I don't have my cell." I tossed the numb words to him. "Would you please hail a cab for me?"

He nodded.

"Certainly, Miss."

His face was soft with compassion. He'd seen me many times before coming in and out of the hotel with Easton. He'd held the door for us numerous times, always smiling and cheerfully greeting us as we came and went.

He wouldn't be greeting me again.

He went out onto the sidewalk and looked up the street. I saw him wave his arm, beckoning a cab to the curb outside. As soon as it arrived, I hit the pavement. He had the door to the cab opened for me. Tipping his hat to me, he wished me a good day.

I prayed Eli was home so he could pay the fare.

The cab ride home didn't even register in my mind. It was a total blur, just like every other thought that was bouncing around in my murky, fog-cloaked mind. I was surprised I'd remembered my address when the cab driver asked.

As he pulled up to our building, I felt myself exhale seeing Eli's car parked in his slot.

"I'll be just a minute with the fare," I said briskly to him. "I'm going right up there to Unit C," I explained. I couldn't imagine what he'd thought when I'd plopped into the back seat of his cab looking the way I looked, sniffling post-tears and looking like the broken-hearted zombie I was!

I ran up the few concrete steps to our townhouse, my fists pounding on the front door, hearing someone's voice screaming, "Eli! Eli!"

The door flew open and Eli was standing there, a look of alarm on his face.

"What the hell, Darce?" he asked, his eyes raking over my face. "Oh God, what is it?" he asked, opening the screen door.

"Please pay the cab driver for me, okay? I'll pay you back, I promise." My voice was strangely calm—and monotone. I saw the look of concern cross over his face.

"Sure," he replied, checking his back pocket to make sure his wallet was there. "I'll be right back, Darce. Let's talk then, okay?"

"I'm really, really tired, Eli," I sighed. "We'll talk in the morning."

He was ready to say more, but the impatient cabbie leaned on his horn.

"Stay right there, sweetie. Don't move," he instructed, loping across the small patch of grass towards the parking lot.

I didn't do as he asked. I couldn't. I wasn't ready to spill my guts to anyone because, if I did, I wouldn't be able to stop. I climbed the stairs to my room and collapsed on top of my bed, drawing my knees up to my chin, wrapping my arms around my calves, essentially drawing myself up into a safe, tight ball, rocking back and forth as I let the tears quietly flow down in rivulets onto my cheeks.

Several minutes later, Eli was pounding on my closed and locked door. "Darcy, honey, let me in. I want to find out what happened. Please?"

"Go away, Eli," I called out. "I just need to be alone for now, okay? We'll talk, just not right now. I've got to work it all out in my head."

"Are you sure?" he replied, reluctantly. "Because I could just…Fuck, I don't know, stand next to you? You don't even have to say anything, I swear."

I didn't answer through the door, but I still knew that he was standing there.

"Darce, you really looked like you didn't need to be alone right now."

"Maybe later," I replied. "I'm just so tired. I want to sleep and then take a shower. Later, okay?"

"Okay," he replied, sounding concerned. "Hey, I'll be right downstairs if you need me. I'm staying in tonight."

"'Kay," I called out. "Later."

324

I heard him retreat back downstairs. I continued to rock back and forth in the fetal position, until, blessedly, I dozed off into a restless sleep.

When I woke up, it was dark outside. I glanced at my bedside clock. It was a quarter till ten. I could hear Eli downstairs, the sound of the television muted any conversation, but I could tell he was on his phone. Probably apologizing to Cain for standing him up tonight so that he could babysit his pathetic roommate.

I crawled out of bed, pulling clean underwear and a nightie from my dresser. I wanted a shower more than anything. I needed to wash off Easton's scent for good.

My hot shower felt nice. I scrubbed my skin so hard it was a dark shade of pink when I emerged from the shower. I'd washed my hair furiously, remembering how he'd touched it multiple times earlier, wanting his fingerprints gone.

I patted my skin dry, pulling up my clean panties, and tossing the silky nightgown over my shoulders. I started towel drying my long, damp locks, spritzing detangler on it. The bathroom was so steamed up that I couldn't see my reflection in the mirror. Maybe that was for the best.

I took a hand towel and wiped the fog from the mirror over the sink. I studied my reflection now. I'd managed to scrub all remnants of the mascara and eyeliner off my cheeks where they'd streaked from my tears.

I picked up my wide-toothed comb, and started trying to run it through my hair, bringing some semblance of order to it. It was well past my shoulders. It was the hair that Easton had loved, forever touching it, running his fingers through it, and breathing in the scent of it. He'd been minorly obsessed with it. Not anymore. My hair, like me, wasn't in his long-term plan.

My comb hit a major tangle and came to an abrupt halt.

Damn! I hate when that happens.

I set the comb down and tried to work through it with my fingers. Shit. I had no patience with this right now. I opened the drawer to the vanity and found Eli's trimming scissors for his goatee. Maybe I should just snip this one extremely stubborn tangle out. I mean, Christ! My hair was super thick. It wouldn't be missed.

I aligned the scissors right above the snarled knot in my hair and snipped, watching it fall to the bathroom floor. That wasn't so bad. I turned back to the mirror, taking the comb that now slid smoothly through that side of my head.

Oops...now this side of my head has a shorter chunk of hair.

Not a problem, I decided. I'll just make a layer cut that same length on the other side of my head so we match. I studied the new length of hair on the left side of my head, positioning the scissors as closely on the right side of my head and snipped a chunk of the length off. There. I turned back to the mirror, combing both sides to see if they were now even.

Not quite. Just a little bit more off the left...

Twenty minutes later, Eli was outside the bathroom door, knocking loudly.

"Darce? You didn't fall in did you?" he said, trying to make light of his concern that I may have gone into the bathroom for the sole purpose of slitting my wrists. I mean hell—what he must've thought seeing me in the state I was in when I got home.

"No worries," I called out. "I'm about done here. I just had to trim some split ends. Gotta pee?"

"Well, yeah," he said, acting as if he really wasn't sure whether he had to pee or not.

I gave myself one last assessment in the mirror. I guess it wasn't so bad. At least most of it was even now, though I couldn't see the back. I'd ask Eli.

I quickly unlocked the bathroom door, throwing it open.

"Ta da," I sang out, my hands fluffing up my damp locks, or what was left of them. "What do you think?" I asked, twirling around so he'd get the full effect.

Eli's eyes widened as he studied my face and hair and then dropped his eyes immediately to the bathroom floor where multiple piles of various lengths of snipped clumps of dark brown hair lay, scattered everywhere.

"Oh, *fuck*," he said, his face a mask of concern. "Do you have Monroe's personal cell number?"

Chapter 47

~ Easton ~

I repositioned myself once again on the soft, leather couch in the cabin of my jet. I'd just finished my second bourbon, my laptop perched on my lap as I attempted to finish this e-mail to Colin. I glanced at my watch. He and Ronnie should be landing at Reagan International right about now. He'd see my e-mail once the flight attendants allowed passengers to resume use of their electronic devices.

I re-read it for the third time:

Colin,

I'm in transit to New York now. I moved my travel plans up for personal reasons. You and I can talk on Monday. Darcy's aware of the organizational change, but I'm not sure what you can expect from her come Monday. Call if issues arise. - E.

There. It was finished. I closed my laptop, powering it off, and downed the rest of my bourbon. I doubted if there was enough bourbon on the continent at the moment to dull the pain I felt over what I'd done. How I'd left. The fucking coward I'd been.

"Easton," my mother said quietly as the limo sped off into the black night, putting distance between me and the corpse she'd just introduced to me as my father. "I want to tell you how this happened. You've a right to know."

I looked over at her, seeing the misery in her eyes that meant she was in pain. Now she wanted to share that pain with me. Thirty-three years later.

"I'm listening, Mother."

"Your fa—Constantine and I were lovers for more than thirty-five years. He was fifteen years older than me, and he was married. His wife, Isabella couldn't give him children, yet he remained devoted to her whilst loving me on the side."

"Don't you mean whilst fucking you on the side, Mother?"

"Come now, Easton. Don't be churlish. It was love. We loved each other, but I knew he'd never leave Isabella. French aristocracy still exists, despite what you believe. Constantine would never dishonour her that way. I realised that after I purposely got pregnant with you." She stopped, pulling a lacy handkerchief from her handbag to wipe her tears. "Yes, I know. The oldest trick in the book. It didn't matter to him, though. He was angry with me and said it was over. Done. He said that he never wanted to see me again." Her voice was filled with emotion as she continued.

"I wasn't quite finished with the games, though. I started hanging out at the various pubs and night spots in Swindon. There was an American Air Force base located close by. That's where I met Trace Matthews. He was immediately attracted to me, so I used that as a weapon against Constantine, knowing it would get back to him." She shrugged her shoulders, as if it was of little consequence. "I told Trace a month later I was pregnant with his child. He was in love with me. I knew his tour was nearly up with the military. I knew I could leave England and go to the States with him, as his wife. I knew it would drive Constantine crazy. And it did."

"Mother," I interrupted, "what's the point of all this?"

"Please, let me finish, Easton," she said, touching my arm for comfort. "I did a cruel thing to Trace Matthews. I didn't love him at all, but I let him think that I did. After you were born, a month early, he knew. Still, he never said a word to me about it, because he loved me and he loved you as his son. The problem was, Constantine wanted me back. He'd located me and was keeping in contact. He knew he had a son. He wanted me to return to England with you so that we'd at least be close. So I did. I admitted everything to Trace Matthews, divorced him and returned to England. Once I did, I resumed the affair with Constantine. I thought for sure he'd want to visit you, but he didn't. He was afraid word would get out that he had a bastard son and it would crush Isabella. So, all of those 'vacations' I took? They were nothing more than me sneaking off to be with him in secret, remote places. Isabella passed away five years ago," she said in a loud whisper, dabbing her eyes.

"Finally," she continued, "I thought we'd be together, that our love could be known to everyone. No more hiding." She laughed derisively, shaking her head in disgust. "It seems when Isabella died, she took Constantine's heart with her. He was a broken man, eaten up with guilt

and regrets. I finally realised that for me, love was a toxic potion. I'd wasted all those years thinking I loved someone who loved me back. It was a cruel realisation. I left him to wallow in his self-pity and remorse. He contacted me several months ago, begging for me to visit him. That's when he told me he was dying, and that he wanted to see you, to talk to you and beg your forgiveness."

"And what about you, Mother?" I asked, focusing my attention on this woman who'd given birth to me, but not much else.

"I don't understand," she replied. "What are you asking?"

"I'm asking when you intend to ask for my forgiveness."

I saw her bristle immediately, her eyes narrowing as she stared at me. "You had a good life, Easton. But don't think for one minute that we aren't cut from the same cloth, you and me. I'm telling you this as your mother so that you don't waste the years I've wasted pining for something or someone that will never honestly love you back. It's not within us to love or to be loved unconditionally. We poison ourselves and those around us with our black hearts, trust me."

I powered up my laptop as the plane was taxiing down the runway of the private airstrip outside of the city. I pulled up the GPS file on Darcy and clicked on the 'Night Moves' link to get the coordinates. The codes populated the field immediately. She was at her apartment.

Good girl.

Chapter 48

It was July 4th weekend. Eli and I'd decided to host a cook-out at our apartment for the hell of it. I'd invited Mom and Dad, Lindsey, Taz and Baby Harper. Eli had invited Cain. It would be a small gathering, as our outside patio couldn't accommodate a much larger group.

It had been a little more than two weeks since Easton had dumped me. Eli had gotten me through that weekend. The following Monday, I'd reported to work with a spiffy new hairstyle that barely hit my shoulders, complete with both high and low lights to give it that "chunky" look as Monroe had called it when he made a special Sunday house call to his favorite crazy-ass customer.

I won't lie, it was a tad uncomfortable being around Colin again. I wasn't sure how much he knew about Easton and me. But by Tuesday afternoon, the veil of discomfort had been blown away and we were back to our usual business banter and personal chatter.

Ronnie had met us for lunch on Wednesday. She'd been condo hunting and had a list of potentials for Colin to visit after work. I even found myself laughing a couple of times during our conversation, but the absence of Easton's name on a daily basis at the office, and even at lunch with Ronnie spoke volumes. I even caught Ronnie looking at me with a sad expression a couple of times. After the whole thing that happened in Easton's hotel room, I was sure I could handle pretty much anything, but someone's pity…That one took a little strength and tenacity; I'm not going to lie.

Eli came through the patio door just then, interrupting my thoughts. "So, you planning on giving your parents the good news today?" he asked, giving me a wink. "Seems like an appropriate theme for Independence Day, yeah?"

I gave him 'the look,' popping a cherry tomato in my mouth from the salad I'd been making. "Funny you should mention it," I replied, "I actually intend to give them the news while they're here."

"No," he said, his eyes widening. "So, I guess you're all about having some fireworks after all."

331

"You know, I actually don't have an issue telling them they're about to be grandparents. I mean, my mom's been practically trying to get me married *for the purpose* of seeing me drive a minivan full of kids—"

Eli let out a shrill gasp, "A *minivan?*" He popped the cap off a cold, bottled beer and immediately took a swig. "Dear God, where have I failed you?"

I rolled my eyes. "You know what I mean. She's like *every* mom, which means she's basically genetically engineered for her Thanksgiving dinners to get bigger and bigger each year." I shrugged, digging through the salad for another cherry tomato. "Telling them isn't the deal. This isn't the fifties, like you said, right?"

He was leaning on the sink next to me, now studying my massacred vegetables. "So, what *is* the big dealio?"

I blew out a breath. "Telling them *who* got me pregnant."

"But you *are* going to tell them…" Eli replied, waiting for me to assure him.

I looked at him with a scrunched-up nose, not answering.

"What?" he asked, cocking an eyebrow. "You know damn well they're gonna ask."

"And you know damn well I've no issue telling them it's none of their business. In a very *respectful* manner, of course."

Eli nodded, picking at his beer label."Okay, I'll buy that, but I mean…why?" He looked back over at me.

"Seriously? You have to ask?" I said, sprinkling grated cheese over my finished—and what I hoped would be delicious—project. "'Hey, Daddy. So, I just wanted to run it by you that I'm currently preggo by the guy you hired to mentor me. P.S. I wouldn't touch that fax machine for awhile, and can you pass me the ketchup?' Yeah, how'd that sound? Because that's pretty much how it would go. I kind of like my dad…and I'm really not ready to give him a coronary."

Eli picked a sliced radish from the relish tray, popping it into his mouth. "That's not the *real* reason, is it?"

"Of course it is," I lied. "What else could it be?"

I heard his soft smirk in response. "You're afraid of them finding out their little girl enjoys it rough and loud, aren't you?"

"Bite me," I replied, flipping him off. "Maybe I'll tell them it's you, Eli. Yeah…I'll tell them I got you drunk one night and tried to convert you back over."

He laughed loudly. "My girl's back," he said, grinning. "And in fightin' form."

We got through the cook-out with no major snafus. Harper kept everyone entertained with the cute little baby things she did. I managed to pull Lindsey aside, asking her to come upstairs so we could talk. I'd already told her about Easton leaving, extremely proud of the façade I'd put up that it was for the best. I was starting to believe that myself.

Once in my room, I closed the door. "You haven't said anything to Taz about me being pregnant, have you?"

"Of course not," she hissed, feigning insult. "I promised I wouldn't, but sooner or later he's going to figure it out, Darce. Like everyone else."

"Well, yeah," I agreed with her. "I totally planned on letting them know when we sent out the baby-shower invites." I smiled at her.

I'm pretty sure I saw her left eye twitch at that comment.

"I know, I know," I replied, testily. "I'm telling my parents this afternoon."

She crossed her arms. "No shit?"

"Yeah, but here's the thing: I'm not telling them Easton's the father, for my own personal reasons. Don't ask. I wanted to make sure you knew that in case my mom tries to grill you somewhere down the road, got it?"

She nodded, her brow furrowed in confusion.

"What?" I asked.

"Well, it's just...who are you going to tell them *is* the father?"

"Darin," I replied, clearly out-of-the-blue. "It's perfect, isn't it?"

"Huh?"

"Yes," I said, my eyes brightening. "It's fucking fantastic. I mean, come on? He's in freakin' Alaska, right?"

"Oh Darce...I mean, I don't know about doing that..."

"Oh, hell," I snapped. "It's not like I'm going to tell anyone *else* that! Geesh, Linds. My parents don't know anyone with the agency, I mean other than Taz, that is."

"Speaking of Taz," she replied, crossing her arms, "when is he allowed to find out?"

"I don't know. Not yet."

She sighed, shaking her head. "Well, I wish you luck with your folks, but I'm betting they're going to be tickled pink."

"Or blue," I said, giving her a wink.

Everyone had left. Mom was in the kitchen, helping me with the dishes. I guessed now was as good of a time as any.

"Mom," I said, rinsing off a platter. "I've got some news to share with you and Daddy."

She looked up from the stove she'd been wiping clean. "Good news, I hope," she said with just a hint of trepidation.

"Well, I hope you think it's *good* news. I'd rather tell you first, just in case it isn't, though."

She nodded, waiting for me to continue. I had her full attention now.

Oh God...

"I'm pregnant. The baby's due in mid-January and the father's in Alaska," I blurted out quickly.

"Oh, Darcy," she breathed, allowing the news to sink in fully. I breathed a sigh of relief as I saw the corners of her mouth turn upward in a smile. "I don't know what to say. I mean, I'm happy if you're happy, darling. I'm not that old-fashioned, you know? A lot of young people don't get married until after the baby arrives...well, look at Lindsey, for example. That worked out well for everyone."

She came over, pulling me into her arms for a "mom" hug, patting my back. "My baby's having a baby," she sighed, sounding all choked up.

"Yeah, Mom, there's just one more thing. Marriage isn't going to happen, I'm afraid. Still okay with it?"

She put her hands on my arms and pulled back to look at me. "Can your father and I at least know who the father of our grandchild is?"

And. Here. We. Go...

"Darin," I said, quickly, turning my face from her. "We uh, we hooked up again thinking we might reconcile, but realized it wasn't gonna happen. My Depo shot had expired, that's why that post-card from my gyno came to your house. Just one of those flukey things, ya know?"

Her forehead creased in a frown. "Darin does plan on taking financial responsibility, though, right?"

"Oh, sure," I lied, nodding my head up and own. There was no way in hell I wanted to belabor the whole 'Darin' topic right now. "Listen, Mom, would you mind telling Daddy on the way home?"

She eyed me warily, shaking her head. "Why?"

"Because," I little-girl whined, "I don't want to know how mad or disappointed he's going to be when he finds out." I totally knew that I was taking the coward's route. I get it, *but* do you a blame a girl for wanting to...I don't know, live? And this talk with Mom was already kind of giving me heart palpitations, so I could only guess how the ol' talk with Dad was going to go.

"I suppose," she replied, giving me another hug. "I'm sure he's going to be as thrilled as I am, so don't stress. Have you been feeling well?"

"Umm hmm," I nodded. "I feel better now that I've given you the news."

"Well, you know there are plans you'll have to make soon about after the baby arrives. I mean you don't intend to stay here in this apartment do you?" She made a point to look over at the living room, probably noting that a baby wouldn't really go well with Eli's surround-sound stereo system.

"Mom," I said, returning to the sink, "I can't think about that right now. I'm taking this one day at a time."

They'd only been gone for five minutes when I looked at Eli who was sitting on the sofa next to Cain. "Well, my ears are burning. Mom's told Daddy," I said.

"Oh, chill," he laughed. "That baby will be spoiled rotten, just like you were. Your dad isn't going to disown his 'wittle' girl," he teased.

"I'm just hoping he doesn't book a flight to Alaska to hunt down Darin and make him do the right thing."

"Shut up! No. You. Didn't!"

"Oh, but I did," I giggled, heading upstairs. "Night, boys."

Chapter 49

It was mid-August and I'd just left Dr. Billingsley's office and was heading to 'Tater's for lunch. I was officially four months pregnant, my blood-work was fine and I'd gained seven pounds, total. No one seemed to have noticed the seven pounds. Maybe it was because I was tall. My tummy had a small baby bump, which wasn't difficult to conceal at all. I figured by the time Colin and Ronnie returned from their honeymoon cruise, my pregnancy would be noticeable, so I wasn't about to spill anything before then.

My mother called me practically every day to make sure I was eating right, getting enough rest and taking my vitamin. *Geesh!* Of course both parents were now quite excited about becoming grandparents, even though my father had told my mother he'd like to "shake the shit out of Darin" for being so irresponsible and leaving me in the lurch.

Ah-hem, yeah, I know.

Ronnie and I usually had lunch a couple of times a week. I was her only girlfriend in D.C. I'd invited Lindsey to join us a few times with Harper (who Ronnie, of course, adored) so now she could add her to her list of D.C. friends. I was meeting them both for lunch today.

I was running a few minutes late. I spotted Lindsey at a table outside in the shaded garden area. I so hated the heat and humidity these days. I figured it must be something with my pregnancy hormones. I parked my car, nodding to Lindsey who was waving wildly, as if I couldn't spot her.

"I went ahead and ordered you iced lemonade," she said, nodding to the seat where a tall, frosted glass of it awaited.

"Thanks," I said, lifting it to take a long drink. "I swear to God I'm so over this fucking summer. Where's Harper?" I asked, finally noticing the stroller wasn't parked next to Lindsey's chair.

"Oh, Taz is with her at home," she replied, sipping her iced tea. "He has the rest of this week off and then next week as vacation. Then he's gone on assignment for the next three to four weeks after that. Guess where?"

I rolled my eyes at her, smiling. "I swear Lindsey, you're like a kid whenever you have gossip or juicy tidbits, aren't you?"

She nodded, giggling. "New York," she said, unable to keep it to herself any longer. "And," she continued, drawing each word out, "he mentioned he's going to be touching bases with Easton while he's there. Apparently there's some drama in the family going on."

"Really?" I commented, not particularly interested in the topic of Easton. It still hurt at times.

"I'd give you the details, but I'm not sure if Taz wants me putting family business out there like that," she qualified.

"Hmm, let me guess. Taz and Easton aren't brothers," I replied, taking another long sip of my drink. I watched as Lindsey's eyes bugged out in shock and awe.

"You *knew?*" she gasped. "Did Easton tell you? I can't *believe* you didn't tell me!" Okay, now she was downright hurt.

"Listen," I said, nodding towards the parking lot, "Ronnie's here. We can talk about it later, okay?"

We enjoyed our lunch together. Ronnie brought pictures of her wedding dress to show us. It was very traditional, similar to Lindsey's. She had her final fitting the following day.

"So," she said, turning her attention to me, "you're still planning on coming to our wedding, aren't you? You haven't R.S.V.P.'d yet, Darcy."

Holy shit! What the hell do I say?

Both of them were watching me, waiting for my response.

"Ronnie," I started slowly, "you know I want to be there, of course. I mean, Colin's my boss, and *both* of you are my friends, but I just don't think I'd be…comfortable."

338

"Rubbish," she said, picking the tomato slice off of her club sandwich. "You've got to face Easton some time, right?"

This was the first time she'd actually come out and mentioned the bastard's name. Up until this point, we'd skirted the issue.

I thought about that for a moment. "No," I said, shaking my head. "I don't ever have to face him again, if I'm lucky."

"So, you're going to let his assholiness keep you from my wedding and what's promised to be a great time?"

How much does she know?

Lindsey piped up in my defense. "Ronnie, there are other circumstances involved here," she said quietly. "It probably wouldn't be a good idea for Darcy to be traveling to New York by herself."

"It's not that," I interrupted, a bit snappish. "I just don't *want* to go by myself, I guess."

Ronnie rolled her eyes. "The invitations reads 'and guest'," she pointed out. "Bring your friend, Eli. Or how about Lindsey, here?"

Lindsey immediately perked up. "I'd *love* to go with you, Darce. I haven't been to the city since my freshman year in college. I'm sure Mom or Grandma would keep Harper. We could spend a few days there, do some fall shopping, and see a play? I haven't been anywhere since my honeymoon," she whined.

"Ha," I said, smiling, "you just want to go because you're thinking Taz might still be there on assignment and you can hook up for an hour or so." I watched as Lindsey's face turned a lovely shade of pink, knowing I'd hit the nail on the head.

"You know we don't communicate much when he's on undercover stuff," she mumbled, poking at her salad. "I just thought it might be nice to have some female bonding with my B.F.F., that's all."

"I'll think about," I said, knowing that I'd give in because, the truth was, I wanted to prove to myself I could face Easton Matthews one more time to show him I'd survived just fine without him.

"Great!" Lindsey and Ronnie both said together.

Yep. It was a done deal...Fuuuuck!

When I returned to the office after lunch, I was surprised to find my father coming out of Colin's office. He immediately brightened when he saw me, coming over to plant a parental kiss on my cheek.

"What are you doing here, Daddy?"

He scrunched up his nose (kind of the way that I do) and said, "I own a good piece of this company, Darcy. I'm exercising my authority to work on site so that I can keep an eye on my daughter while she's in this delicate condition," he laughed good-naturedly.

"Shhh," I hissed quietly. "That's not common knowledge around here." I saw my dad's expression morph to serious and I knew immediately he'd shared this info with Colin.

Dayummmm!

"Oh, I see. Well, I'm off to play some golf before I come back to fill in for Colin," he said, anxious now to get the hell away from me. "See you full-time in a few weeks," he said, giving me another peck on the cheek as he hurried out.

I sat down at my desk and started going through the e-mails that had come in since I'd been out for my doctor's appointment and then lunch. My Outlook In-Box 'pinged' with a new arrival from "C. Devers."

'Darcy - Got a minute? Come on in...Colin'

Shit. Shit. Shit.

I gathered my notebook and pen and went through the door to his office. Easton's old office. The office where lots of lewd and lascivious things had happened when the door was closed. I shook those memories away, just like I did all the others when they came to my mind totally uninvited.

"Yes?" I said, taking a seat as he motioned for me to. He went over, closing the door between our adjoining offices.

"Darcy," he said, sitting back in the leather chair, his hands clasped behind his head, trying to choose his words carefully. "I'm walking a fine line here. I realise that, so please bear with me?"

I nodded, duly noting the sincerity in his voice and his expression. "Your father was just in here at my request to review some of the current projects, bids, submission dates and what-not before I leave in two weeks to prepare for the wedding. He's filling in while I'm gone for six weeks." Colin stopped, swiveling in his chair and looking quite uncomfortable.

"He happened to mention you're expecting a baby in mid-January. Of course, he's ecstatic about the notion as any grandparent would be. It's certainly none of my business, but did you ever plan on letting me know of your...condition?"

Now it was my time to squirm. Legally, I had no responsibility to let my employer know anything until I needed to for Family Medical Leave Act, but I knew Colin wasn't trying to be invasive; he was trying to be compassionate and caring.

"I guess...," I stammered, "I mean I thought once you returned to work at the end of October, well...it would be kind of obvious."

He swung back around and stood up, walking around to the front of his desk, and copping a seat on the corner of it, his long legs outstretched in front of him.

"Listen," he said quietly, "I'm truly not trying to pry, and you're under no obligation to share personal, medical information with your employer. But," he continued, "I consider myself to be your mentor—and your friend. I'm here to support you in any way possible."

I crossed my legs, clasping my hands together and resting them on my knee. "I appreciate that, Colin. I didn't mean to keep it from you indefinitely, you know?" I said with a small laugh. "It's just that I wasn't making it public right away." God this was awkward.

"So, then you haven't told Ronnie?" he asked. "I mean, I get all of that stuff with female secrets…"

"No," I answered, plainly. "My parents know, Eli and his boyfriend know, my best friend, Lindsey. And now you, I guess."

"I see," he replied, scratching his chin "What about Easton?"

God—I so want to bang my head against the desk.

"What about him?" I asked, looking puzzled and clueless, positive I hadn't pulled it off.

"Does he know he's to be a father in mid-January? By my estimation, I'd guess this baby was conceived in mid-April, the same time we were in London for your first presentation."

Now I was scared he'd shared that personal information with my father. Oh God!

"Relax," he said, chuckling, as if reading my mind. "Your father's under the distinct impression that some irresponsible FBI agent by the name of Darin took your 'virtue' and skipped the mainland for Alaska. No doubt Easton played a part in *that* assignment."

Easton must share stuff with him…

Now it was my turn to frown. "How do you know so much?" I asked. "I mean, is Easton your best friend?"

"We've known each other a very long time. I…understand Easton," he replied with a shrug.

"So, what makes you think my ex-boyfriend and I *didn't* hook up in April?"

He shook his head, grinning like a fool. "Darcy, any half-wit could have seen the way you and Easton looked at one another. You pushed his buttons in all the right places and he yours. It was quite obvious there was some high-current chemistry flowing back and forth like lightning bolts between the two of you. It didn't take me long to figure out that both you and he were—and probably still are—totally, undeniably, and irrevocably in love with one another."

I shifted in my seat, not wanting to listen to any more of this because it was pointless. "That's where you're *wrong*, Colin. I admit it. I *was* in love with the

342

son-of-a-bitch. The feeling wasn't mutual and he made that perfectly clear when he told me I wasn't part of his fucking *long-term plan.*"

He was immediately on his feet, coming over to where I was sitting and taking the chair next to it. He grasped my hands into his, forcing me to face him.

"Darcy," he said, solemnly, "listen to me, please. I know Easton probably better than anyone. I've been with him through some tough times, *emotionally*, that is. I understand he's a very *complicated* person—one for the books, I should say. I'm certainly no expert on the male psyche, but I do know him better than most and I have to tell you: this is a first. He loves you more than he ever loved...*her*. And that's presuming that he did love her, which I doubt. So much so, that I'd bet a year's salary that you're the *first* woman Easton's truly loved. It shook him up, sweets. He can't handle it."

I shifted again in my chair. "Well, Colin, he doesn't *have* to handle it because it's been over for several months."

"I see," he said, quietly, gazing over at me. "Then, you're not going to tell him about...the baby?"

"No!" I replied, vehemently. "I know his feelings about women and especially about *babies*...I mean I know all about him *forcing* Bianca to have an...abortion! And even when she did, he still dumped her. I also know firsthand how he treated Devon! Firing her because something slipped through the cracks when she was out on maternity leave...I'm sorry, but I find that *deplorable*."

I didn't miss the look of shock on Colin's face. Was it possible he wasn't privy to *any* of this?

He turned to me, his expression dark and angry. "I'm not sure *where* you got that information, but it's totally *false*. I'm not at liberty to discuss things of a private nature concerning my superior, but I'll say this: none of that's true. Easton is, by no means, a *perfect* individual. However, I'll give him his due when warranted. As far as Devon's concerned, I can and *will* speak to that. Easton didn't fire her when he went to Leeds. He offered her a flex schedule so that she can spend more time with the baby the first year. She's only working half days on site, the rest from home."

343

I was stunned when Colin shared that with me. *What? Why?* Easton had never said a thing about it! I processed all of this recent info, taking several moments.

Shaking my head in wonder, shrugging in defeat, I replied, "It doesn't matter, Colin. He still ended it and I have enough pride not to go where I'm clearly not wanted. As for my condition—I will ask that you keep silent about it. As my employer you are bound by HIPPA restrictions of confidentiality…"

He stood up, turning towards me. "Regardless of U.S law, I can assure you I wouldn't have discussed this with Easton. It's clearly *not* my place. I do think it's *your* place to give him a chance to show you he does truly love you…Please know I respect and will, of course, honour your right to privacy, Darcy. But also know this: Easton's become a better person because of you and I hope somewhere down the road, the both of you wise up and realise what's so blatantly obvious to everyone else. Now, please let me know if there's anything you need."

Dismissed…

Chapter 50

Lindsey and I were seated next to each other in the first class cabin of the 757 bound for JFK.

"This is so exciting," Lindsey said enthusiastically. "Spending four days in New York with my bestie totally rocks."

I gave her a sidelong glance, trying to figure out why she was all pumped up. It wasn't like we both hadn't been there before. It wasn't like I was exactly thrilled at the prospect of having to face Easton again. It'd been three months. I was five months pregnant and had gained twelve pounds. My baby bump was a bit more pronounced, but still manageable with a loose-fitting dress like the one I'd brought for the wedding with a jacket to go over it. The biggest differences were my hair and boobs. One had more, one had less...you get the picture.

"You're just horny for Taz," I teased, noticing the captain had turned off the "Fasten Seat Belt" sign, unfastening mine and adjusting my seat back.

"Am not," she denied, "We've had our share of phone sex over the past couple of weeks, I'm good." She settled her seat back, a smile playing on her lips. She was probably re-playing their last episode of phone sex in her mind.

I smiled as I crossed my legs, squeezing my inner thighs together, enjoying the feel of my clit jewelry as it rubbed against my tight boy shorts. Just because I got rid of the-ass-hat-who-shall-not-be-named, doesn't mean I was ready to part with the jewelry. Let's get real for a sec, okay? I'm pregnant. And I'm pretty sure my estrogen levels are something that could possibly go down in the *Guinness Book of World Records*. And, oh yeah, I'm *single*. So, in case you're still wondering about why I kept the piercing? I love it. My vibrator loves it. The End.

"So, who's keeping Harper?"

"Grandma," she answered. "Slate's on the same assignment with Taz, so Mom's got her hands full with Bryce and Michael. Grandma was dying to keep her anyway. I mean, she's such a good baby."

I had to agree with Lindsey on that one. Secretly, I hoped my baby would be as laid back as little Harper, although considering the gene pool involved, I knew it was highly unlikely.

"So," I said, "we never got to finish our conversation from a couple of weeks ago about the drama with Taz's family."

She peered over at me frowning. "I thought you already knew about it?"

"Well, yeah," I replied, "but I didn't find out from Easton." I filled her in on how I'd found out.

"Ohh," she said, nodding, "then you don't know the part about Easton's biological father?"

I looked over abruptly. "You know who his biological father is?" I asked, surprised.

"Well, sure," she replied, rolling her eyes. "I mean when Taz's dad called a few weeks back asking if he'd spoken to Easton lately, the whole story came out. Easton was furious that Trace Sr. had never told him the truth. He cut off all ties. Taz's dad is *really* upset."

"Yeah, I guess I can understand that," I replied, thoughtfully. "But what does he know about Easton's real father?"

Lindsey leaned in as if on the verge of conveying top secret info to me. "I guess he was an older guy and from French royalty," she whispered.

"Yeah?"

"Uh huh. Like a Duke or something…Marquis," she said a bit louder. "That's his title, *Marquis.* Anyway, supposedly that makes Easton titled as an Earl. But the thing is that the family's upset because of what Easton's mother did in telling him all this crap in the first place. Taz is even upset about it."

"Seriously? I didn't think he cared much for his half-brother."

She shrugged. "Taz says siblings fight at times but it doesn't mean they don't love one another. He says Trace Sr. was a father to Easton by love, if not blood and he's his brother by love if not blood."

I could totally picture Taz saying that and feeling that way.

"Has Taz talked to Easton?" I asked, a bit apprehensively.

"No, but he's tried and left messages, but I guess Easton doesn't want to talk to him either. I think Taz is going to try and stop by his office once his assignment is finished and force a conversation."

That won't be a pretty sight, I'm sure.

"I guess family is family, no matter what," I said.

"Yep. And I'm glad you said that, Darce, because there's something I need to tell you." She said nervously. Her change in tone made me nervous. God—what now?

The flight attendant came by for our drink orders right then. Once he'd gone, Lindsey turned to me, and took my hands into hers. I'd never seen her look so serious before.

"Linds, what's going on?" I asked, almost scared of what she was about to tell me.

"You have to promise, Darcy, I mean *promise* me you won't tell anyone."

I nodded, my eyes widening in anticipation. "Of course. I promise."

"I've been in touch with my dad's mother—my Grandma Lambert, since right after Harper was born."

"Lambert?"

"Yeah. That's the last name of her most recent ex-husband. She lives in New York City. I tracked her down through information I found in my dad's things. It wasn't easy, trust me. I don't know—I just had this need to let her know about Harper and have a connection with someone that was part of my dad. It's hard to explain."

"No, I get it. But why the secrecy?"

"Are you serious?" she asked, incredulously. "If Taz had *any* idea I'd been keeping in touch with her, he'd freak. I mean my dad's still a fugitive from justice,

347

though he's pretty far down the list as far as the FBI goes, but still, Taz wouldn't approve at all. I mean it's not like she and I really talk about my dad. We did at first, but she's just as disgusted with him as everyone else. She thinks he's probably…dead."

"Oh, sweetie," I said, reaching over from my seat and giving her a hug. "I know how hard this has been for you. I sometimes forget all the shit you went through because of it."

She nodded, managing a weak smile. "So you see? That's one of the reasons I really wanted to make this trip with you. There's no way I could've managed a trip to New York without arousing suspicion. I just want to meet her, give her some pictures of Daddy, me, and Harper of course and get to know her a little bit."

"I understand, Linds, but listen, okay? Sometimes you can build these things up in your mind to be something they're not. Just don't be too disappointed if she's not the snuggly, loving grandmotherly type. I mean, I don't blame you for wanting to meet her, but I'm going with you when you do, for moral support anyway."

"Thanks, Darce," she said, smiling. "That means a lot to me."

Once we landed at JFK, we took the courtesy limo to our hotel located on Central Park South. Lindsey and I were staying four nights, returning to D.C. on Tuesday afternoon. It was early evening on Friday, so we just hung around our hotel suite and ordered room service. I felt bad I couldn't party these days, especially since Lindsey rarely went anywhere without Harper. The wedding was set for late afternoon Saturday. Luckily, the church was a short cab ride from our hotel.

Lindsey and I had unpacked, eaten, showered and were now on our respective queen-sized beds watching some trash television. She'd already had Taz checking in on her. Eli and my mother had checked in on me. She'd checked on Harper, so all of the checkpoints had pretty much been covered.

So you can imagine my surprise when I heard the ring of a different cell phone. Lindsey leapt off of her bed, grabbing the hoodie she'd left on the chair. I watched as she fished a different phone out of the pocket.

"Hey," she said, walking towards the bathroom. From there, all I could hear were bits and pieces of the murmured conversation she was having with whomever. A couple of minutes later I heard her say, "See you then, Louise. Okay, take care," as she came back in from the bathroom. She tossed the phone into her handbag.

"So, I'm curious," I said. "Why the two cell phones?"

She looked a little embarrassed as she shook her head. "I know it seems sneaky and all, but I promised my grandmother Louise that I'd do everything possible to make sure Taz doesn't find out we're keeping in contact."

I sat upright on my bed now, looking her in the eyes. "Lindsey, why would *Louise* have an issue with Taz knowing you two are in touch?"

"Because," she replied, "she knows what he does for a living." She was picking at her toenails now, avoiding looking me in the eye.

I went over and sat down next to her on the bed. "Are you sure you've told me everything?"

I could see that she was uncomfortable. Deception didn't come easy for Lindsey. She'd make a horrible criminal. Thank God she'd taken after her mother and not her father. But her naiveté where people were concerned, at least the people that she loved or cared about, nearly killed her a little more than a year ago. It bothered me that she apparently hadn't learned from it.

"Okay," she sighed. "I didn't tell you that my grandmother called me a little over a month ago and said that she'd received a letter from my dad. He'd enclosed one for me and asked that she find some way of getting it to me without mailing it. He was afraid she'd be implicated as an accessory or something."

"How could she be held accountable for receiving mail?" I asked.

Lindsey continued picking at her nails. "Because in his letter to her he asked that she get money to him. She doesn't know where he is, trust me, I know she's not lying about that. But…well, he did give her a drop-off point where she'd be at no risk in getting caught and an associate that's apparently helping him stay underground would know when to pick it up once he got word."

"Oh, God," I breathed. "Lindsey, please tell me you're not giving your father money...please?"

She looked up at me. "Of course not," she said. "I promised Taz a long time ago that if my father ever made contact with me that I'd tell him to turn himself in and face the music. I also told him I wouldn't harbor him or give him assistance as a fugitive."

"Thank God for that," I said, relaxing back a bit.

"But," she continued, "I do feel that since Louise is providing what money she can spare to help her son, my *father*, then the least I can do is help her out financially. She isn't a woman with a lot of means."

Oh God...

"Lindsey, I think the authorities might see that as a fine line between giving someone a gift and money laundering."

She had a stubborn look going now. "I don't care. This money is for Louise and she's free to do whatever she wants with it. She's already emptied her bank account, so it's really a done deal. She's the beneficiary of this cash."

"Can I ask how much cash you're giving her?"

"Ten thousand dollars," she replied, as if that were pocket change.

"*Ten grand?*" I shrieked loudly. "How in the hell did you get ten grand without Taz knowing?

"I borrowed it from my grandmother."

Of course you did, Linds.

I treaded carefully. "I don't feel good about this. You're *seriously* going against what you promised Taz now."

"How so? I don't know where my dad is. I'm giving money to my *grandmother* and I never promised Taz anything where she was concerned. Anyway, I don't want to talk about it anymore, Darce."

She pulled the covers down on her bed, crawling underneath. I could sympathize with her. I mean, she was my best friend and all. I honestly couldn't say what I would've done if I'd been put in that position. But the fact was that Lindsey still loved Jack Dennison (her father) despite the fact that he was a criminal on the run. His criminal activities had indirectly put her in a position last year of being stalked by Kyzer Stanfield at college. She learned too late that Kyzer wasn't what he appeared to be.

Kyzer was involved with his own step-mother, who'd also been Jack Dennison's mistress and cohort in crime, as it turned out. They were certain Lindsey had information or was in possession of something they needed. So much, that Kyzer had abducted her and she was tortured at their hands. I shivered now, thinking how close I'd come to losing my best friend. Thank God for Taz.

It was a tough one. I knew Lindsey wanted to believe there was good in her father's side of the family. I just couldn't quite get there. My instincts were on high alert. Nothing good could come of this, of that I was sure.

Chapter 51

I swirled the last of my brandy in the snifter and finished it off. Colin was sitting across from me at the bar. We were enjoying his last night of bachelorhood. He'd declined my offer of a proper bachelor party, complete with strippers and a mind-blowing lap dance.

Pussy-whipped sod.

"So, Colin," I said with a smirk, "Your last night of freedom, mate. And who're you spending it with? Your boss and best man. Such a pity don't you think?"

Colin looked at me, getting a crooked, drunken grin on his face. "You forgot, *friend*. I consider you a friend as well. Or maybe you don't do *friendships*, either, eh?"

If I didn't know better, I would've thought Colin was baiting me. "Of course," I replied, pushing my snifter over so the bartender could refill. "I'll even bloody toast to it."

I raised my glass, waiting for him to follow, but it was obvious he wasn't going to follow through. "Well?"

"Well...what?" he asked, his eyes now narrowing.

"I want to toast to friendship."

"Bloody hell," he said, smirking again. "You're fucking one for the books, Easton."

I was totally confused as to the reason for Colin's mood becoming dark. I thought we'd had a fairly jovial time throughout the evening. Clearly, he had a burr up his arse at the moment.

"Care to clue me in, mate?" I asked, raising an eyebrow.

"I don't get it, Easton," he said, shaking his head. "Not once, not one fucking time this evening, or for the past several months, for that matter, have you even bothered to ask me how she's been or how she's doing. Is it really that simple for you to dismiss someone so easily?"

I wasn't comfortable with Colin taking me to task on something so personal, so obviously none of his business, friend or not. Apparently, my silence and body language sent the message.

"Oh, I know, I know," he said, derisively, "Easton Matthews answers to no one; he's above reproach and accountability after all, right? Wrong. I'm here to tell you flat out; you were *wrong* in what you did to that girl." He took a drink of his single-malted scotch.

Now I was totally pissed at Colin's badgering. "Just because I don't mention Darcy to you or question you about her, what the fuck makes you think I'm not thinking about her? I know exactly where she is at any moment of any day."

I pulled my mobile out, punched in some digits and hit the field for address location. I held it in front of him, watching him squint to read the address, room number and "time-in" data on the screen.

"What the bloody hell?" he asked, looking at it and then at me.

"Here's a real-time street view if you like," I said, hitting another highlighted tab on the screen.

Colin leaned in, watching as the night vision provided him a clear view of the main lobby entrance of the hotel where Darcy was staying. The live stream showed cars going by and the doorman having a smoke out on the sidewalk.

"Fuck no—you didn't. How?"

I loved it when I could render Colin speechless. It was a difficult thing to do because he'd been with me for a long time, and had pretty much been shock-proofed as a result.

"Remember the clit jewelry I had made for her?"

He nodded, his eyes widening as the blanks were filled in. "Night Moves?" he asked, incredulously.

"Yeah, my own little prototype test module inside the black onyx ball. So you see, my friend, I still keep track of her every day."

He looked at me long and hard. "Why?"

Now it was my turn to be puzzled. "What do you mean…why? Because…I *can*," I stated simply, with a shrug.

Colin laughed, a loud, genuine laugh, his hand slapping my shoulder. "You fucking love her. I *knew* it!"

I gave him a scowl, but it did nothing to deter his laughter. He ordered two shots of tequila from the bartender.

"Colin, really," I started, "I'm not a big fan…"

"Aw, shut the hell up, mate," he said grinning, handing me one of the shots, and raising his up. "To Night Moves—cutting edge technology for the romantic stalker in all of us! Salute!"

He downed his shot, still totally entertained by my revelation. I downed mine quickly, and turned my attention back to him.

"I'm pleased you're entertained at my expense, Colin," I remarked tersely. "I don't have to tell you that what I just shared with you is confidential…"

"No problem, bro," he snickered, his American accent becoming more prominent with his escalating inebriation. "But I have to ask, what if she takes the clit jewelry out? I mean what if her next boyfriend doesn't fancy her having it?"

I gave him a dark glare, signaling the bartender for the tab. Colin was getting too drunk and I'd promised Ronnie he wouldn't be hung over for the wedding.

"There's not been a new boyfriend so far," I snapped.

"Well," he snorted, "with her looks and body, it's just a matter of time, mate."

"Shut up, Colin," I snarled. "You're drunk and I'm getting you back to your suite."

"And you, my friend? Well, you are totally fucked-up over her, and too bloody proud to fix it."

"Is that so?" I asked, handing my credit card to the bartender.

"Bloody right," he slurred. "I don't mean to overstep my place here, Easton, and I've never said something to you that needed to be said a long time ago. I should've said it, but I didn't, but now I am. Your mother isn't to blame for your fucked-upness, you know?"

"Do tell?"

"You're to blame for it. You *allowed* your mother to fuck with your head all these years, knowing damn well she did it for sport, for pure entertainment. I mean, for Chrissake, man, you empowered her and she *still* has the power because you *allow* it! You did the same with that wench of a model...what's her name? Bianca..." He made an at-a-loss hand gesture through the air, "Something-or-other."

I grabbed my receipt and credit card back from the bartender, shrugging my jacket on, and helping Colin up from the bar stool. "You're shitfaced, Colin. Come on, let's get you back to your hotel."

"Wait a minute," he said, wrenching his arm away. "Just listen to me, Easton. Yeah, I'm drunk right now, but it doesn't mean I'm not speaking the truth now, does it? You love the girl, the girl loves you. Take it from your best friend—hell, take it from your *only real* friend. Don't waste one more fucking day *not* doing something about it. You need to fix it, got it?"

He was staring into my eyes and I could see that he was passionate about getting his message across to me. It was something I'd already thought about a million times. I didn't need Colin to point out what I already knew. In my mind, I worried it was already too late.

"I got it, Colin," I replied. "She may just be done with me, though."

"Don't think so, mate. You make it right with her while you have the chance."

Chapter 52

September 14th—Colin and Ronnie's wedding day turned out to be gorgeous. It was sunny, with a slight crispness in the air announcing fall was here. The ceremony was scheduled for 4:30 in the afternoon at Central Methodist Church. I already knew Easton was best man.

The wedding wasn't going to be huge, but the party afterwards was going to be pretty impressive. Apparently, as a gift to the newlywed's, Easton had booked a high-end nightclub called Harmony on the Upper East Side of Manhattan. That had to have cost a fortune, having a trendy nightclub such as that close their doors to accommodate a private reception on a Saturday night, but then, Easton had the means to lavish on the people he cared about.

I'd just finished showering and was getting my make-up on. My butterflies had been restless all day, not to mention a new fluttering that had made its presence known. Our baby. God! Why now? I was already so nervous, not knowing how I'd react to him. These pregnancy hormones were starting to fuck with my mind, it seemed. I'd confided to Lindsey how I would feel happy and fine one moment, nervous and agitated the next, and then an overwhelming desire to see Easton would wash over me. I'd been having dreams about him two to three times a week.

Lindsey had laughed, saying it was all perfectly natural. She said my "nesting" instinct had kicked in. I wasn't sure what the hell that was, but at times I *did* have the urge to fucking climb a tree and *just* hide from everything and everyone.

After I finished with my hair, I slipped into the dark teal knit dress that I had brought to wear. It was trimmed with black fleur de leis scrolling.

"Hey," Lindsey said, coming up behind me, "you aren't trying to upstage the bride today are you, Darce?"

"Puhleeze," I replied, laughing, "You're doing best friend duty, aren't you? What? Trying to make me feel better about my expanding waistline?"

"Yeah, right," she giggled, zipping me the rest of the way up. "God—by the time I was five months pregnant I was already showing like I had twins in there."

I nodded, slipping my earrings in. "That's because you ate anything that didn't eat you first, as I remember."

"Shut up," she giggled. "I learned my lesson on that one. Won't do that for the next baby."

"Are you and Taz thinking of having another one?" I asked.

"Oh no—I mean in a couple more years. I want to go back to work when Harper turns a year old. We're going to buy a bigger place."

I thought how nice it was that she and Taz had plans. I mean it must be great to be a couple that had dreams together and made plans…together.

"Are you nervous about seeing Easton?" she asked quietly.

I nodded, fidgeting with a strand of hair that wasn't behaving. "What if he brought a date?" I asked. "I don't know if I could maintain."

"Sure you could, Darce," she said, encouragingly. "But I'm betting he's not going to do that. I don't care how much of a prick he's been, I think it's a defense mechanism with him."

"You do?" I asked, frowning.

"Well," she giggled, "Taz actually thinks that and I figure since my hubby is the psychological expert in the family, he might be right."

"He said that, huh?"

"Yep," she replied, nodding. "He thinks Easton's mother did a number on him while growing up, big time. He definitely knows firsthand how she used him against Taz's father. He says that Easton has a textbook fear of commitment with a self-loathing undertone."

"A what?" I asked, turning to look at her.

She shrugged. "I think it means he has low self-esteem from being psychologically battered during his formative years, and a general mistrust of people that try and get close to him, along with an inability to let his guard down."

I thought about it and it made sense. He sure as hell was private. "Hey Linds," I said, "Do you think that shit can be passed on through chromosomes?"

"I don't think that *particular* trait could," she replied, "but you may want to ask Taz whenever he's allowed to know about the baby."

"Well," I sighed, "we're ready I guess."

"Let's do it," she said, taking me by the arm. "You'll be fine."

∞ ∞ ∞ ∞ ∞ ∞

The wedding went beautifully. Ronnie was gorgeous in her gown with the long, satin train. Colin looked boldly handsome in his black tuxedo. Ronnie's two sisters were attendants. I felt Lindsey take my hand when Easton came out from a side door near the front of the church with a groomsman, taking his place next to Colin, as they waited for the bride to arrive on her father's arm.

I couldn't take my eyes off of him during the entire ceremony, which was fine because no one would notice. It was the only opportunity I'd have to openly gaze at the man who I'd always love no matter what. I felt a tear and then another roll down my cheek as the bride and groom spoke their vows and pledged their love to one another. I'd give anything to have what Ronnie and Colin had.

As the minister blessed them and pronounced them husband and wife, Easton turned, looking out among the throng of people assembled in the church and his eyes found mine.

He always knew how to catch me staring...

I felt my cheeks flush, but still I couldn't...wouldn't look away.

"Easton's staring at you," Lindsey whispered, her hand over her mouth.

"I know," I replied trying to say it without moving my lips.

He finally tore his gaze away as the ceremony ended and exit song started signaling the wedding party to retreat back down the aisle.

The club where the reception had been booked was decorated in the wedding colors, with a live band ready to play, and tables of catered food being served.

There were way more tables set than needed to accommodate those guests at the church, and by the time Lindsey and I arrived, the main room was starting to get crowded.

"I guess a lot of invitees came here instead of the church," she commented as a hot dude with a British accent brushed against her on our way to a table, giving her a wink and a polite, "Sorry about that, love," as he did.

We found the place cards with our names on them at a table in the center. "God, I hope we aren't sitting with a bunch of losers," I mumbled.

"Shhh," Lindsey, admonished. "You need to lighten up, Darce. This is a happy occasion, remember?"

"Maybe for them, but not for me," I replied, pulling a chair out for myself. "Oh Christ," I said, spotting a place card with a name I recognized at our table.

"Hey," Lindsey interrupted my glowering at the place card, "will you stop reciting the cast and crew members of the Bible, already? We just came from a wedding. And judging from the glares that lady over there, who happens to look like she may have known Jesus *personally*, is giving us, I'm thinking she'd probably like to *smite* you before they start serving wedding cake."

I held up the place card.

"What?' she hissed, clearly not catching onto the name written down on the offensive card.

"Lacee. You know—Lacee *Fitz-friggin'-gerald?*' Geez, it was hard to yell while whispering, but my best friend seemed to finally understand. "What the hell did I ever do to Ronnie to deserve this?" I asked Lindsey, who was now giving me a firm evil eye.

"Darcy, stop it," she warned, taking the place card from me and positioning it back on the table. "Make the best of it, okay? I mean, you work with her and she's known Colin longer than you, so deal with it. They probably put her here because she knows you and she kind of knows me a little even," her voice trailed off.

"Ahh, yes. How could I forget that whole ten minutes you spent with her at *your* rehearsal dinner?"

"I'm going up to the bar. Do you want anything?"

"How about a Royal Fuck?" I asked, with a pout forming on my lips.

"Yeah, got it," she said, heading over to the bar. She returned a couple of minutes later with a Sloe Screw Up Against the Wall for her and a Virgin Daiquiri for me.

"Gee, thanks," I said, taking a sip of the alcohol-less cocktail. "This sucks donkey dicks; you do realize that, don't you?"

"Well, hang with it," she replied. "I wanted to get you something that at least *looked* like alcohol otherwise it'd be…well, *suspicious*…"

Nice, Linds…

"You know," she said after drinking half of her drink. "I just may say something to Easton myself about not returning Taz's calls. I think it's really rude."

"Hey," I said, leaning closer to her, "why don't you have about three more of those and then go up and ask the band if you could use their microphone, and then *publicly* bash the guy Kathy Griffin style?" I waggled my eyebrows at her.

"Stop it," she said, giggling and taking another sip. "You know I'm not as bold as *you*…oh, look there, speak of the devil," she nodded towards the entrance as the bridal party arrived and took their places at the head table.

I caught a glimpse of Easton talking to Ronnie, laughing and then leaning in to give her a kiss on her cheek. I was still gawking when a familiar voice got my attention.

"Well, imagine that. We're sitting with someone I work with, Austin."

I looked up and saw Lacee, dressed in a tight black low-cut dress with a tall, blond-haired man in a suit. He looked to be older than her, maybe early 40's.

Lacee introduced both of us to Austin Devers, a cousin of Colin's. He seemed nice enough, probably too nice for Lacee, but that was his lesson to learn. We all made small talk for a while, Lindsey getting more drinks for us before dinner was served.

I sat through the toasts, the speeches, and the bride and groom's first dance, finally turning to Lindsey once Lacee and Austin got up to dance. I leaned in to ask if she wanted to leave, just as I felt a hand on my shoulder. I saw the look in Lindsey's eyes and I knew who it was.

I turned my head, and gazed up into familiar gunmetal eyes, feeling my heart come alive with his nearness to me.

"Darcy," he said softly, holding his hand out for mine, "would you please do me the honour?"

Holy shit? Is this actually happening…?

My hand slipped into his and, like an idiot going back for more torture, I allowed him to lead me to the dance floor. His arms encircled me as he pulled me gently against him for this slow song. I recognized it. The same song we'd danced to at Lindsey's wedding.

I kept my face blank, as I picked a spot in the room and kept my eyes focused on it. I kept trying to imagine (or make-believe) that this could be any man. We were just two strangers dancing together at someone's wedding, never having met before. Even as I breathed in his familiar scent, and tried to place titanium into my spine in a vain attempt not to completely melt in his arms, it was working.

Until I heard his voice.

"I apologise," he said softly. "I've a tendency to try and lead when slow-dancing."

I immediately felt my lips twitch, and it literally took everything I had in me not to laugh at the almost forgotten words that I had spoken to *him* the first time we danced which felt like years and years ago.

Bastard stole my line...

The laugh that I was trying to hold back compromised with my lips as a smile immediately broke through, and I had to tilt my head down so that he wouldn't see.

I couldn't help it. "I don't intend to allow that," I replied, reciting the same words he spoke to me that day. "You'll learn to follow, I promise."

I brought my eyes back to that place in the room I was staring at before, and vowed that I wouldn't take my eyes away from it until the song stopped. But that didn't stop me from feeling his soft chuckle work its way through his chest.

"You're more beautiful now than ever," he whispered against my hair. "Something's changed."

I felt my guard slowly withering away, and I tried like hell to build it back up again. "My hair," I whispered very softly, leaving it up to fate and to chance whether or not we should be having this conversation. I couldn't decide if it was a good or a bad thing when I found out he heard me as he brought his hand gently to the nape of my neck to finger a loose strand. "I'm wearing it shorter now," I explained with a bit more voice.

"I can see," his voice floated softly to my ear. "You did that to *punish* me, didn't you?"

That's when I said screw it, and started to pull back, as a reflex, so that I could finally look at him. His arm tightened, though, keeping me firmly in place. I think he thought that I was getting ready to bolt from the dance floor.

I reassured him by simply turning my face up and over to his. Big mistake. I wasn't expecting the emotion I found settled deep in his eyes. I couldn't make it out, but I kept my gaze fixed onto his nickel-gray one. "Why...?" I tried to clear my thoughts. "Why do you feel you deserved punishment?"

I felt his deep sigh, the moment of silence while he decided whether or not he was going to engage in a game of banter with me or simply put it out there. "Because I broke you," he replied, as his fingers traced a pattern on my lower back, sending delicious tingles to my spine, and breaking through the titanium. "Because I couldn't bear the thought of loving you," he finished, his lips brushing lightly against my brow.

I could almost feel the light tears glistening beneath my eyelashes from having heard the words he never said, the words I didn't think he'd *ever* say. And here Easton was, handing them over like we were trading wishes.

Jesus…Get it together, Darce. He left you, remember? And when he should've said them, he didn't.

"I'm still in one piece," I said softly. "You didn't totally wreck me. You left me with something."

I felt his lips graze my forehead, his hands pressing me closer against him. "I can't let you go, love. Not again."

"You have to, Easton," I replied, trying to play it off as casual. "Because I'm not yours and I don't love you anymore."

I heard his smirk of disbelief. He lowered his head so that his lips were nearly touching my ear. "I don't *blame* you for hating me. I deserve that—and more. But it's not over, Darcy. It'll never be over. This *thing* we have…this complicated and beautiful thing that you and I share with one another? I won't allow it to be finished because I *do* love you, in spite of my black heart and my flawed emotions."

I felt his lips on my ear, his warm breath against my neck as he whispered again that he loved me. Mercifully, the song ended and I pulled away, his arms reluctant to release me, his gaze penetrating every inch of me.

Walk away.

But before I did, I had to tell him, because *I* still had a wish to trade. "It's too late, Easton," I said through the sounds of couples going back to their chairs and idle chatter. "And I'm sorry." His eyes burned through mine as I continued. "It's not that I could *ever* hate you, because that's just not possible…It's just that I don't *love* you anymore."

I half-expected him to call my bluff, but he didn't. So before I joined the couples around me and made my way back to my own place card, I told him with shaking hands, "I could never allow myself to take that risk…again."

Without seeing or hearing his reply, I turned around.

And walked away.

Chapter 53

Lindsey and I were sitting in the back of a cab in front of a fountain somewhere in mid-town Manhattan. It was Sunday and we'd survived the night. I hadn't slept well after the dance and conversation I'd had with Easton. I'd insisted on leaving right after that. Lindsey hadn't argued, but Lacee had been nosy as hell, asking if I felt alright and if Easton had done anything to upset me.

I told Lindsey about it once we got back to our hotel. She had told me she was proud of my strength, but then asked me if I felt absolutely certain about what I had told him. I told her "no" because I wasn't sure. In fact, I was fairly certain it had been a lie.

I wasn't about to lie to my best friend.

It was my turn to tell her before bed that I didn't want to talk about it anymore. She'd given me a heavy sigh, and I could see her shaking her head in my peripheral vision. I heard her on her super secret cell phone later, making arrangements to meet Louise on Sunday to give her the money and get the letter from her father. She told her she had some pictures for her of the baby, too. There was no way in hell I was letting her go by herself.

Another taxi pulled up in front of ours. We watched as an older woman, most likely in her mid-sixties, got out and paid the driver. She was average height and build, her clothing was non-descript, definitely not showing signs of wealth, but not poor either.

"That's Louise," Lindsey said, all smiles, paying the driver.

We got out and, immediately, Lindsey waved to Louise. The woman came over, giving Lindsey a hug and me the hairy eyeball. Lindsey broke away and introduced me as her best friend in the world.

I smiled and shook Louise's hand, noticing she didn't have much warmth to her. Lindsey had said she was meeting us here because she lived in the Bronx and it was a good distance. She said she knew of a quaint coffee shop nearby where they could "catch-up." I so wanted to point out to Lindsey that 'catching-up' was a term used between people that are already friends or have an established relationship. I didn't think this qualified.

366

We walked the half-block to the coffee shop, finding a table near the window. I knew Lindsey wanted some privacy while she turned the cash over to Louise, so I made it a point to excuse myself to go to the restroom, as she'd instructed me to do before we'd left the hotel.

I returned five minutes later, getting a nod of approval from Lindsey and seeing a cup of coffee at my place. I sat down, feeling sort of out of place in this family moment. Maybe I'd made too much of an issue out of it. It was likely that, as a result of the whole ordeal with Easton, some of his "genuine mistrust of all mankind" had worn off on me.

Lindsey was busy sharing photos of the baby with Louise, who was giving her the obligatory "oohs and aah's" that any proud grandma would. I sipped my decaf, watching the traffic outside the coffee shop and noticing, after ten minutes or so had gone by, that a dark blue panel van had driven by three times since I'd returned to the table. It might not have come to my attention, since this was New York City after all, and there were likely hundreds if not thousands of older model panel vans in dark blue around, but the fact that the passenger door was caved in made it stand out. I was getting a feeling of uneasiness after it went by a fourth time and Louise looked at her watch right afterwards.

"Lindsey, I'm afraid I've got to get going. My ride's going to be here in just a couple of minutes and if I'm not out there waiting, she'll probably go back to the Bronx without me," she chuckled. "Norma comes to mid-town every Sunday to visit her mother who's not well. She agreed to swing by here, so that I didn't have to pay cab fare back, honey."

"No," Lindsey said, smiling, "it's okay, Grandma." She left a $20 bill on the table, standing up to put her jacket on. "When will we talk again?" she asked.

"Soon, honey. I'm so appreciative of you giving me this money, though you know I didn't ask you to do that."

"I know, Grandma. I just don't think that it's right for you to deplete your life savings on account of...Daddy. I mean, can't you talk him into turning himself in? I can't imagine how his life must be, always...I don't know—looking over his shoulder?"

"I've tried; I really have," she said with a sigh. "He always had a mind of his own. Even as a child, he always had to be in control. I guess he got that from *his* daddy."

We walked out of the coffee shop and Louise looked up and down the street for her friend, Norma. Just then, the dark blue panel van slowed and pulled into the tiny parking lot next to the coffee shop.

"There's Norma," she said with a smile. "Come meet her. She's my best friend, just like Darcy here is yours."

Don't even think about it, Lindsey—

"Sure," I heard my trusting and naïve best friend say, holding on to Louise's arm as they trudged to the alley that ran alongside the building and led to a small, obscure parking lot.

I followed behind, because there was no way I'd let my best friend get anywhere near danger without having her back. Lindsey and Louise walked over to the driver's side door which faced the back of the building, with me right there with them.

"Norma?" I heard Louise say, wrapping her arm around Lindsey's shoulder as they walked up to it. "Norma, I want you to meet my…"

The door to the van opened and I watched, as if it were playing out in slow motion, the look of surprise that engulfed Lindsey's face.

"Daddy," she shrieked, as the man stepped down, holding a Glock in one hand, and tossing a set of keys to his mother with the other one.

"Quiet, Lindsey," he warned. "Just get in the back. We'll talk once we're out of here. You too," he said, nodding towards me.

Who me? Naw—dude I'd really, really rather not…

He watched with his presumably loaded gun pointing towards us as Louise opened the side panel door, waiting for Lindsey and me to climb in before she shut and locked it. I noticed it couldn't be opened from the inside. The door lever had been taken off.

Fuck.

∞ ∞ ∞ ∞ ∞ ∞

I seriously hadn't thought I'd find myself hog-tied and gagged once things had ended with Easton and me. Given the fact that, this time, there wasn't a clean, soft mattress underneath me, but instead, a dirty, rodent-dropping-infested concrete one did little to conjure up more pleasant memories.

It was probably my own fault, running my mouth the way I had in the van after I'd been told to keep it shut more than once. I finally got the message when Lindsey's dad pressed the barrel of his weapon into my back, once we'd reached this deserted warehouse and parked inside.

Lindsey was, of course, trying to plead and reason with the son-of-a-bitch, but that wasn't working. Apparently, the dude inherited his sociopathic personality from his maternal side, despite what she'd said earlier about his need to control coming from *his* father.

Yeah…right.

Grandma Louise was holding the gun now, making sure that Lindsey (who was not tied up or gagged) stayed put in the chair she was provided. Daddy-dearest was counting the cash, not only the wad that Lindsey had given his mother, but what he'd taken out of our purses once we'd arrived here. Fuck! I'd brought over fifteen hundred dollars in cash with me to shop, since my one and only credit card was at its limit. He'd scarfed another six hundred from Lindsey, plus her wedding set, the *fucking* rat bastard. I'd given him my jewelry without hesitation. He wasn't going to get all that much out of it.

Louise had removed the batteries from both of our phones and tossed them into a trash can before we'd left the lot. No tracking technology for this heist.

"Daddy," Lindsey said once again, "how could you do this to me? I'm your own daughter for Chrissake? I can't believe this…"

That was probably the tenth time she'd asked him that since we arrived here and I'd been forced to stop yapping with the scarf that was being used as a gag.

"Listen," he said, his voice carrying the desperation he must be feeling. "Do you think I *wanted* to? Do you think if there were *any* other way possible for me to get out of the country without involving you, I wouldn't have grabbed it? Honey, it's about surviving and, without this money and my mother's help, I'd be dead in a week. There are more people after me than the authorities…people that are more threatening to me than the authorities. I have no choice. This money will buy my way out of the U.S."

"And then what?" she asked, now getting a bit louder. "What will you live on once you get where you're going? What kind of life are you going to have?"

He gave her a sardonic smile. "One where I'm free to pursue other money-making interests without drug lords, thugs or the Feds breathing down my neck. Yeah, I made some mistakes, Lindsey, but I can't undo them now. And I won't go to prison. I'd never survive inside, considering who I've sold down the river in order to survive this past year and a half. I wish there were another way, sweetheart."

"Don't call me that!" she hissed. "I'm ashamed of you and the fact that you're my father. Most of all, I'm sorry that I ever loved you." She buried her face in her hands, the sobs coming full force.

"Well, I'm sorry you feel that way, Lindsey, but after tonight, you'll never have to lay eyes on me again." He turned to his mother, instructing her to keep the gun on us until he returned. She nodded, handing him a key.

"It's locker 247," she said. "Tell your contact that it's right down from the south entrance. He nodded and took off, telling her he'd be back before dark. He pulled his dark hoodie up around his face. I wasn't sure what he'd looked like before, but with a full beard and mustache and a knit hat covering his hair, he looked like someone that had been living on the street for a while.

"Grandma," I heard Lindsey implore, "Can you at least untie Darcy so she can sit in a chair? She's pregnant."

"No," Louise snapped. "She doesn't know when to keep her fuckin' mouth shut. I don't need the aggravation."

"What are Daddy's plans for us?" she asked, timidly.

"You'll know soon enough," she said. "Now you keep quiet or I'll find a gag for you too, girl."

I closed my eyes, and for the first time in a very long time, I prayed and meant it.

Chapter 54

~ Easton ~

It was after six in the evening when I finally pulled myself up and out of bed for a shower. I'd definitely imbibed too much at the reception. I'd consumed even more when I returned to my loft afterwards. I should've known by now, it never did any good trying to drown my thoughts and feelings about Darcy with alcohol. There was nothing that could take her words out of my head. Yet I couldn't blame her one bit.

I checked my mobile once I was out of the shower and dressed. Just more missed calls from my non-related brother, Taz. He'd called several times leaving messages over the past couple of months that I hadn't bothered to return. What was the point? We'd never been close and now there was no reason to even try. I deleted the voice messages without evening listening to them.

I ran my hands through my still-damp hair, trying to figure out if I should even attempt to salvage what was left of Sunday. I sat on the sofa and pulled my laptop over to check e-mails. There was one that had come in from Dobbs about eight this morning. It was a reply to mine that I'd evidently sent to him at four-thirty this morning (while clearly under the influence) instructing him to de-activate the Night Moves chip that had been embedded in *"Farcy's"* clit ring.

Bloody Christ—my inebriated fingers couldn't even get her name spelled correctly. Drink much, Easy-E?

Oh, hell. That's what *she* used to call me when she was being playful...or maybe when she was just being a pain...either way, I'd loved it.

Dobb's wanted clarification from me that I'd been referring to *Darcy*, not someone else named 'Farcy'...Seriously, Ryan? And he wondered if I also wanted the navel piercing de-activated if, in fact, I had meant 'Darcy.' I must've forgotten about that one in my drunken stupor.

He'd sent another e-mail at two-thirty this afternoon, clarifying that he'd taken it upon himself to presume I'd meant "Darcy" and had de-activated the chip in the clit jewelry and now awaited instructions from me before de-activating the matching jewelry for her navel.

How anal is he?

I hit the reply button and started typing my instruction for him to stop being so fucking anal and just get it done, but the loud pounding on the door to my loft interrupted me mid-sentence.

"Bloody hell," I shouted, getting to my feet to see who the hell was pounding the fuck out of my door. Where the hell was the doorman, anyway?

I opened the door, and my former brother stepped through it as if *he* were being inconvenienced by the interruption.

"Don't you fucking return calls, ass-hat?" he asked, pointing his finger at me, his eyes definitely showing some flashing rage.

"If I feel there's something to talk about, *Trace*," I replied. "Thing is, mate, we've no blood between us so really, what's the—"

"Shut the fuck up, Easton," he snarled. "I'm not here about that right now. I'm here about my wife. She's missing and it seems that you were the last one to see her and Darcy last night before they left for their hotel. I got that information from your former fuck-buddy, Lacee."

"I see," I replied, with a smirk. "The same Lacee that most likely provided you with my address here?"

"I work for the bureau, bro. I can get this information whenever I want it."

"Touché," I replied, closing the front door and turning back to face him. "Have you asked Darcy where your wife might be hiding?"

"She's missing as well," he growled, fisting his hands at his side.

"Taz, I haven't seen either one of them since last night. They're certainly not here, but you're free to check. No search warrant required," I added.

He looked around, as if he were contemplating doing just that, as if I would've lied about it. He was rattled. I needed to stop antagonizing him at the moment.

"What about their mobiles? Do you have the means of tracking Lindsey?"

"I've called both of their phones and they're shut off, or the batteries have been removed."

"What are you doing in New York, anyway?" I asked. "Did you just get in?"

"No," he said, impatiently. "If you'd have listened to any of my messages, you'd have known we've been working a case in the area for the past month or more. I was supposed to stop by the hotel to visit Lindsey this afternoon and she wasn't in. The staff said they hadn't seen either one of them all day," he shrugged, "I guess I thought maybe Lindsey had come along with Darcy to visit you...I mean, I know you and she were...involved at some point."

Taz was clearly rattled. For a senior agent to be rattled like that told me there was definitely something very wrong here. I grabbed my mobile and called Dobbs.

"Ryan," I nearly shouted when he answered, "Do not deactivate the other chip Darcy's wearing. Do you understand?"

"Sure. No problem, Easton. I didn't intend to until I'd received further clarification."

Thank God he's so fucking anal.

"We may be in luck," I told Trace, pulling up the Night Moves program. "If they're together, and if Darcy's still wearing her bellybutton stud, we're in luck."

Taz didn't even question the correlation as he stood behind me and watched as I pulled up the coordinates, quickly transforming them into a street address, and then pulling up the real-time stream of the building, which showed the front entrance. And a huge building it was.

"What the fuck," he commented, looking at it closely. "It looks like an abandoned warehouse." Taz was immediately plugging the info into his hand-

373

held GPS, pulling up a map and directions, which of course, I had already at my fingertips with this newly developed track-ware.

"It's in Washington Heights," he said, "Right across from Mullaly Park." He pulled his mobile up to make a call. "Slate," he said into his mobile. "I've got an address where Lindsey might be…and Darcy."

Just then, as we both watched the live stream, a dark panel van pulled up onto the sidewalk in front of the building. Someone jumped out, and headed up to where an overhead door was located just down from the main entrance. Whoever it was, pressed a button next to the door to raise it, turned and started back toward the van.

"Holy fuck," Taz said. "Can you freeze-frame that, Easton? Or maybe save the feed somehow?"

"Of course," I replied, hitting the menu to do both. "Done."

He went back to his conversation, his voice exuding emotion. "Slate, I can't be sure, man, but I'm going to send you this video feed. You'll know better than me, but I think it's the rat bastard."

This can't possibly be a good thing.

Chapter 55

Something was definitely going on outside. I wasn't sure how long we'd been in this hell hole. All I knew was that I couldn't feel my left side anymore. It was the side my weight was resting on against the cold, dirty concrete. The rats weren't even all that shy in this building, now that it had started to get dark outside. *Which was just awesome*, said no one…ever.

Lindsey's father had returned with a satchel and a newly purchased pre-paid phone. He'd been on it most of the time, arranging for a drop somewhere tonight at ten-thirty to pick up the weapons. God only *knew* what kind of weapons he was dealing in. Lindsey had come over and put her jacket under my head for comfort, sitting beside me, instead of in the chair she'd been provided.

'Geez-Louise' continually watched us, making sure we both saw the Glock being held steady in her hand. I had no doubt in my mind that she would use it just as easily on Lindsey as she would on me. There had to be something in this for her, and I doubted it had anything to do with loving her son.

A thunder storm was rolling in—yeah, I know. Just what I needed to make this horror story perfect, right?

Lindsey was patting my arm every time the crack of thunder sounded outside and I jumped. As much as anyone who's been hog-tied can jump, that is. She was trying to soothe me, when in reality, I truly believe she was more frightened than me. She didn't know just how far her father would go to save his own ruthless hide.

Jack Dennison's current call was cut short when the blaring sounds of sirens could be heard over the thunder and rain pelting against the building, screeching to a halt outside. When, soon after, the sound of a helicopter could be heard overhead, it sealed the deal as far as I was concerned.

Yes! The cavalry is here!

I saw a look of relief flood over Lindsey's face. It was short-lived however.

"Lindsey," her father bellowed. "Come here. Now!"

She scrambled to her feet and approached her father tentatively. It was almost as if she wasn't sure whether she was walking into a death trap, or into her father's arms for comfort. He bent down, wrapping his arms around her. And, for a second, I actually thought he was trying to comfort her before he had the good sense to blow his own brains out. He motioned for Louise to give him the gun, and to follow him.

He pulled Lindsey in front of him like a fucking human shield, his own mother falling behind him to serve the same purpose as they left me there on that, cold, dirty cement floor to kick at the rats who seemed to get braver by the second. He was going to try and escape. What a stupid fuck!

By now, it was difficult to distinguish the flashes of lightning from the headlights and spotlights directed on the building. I heard the van start up, most likely Lindsey was forced to drive it out of there, while Jack and Louise cowered in the back like the cowards they were. I could see the light from the street as the door opened and the van pulled out and then nothing. It was relatively quiet for several seconds until I heard the loud sounds of 'Pop! Pop! Pop!'

Oh my God…Lindsey!

I was cold, tired, dehydrated, and hungry; yet tears still formed in my eyes and rolled down my cheeks. I could even hear my own muffled sobs from beneath the scarf that was tied tightly over my mouth and seemed to get tighter by the second. I didn't need to hold my sobs back. There was no one here to see me break this time. The rats didn't care. So I let loose, but I couldn't really and totally let loose because the fucking scarf was muffling everything that I wanted to let out: the anger, the rage, the total fucked-upness of how a father could do what Jack Dennison had done. It was unfathomable to me.

Maybe my pregnancy hormones were making me feel things more deeply and more personally then I ever had before. Maybe it was the fact that, when I'd first felt that fluttering within my gut, I had insta-loved this little tad-pole inside of me that I'd named "Junior." At five months pregnant, I already loved him or her. My God! Jack Dennison had 19 years with Lindsey before he split. What the fuck?

My musings were interrupted as I heard footsteps coming down the metal stairwell that led to the floor above this one.

I squeezed my eyes shut, as if that would make the sound go away. I willed my ears to not hear what was approaching. Then, I opened my eyes. What could be any worse than what I'd been through? Having a homicidal vagrant come through the door would beat laying here and getting chewed on by rats. Darcy Nicole Sheridan was made of tougher stuff than this.

As my eyes, once again, adjusted to the darkness settling in, with only the occasional flash of lightning to illuminate my surroundings, I heard the sound of the footsteps on the concrete getting closer and closer.

And then I saw them. Bruno Magli Micolino braided-strap loafers in black. And as they got closer, I knew that everything was going to be alright. Who else would be wearing black Italian leather in a shit-hole like this?

Easton...

I felt his hands on me, untying my binds, talking to me in his very soothing voice, telling me that he loved me, that I was going to be fine and not to worry, and I knew that it was true. I didn't say a word, even when he removed the scarf that had been tied around me. I simply crawled up into his lap as he rested on his haunches just inches from me, and tucked my face into his broad chest, not wanting to look at anything right now. I was just listening for the sound of his steady heartbeat. There it was.

"I lied," I whispered against him.

"It doesn't matter," he replied, lifting me up and carrying me towards the door.

"It matters, Easton. I love you. I never stopped."

"I know," he replied, his arms tightening around me. "I know, baby."

I felt the cold chill of the wet, night air hit my face as he carried me outside. The rain had diminished to a slow drizzle. The flashing lights were everywhere and as I gazed about, I could see that New York's finest were perched all around the building, along with FBI swat team members dressed liked ninjas in black, with knit ski-mask type head coverings on, and an arsenal of semi-automatic weapons aimed to fire. They were on top of buildings as far as I could

377

see down the street, the reflective lettering "F B I" visible on the back of their field jackets.

I pulled the collar of Easton's trench coat up to my eyes, as if to shield them from seeing whatever it was that was about to go down.

"Easton," I said, my voice cracking. "Where's Lindsey? I heard gun shots a little while ago." Before he could answer, I saw the van they'd left in sitting cock-eyed on the sidewalk a half-block down. The tires had been blown out and the panel door was ajar, but no one was around it.

"She'll be fine, love. They're seeing about getting her back right now safe and sound. Don't worry."

"Stop!" I cried out, now struggling to get released from his arms. "I need to wait for Lindsey. I have to know that she's safe. Where is she?" The shock I'd been in was wearing off enough to allow the panic to now seep in.

He lowered me to my feet in front of him, keeping his arms around me as he nodded to the park across the street that seemed to be surrounded on the ground and on rooftops with agents that looked more like terrorist snipers than law enforcement. I could see that they were keeping in contact by wireless radio.

"Listen, sweetheart," he said cautiously. "Her father has her in the park with him. He's trying to use her to protect himself—the bloody bastard," he snapped. "I don't want you to worry, love. She won't be harmed, I promise you. They know what they're doing out there."

"And her grandmother?" I asked.

His furrowed brow told me he hadn't a clue as to whom I was talking about. Hopefully, the old bitch had caught a stray bullet.

I could tell something across the street had just heated up. I could feel the tension rise. Easton felt it too as he pulled me into an alcove doorway on the side of the building facing the park across the street, shielding me with his own body. From the rooftop of the building directly across from us, I could see the red glare of the infrared night scope atop a weapon as it searched for a target. It then stopped and held position. A second later I heard a shot ring out. Only one. But I knew it had met its mark when seconds later I heard the blood-curdling scream of my best friend coming from a cluster of trees fifty yards away in the darkness of the park. Her plaintive wail seemed to go on and on.

I started to push away from Easton, so that I could go to her, but he immediately pulled me back, encasing me tightly within his arms. "She's okay, love. They got him, not her. She's fine."

"She's not fine, Easton," I persisted. "Don't you understand? That was her *father* and she loved him…no matter what! She *loved* him. I need to go to her!" I was on the verge of hysterics.

"No," he said, firmly, drawing me back closer, lowering his lips to my ear. "That's Taz's job, baby. Not yours," he continued, nodding his head toward the park.

Oh Friggin' Hell…God, please don't let Taz be the one that took the son-of-a-bitch down!

I looked across the street to the building where the sharpshooter had been positioned and watched as he hoisted himself down to ground level, dropping to the pavement from the fire escape. There were two agents in FBI jackets waiting for him. Another had taken off in a fast sprint in the direction of Lindsey with several NYC police officers on his flank.

The sniper-agent turned his weapon over to one of the others, and then pulled his ski mask cap off, revealing his seriously handsome face.

Thank God! It's Slate…

I looked back across to the park, seeing the white reflective letters of "F B I" on the back of the jacket of the agent that had taken off like a rocket once the single bullet had met its mark. *That* had been *Taz*, thank God! Lindsey's Taz— and he'd be grabbing up his baby girl any sec, letting her know that she was safe and loved, and that he was taking her home.

I looked up at Easton, who still had his arms wrapped around me, using his body as a shield of protection for me, even though the threat of danger had been eliminated. "Can we go home, Easton?"

"Yes, love. We're going home. That's why I'm here, baby—to take you home."

Chapter 56

I awoke the following morning, still ensconced in the warm cocoon Easton had made for me with his body. He'd taken me to his loft and carefully bathed me from head to toe, washing my hair of the filth that had accumulated during the hours spent as the late Jack Dennison's hostage. He'd given me one of his long-sleeved shirts to wear, and a clean pair of his boxers.

We hadn't talked a lot last night. Easton had insisted I get my rest and had molded his body against mine perfectly, where we'd fallen asleep together and remained that way until now. I snuggled into him with my backside, eager for him to be awake with me.

"Morning, love," I heard him whisper against the back of my neck. "Sleep well?"

"Umm," I said with a sigh nodding, "Better than I have in a long, long time. You?"

I felt his smile. "No complaints...though I'm a bit puzzled about something," he said, his hands now gently massaging my small baby bump.

It's time, Darce.

"What's that?" I asked, innocently, holding my breath.

"You seem to have a bit...*more*...here, love," he whispered against my neck. "Of course, I've nothing against full-figured women, but during the night it seemed to me as if...well, for lack of a better word, my hand *felt* some vibration as it rested against your abdomen."

Oh God...

"Easton," I said, slowly, glad that I wasn't facing him at the moment. "I'm pregnant. It must've happened the night of the storm...when we were...together at your estate."

"I see," he replied, his tone giving me no indication as to how he was taking the news.

I swallowed nervously and continued. "I know how you feel about…well, *babies* and all, and the reason I didn't tell you was because I was afraid you'd try to force me to have an abortion…and there's just no way—"

"What?" he growled; anger now very evident in his voice. He sat up, pulling me with him, but I was too scared of what I'd see in his eyes after what I'd just told him.

So I busied my focus by watching my hands pluck at the sheet covering my body.

"Look at me," he ordered.

I turned to face him, looking up into his angry eyes from beneath my lashes.

"What in God's name are you saying?" he demanded.

"Bianca…," I explained, fumbling for words, "I was told that you forced her to have an abortion."

"Good Lord, woman," he said, eyes flashing, "What kind of a man do you think I am?"

Is that rhetorical?

I shrugged my shoulders, still watching him. The anger was slowly dissipating. "I was told that by Lacee," I murmured. "She was told that by Bianca."

"That bloody figures," he mumbled, taking my hand into his. "I know I've been an arse and that you've seen first-hand some of that with Devon, and in the way that I treated you. You have to know now that I'd never react that way to news like this. I wouldn't have with Bianca, and certainly not with you. None of that's true, love. Do you believe me?"

His eyes were searching mine for an answer and I realized it was important to Easton that I knew the kind of man he was and that I believed him over idle gossip and vicious lies.

"Then tell me, Easton. If *you loved* me, why did you leave me? Convince me that it'll never happen again."

For the first time ever, I saw a look of pain cross over his face, but it was quickly replaced by a look of resolve. He looked over at me, his eyes brilliant with some self-revelation, some understanding of why he'd done what he'd done.

"It's difficult to explain, Darcy, but I promise you that I *will*. Because you deserve to know, not only what I've just recently figured out, but where I want our future to go. The demons are gone, baby, I promise you that. Forgive me for ever making you the recipient of my anger and hostility. I had no right to do that and I *will* explain some things to you about my past, but please understand, I'm not using those as excuses for my behaviour, alright?"

I nodded, giving him a hesitant, but *very* relieved smile. "I understand," I said. "I mean, I don't know the details of the stuff Lacee told me about your mother and Bianca, but Colin did share with me the fact that you didn't terminate Devon, and instead you offered her a flex schedule. He didn't believe the vicious lies Bianca spread either. He told me he believed you loved me," I finished a bit sheepishly. I wanted to trust in his sincerity.

He looked at me, his eyes full of passion. "I do love you, Darcy. I adore you. And I *will* show you that for as long as you'll permit it. But for the moment, I'd like to know when our baby's due." He was looking at me with tenderness and his eyes were full of love.

"Mid-January," I replied softly. "And I hope you know I didn't do this on purpose. You see, my Depo shot had expired and—"

"Quiet, love," he gently admonished, pulling me onto his lap, wrapping both arms around me so that his hands were massaging my belly. "I don't *care* how it happened. I'm just pleased that it did. I love the thought of having a baby—our baby. By the way, I'd prefer a boy first, if you don't mind. Daughters can follow later."

"I'll try to accommodate you on that, Mr. Matthews," I said with a stern tone, but my lips were already curling into a laugh-like grin. I leaned back against him as we enjoyed our "tummy time" together. "However," I began to inform him, trying and failing miserably to hold onto that stern tone, "it is the *male* that determines the gender, just so you know. I mean, I'd *hate* for you to punish me if you get a daughter first out of the gate."

383

I heard his rich laughter against my hair as he slowly and methodically relieved me of my clothing, kissing, caressing and loving every part of me with slow and deliberate measure. My body responded to his, just as it always had, taking his fullness inside of me and rising up to meet him thrust for thrust as his lips devoured me.

"I love you, Darcy," he whispered against my ear, his fingers teasing the soft peaks of my breasts. "And I'm going to love this baby and all the rest of the children we'll have together."

My heart fluttered at his words because they'd come from his heart, the one he swore he didn't have.

"I love you, Easton," I replied, my hands, capturing his face, pulling him down closer so that our eyes locked. "Thank you for saving me. *For everything*," I whispered.

Later, as we were curled up on his sofa together, his cell rang. It was Taz. I'd been curious about how they'd hooked up, in light of what Lindsey had shared with me earlier. They talked for a few minutes. At first it sounded as if Taz might've been bitching him out over something, but Easton seemed to be taking it in stride.

For real?

I watched as he held his phone away from his ear, rolling his eyes and giving me a smirk. Finally, when Taz had said what he'd called to say, Easton spoke up. "Let me remind you, *bro*, that if not for my patented track-ware, you and the rest of the bureau wouldn't have had a clue as to the location of your wife, the rat bastard fugitive, along with the perps that were assisting him that you've been trying to nail for a month now. So, if someone gives you shit about me having my helicopter land rooftop on the building yesterday without the knowledge or the *authorization* of the FBI, you might want to make a case for me. Besides," he continued, giving me his sexy wink, "It all turned out for the best. You got your collar...and I got *mine*."

I could tell that Taz was thanking him and that the conversation had been amiable all along. Easton inquired about Lindsey and, right before they ended the call, Easton made his plane available for our return to D.C.

"So," I said, sticking my big toe up to his face and waggling it. "You two make up?"

He gave me his signature smile, grabbing my foot to tickle it.

"Stop, Easton," I laughed, finally getting it away from him. "Answer my question."

"Taz and I are fine," he replied. "We're brothers who occasionally disagree, that's all. It's what families do, I guess. He thanked me for finding you two, right after he attempted to chew my ass about coming to get you once I'd found you."

"Yeah, about that," I replied, "wanna clue me in how it came to be it was *you* that found us?"

"Why, Miss Sheridan," he replied, seriously. "Did you not pay attention to your own presentation on the cutting edge technology of Night Moves Track-Ware®?"

Huh?

"What? Where?"

He was amused by my inability to figure it out.

"I don't just give *anyone* clit jewelry, you know?" he teased. "Only very special people that I want to keep *track* of…"

No he didn't…

"Seriously?" I asked, my eyes widening. "You had chips put in my clit jewelry?"

"And your belly-button stud as well."

I couldn't help it, I started laughing. He watched me with a bemused look on his face.

"You're definitely a piece of work, Easy-E. But hey? For once, your odd proclivity for ultimate control, along with borderline stalking worked out for everyone concerned. Well, except for Jack Dennison, I guess. How's Lindsey?"

385

"Taz said she's doing better, but it'll take time for her to get over the shock of what her father did and who he was. I guess I know a little bit about that. She'll work it out. Taz will be right there with her. As it turns out, the old lady—Louise is it?"

I nodded.

"She apparently sang like a bird. She and her son were heavily tied into some weapons smuggling in return for getting across the border with brand new identities."

Holy shit!

"Now," he said, as he pulled my feet into his lap and started massaging them, "let's talk about us."

"Okay," I replied. "Shoot."

"Do your parents know about the baby?"

Uh oh.

"Well, yeah," I replied, "But…they sort of think it's Darin's," I said, wrinkling my nose up, knowing he wasn't going to be happy hearing that. I was surprised when he calmly continued administering his kick-ass foot massage.

"You and I will remedy that as soon as we get back, understood?"

"Yes, sir," I replied, giggling. "But they're going to freak—just so you know."

"They'll get over it," he replied. "After all, it won't do for them not to welcome their soon to be son-in-law with open arms."

"And open minds," I mumbled under my breath. "Wait—hold up. Was that a proposal?" I asked, jerking my foot from his grasp. "No—I think you can and *will* do better than that, Easton Jamison Matthews!"

He pulled me onto his lap, brushing the hair back from my face.

"Darcy Nicole Sheridan," he said quietly, gazing into my eyes. "Will you do me the honour of becoming my wife?"

Of course, you all know what the answer is, right?

~ **Friday, January 13th** ~

It was official. My aversion to 'Friday the 13th' had been forever banished. Never again would that be a sign of bad luck or karma. This Friday the 13th had been perfect. Our son had made his debut into the world on Friday the 13th—my new *lucky* day.

"Mrs. Matthews," the nurse greeted me, coming into my hospital room with yet another large bouquet of flowers, this one in a baby-blue basket containing a brown stuffed teddy-bear wearing a baby-blue bow tie and hat in it. "Looks like this little fellow already has a fan club," she finished with a smile. She set the latest delivery down on the table that was nearly full of flowers, stuffed animals, balloons, and musical planters playing all kinds of popular nursery rhymes.

"Yes," I replied, smiling and wondering where the hell Easton was with the baby. I'd waddled to the bathroom for a quick sitz bath at the nurse's direction and when I'd returned, Easton and the baby were both gone.

"Would you happen to know where my baby is?" I asked, as she prepared to take my blood pressure again for the umpteenth time since I'd delivered our 7-pound, 6-ounce bundle of joy three and a half hours prior.

She pumped the rubber ball, inflating the cuff. "No worries, sweetie," she gushed. "Oh, that *husband* of yours sure is serious about his responsibilities as a new daddy. He's down with a couple of the other new fathers at "Daddy Training" offered by the pediatrics ward. We encourage it so they can be of help to Mom and Baby once you both go home."

Easton had easily won over all of the female nurses, aids, technicians, and dieticians since our arrival. They had gushed, blushed, flushed and openly gawked at him, not giving a shit whether I saw them or not, from the time we'd arrived at the hospital. I suppose the fact that he'd been constantly fussing over

388

me the whole time I was in labor and throughout the delivery had further ingratiated him to the staff.

I had no complaints, though. He'd been awesome with me throughout my pregnancy. True to his word, once we'd returned to D.C., he'd stayed at Eli's and my apartment until he found permanent living quarters for the two of us. He'd opened up to me about some of the horrific things that had occurred during his childhood and shared some memories that weren't so pleasant. I'd been given the facts which, of course, had differed from Lacee's version relative to Bianca.

He insisted we be married *before* the baby arrived, promising me a lavish ball to celebrate our nuptials once the baby got here and I felt up to it. So, we'd flown to Monte Carlo for a long weekend, becoming husband and wife in a private and intimate ceremony.

My parents had taken the news better than I'd anticipated. It probably had helped that Easton did all of the talking, relaying to my parents our mutual love, respect, and commitment. I'd kind of hung back, Easton's arm wrapped around me, watching my father's expression go from shock, to numb, to acceptance once Easton explained (amidst my deep blush) that anything they'd overheard in Belize the previous year was certainly not indicative of the current love relationship we shared.

I think it had sealed the deal when he assured them we'd be making our home in the States, having a home in New York and another one in D.C., so that they'd have plenty of interaction with the first of *many* grandchildren we planned to give them. I'd raised my eyes to look at him, my mouth going slack momentarily at *that* one. He'd only squeezed me a bit tighter, the corners of his mouth turning up.

I was glad we'd found a new home not far from my parents house once we returned from getting married. It worked out well for Eli, too. Cain had moved into the apartment and those two were as 'in love' as Easton and me. My old room was now serving as their "walk-in" closet, Cain being every bit as much of a clothes whore as Eli, possibly worse. They'd hosted a bridal/baby shower for me.

Lindsey had come to terms with the death of her father. Her grandmother was serving time in prison and Lindsey said she hoped the old bitch rotted there until hell wouldn't have her. (Not sure *exactly* what *that* meant, but knowing Lindsey and the way she always tried to see the best in people, I'd say she parted with some of that naivety that didn't seem to work in her best interest at times.)

Taz, of course, had seen to it that Lindsey wasn't made aware of the fact it'd been Slate that took the rat bastard down. My money said Sammie had likely fucked Slate raw all night long after *she* found out, though.

Lindsey felt so damn guilty and repentant that she'd involved me in the drama. I had to keep reminding her that it was at *my* insistence I'd gone with her that day, and the fact that Easton was so freakin' possessive and had that clit jewelry imbedded with tracking software, just may have saved both of our lives. Hey, it was her dad's choice to run with her as a human shield, rather than give his sorry ass up.

Taz and Lindsey were expecting a baby boy in mid-May. I figured Taz had gone out of his way comforting her after the scene that night in the park, giving her another baby in the process. She was so happy, especially since they had a home under construction that would be ready in mid-April.

She and I'd decorated the nursery for my baby in primary colors that were gender neutral. Easton had insisted we be surprised and not know the baby's gender until it was born. I had really wanted to know the sex of the baby beforehand, because I was dying to shop for baby couture, but I'd finally relented and agreed on one condition: if the baby turned out to be a boy, I selected the name, if the baby turned out to be a girl, he selected the name. He agreed, on the condition the baby not be a 'junior' anything.

Problem solved…almost. Once Easton had shared his girl name choice for me I was tempted to devise a sure-fire scheme that would allow me to successfully pull off a baby-swap at the hospital, if necessary.

So, are you ready for this?

Easton's girl-name selection*: **'Prudence Stormy Matthews.'**

I know, right?

He seemed to think it reflected her conception beautifully: It was a *stormy* night and he'd used *good judgment* (prudence) in comforting me with his body.

I'd refused to divulge my name selection until 'Junior' made his screaming debut. I was all about making sure that a baby's name matched their looks, and I was hoping like hell it *was* a 'Junior' and *not* a 'Juniorette' because I was so regretting the deal I'd forced on him.

Just then, the proud daddy came into my hospital room, cradling our son against his chest, cooing softly to him, as the baby's finger was curled around Easton's thumb. The nurse had fluffed my pillows, checked my temperature and pulse, and was on her way out. She stopped to gaze at the baby, giving him a smile and murmuring how much he favored his daddy.

Yeah—okay, thank you very much, but I can actually see some of me in his cute little face.

"Easton," I said, holding my arms out. "Do you think you might allow me to hold our baby at *least* once?"

His smile lit the room as he came close, carefully transferring the baby into my waiting arms. I loved both of them so much.

"Make sure you support his head, sweetheart," he cautioned me and then, quickly catching my eye roll, continued. "Hey you, I'm sorry, about disappearing like that," he said, taking his place on the edge of my bed. "I didn't want to miss the class. The nanny teaching it was brilliant. I even changed his nappy." He beamed proudly.

Probably a first for him—and likely the last…

"It was even a bit of a pooey one," he bragged. "So, on those, you'll need to be extra vigilant with boys," he explained. "Make sure you put something over his Willy whilst you're cleaning his bum, Darcy, otherwise, you're likely to get whizzed on." He was beaming like a fool who had single-handedly discovered fatherhood.

Who'd a thunk?

If I hadn't realized it before, I did at that moment. Easton truly had shed the demons of his past: his mother, Bianca, Miss Gennifer (the fucked-up, perverted bitch!). We'd discussed his overly-possessive tendencies, and I'd explained to him that, while I loved gifts of jewelry, I'd prefer from here on out they not contain track-ware. Easton had finally learned to trust women. I'd finally learned to trust love.

I looked over at my husband, who was clearly mesmerized by the little baby sounds and movements coming from the newest member of our family.

"Thank you for the diaper-changing tips, Easton," I replied, smiling down into my beautiful little cherub's face. He had a mass of nearly raven-black hair and dark, smoky blue eyes. "Tell me, Easton? Did they show you how to feed him?" I teased.

He cocked his brow, gazing at me, as I unhooked my nursing bra and got the baby situated to latch on. He nuzzled into me, his little head rooting and bobbing until I helped guide him on to a successful latch. I gave Easton a smug smile as I one-upped him.

"Don't tell me you're jealous of the attention I'm giving our son?" Easton asked, leaning forward to brush his lips against my cheek, his fingers, pulling an errant strand of hair behind my ear, and then kissing me softly there. "I love you, Darcy," he said gently. "And I adore the son you've given me. Well done, sweetheart."

I traced my finger softly against the baby's finely arched eyebrow. It was just like Easton's. I was glad. I looked up at my gorgeous husband as he watched me, fascinated by the closeness and the cute little, sucking noises our baby was making as he nursed.

"Maybe you're the jealous one, Easton," I teased him softly. "Someone else seems to be enjoying one of your favorite places."

I saw Easton furrow his brow and I couldn't stifle a giggle. "Yes, well the doctor said six weeks, but I assured him you're a quick healer, Mrs. Matthews."

"I love you, too, Easton." I sighed. "I adore our baby and the life we have together. And, Mr. Matthews, you deserve some credit here, too. I mean, I couldn't have done it without you, right?"

He nodded. I could tell he was getting kind of choked up with us being a little family now and our baby making that part of it official. Easton took my free hand in his, raising it to his full lips, kissing each one of my fingers softly. I hadn't seen him quite so emotional since our wedding night.

We'd taken a walk on the beach after the ceremony, talking and making plans about where we'd look for our new home. Easton had stopped suddenly, a look of determination on his face as he pulled something from the pocket of his trousers. It was a ruby-encrusted, gold-filigreed ring. He looked at it for only a few seconds and then hurled it into the waves of the ocean. I'd asked him about it, curious as to what the ring had meant. He told me it had meant nothing, that everything that meant anything to him was within inches of his reach.

"So, Mrs. Matthews," he said now, his eyes smoldering as he looked into mine. "Do you plan on keeping me in the dark forever as to what name we're giving this little chap?"

I shifted the baby a bit, looking at his face to make sure the name I'd selected fit. That had been important to me. I decided it fit perfectly. I only hoped Easton liked it.

"Weston Jamison Matthews," I announced proudly, watching Easton's expression for a reaction. "I think it signifies 'east meeting west' and making it work out," I explained. "Do you like it?" I asked tentatively.

He leaned in, capturing my lips with his. "I love it, baby," he said, between his soft kisses. "It's perfect. And we can save the name 'Prudence' for one of our daughters."

I kissed him back, making sure he could feel the smile passing from my lips to his.

"I think I'm going to want more sons, Easy-E."

About Andrea

Andrea Smith is a *USA Today* and *Amazon* best-selling author. She is a native of Springfield, Ohio, currently residing in southern Ohio. Having previously been employed as an executive for a global corporation, Ms. Smith decided to leave the corporate world and pursue her life-long dream of writing fiction.

Indie Authors appreciate readers taking the time to leave reviews on Goodreads, B & N and Amazon to help raise awareness of their books.

G-Man Series:

"Diamond Girl" (Book #1 in the G-Man Series)

"Love Plus One" (Book #2 in the G-Man Series)

"Night Moves" (Book #3 in the G-Man Series)

"G-Men Holiday Wrap" (Book #3.5 in the G-Man Series)

"These Men" (Spin-off)

"Taz" (Book #5 in the G-Man Series)

Baby Series

This is a 4 Series which needs to be read in order.

"Maybe Baby" (Book #1)

"Baby Love" (Book #2)

"Be My Baby" (Book #3)

"Baby Come Back" (Book #3.5)

Limbo Series

"Silent Whisper" (Book #1)

"Clouds in my Coffee" (Book #2)

September Series - New Adult Romance

"Until September" (Book #1)

"When September Ends" (Book #2)

Made in the USA
Charleston, SC
11 April 2016